PRAISE FOR *THE SIGN FOR HOME*

"As if complex characters, a compelling voice, smart stylistic choices, and the fierce defense of diversity, accessibility, and equality were not enough, *The Sign for Home* also immersed me in an engrossing and important conversation I knew too little about. I closed this book more enlightened, more engaged, and more hopeful than I was when I opened it, and I enjoyed every page along the way."

—Laurie Frankel, *New York Times* bestselling author of *One Two Three*

"A hilarious, peculiar and very touching story about a deaf, blind Jehovah's Witness boy and his gay interpreter."

—James Hannaham, author of the PEN/Faulkner Award winner, *Delicious Foods*, *New York Times Book Review*

"Fell writes with a deep compassion and keen attention to the experiences of living with deafness and blindness. This heartfelt romance is hard to resist."

—*Publishers Weekly*

"A unique coming-of-age romance."

—Buzzfeed

"Tender, hilarious and decidedly uplifting."

—BookPage

"Poignant. . . . Riveting."

—*Los Angeles Times*

"Reading *The Sign for Home* will cause you to experience many emotions, from indignation to horror to heartbreak. Ultimately, though, this is a novel about the power of love—not just romantic love but the love that evolves from friendship. It's a beautiful story that's powerfully told."

—BookReporter.com

the sign for home

A NOVEL

Blair Fell

EMILY BESTLER BOOKS

ATRIA

New York   London   Toronto   Sydney   New Delhi

EMILY
BESTLER
BOOKS

ATRIA

An Imprint of Simon & Schuster, Inc.
1230 Avenue of the Americas
New York, NY 10020

Copyright © 2022 by Blair Fell

First Emily Bestler Books/Atria Paperback edition March 2023

EMILY BESTLER BOOKS/ATRIA PAPERBACK and colophon are
trademarks of Simon & Schuster, Inc.

For information about special discounts for bulk purchases,
please contact Simon & Schuster Special Sales at 1-866-506-1949
or business@simonandschuster.com.

The Simon & Schuster Speakers Bureau can bring authors to your live event.
For more information or to book an event, contact the Simon & Schuster Speakers
Bureau at 1-866-248-3049 or visit our website at www.simonspeakers.com.

Interior design by Kathryn A. Kenney-Peterson

Manufactured in the United States of America

3   5   7   9   10   8   6   4   2

The Library of Congress has cataloged the hardcover edition as follows:

Names: Fell, Blair, author.
Title: The sign for home : a novel / Blair Fell.
Description: First Emily Bestler Books/Atria Books hardcover edition. | New
York : Emily Bestler Books/Atria, 2022.
Identifiers: LCCN 2021032648 (print) | LCCN 2021032649 (ebook) |
ISBN 9781982175955 (hardcover) | ISBN 9781982175962 (trade paperback) |
ISBN 9781982175979 (ebook)
Subjects: LCGFT: Fiction.
Classification: LCC PS3606.E38847 S56 2022 (print) | LCC PS3606.E38847
(ebook) | DDC 813/.6—dc23
LC record available at https://lccn.loc.gov/2021032648
LC ebook record available at https://lccn.loc.gov/2021032649

ISBN 978-1-9821-7595-5
ISBN 978-1-9821-7596-2 (pbk)
ISBN 978-1-9821-7597-9 (ebook)

*To all the Deaf and DeafBlind people I have known,
befriended, and worked with over the last thirty-nine years.
Through your kindness and patience you've allowed me to
be part of your world and taught me about your beautiful
language and culture and for that I am forever grateful.
This is for you and in memory of my brilliant teachers at
Gallaudet University, Gil Eastman and Bernard Bragg.*

the sign
for home

1

SNIFF

Sniff.

The air of your room. The odor of sheets and blankets, hot summer dust, old technology equipment, an Old Spice deodorant stick worn to a nub. The stinging smell of detergent from the washing machine outside your door burns the lining of your nostrils.

You are sitting alone at your desk in your T-shirt and shorts. The undersides of your thighs are sweaty and stick to the fiberglass chair. The tips of your fingers rub themselves against the cool plastic keys on the keyboard. You tilt your head down close to it.

Sniff.

Plastic-and-dripped-coffee smell. Maybe the sticky crumbs of old peanut butter and grape jelly sandwiches? You lift the back of your wrist to your nose.

Sniff.

Soap, hair, and skin.

You look toward the computer screen, your face just inches away. *Making love to the screen*, your trainer from the Abilities Institute called it. The white screen has been inverted to black because it's easier on your eyes—or eye, rather, as there's only one that has any usable vision left. The giant white cursor, magnified with your ZoomText software, winks at you over and over again, calling you to write, demanding you take control of your sinful mind. You begin to type three-inch-tall white letters that march across the screen one at a time . . . T . . . O . . . M . . . R . . . S . . .

To Mrs. Clara Shuster, MSW

I have getted your email. Please telling potential MALE interpreter (10 a.m.) and female interpreter (11 a.m.) with TOP TACTILE ASL SKILLS I will meet them and YOU tomorrow on ABILITIES INSTI-TUTE FOR THE DISABLED, 114 Skidmore Street, Poughkeepsie, NY, at SECOND floor conference room. After meeting BOTH MALE AND FEMALE ASL interpreters I will then DECIDING which will team with my OLD LONG TIME INTERPRETER MOLLY CLINCH.

You stop typing. Molly has been your interpreter and Support Service Provider, or SSP, since you were thirteen years old. Other than Brother Birch, Molly is the most important person in your life who is still alive. She was there when all the worst, unspeakable, sinful things happened.

Your fingers find their place back on the keyboard.

Tell INTERPRETERS bring jacket or sweater for interview, because Second floor of ABILITIES INSTITUTE on 114 Skidmore Street can getting COLD like refrigerator. (FROWNING) Cold, I guess, make Mrs. Clara Shuster SMARTER and WORK HARDER. HA HA. This is JOKE. (BIG SMILE)

Writing English is hard. Brother Birch says when hearing people read your writing they think you're a small child. (You aren't.) Or that you have developmental disabilities. (You don't.) English is just not your first language. American Sign Language is. Writing in a language that you've literally never heard is like battling monsters with your hands tied behind your back. No matter how much you try to butt them with your head, they keep knocking you down. The worst are the confusing Preposition Monsters and the giant Verb-Tense Rodents, sharp-toothed beasts who time and again . . . *have eat you? Have eat-ed you? Has ate you? Have will eaten you?*

This is why Brother Birch is letting you take a class at the community college this summer to make you a better writer, which will help you to write sermons and preach the word of God. Hallelujah.

Gold star.

And maybe you will also be able to meet new people, including girls, and that will help you to stop having sinful thoughts about the person you are never supposed to think about ever again.

Red star.

You return to typing the email to Mrs. Clara Shuster.

When male and female interpreters comes to Abilities Institute they will recognize ME since I will be ONLY 23-year-old MAN with a WHITE cane and DOG who does NOT look up when Interpreters CALLS OUT NAME. Again JOKE. (Big Smile) DARK HUMOR. I am not RUDE MAN. Of course I DEAFBLIND. HA HA HA. Please tell all interpreters I DO NOT LIKE SWEATY HANDS or bad breath or too much perfume which stings my nose.

Before, when you were small, everyone at the Kingdom Hall was taller than you, so your head would come up to their chest and shoulders. They always smelled like armpit. Now you smell the tops of their heads, which smell like hair cream, shampoo, or dust.

You like short people better than tall people.

Mama was short. Molly is short. Your old friends from the Rose Garden School, Big Head Lawrence and Martin, were short. Martin also had lots of fat on his body. (You also like fat people.) The person-who-you-are-not-allowed-to-remember was also short, but thin, with black eyes, thick black hair, and smelled like . . .

Quiet! Quiet, stupid brain! Quiet!

Red star.

Down at the Kingdom Hall hearing members will do very basic Tactile Sign Language with you, so if they ever meet another DeafBlind man they will know how to talk to him about Jehovah God. Some of the girls take a very long time to spell their names and mix up the letters. Sometimes they let their hands linger longer in yours than is proper, and you'll let your own hand wander up to their wrists. And that's when things get different inside you. Sometimes, if they have nice hands—soft, smooth, expressive, not sweaty—you ask them to fingerspell their names a second time even though you understood the first time. You'll pull their hands in a little closer, so you can feel the warmth of their bodies. You'll inhale their perfume, powder, skin, breath. Then sometimes you daydream about asking the girls to put their fingers inside their soft place, the way you-know-who did, and let you smell them.

Red star.

You pray again to Jehovah God: *Please, Jehovah God, let me stop having sinful thoughts every five minutes. Please let me take Brother Birch's kind and loving advice to "Not be like Lot's Wife and look back at the past"—especially about you-know-who—and please let me be a spiritually strong man and servant to you and your son, Jesus Christ.*

You take a deep breath and finish writing the letter to Mrs. Clara Shuster:

Let BOTH interpreters with HIGH SKILLS know my old GUIDE DOG is name "SNAP" . . . (SNAP FINGERS is name). She is old secondhand guide dog. She do not BITE a lot. But tell interpreters with HIGH SKILLS NOT to BANG BANG on table to show they am HERE. SNAP does not like it and BARK ANGRY. GASP. GULP. Embarrass! Better way, gently TAP on my shoulder, and hold, do not move so don't LOSE YOU. After that I will interview potential

INTERPRETERS and then pick one to work with me and Molly this summer. Okay?

Thank you for all helping me so much. I am very exciting going to WRITING CLASS at Dutchess Community College. I promise work very hard and get good grades so Brother Birch, Jehovah God, and you WILL HAVE be proud with me.

Blessings and Hugs,
Your friend
Arlo Dilly

2

THE TERP

"I'm here to see Clara Shuster," I said to the Abilities Institute receptionist. "The name is Cyril Brewster. I'm here to interview for the interpreting gig."

"Clara will be with you in a moment. You can wait in there."

The receptionist pointed to the door of a waiting room just off the hallway. I went inside. The decor of the Abilities Institute, like most decent purveyors of social services, strained for an aura that said *We really, really care . . . no, really*. Everywhere I looked there were racks of helpful brochures and cliché posters of sunsets and waterfalls with inspirational quotes written in script. One said: "It Is During Our Darkest Moments that We Must Focus to See the Light."

Irony, I thought.

As I passed a mirror, I took note of my face. As always, I sucked in my cheeks and widened my eyes. My ex, Bruno, used to call this my fake mirror face. For a man in my middle years, I'm still decent looking—for a redhead. I stretched the crow's feet around my eyes, and once again considered whether Botox would be feasible. It was always the same conundrum: Which do I follow, my desire to be attractive or my desire to be a good interpreter? I have what people call "Deaf face," meaning I wear my emotions—and the hearing consumer's emotions—like a billboard on my face. Facial expressions are a big part of ASL grammar, signaling questions, mood, anger, joy, confusion, and more. I wouldn't have been as popular with Deaf consumers if my face were always frozen into a dashing look of sexy disinterest. *Nope. No Botox for me!*

Of course, my face won't matter if I get this job.

I felt nauseated. I had a strict policy about not taking gigs with the Deaf-Blind where I'd have to interpret in Tactile ASL (TSL). DeafBlind people who use TSL will express themselves the same way as any sighted ASL user. But when they "listen," rather than using their eyes, the DeafBlind consumer will place their hands on top of the person's with whom they are communicating, *feeling the signs.* Think Helen Keller talking to Annie Sullivan in that movie *The Miracle Worker.* The problem was, I was no Annie Sullivan, and I knew it. You'd think they'd require a certain skill level to take a job like this, but that's not how this business works when there aren't enough interpreters. If you're smart, you don't take jobs you can't handle. But sometimes you don't know you can't handle it until you do.

Before that day I had accepted exactly one DeafBlind assignment in my entire career. I was a baby interpreter, just out of my training program, and it was a medical gig. The agency that hired me said it would be *exactly like regular ASL interpreting.* It was a lie.

We'll call the DeafBlind client "Shirley."

Shirley was in her forties with prematurely gray hair and eyelids that drooped to the point of being almost closed. As soon as I arrived at the job the nurse informed me that the doctor would be giving Shirley the awful news that her daughter was dying of cancer. It was bad enough I didn't understand the ins and outs of Tactile Sign Language, but I was being asked to transmit the worst news of this woman's life.

Shirley's daughter was lying in the bed unconscious, tubes coming out of every orifice. Her hands were resting on her daughter's forearm, waiting for her to wake up. I tapped Shirley on the shoulder to introduce myself. She stood up and faced me, placing both hands on top of mine, her breath heaving onto my face, no boundary between our bodies. The Tactile thing felt awkward, like someone was putting their tongue in my ear in order to speak. My heart pounded. Sweat poured down my temples. Due to my ignorance and panic, I envisioned myself being smothered by an elderly, fragile DeafBlind octopus.

Before I could even attempt to practice some Tactile sign with her, three doctors, two nurses, and a social worker entered the room and introduced themselves. Still feeling so unsure of myself, I awkwardly jammed my signs into Shirley's hands, as if by sheer force I would be able to convey the message more clearly.

"I'm sorry, Shirley," the doctor said. "Your daughter's tumor is m-a-l-i-g-n-a-n-t. Unfortunately, there's nothing we can do."

Shirley didn't react, so I assumed the doctor's words weren't registering. Was my Tactile interpreting totally off?

I repeated the doctor's words again, changing my vocabulary and trying to slow myself down.

"Your daughter's tumor is very very bad. Can't operate. Can't help. Short time, and then will pass away. Sorry. Understand?"

Still no reaction. Just as I was about to take a third stab at the interpretation, Shirley's body started shaking. A moment later she was weeping and squeezing my hand close to her body to steady herself. Her tears fell onto my wrist, and suddenly my own eyes began to well up. But, being new, I was so concerned about being "professional" that I pushed Shirley away so I could interpret "properly" for the doctor again. *Comforting her wasn't my job*, I thought. But Shirley didn't want the doctor at that moment. She wanted me, the person who allegedly knew her language. I should have hugged her. I should have done something other than what I did.

My head began screaming: *You useless idiot! You should never have taken this job! Fuck that agency for sending you here.*

That was the moment I promised myself I would never take another DeafBlind gig.

And I didn't—until that morning at the Abilities Institute. Until I met Arlo Dilly.

I was desperate. I needed money—a lot of it. Now past the age of forty, I sensed myself beelining for homosexual obscurity. In Poughkeepsie some of the local queens had a saying: *If you wanna meet a man the odds are good, but the goods are odd.* And boy were they. You could sleep your way through the locals in a week and a half. Otherwise you had to travel up to Albany (Smallbany, we called it) or try your luck with random weekenders up from Manhattan. They usually already had partners and looked at hooking up with the locals as some kind of bucolic novelty, like apple picking in the fall. If I was ever going to fall in love again, and not end up some depressed, lonely country queen who watched QVC and *Golden Girls* alone in bed every night, I knew I had to get the hell out of Poughkeepsie.

And then I had my chance. Just two weeks prior an old Deaf friend called about a potential staff interpreting job outside Philadelphia. It was set to start in the fall if I could only save enough money for the relocation and tie up some loose ends (aka a boatload of credit card debt). Unfortunately, my five-day-a-week gig at the French Culinary Institute canceled at the last minute. (Deaf student became a vegan and dropped out.) The thing is, if you don't have your summer booked by the end of May you're screwed until September. It looked like my plan for escape had once again fizzled. So when Ange from the agency called and said there was a potential summer class, working with a DeafBlind guy for three hours a day, and the job would pay ten bucks an hour over my usual rate, I jumped at the chance. Fuck my rules, I thought. If I wanted to free myself from Poughkeepsie, I would have to get over my fear of working with the DeafBlind for three months.

So the only question was, could I actually do it? And would the Deaf-Blind guy want me?

3

WHAT'S IT LIKE?

You have been waiting forty-five minutes for the Able-Ride to take you to the Abilities Institute to interview the two interpreters. It's hot outside, and you have to wear your sunglasses because it's far too bright. Even though the Abilities Institute is only fourteen minutes from your house and your meeting is at 10 a.m., you told the driver that your meeting was at nine so you would get there on time. But still the van is late.

When you first moved in with Brother Birch, your orientation and mobility instructor taught you to walk from your house to the bus stop and stand and wait with your laminated travel card. The travel card explains to strangers that you are DeafBlind and that you need help with things like crossing the street and getting on the right bus. You are also supposed to show the travel card to the driver with the destination written in Magic Marker. This way he knows when to stop the bus and have someone tap you and let you know to get off. The problem was that almost every time you attempted to travel somewhere on your own you got very anxious and made mistakes. Once, you got on the wrong bus. Twice, you got off at the wrong stop because you were impatient. Brother Birch said he was worried about you and also tired of getting calls from ungodly strangers asking him to come get you when you got lost in the dangerous parts of Poughkeepsie. So now you are forbidden from traveling on public transportation alone and, if Molly or Brother Birch aren't taking you,

you have to use Able-Ride if you go anywhere more than two blocks from your house.

Your legs hurt from standing.

Your guide dog, Snap, lies on the ground and rests her chin on your foot.

Sweat pours down your temples.

Smells like cut grass, gasoline, street tar.

When the driver finally arrives twenty minutes later, you sit in the back seat and lean your head against the cool window. During the fourteen-minute drive to the Abilities Institute you think about yesterday. Two of the girls at your Kingdom Hall have started learning sign language. One of the girls, the one who signs a little better and has a wart on the side of her middle finger, asked you "What's it like to go blind when you're already deaf?"

You would like to have told her that it's really really bullshit and you wouldn't wish it on your worst enemy. Or how you are sick and tired of explaining your disability to girls like her since it's the only thing they ever notice about you. Or maybe you could have told her she better be careful because Jehovah God will get mad at her for being rude and make her lose her sight as well.

But you didn't say any of those things. You told the girl that not every-one with Usher syndrome type 1 goes blind the exact same way. Some people might just experience night blindness and tunnel vision, while others might go completely blind. Some people are lucky, some are not. You are not. You've had night blindness for as long as you can remember, and your tunnel vision got really bad by the time you were eight. You lost all sight in your right eye by the time you were eleven. That was the first time you actually learned the word and sign for *retinitis pigmentosa*. RP is the part of Usher 1 that causes the blindness. Then the vision in your left eye got even worse when you were thirteen, and again at fourteen, and again at fifteen. And later, each time you had to relearn how to "see" the world with whatever vision was left. A doctor once told your mama that you would probably be totally blind by the time you reach thirty.

The wart-finger girl said, "But I saw you reading something last week with a magnifying glass. You're not really 'blind.'"

That's when you wondered, *Have they not been paying attention at all?* Have they not noticed that you've been using Tactile Sign Language and have a guide dog and a white cane? Did they think you were doing this for attention? You tried not to say something insulting about their intelligence. If you were rude, the girls might refuse to tell you when your Able-Ride arrived or point you to the wrong bathroom or not let you touch their wrists a little longer than was proper.

Rule number one of being a successful DeafBlind person: BE NICE ALL THE TIME. If you don't want to be stuck standing on a busy street corner or staring at a shelf in a food store wondering if you've picked up a can of peaches or a can of beans, then you will need the help of other people sometimes. This means you might need to flirt, seduce, and charm people into being your ally. It's not smart to tell people to go fuck themselves like you sometimes want to.

Red star.

So, you politely explained to the girl with the wart on her finger that many people think the "blind" part means total darkness, this great black mass of space. That's not how it is for you. For you, today anyway, when a good light is shining on a piece of paper and the writing is large enough, or maybe you have a magnifying glass, you are able to read with the tunnel vision in your left eye. But if there isn't enough light or the print is too faint or small, then you'll just pretend that you can see it and nod your head like you understand.

The other girl changed places with the wart-finger girl and put her hands in yours. The second girl smelled like sweat and a little bit like metal or blood. It was probably just her braces cutting into her gums. But your sinful brain forces you to think of someone else, the person you're not supposed to ever think about. Against your will, you recall that first time at the Rose Garden School: the blood, the worry that you hurt her, the warm small body, her scent.

Stop it! Stop it!

Red star!

Because of your undisciplined and sinful mind, you had to ask the sweaty-metal-smelling girl to repeat what she just attempted to sign.

"So that's great! Sometimes you can see!"

And the explaining continued. To "see" you need the conditions to be perfect: right light, right contrast, not too much movement. And even then you can usually only see parts of something you're looking at and you have to piece them together in your mind. To capture something in that small remaining area of vision, you also need everything to stay still. But nothing stays still, including your own DeafBlind head.

You dropped a pen on the floor to demonstrate. Gravity has other rules when you have tunnel vision. Nothing ever seems to go straight down. For the sighted person it is obvious where the pen landed. But for you, it is like the pen completely disappeared off the end of the earth. *Here there be monsters!* You look to the floor and move your head, signing as you go: *Can't see it. Can't see it. Can't see it.*

There isn't a clear distinction between the "blind" area of your peripheral vision and what you can see. No. That would be too easy. Your mind samples the shapes and patterns from what's contained in your vision field and fills in the blind area with all these geometric shapes. Your mind tricks you into thinking you are seeing things you really aren't seeing. So finding something real gets harder.

Can't see it. Can't see it. Can't see it.

There!

Suddenly the dropped pen appears like magic, but if you move your eyes even a centimeter then the evil magician that lives in your malfunctioning retina makes the dropped pen disappear again. This happens not only with pens but with books, with words, with your lunch, with the face of your friend. It's like constantly being Sherlock Holmes in "The Case of the Hidden Visual World."

The sweaty-metal girl and the wart-finger girl said they understood, but by that point they had grown tired of talking to you. Who knows if they understood anything you told them? They could have been rolling their eyes and telling each other they wished you'd shut up. Despite answering their questions in far too much depth, despite not being rude, despite all your efforts to be the perfect DeafBlind young man, they eventually left you alone in the middle of the room without even a wall nearby to anchor yourself. You were once again like a small piece of useless but pleasant Styrofoam floating in the middle of the Pacific. This is what it's like to be a DeafBlind man with Usher syndrome type 1. You would probably die without the hearing-sighted to assist you, and sometimes you absolutely hate them for that.

4

THE MEETING

"You must be Cyril!"

Clara Shuster, MSW, entered the conference room clutching a stack of files. Her honey-colored hair was swept back with a black velvet headband. A string of real pearls made it clear that she wasn't doing the shit-paying job for the money.

"Welcome to the Abilities Institute!" Clara gushed in a singsongy voice. "Thanks so much for coming in to meet Arlo!"

"No problem," I said, trying to match the kilowatts of her smile.

"I'm a bit flustered. I just spent the morning at the Social Security office with one of our clients. The workers there can be so frustratingly insensitive, but I'm sure they have their own battles they're fighting, right?"

"I totally get it," I said, nodding my head empathetically. "Social work is the hardest job out there. I have the utmost respect—"

"I don't know about that," Clara volleyed, touching her heart. "What *you* do is . . ." She searched for the word. "Remarkable."

"Oh, yeah, right," I muttered. "It's good."

Nothing annoyed me more than hearing people getting all gooey about the sign language interpreter thing. Sure, it was a cool gig. But I wasn't an ASL interpreter because of some innate goodness. I did it because interpreting was fun, it paid decently, and I really liked most Deaf people.

"Don't be modest," Clara said, pulling the student's file from her desk. And then, just like that, her demeanor shifted to *all business*.

"The DeafBlind student's name is Arlo Dilly. Twenty-three years old. Lives with his guardian, an uncle . . . or rather a great-uncle. Arlo has Usher syndrome 1. I'm sure you're familiar with the condition."

I was, but only barely, which apparently showed on my face, since Clara started to explain.

"In Arlo's case, he was born deaf, followed by night blindness as a child, balance issues, and then a progressive loss of peripheral vision. Lost the sight in his right eye completely, and the left is on its way out. He uses two-hand Tactile. Angela says you have experience?"

"Um . . . a little."

"I see. Well, Arlo will be interviewing you and the other applicant, and he'll make the final decision quickly since the job starts Tuesday. He's a nice young man. Very bright. But this will be the first time he's in a classroom setting since he left high school. He needs someone comfortable with Tactile ASL."

"Of course!" I said, feeling myself being overly eager. "It's important that he find the right match."

Clara looked me over, stopping her gaze at my hairline, smiling curiously, then continuing as if I hadn't said anything.

"You would be teaming with his regular interpreter, Molly Clinch. Do you know her? She's been with him since he was thirteen."

Working with a team interpreter was never my favorite thing, but anytime you have a gig that goes over an hour, and where there will be incessant talking, a team is a necessary evil. The brain starts to miss things after just twenty minutes of nonstop interpreting, and sign language interpreters are at risk of repetitive stress injuries, so we'd switch on and off every twenty minutes to keep the brain fresh, the body safe, and the message accurate.

"Molly Clinch?" I repeated the name. "Is she new to the area? I thought I knew almost every terp north of Yonkers."

"Ah," Clara said. "Interesting. Well, as far as I know, she mostly just works with Arlo. It's important to know that he comes from a strict Jehovah's Witness family so has lived a fairly sheltered life. There's also been some trauma in his past, but, well, if he wants to explain that I'm sure he will."

Trauma? I thought. *More than being raised Jehovah's Witness?*

"Hmm," I said, nodding my head.

"Now, I need to run and make sure the other applicant is on her way." Clara stood and made her way to the door of the conference room. "Arlo should be here any minute. I'll be right back."

And there I was, left alone to stare at the walls again. Opposite the inspirational posters were a series of vintage photos of former students of the Abilities Institute. By the cut of their bell-bottoms and David Cassidy feathered mullets I'd say they were taken back in the 1970s or early '80s. Some were in wheelchairs, some had crutches, a few had white canes, and two were teenagers with Down syndrome. Each had a gigantic smile as if the photographer had tickled them into a state of euphoria.

Where are they now? I thought. Would this Arlo Dilly's photo be up there someday? Where did the students go after here? Were they stuck in Poughkeepsie like me? Holed up in some state-run facility? Dickensian lite? Or were they able to actually get out and have a life?

I wanted a life. *I needed this job.*

A moment later the door pushed open and in popped the head of an old yellow service dog, followed by her slow lumbering body, and then, finally, at the other end of the harness, the DeafBlind consumer himself. *So this is Arlo Dilly?* He was taller than me, six foot at least, and could have been mistaken for any other twentysomething on the streets of Poughkeepsie. I mean, if you ignored his bad haircut, his uncertain and wobbly walk, his giant BluBlocker sunglasses, his dirty backpack the size of a small island, his shirt nerd-buttoned up to his neck, and his saucer-sized yellow button that proclaimed (for safety reasons), I'M DEAFBLIND.

He certainly didn't look as scary as the DeafBlind octopus my mind had created.

Arlo's guide dog, with her gray muzzle, pink nose, and intensely languid eyes, stared up at me almost witheringly, like she was the canine equivalent of a beleaguered and bored secretary portrayed by Agnes Moorehead. As the dog led Arlo farther into the room, he slapped his feet on the floor with loud determination, as if he was killing a bug with every step. When he accidentally sideswiped the arm of one of the conference-room chairs with his leg, he groaned in pain and angrily grabbed the offending chair as if it had tried to hit him on purpose. But then, just as quickly, he started feeling the chair, memorizing its size, shape, and place in the room.

A wave of guilt flooded over me. With any regular client, I would have immediately introduced myself and chatted. Besides being polite, it was the way I could study how the consumer signed and adjust my interpreting accordingly. But the memory of my failure with DeafBlind Shirley still haunted me. So, instead of engaging, I just sat there watching, as though Arlo were some criminal suspect behind a one way mirror of blindness.

Arlo snapped his fingers, signing *sit* to his dog. The old dog obeyed and looked up at her DeafBlind boss adoringly, as if Arlo were the perfect combination of God and a raw bloody steak. Then Arlo removed his gargantuan backpack, placed it at his feet, and unzipped it. Then, step-by-step, he began transferring things between his backpack and his various pockets. A small notebook and black Sharpie were placed in the front right pocket of his khakis. He pulled a folded white cane from his back pocket and transferred it to the front pouch of the bag. His baseball cap he placed in the main compartment. He checked the contents of his wallet and replaced it in his front left pants pocket.

Finally, after everything was in its place, Arlo pulled out a bottle of eyedrops and removed his gigantic sunglasses. I could finally see his entire face. Despite the hair, despite the awful clothes, despite his whole awkward manner, he was a nice-looking young man with a firm jaw and blue eyes that were slightly crossed. He squeezed the drops in each eye and then let them adjust. A moment later he appeared to look around the room until his eyes settled on me.

He sees me. I expected him to confront me about not declaring my presence. For even then, I knew that not announcing myself was considered incredibly rude. I held my breath, ready to accept a scolding. But a second later his eyes floated past me, and he hunted for the chair he had recently bumped into and sat down. *He didn't see me.* So, I continued to observe for a minute more. His Disney-animated eyebrows conducted an orchestra of internal emotions: a sweet memory, an annoyance, anxiety, sadness—something darker. Shirley's face had shown nothing; Arlo's was a full-on carnival of secrets.

"Growlf!" Arlo's old dog glared at me reproachfully. Guilt-stricken, I tiptoed over to the door, opened it, and slammed it hard to indicate I had just arrived. Arlo's head turned toward the door, a look of anticipation on his face.

"Hello? Interpreter?"

Arlo quickly squeezed some sanitizer onto his hands and then reached out two feet to the right of me. I scooted over to shake.

"Hello?" Arlo signed. "My name A-R-L-O. Name-sign: (Arlo twists the letter A into his cheek. Name-signs like this usually mean the person has a dimple there). You certified interpreter?"

Arlo's hands floated in the air in front of me, palms down, waiting. I hesitated. My hands were shaking. Finally, I lifted them into his.

"Hi. Yes. I'm C-Y-R-I-L. My name-sign is (my pointer finger lies flat above my eyebrows and wiggles in imitation of my forehead's tendency to twitch when I'm excited—my Deaf ex gave me it when we first met). Nice to meet you."

I removed my hands so Arlo could answer.

"People here [in the room] . . . how many?" Arlo asked, his expression puzzled. "Before, someone here. Maybe other female interpreter?"

Again, I placed my hands back into Arlo's. That's how it would go from then on. He talks: ASL in the air as usual. I talk: his hands on top of mine, feeling my signs.

"Yes . . . I mean . . . no," I lied. "I just got here. Just you, me, and your dog, who I hope doesn't like to eat interpreters for lunch. Ha ha."

I added a *ha ha* sign at the end so he knew I was joking.

Sign HA HA: *Upside-down "H" hand with thumb out. The two fingers casually jiggle like legs kicking in laughter. Also an abstracted spelling of H-A-H-A.*

Arlo smiled. Dimples. Teeth. Wattage. But a split second later it was all gone, swallowed by a look of concerned curiosity. Meanwhile, I felt myself attempting to combat his blindness with a kind of visual shouting, broadening my own smile to the point of ridiculousness. My expressive face, my greatest tool, was worthless.

Arlo nudged his dog with his knee and snapped his fingers, commanding her to lie down. She hesitated, still staring at me, like she didn't trust me.

"Sorry," Arlo signed. *Snaps fingers.* "Very old guide dog. Grumpy." *Snaps fingers.* "Letting you know she will angry if you hurt boss. That's me. Ha ha."

Suddenly I got it: The dog's name was Snap. With Arlo's hands atop mine, *listening,* I talked to the dog.

"Don't worry, Snap! I'm a good guy. Although I'm a cat man by nature. Ha ha."

Arlo didn't laugh. Neither did Snap. All three of us simply waited. Me staring awkwardly at him. Him staring three inches to the right of my head. Snap, her ridiculously expressive brown eyes on the verge of rolling at the absurdity of my discomfort.

"Excuse me," Arlo finally signed. "Personal question. You JW?"

It took me a second to understand what he meant. Then I remembered: J-W was the sign for *Jehovah's Witness*. Usually, a new Deaf consumer would first ask whether or not I came from a Deaf family and then if I was married and had kids. They never began with a question about my religion.

"So is this your first time taking a college class?" I asked, attempting to deflect.

Arlo's eyebrows furrowed.

"Believe in Jesus?" he asked, clearly not letting it go. "Catholic? Jewish?"

How much was I willing to hide my heathen homosexuality in order to get the job? A bad interpreter-client match is the worst thing in the world.

"I don't usually talk about that," I said. "But if you want to know, I wouldn't say I'm an atheist. That's way too committal. If not knowing or caring were a religion, that would be the one I'd join."

Arlo appeared confused by my response.

"Is that a problem?" I asked.

Snap half barked, half growled, nudging her gray muzzle between Arlo and me. Was the dog religious too? Arlo pushed the dog's snout down and pointed his finger admonishingly. Snap lowered her head, her judgmental eyes still glaring at me. *Imposter!* she seemed to be thinking. *He's not suited to this job!*

"Okay," Arlo signed to me. "Understand. But you will die forever. Not afraid? Sorry. Sorry. Right. Too personal."

Arlo tilted his head away from me, his eyebrows indicating some inner dialogue was happening. I was certain I had lost the gig. My escape plan to Philly would crumble, but at least Arlo would get some devout Tactile interpreter who could share her favorite Bible passages with him. And I wouldn't have to break my promise to myself. Still, I felt disappointed.

"One more question?" Arlo suddenly signed. "Maybe later when Judgment Day happen, then you will believe in Jehovah God?"

I was just about to answer a decided no when Clara Shuster suddenly entered, causing me to nervously shove my hands into my pockets. Seeing Arlo's hands hanging in the air waiting for me, Clara raised her eyebrows in a gentle reprimand.

"Remember, he's tactile," she said. "He looks like he sees you, right? He's probably faking."

I started to explain myself, but Clara held her hand up, her thumb and pointer finger indicating a pea-sized hole.

"He can only see about this much in his left eye these days, and even that's starting to get foggy. With the right magnification equipment he can see enough to read, but tends to use braille for anything really long."

"Other person here?" Arlo asked.

Arlo had noticed from my movements that I was talking to someone and not interpreting—something I usually would never do, since it's incredibly impolite. I apologized and quickly, without voicing, caught Arlo up on everything Clara had said. A faint smile appeared on his face. I couldn't tell whether it was due to Clara's comment about his "faking it" or simply because I had interpreted everything.

While this short, silent exchange between us happened, Clara, who didn't know sign language, stood there looking uncomfortable.

"What are you two signing to each other?"

"Um . . . just interpreting," I said.

Clara looked at me and smiled knowingly.

"You know he perceives a lot more than we think. Trust me. He's a smart one, and adorable, as you can see. Don't tell him I said that."

I already had, including her request not to interpret what she said. (Never tell an interpreter *not* to interpret something said in front of a Deaf person.) Arlo smiled as his cheeks flushed. Snap pricked up her floppy ears, gave a funny little happy growl, and banged her tail twice on the floor.

"Oh hush, Snap!" Clara said playfully. "They need to retire that old dog soon. She's got arthritis in her hips and her eyesight is somewhat questionable. Sometimes I'm not sure who's guiding whom. Now, if you wouldn't mind interpreting some business I have with Arlo? It will be a good way for him to see your style. I'll do the same with the other applicant."

What followed was a typical case manager–client conversation about things related to school: access to the library's computer, mobility issues that could arise on a campus built on a hillside, how the state would cover the cost of books and provide a vibrating alarm clock for free.

Arlo appeared to understand everything I was interpreting, with only some clarifications on whether I was fingerspelling a D or an L. In the middle of one of Clara's sentences Arlo interrupted, indicating he was just talking to me, and not to voice what he was saying.

"Clara Shuster's face?" he asked. "Smiling, frowning—which?"

"Her expression is, well, *in between*. But not angry. Professional."

"Okay. Thank you."

Then it hit me. To do the job right for Arlo, it wasn't just about the language; I would need to describe people's expressions, the room where they stood, whether they had food in their teeth. Everything. Distracted, I completely lost what Clara was talking about and had to ask her to repeat herself. When she did, I noticed my hands were shaking again. Then I started to worry whether Arlo smelled the half bottle of red wine I had the night before. I suddenly couldn't breathe. A pipe-burst of sweat poured down my armpits. It was the DeafBlind octopus thing. It was back.

"You okay?" Arlo asked.

"Yes, yes, sure! It's just very hot in here."

I took a deep breath and tried to focus. *Just do the job!* Then, as Clara talked about Arlo's goals for the class, I wanted to somehow replicate her demeanor, so I let my wrists go a little limp to indicate the languid lilt of her snooty, Connecticut-raised accent. She talked about how Arlo's uncle felt it was necessary that Arlo improve his written communication since he was set to go on a yearlong mission to Ecuador with his church at the end of summer, and one of his tasks would include putting together written material. Finally, as I worked on "embodying" Clara's voice in my signs, my interpreter "flow" kicked in. Arlo was nodding at all the right places. He was getting it. Also turning Arlo's ASL into spoken English—what we call "voicing"—went incredibly smoothly. When the Deaf person and the interpreter are a good match it can feel a little like channeling a vocal spirit. My shaking stopped. My sweating stopped.

I can do this!

"Well, it seems like you two work well together," Clara finally said, noticing Arlo's engagement. "So Arlo just needs to meet the other interpreter applicant, and then we'll give you a call."

"No. Wait!" Arlo signed, interrupting Clara. "Other interpreter . . . Don't need. I decide finish. I want Cyril!"

Arlo searched for my face.

"Cyril? Interpret for me? Will?"

Suddenly, Arlo was making it my choice. If I didn't leave then, it was going to be a long, complicated summer. The job frightened the hell out of me, but it was also beginning to excite me.

"Sure," I said. "I'm available."

Arlo smiled while Clara clapped her hands, like a baby had said "Mama" for the first time.

"Great! I'll have the secretary let the other interpreter know we'll keep her on our list as a sub or if something changes. Now, Cyril, if you wouldn't mind, could you interpret just one more thing I need to tell Arlo?"

"Sure, no problem."

Clara explained how she was going to need to either cancel or reschedule Arlo's campus orientation over the weekend since Molly, his regular interpreter, wasn't available.

"But class start Tuesday," Arlo said, looking distraught. "I finish touch campus—haven't. First time. Cafeteria . . . where? Library for internet . . . where? I know nothing. Campus very big, complicated. Molly told me maybe one thousand stairs."

Arlo indicated the warren of stairways that made up the hillside campus.

"Cyril interpret—can?" Arlo asked.

"I'm afraid I'm not available until Tuesday," I signed and voiced. "I wish I was."

"If Cyril can't," Arlo signed, frustrated, "can find other interpreter? Okay? If can't . . . no problem. Sorry."

If I were to describe my first impressions of Arlo, I would have said he was a smart, humble, and polite young man on the surface, but there was something underneath. It was as if he carried a heavy vessel filled with sorrow inside his chest. He reminded me of someone, but, at that moment, I couldn't figure it out.

"I'm sorry, Arlo. It's just not possible," Clara said, exaggerating her disappointment. "You know how hard it is to find an interpreter last-minute. Of course, you could just use your SBC to communicate with the trainer?"

Arlo's brow knitted and he pursed his lips. He explained how the SBC (screen braille communicator), a device on which Arlo would type to the non-signing trainer, was an older, cumbersome model. Using it would require him to sit at a table every time he needed to say something. Definitely not ideal while one was learning his way around a hilly campus with a dog and/or white cane. Clara apologized, saying she knew his equipment was out of date, but quickly got off the topic. (Clearly there was a story there.) Then she reiterated that an interpreter just wasn't possible. I waited for Arlo to put his foot down and demand Clara try harder to find one.

"Okay," he finally signed, forcing a smile. "Never mind."

"Fantastic!" Clara said, ignoring Arlo's obvious distress. "Then we're all set."

My redheaded temper began to flare. I desperately wanted to quote the law to Clara that gave Arlo the right to have an interpreter there. But it isn't kosher for an interpreter to just interject their opinions while working.

More importantly, it's best to let the client advocate for themselves. However, I also knew how some Deaf, unaware of the law, would simply accept when hearing people would intentionally or unintentionally deny them their legal right to accommodation. I held my breath. *Say something, Arlo! Please, say something, so I don't have to!* Then, after watching Clara Shuster, MSW, write a note that Arlo would forgo the campus orientation, I couldn't control myself. Without voicing, I quickly asked Arlo if he wouldn't mind if I said something to Clara myself. He looked puzzled but told me to go ahead.

"Pardon me," I blurted out nervously, speaking and signing simultaneously. "This is Cyril talking now. Mrs. Shuster, I know it's crazy hard to get an interpreter last-minute, and I'm sure you've tried your best. But, as you know, the ADA requires *appropriate, qualified access for communication*. And Arlo's correct. That campus is nuts with stairways, so he'll clearly need an interpreter and the orientation. Sorry if I'm speaking out of turn, Mrs. Shuster, but I'm wondering if you've tried some of the other agencies?"

I then listed all the other good interpreting agencies within fifty miles of Poughkeepsie. Clara's face made it clear she did not appreciate my supplanting her position as the chief social justice warrior in the house, but still she copied down the names and said she would try to find someone. When the interaction was completed, I noticed Arlo spell out the letters A-D-A to himself, like they were some magical incantation to which he was not privy.

"You do know what the ADA is, right?" I signed to him, still simultaneously speaking so Clara could hear me. "Americans with Disabilities Act?"

"I think that's enough for now, Mr. Brewster," Clara whispered, her teeth bared in an outsized smile. (Social worker lingo for *I want to kill you.*) "I'm sure Arlo is well aware of his rights but thank you for reminding us."

I tried to imbue Clara's terse yet placating tone into my interpretation.

"Cyril, question?" Arlo asked me privately. "Clara . . . angry now?"

"Not angry. Just a little annoyed—with me. I get the feeling she didn't like me talking so much about the ADA. But I'm only guessing."

Arlo nodded, affirming that he understood. Then, as Clara was about to end the meeting, there was a knock at the door. Clara called for whoever it was to come in. There at the door was a thin, short woman, probably in her early fifties. Her brown hair was streaked with silver and pulled back with a velvet headband, the sort women wore in the 1980s. She was not unattractive, but her face looked sullied by weariness and disappointment. She wore a neat polka dot skirt and a solid black sweater. *Black* in the *summertime?* She had to be another sign language interpreter, but one I didn't know. She was clearly disturbed to see my hands atop Arlo's.

"Oh, good!" Clara exclaimed. "Cyril, this is Arlo's regular SSP and longtime interpreter, Molly Clinch."

As soon as I fingerspelled Molly's name, Arlo's body tensed, and his eyes darted nervously around the room.

"Molly, I'm so sorry," Clara continued. "I'm afraid we won't be interviewing your friend. Arlo has decided to go with Cyril here as your team for the summer. So we're all set."

"Pleased to meet you, Molly," I said, my hands still in Arlo's, interpreting.

Pursing her lips so tightly they virtually disappeared, Molly gestured at me like a shit stain on a new white carpet.

"Does Brother Birch know about this?"

5

LEAVING HOME

Just after you finished eating a peanut butter and grape jelly sandwich for lunch, you are surprised when Molly walks into the kitchen of Brother Birch's house. You can instantly recognize her propulsive, angry footsteps, which tap the floor like the end of a wooden broomstick. Molly rarely comes over to interpret without you knowing first.

A minute later you find out why.

"You never should have made a decision about the interpreter without consulting me," Brother Birch says, via Molly's interpreting. "You put us in a very awkward situation. Didn't you know Molly had already told her friend she had the job?"

You explain that Mrs. Shuster was the one who said it was better to have a male interpreter voicing for you to reduce confusion when you speak. This is a lie.

Red star.

"But we know nothing about this man," Brother Birch says. You can tell he is getting aggravated by the way Molly is interpreting. "You know how much I care for you, Arlo. You've done so well over the last several years. But remember: The Devil will find every opportunity to corrupt our hearts. We don't want a repeat of what happened before."

Brother Birch doesn't finish his thought. You ask Molly to repeat her interpretation in case you missed something. She says: *Doesn't matter.*

Then you remember. Even talking about what happened five and a half years ago at the Rose Garden School is forbidden. It lives in phrases like "before" or "doesn't matter" or in the dangling stillness at the ends of sentences.

You lower your head, squinching your eyebrows so you look very sad that you disappointed anyone. Then you tell Brother Birch that you can write Mrs. Shuster in the morning and ask that they hire Molly's friend instead. Molly's hands pause and you feel her shift in her seat. You know they won't be able to do this, because Mrs. Shuster explained that canceling interpreters at the last minute is *very expensive*. But you pretend not to know this.

Ha! You got them!

"Unfortunately, we're stuck with him now," Brother Birch says. "Luckily Molly will be there to make sure he's a good fit."

Smiling is the worst thing to do at this moment. To prevent yourself from smiling you tilt your head downward and suck in your lips, crushing the smile inside your face. Brother Birch asks you if something is wrong. You tell him you have a headache.

"Get a glass of water and then go prepare for Bible study tomorrow. I need to speak with Molly alone right now."

While Brother Birch and Molly tell secrets, you and Snap walk down to your bedroom in the hot basement. You sit at your desk. Snap lays her warm body at your feet and licks your pant leg to remind you she loves you. You turn on your computer. You go to the website JW.org and try to read *The Watchtower–Study Edition*. The question is: *How Can You Safeguard Your Heart? How Satan Tries to Infect Our Heart*. Your left eye immediately becomes tired, so you stop reading. You let yourself think about the new college class on Tuesday with Cyril, the new male team interpreter working with Molly. A new interpreter who will interpret *everything*. This makes your body rock back and forth, and you allow your face to smile. It's not often that something new happens in your life lately. Other than visits to the ophthalmologist and the Abilities Institute for training, the last several years have been about one thing: becoming a *spiritually strong* young man. Being spiritually strong means preparing for and going to the Kingdom Hall for Public Talk, Watchtower Study, Theocratic Ministry School, Bible study, and, if you want to keep your auxiliary pioneer status, a minimum of seven and a half hours of field service a week standing at the mall or going door-to-door with Brother Birch. It's exhausting. A big portion of your free time is spent alone in your room reading JW.org, trying to avoid being tempted by forbidden websites, thinking about committing red star sins, praying not to commit them, and, more often than not, committing them and then praying for forgiveness. Every single other moment, when you're not sleeping, bathing, or eating, you get lost in the fantasy place inside your mind. And, to be totally honest, even when you're doing most of the other activities, you still spend much of the time in your fantasy place. The outside world can be tedious, but in the fantasy place you can time travel, and remember forbidden things, and pretend things are different than they are.

But starting Tuesday, for three hours a day, your outside life will be different. You will learn to improve your writing, and there will be new people sitting right next to you in class. Being friends with worldly people is forbidden, but it's okay if you witness to them. How many of the other students will be your same age? How many will be men and how many will be women? Inside your fantasy place you imagine a young woman who will be shorter than you, who will sit right next to you. You will be surprised to learn that she knows sign language too, and is a spiritually strong JW with smooth, soft, dry fingers that say funny things. Her wrists will be thinner than yours, and her skin will smell of baby powder and body odor and when no one is looking she will let you . . .

Red star.

Your eyes focus again on the big white letters on the black screen: *Satan.* You switch the screen from JW.org to the search engine, and try to remember what the male interpreter told you today about the . . . what was it? A-D-A law? It meant the America . . . Disable . . . something. ADA. Why has no one ever told you about this law before? You type the letters ADA and the word *law* into the search bar and press Enter. Suddenly the page fills with selections. The first link your vision settles on says: *What is the Americans with Disabilities Act (ADA) of 1990?* That was it! That's what the interpreter called it: the Americans with Disability Act.

In the middle of reading the page about the ADA you feel someone coming down the steps to the basement. The footsteps are of moderate weight and irregular. It's Mrs. Brother Birch, who is always trying to reduce her weight to take the pain off her arthritic knee. If she catches you not preparing for Bible study, she will snitch to Brother Birch. Your hands are shaking as you switch back to the JW.org page and start to nod your head thoughtfully in case she's looking. A moment later the *thump-womp-thump* of the dryer vibrates through the floor, followed by Mrs. Brother Birch's uneven footsteps clomping back up the steps until they are gone. You are safe.

Sniff.

The laundry machine: wet metal, soiled clothes, and soap.

The dryer: electric fire and . . .

Sniff sniff.

Your mind attaches to something else: orange-smelling fabric softener. A memory flashes across your brain: A dark room. A chilly morning. Folded clothes piled on the bed. A suitcase?

"MAMA? What?" You signed into the darkness.

That chilly morning you first went away to school. Early September? Late August? Your mama's living room. Ten years ago. You were thirteen. The dim light rendered you totally blind, but you could smell her scent: coffee and milk, the orange blossom perfume she'd buy at the Walgreens because she knew you liked it. Something was wrong. You could read your mama's moods by the pulse of her blood, the flick of her finger, her breath. She was the Earth; you were her moon.

"Mama? What?"

You waved your hands in the air in front of you. Your knowledge of real ASL was still limited, but your mother's was almost nonexistent. She never studied sign language, so your entire relationship was contained within the boundaries of homemade gestures, bad lipreading (when you could see better), and a handful of signs she had learned from the interpreters at the Kingdom Hall: *want, toilet, bad, good, boy, girl, where, please, sorry, when, now, later, hamburger, tomorrow, eat/food, Jehovah, God, Jesus, funny, thank you, Mama*, and your name sign.

Mama's real name was Alma Dilly. Because you knew her before you lost most of your vision, her face remains one of the only ones you can still see clearly with your mind's eye. Her eyes were hazel. Her face was very pale. When she smiled, one side of her mouth went higher than the other, and she smiled at you often. But that morning you couldn't see her face. It was far too dark. You could only feel her body walking back and forth across the room, first to the bureau, then the bed. You chased her vibration.

"What do?" you begged, forcing your fingers into her face. "Me red star? Me bad boy?"

She said nothing.

Following her to the bed, you felt the piles of clothes: your favorite polo shirt, underwear, corduroy dungarees—the kind you liked to run your fingers across, feeling the scratchy velvety ribs. Why were *your* clothes out? Your hands searched across the span of the bed until they hit something large and hard with a texture like the sandpapery skin of a snake.

Sniff.

The smell of old shoes and cardboard. Your mother's big suitcase. *Packing?* Yours was always the smaller suitcase. Why were *your* clothes going into *her* suitcase? A waft of cold air blew against your face. The front door opened.

Sniff.

Your stomach clenched. The oily smell of Tiger Balm and a bacon breakfast: *No, no, no! Brother Birch is here.*

Brother Birch, your mother's uncle, the most respected elder in your entire Kingdom Hall. You hated him when you were little. Brother Birch, who forced you to sit motionless during the long and boring Public Talk, and if you squirmed he would press his fat thumbnail into your thigh, clamping his thick, hairy, calloused hand across your mouth if you dared to scream out. Back then, like your mother, he knew no sign language.

"Brother Birch drive us?" you asked anxiously. "Your clothes . . . where? We go together? Please talk something! Mama!"

You shook her cold hands, hoping words would free themselves. When they didn't, you reached up to her face and met her quivering lower lip, a worried brow, and wet cheeks. You traced the liquid to the source at the corners of her eyes.

"Crying? Mama? What for? What for? What for?"

Suddenly, as if a tornado had lifted you, Brother Birch yanked you by the waist from your mother's side. Instinctively, your feet kicked backward, landing your heels squarely into his shins. He dropped you and your elbow cracked onto the hardwood floor. Weeping, your screams vibrated through your body. Mama pulled you up to her chest, stroking your hair, kissing your forehead.

"Don't want go with Brother Birch! Please, Mama, please!"

"No . . . bad boy," she signed, awkwardly. "Yes . . . good . . . boy."

Again Brother Birch wrestled you from your mama's arms and dragged you, screaming and kicking, across the floor and out the door. The cold morning air stung your tear-spattered cheeks. The rising sun shot stinging glares into your eyes. But when your limited vision adjusted, you saw a large, strange woman opening the door of a white van. The suitcase with your clothes getting put in the back. *Where are they taking me?* Despite fighting for your freedom, Brother Birch managed to get you into the back of the van. The van driver laid her fat body across yours, suffocating you. They intended to break you. You had no choice. You pushed the air from your lungs up and across your vocal cords until the sound vibrated behind your nose.

"Sss . . . sorry!"

Finally getting off you, they strapped the buckle tightly across your lap. The cold, scratchy vinyl seats smelled like plastic. The van's engine rumbled. Gas fumes and the stink of a freshly lit cigarette burned your throat. You thought your body was quaking from its tears until you realized the van was moving. How would you find your way back home if you could no longer see? You pressed your face into the cold window, screaming and signing as large as you could.

"Mama! Mama! Please! Can't see! I want stay home! Please! Stay home!"

The van jerked to a stop.

Had your mama heard? Any moment the door would slide open and she would pull you into her soft-as-pillows arms and take you back into the house and feed you Tang and Oreo cookies, just like the two previous times this happened. She would kiss you a hundred times all over your face, then press her fist into her chest, signing SORRY, SORRY. But you would turn your angry head away and cross your arms just so she knew how much she had hurt you. But then you would forgive her.

You waited. You waited. You waited.

◇ ◇ ◇

When the sad memory is over your fingers are curled into fists. You are back inside your basement room, sitting in front of your computer. You are twenty-three years old. Your mother has been dead for six years. Brother Birch takes care of you now and he often pats you on the back and can sign "*Good boy. Good Arlo. Jehovah God loves you. I love you.*" You take a deep breath. The giant white cursor is still flashing on the screen. There are no footsteps any longer, only the constant vibration and rhythmic throbbing of the clothes in the dryer. You return to the page that talks about the ADA law. You start to read.

6

FIRST DAY OF CLASS

One of the best things about working as a freelance sign language interpreter was that I rarely had to work in one place for very long. Most gigs were two-hour-minimum one-offs: doctor's visits, Social Security appointments, job interviews, that sort of thing. Even the longer assignments, like semester-long college classes, never lasted long enough for me to start disliking any one place or person very deeply, or vice versa. I have always been someone who could love just about anyone or anywhere for about two hours. After that it's diminishing returns.

While Dutchess Community College isn't nearly as stately as nearby Marist or Vassar, its lovely setting on the side of a hill gives it some of the best views of the countryside outside of Poughkeepsie. As soon as I got off the elevator on the third floor, I got a whiff of that "first day of school" smell. Even in middle age it immediately made my stomach slightly queasy. Being the only redheaded, gay kid growing up, I was a target for bullies and hated school. My best friend, Hanne, was the one saving grace during my junior and senior years. Then again, I spent half the time blowing off classes so I could cruise older, married guys during lunchtime at Kaal Rock Park or in the JCPenney bathrooms upstairs at the Galleria. As irony would have it, I often ended up interpreting the same classes I used to skip.

As soon as I turned the corner toward the Office of Accommodative

Services, I saw Arlo and his interpreter, Molly Clinch, standing by the door, with Snap lying at Arlo's feet looking bored. Arlo wore the same outfit I saw him in at the Abilities Institute: khakis and blue oxford shirt buttoned to the neck. The look seemed out of place next to all the T-shirt-and-shorts-wearing students swarming the hallway. Molly looked exactly the same as that first day: same headband, same world-weariness, but instead of a polka dot skirt, this one was black and printed with violets. I decided to hang back for a moment just to get a handle on how Molly worked with Arlo. I quickly figured out that she and Arlo were having some sort of disagreement.

"Please," Arlo begged. "Maybe just try, okay?"

"No," Molly signed, her eyes widening in annoyance. "That's not your section for the class. The booklet says it's closed. That means it's full. Finish. End of story."

"I know. But yesterday Disability Office advisor email me. Say if professor sign permission paper . . . then . . . fine. Join class . . . can!"

I missed what Arlo signed next but was able to glean that he found something on a website that rated the professor as the best writing teacher at the college.

"Website said other teacher 'boring' . . . very low rating. Can we try join class? Please?"

Molly shook her head, her thin lips squeezed tight. She looked at Arlo more like an aggravated mother than an interpreter.

"No. That's enough. We will follow the schedule you were given. That's how college works!"

Molly's ASL, while not exactly beautiful, was fluent, which was a relief. An ASL interpreter being qualified for a job is never guaranteed in a state that doesn't require interpreters to be licensed or certified. It was what Molly said that bothered me. It was never an interpreter's place to make a decision for the Deaf. Our job is to interpret the message well enough so that the Deaf can make decisions for themselves. I might have said something, except that Molly had been Arlo's interpreter for a decade. I was the new guy. Still, there was something *off* about their whole interaction. Then I caught sight of *The Watchtower* magazine sticking out of Molly's purse. She was a JW too. I was about to spend my whole summer with two JWs. *Yippee for me.*

I had nothing against JWs. Some of the best and nicest interpreters in New York State are Jehovah's Witnesses. And I was certain she'd have had plenty of experience working with a gay guy. One of the weirder aspects of the interpreting business is that it is, for the most part, composed of four discrete groups: children of Deaf adults (known as CODAs), brainy progressive women, overly zealous religious folks, and finally, queers like me. CODAs become terps because ASL is their native language and practically a ready-made career. Brainy progressive women because it is a profession where they never stop learning and get to make a positive difference in the world. Religious zealots because interpreting offers a flexible schedule to do missionary work and knowing ASL allows them to proselytize to a marginalized group. Out west the Mormons fit this slot. Here in the Northeast we have the JWs. As far as we queers go, I suppose it's because we understand what it is to be an outsider, not to mention we look hot in black and are great with our hands.

"Hey there!" I finally shouted, hoping my interruption of the disagreement would work in Arlo's favor. "Hope I'm not too late."

Molly looked at her watch and let Arlo know I had arrived.

"I was always taught it's customary to arrive at a new job at least fifteen minutes early," Molly signed without a hint of humor.

So much for her being the nice kind of Jehovah's Witness. It was far too soon to tell her to shove it up her skinny, sour JW butt, so I forced a smile and lied about not being familiar with the campus.

"So where's this class?" I asked.

"Arlo's schedule says to go to room C-122," Molly said, simultaneously signing to Arlo. "We can't change that now."

Arlo looked distressed. I tapped him on the shoulder, and his hands lifted into mine.

"Hi! Sorry I was late," I signed. "You look upset. Is something wrong?"

Arlo shook his head no, but his face twitched with dismay.

"I just want take different professor's class," he signed. "Molly say: *Impossible. Class full. Close finish. Sorry.*"

"I'm sure Molly is just following rules," I signed, trying to appease Molly a little. At first anyway. "When I was in college up in Rochester, I used to always get into classes that were supposedly full. You don't mind if we try, do you, Molly?"

As she had done that first day at the Abilities Institute, Molly looked at me with such disgust, you'd think I just ate a baby. She quickly shoved her hands under Arlo's, nearly knocking me out of the way in the process.

"That's very nice of Cyril to offer his opinion. But this isn't Rochester. Let's go before you miss the start of *your* class."

Molly began leading Arlo toward his originally scheduled class. No longer able to control myself, I headed them off, stopping them, and addressed Molly while I interpreted for Arlo.

"Whoa there, Molly! Remember, you and me, we're just the interpreters, right? Isn't it, you know, better to support Arlo in making his own decisions? Can we agree on that?"

Molly rubbed her hands down her flowered print skirt, wiping the fury into the folds of violets.

"Excuse me, Mr. Brewster?" Molly's voice dripped with sarcasm. "How long have you actually worked with Arlo? A day? An hour? By my watch I'd say between five and seven minutes, if we include the walk from your car to arrive here—*late.* Now, shall I suggest we get to the class and do the jobs we are paid for?"

Molly rolled her eyes and again offered her arm to Arlo. Annoyed, I yanked Arlo's hands back into mine.

"Of course, as all interpreters know, Molly"—my voice wavered with nervous anger—"the Deaf consumer is the boss, right? So, Arlo, what would *you* like to do?"

There we were, me and another interpreter, standing in the middle of a hallway using the DeafBlind student in a game of tug-of-war. *How did it all fall apart so quickly? I will surely be fired before the day is out.* But then I saw it: while Molly was seething, Arlo was suppressing a smile.

"Calm, calm," Arlo signed. "Everyone confuse. Hold on. Idea! Maybe this time I decide? Okay, Molly? I will ask professor sign paper—okay? Suppose say 'no'? Then accept! We go back regular class. Okay, Molly, okay?"

At first Molly looked annoyed. But then, as she stared for a second at Arlo's nervous smiling face, I caught the quickest glimmer of something: her heart, it appeared, did beat.

"Fine," Molly signed, rolling her eyes. "But it's a waste of time."

Then, without interpreting for Arlo, she whispered at me through her teeth: "So this is how you are? They warned me about you."

7

BANISTERS AND BALONEY

You are walking down the hallway with Snap, Molly, and Cyril, your new interpreter. You grasp Molly's elbow. Some people get fat when they are older. Molly has gotten skinnier and smaller as if she has been shrinking. When you first met Molly ten years ago at the Rose Garden School you were only thirteen and had just woken up in the strange bed after having cried yourself to sleep. It was dark, and you didn't know where they had taken you. It was Molly's cold fingers that told you everything.

"It's called the Rose Garden School," she signed.

"Roses?" you asked, sniffing the night air. "Can't smell!"

"There are no rose gardens here. It's just a name."

"You my interpreter?" you asked in your hodgepodge of basic ASL and homemade signs you used with your mother.

"I'm called an intervenor. It's like a teacher and an interpreter all in one," she signed.

"I want go home!"

Many of Molly's signs were unfamiliar, but you could already tell she was more accomplished than any of your previous interpreters. She told you that the Rose Garden School would be your new home, and that you would sleep in a dorm called Magnolia House, which was also named for a flower, and no, there were no magnolias anywhere near Magnolia House.

"I want see Mama!"

"Try to stop crying," Molly signed. Her hands were chilly but not unkind. "You'll see her at winter break and in the summers. But you need to be an example when the other children arrive. Jehovah God is depending on you!"

For the first two weeks Molly and Costas, the orientation and mobility instructor, were the only people with whom you interacted. Costas showed you how to find your way around the school, teaching you things like running your cane along the side of the pavement—"shorelining"—and then to turn right when the grass starts in order to find the cafeteria.

"Make sure you don't only tap your cane in front of you," Costas signed. "Sweep it back and forth like this. Remember the cane is there both to alert you to obstacles and also to signal to others that you have vision problems."

At the start of the second week, the school was officially open, and Molly guided you to a giant hall that was very bright and painted orange and yellow. You felt the breeze and bump of hundreds of children's bodies. The floor rumbled like an earthquake of feet.

"This is the cafeteria," Molly signed, seating you at a big long table. "Don't move. I'll be back with your lunch in a few minutes."

You sat there waiting, frightened and excited. But no matter how you strained to see the other students with the vision in your left eye, their faces flew by like the rapidly flipping pages of a book. If you looked farther off, you could catch glimpses of Deaf children releasing thousands of words into the air with their hands. They all seemed to know one another. A wave of homesickness crashed over you and you squeezed your eyes closed so you wouldn't cry.

A moment later someone's hot breath huffed onto your cheek.

"Molly?" You reached out your hand, but whoever it was jumped out of the way too quickly for you to see.

Sniff.

An unfamiliar spicy-sweet smell filled your nose.

"Who?" you asked, turning toward the scent. "Stop playing!"

A breeze of a hand waved at the other side of your head. You snapped your head toward it, but just as quickly it disappeared. Then a purposeful blast of air blew into your hair. This time you swung your arm, but the sneaky child disappeared into the chaos of the cafeteria.

"What's wrong?" Molly asked, after setting a food tray in front of you. "Why did you try to hit me?"

You explained to Molly about the mysterious child blowing on you, but she dismissed it as unimportant and told you to eat. Your fingers found a glass of milk, an apple, two slices of bread with something in the middle.

Sniff.

The "hamburger" had an unfamiliar smell.

When you chomped down, your mouth was suddenly awash with brand-new textures and tastes: creamy eggy mayonnaise, soft sweet bread, and a slippery, savory, meat-like substance. You waved the bread and meat into Molly's face.

"Wow!" you exclaimed. "This *hamburger* delicious! New *hamburger*, name what?!"

"That isn't a *hamburger*," Molly signed. "It's called a S-A-N-D-W-I-C-H. Sandwich."

Sign SANDWICH: *One hand folds over the other hand like it's the bread making a meat sandwich. Then you raise the hand sandwich to the mouth.*

Your face flushed warm from embarrassment.

"Okay. Okay. Right. *Sandwich*. I forget."

But you didn't forget. You didn't know the sign for *sandwich*. Your mama would use the sign *hamburger* for all foods formed with two pieces of bread. It didn't matter whether the *hamburger* was made with peanut butter and jelly, a fried chicken patty, or the especially delicious sloppy joe *hamburger*, which she would sign "bad boy hamburger."

"You really need to learn more ASL," Molly signed. "Especially the signs for food so you can ask for it. This is called a B-A-L-O-N-E-Y sandwich."

Then Molly taught you her sign for *baloney*, which she explained was also the sign for *hot dog*. You repeated the sign over and over, burning it into your brain.

"Baloney, baloney, baloney! Hot dog, hot dog, hot dog!"

You decided to request the same kind of delicious sandwich the next day, and also the day after that, and maybe forever.

Molly turned away to talk to another intervenor named Sybil. You had met Sybil the day before. She smelled like flowers and had soft squishy hands. Unlike Molly's brittle, awkward hugs, Sybil's hugs were thick and warm. Sybil had worked at the Rose Garden School longer than Molly and was the intervenor for the two boys who would be your roommates.

"Hello, Arlo!" Sybil signed, sitting next to you at the table. "Good news! Your roommates came back to school today. You will meet them later!"

Your body rocked back and forth with excitement. Would your roommates like playing games, telling you stories, and sharing their dessert? *Do they have Usher syndrome 1 as well? Is their vision better or worse than mine?* Then a chilling thought entered your head: *What if they know more ASL than me? What if I can't understand them?*

"Molly!" you cried, turning away from Sybil. "Molly! Teach me better sign language! Must! Now!"

"What? Finish your baloney sandwich—"

"No time!" You pulled her from the table.

For the next two hours Molly became your flesh-and-blood ASL-English dictionary, as you pointed at nearly everything and everyone you encountered.

"That . . . name what?" you demanded. "Sign what? That . . . what do? Name what? Sign how? Fingerspell?"

They tried to teach you to lipread at your old mainstreamed school (which you never could do very well, even before your sight got worse), and the little ASL you did know was from the hearing JWs at the Kingdom Hall who studied sign language so they could preach to the Deaf. Many of the signs Molly was using, like "ketchup" and "fork," you already knew, but then there were dozens of others that were completely new. Signs like *Coke machine, cake, lunch lady, nosy,* and *rude.*

You pointed to a big cylindrical metal object near the door.

"That!" you begged. "Spelling? ASL . . . how?"

Molly fingerspelled the term *trash can* then followed it with the ASL sign. Molly said that some people also liked to sign *trash* the way you signed the words *lettuce* or *cabbage.* That version, Molly said, was probably invented because the word *garbage* looked like the word *cabbage* to some long-ago Deaf person who read lips.

Within the first hour you learned over fifty new signs from Molly.

"Wow!" you signed. "Too many words! Head is full! If not remember . . . Wow! My face will red!"

"Maybe it's time we stop?" Molly begged, her previous willingness deflating.

"No time! Teach more! That!"

You pointed to something on the wall behind Molly: orange and black paper formed into circles and connected, pumpkins with faces, the word *Halloween.*

"H-A-L-L-O-W-E-E-N?" you fingerspelled, already knowing you were crossing a line. "ASL . . . what?"

"Never mind about that," Molly's hands reprimanded gently. "Didn't your mother teach you? It's sinful to celebrate P-A-G-A-N holidays."

You nodded, but still had hoped for a loophole at the new school.

"You are good boy," Molly signed. (*Yay! She likes you!*) "You love Jehovah God. Same as me. When goats talk about H-A-L-L-O-W-E-E-N or C-H-R-I-S-T-M-A-S, we'll just smile and say 'Excuse me. Need to go now!' Remember, the children here aren't meant to be your friends. They aren't special like you."

"Me special . . . why? 'Special,' what mean?"

Molly folded your hands in hers. Was she praying? Or was she just killing time to figure out what to tell you?

"You know what the word *saved* means in the Bible?" she finally asked.

"Yes! I know meaning *saved!*"

Before you knew the word for *hamburger* you knew the words for *saved* and *the Anointed Ones*. The Anointed Ones were like JW movie stars. They were 144,000 individuals specifically chosen by Jehovah God. The Anointed Ones would never have to die or face Judgment Day like the rest of us. Instead, all 144,000 would be gathered up and go directly to heaven to help Jehovah God rule and get everything ready for the end times. The un-anointed must follow God's law, be spiritually fit, and await Judgment Day. Then and only then will you know if you are saved.

Sign SAVED: *Your two fists are crossed as if bound together at the wrists, then you twist your wrists outward and apart as if you've broken your chains.*

"But do not wait to know if you are a member of the Great Crowd!" Brother Birch would always say. "When the Great Tribulation comes, there will be no time to make your peace with God. That time is now! For those who wait, the sinners, the unbelievers, the blasphemers, it is the Lake of Fire!"

While you could not comprehend everything Brother Birch said when you were young, you knew that whenever he spoke of the Lake of Fire you felt a sickness in your stomach, and not because you didn't know how to swim or because of how hot it might be. The Lake of Fire meant one thing:

"Oblivion!" Brother Birch would warn. "That's right. The righteous shall have the kingdom of heaven for eternity. For the wicked, upon death, they shall instantly become nothing."

Yes, you knew what "saved" meant.

As you walked back to your dorm with Molly, the dozens of new signs and words swirled around your mind, but still you felt unsettled by the memory of Brother Birch's lessons on salvation and the Lake of Fire. You stopped Molly and tapped her shoulder.

"Question. Jehovah God, friendly, strict . . . which?"

Molly, who had been so exhausted a minute before, became energized again.

"Jehovah God is wonderful! He cherishes you! He is your Heavenly Father."

"Father?" you asked, perplexed. "Long long time ago, Mama say my father ran away. Mama stuck all alone. Broken heart. Crying because father."

"That was your earthly father. He was wicked. Brother Birch told me. Jehovah God is your real, most important father. Jesus is His son. If you obey Jehovah God's word, He will take you to live with Him in heaven."

You repeated the sign for *heaven*, which you'd known all your life.

Sign HEAVEN: *Both hands, palms down in front of the face, twirl around each other and rise like ascending souls. When they arrive above the head, they separate, creating the floor of heaven.*

"Heaven? Looks like what?"

Molly took a deep breath. "Wow! Heaven is the most beautiful place anywhere. In heaven, no one is ever sad or sick or lonely. Never. I'll tell you a secret."

Molly leaned in, hiding her signs from snoops.

"In heaven you will be able to hear and see again perfectly."

Molly's words thrilled you. You didn't care about the hearing part, but you longed for your vision to get back to where it had been.

"I want vision strong again! I go heaven . . . when?"

"When Judgment Day comes. *If* you're good. Right now you need to learn to read and write and improve your ASL so you can preach the word of God. Then you'll be able to bring the goats to the Lord."

"Judgment Day . . . when?"

"That's enough," Molly begged. "Lunch is over now. Go up the stairs like I taught you. I'll see you at your afternoon class."

"One more question . . ."

"Go!" Molly demanded.

As you headed up the stairs your hand touched the strange wooden object that sat at the very end of the banister. It was shaped like a pineapple without its top. Surely you needed to know its name. You ran back and found Molly, pulling her back, pointing to the mysterious item.

"Last question! Promise! This? What name?"

"This is why you dragged me back?" Molly asked, all her niceness seeping out some hole at the bottom of her exhausted being. "I don't know what it's called. It's just the end of the banister. Now go to your room. Not everything has a word, Arlo."

Not everything has a word? That can't be. Molly just didn't *know* the word, and was too lazy to ask anyone, and now you would be embarrassed in front of the other students.

"Liar!" your hands yelled. "You lie because I Deaf and low-vision!"

"Bad boy! You should not call people that here! That's a sin!"

"Then lying—what for?! Wow. Lying very serious sin! Future, when you die, Jehovah God will throw you Lake of Fire! Will!"

For a moment Molly said nothing. You think: *Ha! Take that! I have crushed her!* But when she spoke again, her signs felt weary and bloodless.

"Okay. Okay. Finish," Molly signed, her gentleness returning. "I'm sorry for getting upset. I'm just so tired. I promise you'll have the whole semester to learn new words. Okay?"

You pulled your hands from Molly's and took out your cane. With your other hand you reached out for the banister and caressed the cold, knobby end. What if Molly was telling the truth? Suddenly you felt such pity for the strange object. Like you, it was alone and had no friends. Worse than you, it did not have a name.

PROFESSOR LAVINIA BAHR

The three of us made our way toward the classroom in silence. Even the guide dog seemed uncomfortable. I kept ruminating over Molly's cheap comment: *They warned me about you.* My mind sorted through all the interpreters I might have offended over the years. The list wasn't long, but it wasn't short. It's like that interpreter joke: "How many interpreters does it take to interpret the changing of a light bulb? Five. One to interpret it, three to complain about the interpretation, and one to be looking at their iPhone."

With ten minutes left before the class was set to begin, we walked into the room like the smallest of traveling circuses. Almost every seat was full. This worried me. The class title, English Comp 101, section 4, and the name Professor Lavinia Bahr had been written on the whiteboard in cursive so precise it could have been done by a nineteenth-century nun. The professor herself was a fabulous cross between Maya Angelou and a bedazzled tank. She sat behind her desk draped in a royal-blue African-style calico dress, with huge beaded drop earrings and a vibrant blue silk scarf wrapped around her head. I watched as Molly described the professor to Arlo, taking special care with her dress, her earrings, her size, her race, the *strict* expression on her face, everything to paint a full picture for Arlo.

"We'll wait a few more moments for any latecomers," Professor Lavinia Bahr announced to the class, her low, sumptuous voice almost British in its precision and flavored with what I would eventually learn was a Saint Kitts accent. "Meanwhile, please take out your notebooks and writing instruments!"

Upon seeing Molly interpreting, Professor Bahr raised her dagger-sharp eyebrows and pointed toward us like we were the mistake of some misbehaving child.

"Excuse me, class!" she barked. "Who owns this family? They seem to be lost."

Both Molly and I grimaced at the suggestion that she and I might be married with Arlo as our son.

"Tell Arlo to show her the drop/add form now?" I signed to Molly.

But while Arlo just stood there, lost inside his head, Molly simply sighed and passed Arlo back to me, with a fed-up lift of her eyebrows. Her meaning: *You brought this on yourself; you tell him.*

◊ ◊ ◊

Sniff.

The air of the classroom smells like Magic Markers, pencils, waxed floors, wood and metal furniture, fresh paint, and . . . books. To read a book made out of paper, you need to put it on a machine that magnifies it so large you are only able to read a few words at a time, or have the book translated into acres and acres of raised paper dots, minuscule mountains of braille.

There's something else. Your feet and skin perceive other vibrations in the room.

Sniff.

Bodies of other people in the room. Giant unread flesh-books. You try to catch an image of a face, but there are only flickers and shadows. A light flare blinds you when you look toward the window. You close your eyes.

Sniff.

The smell of a woman floats into your nostrils. Perfume, skin, clean. Your mama smelled like soft cotton, orange blossom perfume, and sometimes eggs. Molly smells like The Watchtower *magazine and flowery deodorant.*

And the other one? The one you are forbidden to think about smelled like . . .
Don't think about it. Don't think about it. Forget. Forget.
   Breathe in deeply.
   Other people's bodies can help you forget.

◊ ◊ ◊

"Hey!" I said to the professor. "Sorry . . . um . . . Professor. No one *owns* us. Ha ha. Arlo here is a student. He'd like to ask you something."

Then to Arlo:

"Hey! Are you paying attention?" I signed with desperation. "You zoned out. The class is starting soon. Show the professor the drop/add form!"

Arlo, misunderstanding the location of the professor, began signing to a large-boned male student sitting right next to us.

"Excuse me, Professor . . ."

I stopped him, and steered Arlo and Snap toward the professor's desk at the front of the classroom.

"Go ahead," I signed. "She's there."

"Excuse me, Professor," Arlo began again, with me voicing. "My name is Arlo Dilly. It's nice to meet you."

Professor Bahr shook her head, then spoke directly to me as if I were the one speaking.

"Can't you see I'm about to begin a class, sir? If you need assistance, I'm sure the office can—"

Before I could stop him, Arlo went in to shake the professor's hand, clipping her in the left breast in the process. The professor, who had been looking at me, jumped back in shock, with a small scream.

"What in God's name?!" she snapped. "If you could please tell your son he cannot randomly grab people."

At that point Arlo had located her hand, and began shaking it with one hand while his other hand held her wrist. By the look on the professor's face, she felt the shake was going on far too long.

"Um . . . excuse me, Professor," I said, gently taking Arlo's hands from hers and putting them back into mine. "I think there's a misunderstanding. Let me explain. Um, I'm Cyril, an ASL interpreter. The person who was speaking a moment ago was Arlo here. He's not my—*our*—son. We *work* for him. I know it's confusing. If I speak or Molly speaks—that's his other interpreter standing by the door looking annoyed at me—when either of us speaks, we'll say something like 'This is Cyril speaking' or 'This is the interpreter speaking.' Otherwise, when you hear 'I' or 'me,' that's Arlo speaking. Do you see what I—meaning 'me,' the interpreter—am saying?"

The professor heaved a deep sigh and massaged her brow with her fingers.

"What in God's good name are you talking about, sir?" she barked. "I? Me? He-she-it? Is this some old Abbott and Costello television routine? Once and for all, I cannot help you. Now I need to start class."

With that the professor turned her attention to her roll book, dismissing us completely. At that point Molly came over, shoved her elbow into Arlo's hand, and started guiding him back to the hallway to leave. Arlo was clearly confused, but still signed nothing.

"Molly! Wait!" I quickly blocked their exit, then placed Arlo's hands onto mine to interpret. "Of course, Molly, we're not the ones who make decisions, right?"

"This isn't his class," Molly signed to me sharply. "Also, that teacher seems mean. We had to work very hard for him to be able to take this class. I don't want it to be a waste of time for him."

"But that should be up to Arlo," I signed. "He's the boss. Not us. What would you like us to do, Arlo?"

Arlo hesitated, then nervously addressed Molly.

"I ask professor one more time? Can?"

"Of course," I answered before Molly could interject. Then I guided Arlo back toward the professor, who had begun her lecture. I coughed to get her attention. She ignored me, so I coughed again. This time a bit too aggressively, as if I had the mildest case of tuberculosis. Her head snapped in our direction.

"Excuse me, Professor," I said. "Arlo just wants to ask you one thing real quick."

I nudged Arlo to start talking.

"Professor," Arlo began, as I voiced. "Sorry to interrupt. I would like to switch to your class. A website I read says you are a great teacher. I know I will learn better with you and promise to work very hard. So will you sign my drop/add form?"

Arlo pulled the drop/add form from his pocket and held it out thirty degrees to the left of where the professor stood. The professor's expression softened while she heaved a surrendering sigh.

◇ ◇ ◇

Sniff.

A gust of air from the professor's lungs tells you stories. Your mind attaches to a time at the Rose Garden School. You were fourteen years old. It was the September after your first summer break. You were no longer homesick. Martin had brought an entire chest filled with his favorite food from his grandmother's house. He fingerspelled each dish for you: jerk chicken, goat curry, beef patties. Professor Lavinia Bahr must have eaten this kind of food for breakfast.

◇ ◇ ◇

Professor Bahr's eyes filled with pity as she gazed at the drop/add form in Arlo's outstretched hand, his slightly crossed eyes gazing just past her head.

"I'm so sorry, Arlo or Cyril or Molly or Doggie or whomever I'm speaking to at this moment, but I'll have to say no."

I tapped Arlo on the shoulder. He put the drop/add form back in his pocket, so I could interpret what Lavinia was saying.

"I'm talking to you now, Mr. and Ms. Interpreters." Professor Bahr folded her hands and looked down at the class roster in her binder. "You need to understand the school is supposed to limit these classes to fifteen students. Yet I have one class with seventeen students, and this one, which is already overbooked with twenty. I only have so many hours in the day. Have you ever read thirty-seven response essays written by first-year community college students? Most of which have been written on a bus thirty minutes before class? Twenty-seven of which repeatedly misuse 'it' apostrophe 's' dozens of times?"

It was only at that moment that Professor Bahr registered that I was still interpreting for Arlo.

"Excuse me?" she snapped. "Are you telling him what I'm saying? I was just talking to you two! Not him!"

"I'm sorry," I began. "This is me the interpreter, Cyril, talking now. You understand, we have to interpret everything. Providing *equal access* is our job. It's not *ethical* if we don't. You understand?"

While fingerspelling and clarifying the sign for *ethical* for Arlo, I looked over at Molly for support, but her face was a mask of disapproval. Arlo, however, was smiling.

◊ ◊ ◊

A secret hatch opens in your skull and fresh air fills your brain. New fact: Interpreters are supposed to interpret everything. It's a rule. New word: ethical.

Sign ETHICAL: *The edge of the "E" hand touches the outward-facing palm twice, once at the top, once at the bottom, as if it were placing the stamp of the "E" on an official document.*

You've seen the sign before. But what does the word really mean? What is ethical? *If everyone else gets ethical, then you want ethical.*

◊ ◊ ◊

Arlo began to talk as I voiced.

"This is Arlo speaking now. Yes, Cyril is right. It's good for the interpreter to interpret everything. That's ethical. If you let me join your class, I promise I won't be any more work than other students. I really want a"— *Arlo signs hard + require + checks off five fingers like a list. I interpret this as—"demanding* teacher."

Professor Bahr began repeating herself about the class-size limits, but Arlo wasn't finished so I kept voicing. His former timidity vanished, and his tone grew more adamant, which I tried to reflect.

"You're the best teacher of English composition here at DCC," he signed. "So, yes, you can say, 'No, I don't want Arlo in my classroom because there are just too many students!' But you cannot reject me just because I'm DeafBlind."

"I never said anything like that!" Professor Bahr interjected.

I attempted to get my hands into his to interpret, but Arlo was on a roll and refused to listen.

"Have you heard of the ADA law?" he signed proudly. "That stands for the Americans with Disabilities Act of 1990."

I was stunned. Arlo had obviously researched the ADA after I had mentioned it at the Abilities Institute the day we met. I did my best not to break into cheers. And even Molly was trying to subdue a proud smile.

"The ADA is a very important law from 1990," he went on. "President George H. W. Bush approved and signed it. The law says a person or business cannot discriminate against someone for being disabled. What does that mean for me? Schools and doctors must provide an interpreter free of charge. This is called equal access. So, if you let the hearing and sighted students into your class above the fifteen-student limit, why not me? Because I'm DeafBlind? This would be ignoring the ADA law about equal access. But also, it's just not fair . . ."

Fuck me! I realized "fair" was not the right gloss on the sign Arlo had used. *Think! Better word, better word . . . Got it!*

"Or rather, *just*! To not let me take your class is *unjust*."

Pleased with the interpreting adjustment, I totally missed what Arlo signed next. I asked him to repeat it. But then, seeing what he wanted me to voice, I thought, *No, no, no! You do not want me to say that! You are going to screw this up, buddy!* Compared to hearing people, Deaf folk, in general, tended to be far blunter—sometimes shockingly so. In certain circumstances interpreters will do something called cultural mediation where, if it matches the Deaf person's intent and tone, we mediate the language to prevent cultural misunderstanding. This doesn't mean censoring a Deaf person who intends to be offensive. Deaf folks have the right to be rude, wrong, or downright offensive. It is always a delicate call. I looked over to Molly for support, but she just shrugged her shoulders in an unsympathetic "better you than me" gesture.

"Pardon me," Professor Bahr asked, annoyed by my delay. "Is Arlo saying something I should hear?"

Taking a deep breath, I asked Arlo to repeat himself. What he was saying didn't need cultural mediation, but my stomach still clenched at the content.

"Well, Professor," Arlo signed, as I voiced. "You should accept me into your class because you are a Black person. Because your ancestors were from Africa and you have lived through the civil rights struggle, meaning you understand discrimination."

"I beg your pardon?" Professor Bahr said indignantly, her eyes widening.

It felt like the entire classroom leaned forward to smell the impending bloodbath. I just wanted to hide until it was all over. But it was my voice delivering the message. Molly shook her head as if I was the one to blame. Professor Bahr pointed to Arlo but spoke directly to me.

"Why does he think I'm old enough to have lived through the civil rights struggle? How old does he think I am? Did you coach him on what to say?"

"No. I'm sorry," I said. "This is Cyril talking now. Again, if you could please just direct the questions to Arlo. I'm really just an interpreter."

"Yes, yes!" she hissed, frustrated at both me and herself. "You've said that over and over. I'm sorry!"

The class was hanging on Professor Bahr's every word. She steadied herself and looked directly at Arlo, the DeafBlind young man who may or may not turn out to be a DeafBlind racist.

"So, Mr. Dilly. I'm curious now. Why do you assume so many things about me? You don't know me."

"Right. I don't," Arlo signed. "But I can guess a lot of things."

"Oh, really?" Professor Bahr responded. "Like what? What else can you guess about me?"

Arlo paused.

"I think maybe you're from somewhere in the Caribbean," he began, as my voice tried to maintain his matter-of-fact tone. "Molly described you to me and said you have an accent. I think maybe you're from Jamaica. At my old school I had a friend whose grandmother was from Jamaica. After vacations he would bring food back from her house and it smelled just like your breath today."

Some of the students choked on their laughter while others squirmed in nervousness. My own queasiness was suddenly replaced with astonishment. Arlo, like a DeafBlind Sherlock Holmes, was completely able to infer significant things about the people and places around him based on the slightest shards of information. How much had I underestimated him? (How much had I underestimated Shirley and all DeafBlind people?) Truly knowing the world is less about whether you can see and hear and more about the intensity of your curiosity and intelligence.

"Interesting," Professor Bahr finally said, placing a hand over her mouth. She looked embarrassed, but not angry. "I would like to point out I am not in the habit of eating beef patties for breakfast. I happened to be preparing lunch for myself and my husband this morning and, well, took a few nibbles and . . ."

She reached into her purse on the desk, pulled out a small white mint Life Saver, and popped it in her mouth, then broke into a broad smile. The class, in a collective sigh of relief, started to laugh.

"You appear to be quite perceptive, Mr. Arlo Dilly. That's a good quality for a writer. But tell me something. As an experiment. What else can you tell me about *myself*? Don't be shy! Tell me everything!"

As soon as Professor Bahr said this, I decided to increase my lag time, allowing the gap between Arlo's signing and my voicing to increase. Then, if I did need to do any cultural mediation, I'd have the time and space to do a better job. And this time I needed it.

Arlo in ASL: "*What I know about you? Honest? You big woman (gestures a large frame). Your hands—very wrinkled, tired, old feeling. Work hard! Weigh? How much? Maybe 190 to 200 pounds. Maybe more. Wow, very big fat strong! Not young. Maybe fifty or sixty. You big ego. Attitude . . . strong. Smart! Wow! Impress me!*"

My voicing: "Professor, to be honest, I'd say you weigh about 190 pounds. In your middle years. Fiftyish. From the feel of your hands and what you're saying, I'd say you're probably exhausted from your hard schedule, but you have a very strong personality and are extremely intelligent. Wow. Very impressive."

It was then that I realized how in sync I felt with Arlo. It was almost as if I was channeling his voice. Which, of course, I wasn't, but it felt that way.

Arlo continued:

"When I was young, Molly helped me to improve my ASL, but my best ASL teachers were my two DeafBlind friends, Martin and Big Head Lawrence." I had to clarify the second name with him twice! "When I first met them my signing was pretty lousy. But my friends were both experts with ASL. Whenever I didn't know how to sign something, Martin and Big Head Lawrence would teach me and insist I sign it right. Finally, I knew my own language, and the world opened up more for me. Understand? So, it seems only natural that I'd want to be taught by the best writing teacher at the community college." At this point he again described her using signs that could mean *old*, *tall*, *fat*, and added *mean* . . . but he signed them with admiration. "And I'm not intimidated by your strictness or formidable presence. I just want to learn to write better. So please let me switch to your section."

Finished. I felt exhilarated but also a little spent, like after good sex. I asked Molly to switch with me. Even she looked impressed with how it went, though she said nothing.

Everyone in the room waited in anticipation, including Snap, whose ears aimed directly toward the professor, expectantly. Professor Bahr gave nothing away. She just stared at Arlo's wandering gaze until she suddenly threw her head back and detonated a huge bellowing laugh from the depths of her lungs.

"HA HA HA! Oh my God! This handsome boy is brilliant! And so perceptive! That's unbelievable. He really understood all that about me just by his sense of touch and smell? And by you two making those signs? I'm sorry . . . You, Arlo—this is who I am talking to—you were really able to deduce all that about me?"

"Yes," Arlo signed, but with Molly voicing now.

"Oh, my goodness," Professor Bahr exclaimed. "Now you have a woman's voice! This is going to get so confusing and also fascinating!"

Arlo started to rock back and forth, his own smile acknowledging that he had made a connection with the professor.

"Mr. Arlo Dilly, I am thrilled to have you in my class! Will I need to grade your interpreters' essays as well? And your doggie's?"

"No," Arlo signed, getting the professor's joke, but his demeanor remained deadpan. "Interpreters are here so everyone understands each other. And my dog, Snap, writes even worse than me. That's a joke."

Suddenly Arlo started laughing so hard his shoulders shook. This led the way for the entire class to erupt in joyful hysterics. As for Molly, there was finally the slightest hint of a smile.

9

MARTIN AND BIG HEAD LAWRENCE

On Tuesday afternoons you, Brother Birch, and Mrs. Brother Birch stand outside the entrance to the food court at the Galleria to do field service. Brother Birch and Mrs. Brother Birch engage passersby by saying things such as "Does God really care what happens to us humans?" or "Do all good people go to heaven?" Your job is to hold up brochures like a Deaf-Blind billboard. Today you're not even sure which brochure Mrs. Brother Birch put in your hand. All the brochures smell and feel the same. The titles are usually something like *Can the Dead Really Live Again?* or *Good News from God!* or your favorite: *How Can You Have a Happy Life?* It answers important questions such as "What do we need to do to be happy?" and "What hope do we have for future happiness?" The brochure says, because of war and hunger, we're not really happy. Then it points out what we would need to be happy, like peace and security, loving family and friends, good health, enough food and housing, purpose in life, and hope for the future. The first time you read this brochure enlarged on the internet you exclaimed: *Yes, yes, yes! If I had these things, I certainly would be happy!* The literature goes on to say that these things that will make you happy are very difficult to achieve. *(Okay, and?)* Then it promises that you will definitely get them if you just do certain things. *(Great! How?!)* This is where Jehovah God plays a trick on you. It turns out that you'll only get these gifts from God if you live a spiritually strong life and follow Scripture in every detail—no lying, no sinful actions like masturbating, disobeying Brother Birch, or telling sinful secrets, and you must spend lots of hours standing around holding up brochures outside of food courts. And even if you can achieve all these impossible goals, you still won't even know if you've succeeded in being "truly happy" until *after* Judgment Day, which, the elders say, could be any day now, or not for a hundred years. In other words, don't hold your breath.

You hold your breath.

You sniff the brochures a few times.

You rock from one foot to the other.

Professor Bahr said to become a good writer you need to "find your voice." She said "voice" meant *connecting your true soul to the words on the page*. You will need to write tens of thousands of words before you can find your voice, which seems too many to write in one summer. You also have to be "willing to write very badly," she said, before you can write well. Luckily, you are an expert at writing badly, so that first part is done. Professor Bahr also said you should keep a journal and tell yourself all your secrets. But if you write down your secrets, you will be breaking your promise to Brother Birch and Jehovah God to try to forget them. How can you remember just some secrets but forget the rest? How can you select only certain parts of the air to breathe?

◇ ◇ ◇

After two hours of standing at the mall, your feet hurt and your arm is tired and you wish the Second Coming of the Messiah would happen in the next fifteen minutes. Saturday field service is better because you get to go door-to-door. Brother Birch likes to do door-to-door field service with you. When people see that you're DeafBlind they feel guilty for slamming the door in your face, so sometimes they invite you in. Brother Birch does all the talking. You just get to feel what it's like to be in strangers' homes. Some smell really nice and warm. Some smell like dog piss and dirty socks.

Brother Birch promises that someday, after you do better in Theocratic Ministry School, you will get to spread the word of the Lord as well. But, for now, your job is to just get Brother Birch into the strangers' houses, or stand in the hot sun, just outside the food court, bearing witness to how great Jehovah God is for making use of a DeafBlind man.

Someone stops at the brochure rack. You push the brochure in their direction. They come closer.

Sniff.

A gust of sweet and salty peanut butter air from their mouth.

A memory of a person. Short. Squat. Thick chubby fingers. Wiry hair. You go into your memory place.

Martin. You told the professor about him, one of your best friends from the Rose Garden School. The one who really taught you ASL. You were thirteen. That first day after all the students had come back. Gym class. Late afternoon.

The climbing rope . . .

◊ ◊ ◊

"The gym teacher wants you to try to climb it," Molly signed, handing you the rope that was as thick as your wrist, and scratchy like a hairbrush.

"Top far away?" you asked, looking up toward the very, very high ceiling, seeing only oblivion.

"Yes," Molly signed. "You don't have to climb all the way. Gym Teacher said you just need to pull yourself up about ten feet above the ground. It's only about twice your height. Gym Teacher will make sure you're safe."

"Teacher crazy!" you exclaimed, pushing the rope away. "Too dangerous! Will fall and die!"

"Just try!" Gym Teacher demanded, signing to you with his own thick, calloused fingers.

Gym Teacher was a hearing man who had Deaf parents, so it wasn't as easy to garner his sympathy like the other hearing teachers.

"Don't be a baby!" he signed.

Your face flushed hot. Did the other students see what Gym Teacher signed? You squeezed your face closed because if you cried it would make it worse.

"Just hold on to the rope and pull yourself up to the next knot!"

Before you could object, Gym Teacher led you to a place where the thick hairy rope hanging down from the ceiling hit you in the face. You grabbed it. He guided your hands to another knot a foot above the first and you clutched it with both hands, squeezed your biceps and lifted yourself higher. Then you reached for the third knot and pulled higher. Then the fourth, and fifth, higher still. And just as you had lifted your body to the sixth knot, flames of pride ignited inside your brain. Were you at the ceiling yet? You wished you could see something. How high had you gone exactly? Suddenly you felt the rope begin to swing. Paralyzed. You held your breath. The weight of your dangling body grew heavier. Your arms began to ache. Your sweaty hands started to slip. You were about to die. When you let go you fell instantly into the gym teacher's arms, causing both of you to tumble onto the soft mat.

"Why did you let go of the rope?!" Gym Teacher yelled. "You weren't even that high off the ground! Now try again!"

"No! No! No! Dangerous!" You hid your hands inside your armpits, protecting them from Gym Teacher's mean, angry fingers.

After a few moments Molly tapped your shoulder.

"Okay. Gym Teacher said you don't have to do the rope today. Go do sit-ups by the bleachers and wait for class to end."

A brush fire of embarrassment crept from your cheeks to the tips of your ears.

"Other kids laugh at me?"

"No," Molly signed—probably lying. "I'll make sure the gym teacher doesn't make you do that again. Go do your sit-ups and I'll take my break."

Alone on the mat you lay there, faceup, imagining you were back at your mama's house, safe and sound. No Rose Garden School, no gym teacher, no scary rope, no mean Deaf students laughing at you. Two minutes later, you felt the ball of the stranger's cane hit you on the side of your ribs. You leaped up and confronted the attacker.

"Who?!"

Sniff.

Not Molly. Not the gym teacher. Not the spicy-sweet smell of the mysterious bully in the cafeteria. Peanut butter? Suddenly, a heavy hand clumsily felt your hair, your cheek, your chest. Why would the person be touching you that way? *Who there?!* You grabbed the thick wrist, holding it still so you might get a glimpse of his face. But his dark features, along with the dimly lit corner of the gym, made it impossible. The boy was shorter than you, with a plump round body. In one smooth move, he pulled his wrist from your grasp, then jammed his sausage fingers into your hands.

"Stop grabbing me!" the boy said using Tactile Sign Language. "You new boy, right? A L R O? A R O L? A-O-L-R-A? Whatever. We roommates!"

Roommates! It was one of the students Sybil had mentioned. In the chaos of everything, you had forgotten. You had never met anyone your own age who also had low vision. You corrected him on the spelling of your name and then told him your name-sign.

"Got it!" The boy patted you rapidly on the shoulder, which made you smile. "My name M-A-R-T-I-N! Name-sign ("M" pressed into his right temple). Why? Because of my eyes."

Eyes? What was different about his eyes? You pulled Martin across the floor to a brighter part of the gym and positioned him so the sun from an upper window streamed onto his face. Then you stepped back several feet until you could at least capture parts of his face, but not all at the same time. He had a friendly smile set inside a very round head, a wooly short cut of black hair, and very white teeth. His eyes looked closed, which was frustrating. Martin started signing. Back then, given the right light and distance, you could sometimes see well enough to read visual sign language. But because Martin's skin and shirt were the same dark shade, it was hopeless. Frustrated, you crossed back to him.

"I can't understand!" you told him. "Must wear light shirt. Different from skin. I low-vision, same as you."

"I not low-vision!" Martin signed. "I full blind!"

Martin guided your fingers to his soft, velvety eyelids. It took you a few seconds to realize what you were feeling. Behind those eyelids was nothing. You jerked your hands away. Martin instantly pulled them back, insisting your fingers linger on the soft emptiness, as if to say, *This is who I am.*

"When I grow up, Mama will buy me beautiful glass eyes. Green! I will look really handsome and sexy!"

Martin laughed. But that word squirmed like a hungry worm inside your brain: *blind.* Martin didn't even see the blur, the shapes, or even your one elusive and diminishing perfect spot of vision. Martin saw nothing. You had never called yourself *blind* back then. Yet it was the unspoken fear that awakened you every morning and put you to sleep at night.

"You dreaming?" Martin signed, annoyed at your silence. "Wake up!"

Martin pulled your hands in close between your bodies, making it harder for any nosy sighted kids to see what he was saying.

"I tell you secret. Understand? Last semester. Dorm boss name: Fat One." He showed you her name-sign: upside-down "Y" walks like an obese person across the palm of the other hand. "You know Fat One? Gross. Hate her! Fat One hit my best friend." Martin showed you another unfamiliar sign: an "L" hand lifted outward from the temple.

"Sign means what?" you asked.

"That name-sign of other roommate, my best friend: L-A-W-R-E-N-C-E. Big Head Lawrence." Then Martin repeated the strange name-sign.

"Can meet?!"

"Hold on! Finish story first!" Martin continued. "Fat dorm boss hit Big Head Lawrence! Why? She catch jacking off!"

Martin makes a gesture grabbing at his throat. You have no idea what it means. He continues the story, acting out the parts of the dorm boss and Big Head Lawrence.

"*Dirty boy! Disgust!* Then dorm boss smacked his hands and butt! *Many times I tell you! Bad boy! Bad boy!*" Then Martin addressed you: "Understand? Must careful. If jack off too early, will get caught. Wait until later—lights out—when dorm boss asleep. Same everyone else. Understand?"

"Yes. *Understand,*" you answered, but it was a lie.

You wouldn't fully comprehend what Martin said for weeks. But still you hung on every sign that sprang from his fingers. His ASL was a hundred times better than anyone's you had ever met. Certainly better than Molly's and your other teachers' growing up. Martin's signing was fast, vivid, acrobatic. It was one of the most beautiful things you had ever experienced.

"Shh! Don't tell anyone!" Martin went on. "If Fat One helps you with lunch plate—throw down [on] floor. Mess up. Splatter. All over floor. We . . ."

Martin used another sign you had never seen before, but then fingerspelled the word for emphasis.

"R-E-V-E-N-G-E!"

"Wait," you signed. "Not understand. Word: R-E-V-E-N-G-E. What mean?"

"Ha ha! Don't know meaning of word *revenge*? Wow! (Again he used the gesture of grabbing at his throat.) Revenge means when someone does something bad to you, you do something worse to them. Why? So they won't hurt you again."

Yes! Revenge! You desperately needed that word! Revenge for how Brother Birch stole you from your mother! Revenge for the van driver who lay across your body! Revenge against Gym Teacher for forcing you to climb the rope! Revenge for all the hearing people who ever ignored you all your life! But it wasn't just that sign, it was all of them: *Fat One? Jacking? Disgust?* The sinful signs felt hot in your hands. As Molly had warned, Martin and his best friend, Big Head Lawrence, were clearly not "saved." But you didn't care. You wanted more.

"What mean?" you asked Martin, repeating his gesture where he grabbed at the base of his throat.

Martin thought for a moment and then explained it was a gesture someone did if they got caught doing something and felt embarrassed. Like if a teacher catches you cheating, or someone walks into your room and you're playing with yourself.

"Wait! Wait!" you say. "What spoken word for . . . (you repeated the gesture)?"

"Hmmm. Good question," Martin signed. "I remember! Intervenor Sybil told me! English two words! You can write G-A-S-P or G-U-L-P!"

"Gasp or gulp? Smart kids use which word?" you asked.

"Both!"

Martin makes you repeat all the signs he just taught you, correcting your hand positions.

"I ASL and writing top skills!" Martin bragged. "My family Deaf family. They ASL experts! Wow. They beat everyone . . . ASL champion! If you don't know sign or English word, ask me!"

"Okay. I will. I curious . . . other roommate? Big Head Lawrence? Name-sign why?"

"Wait here," Martin demanded, returning three minutes later, dragging along another boy. This new boy was also shorter than you. But while his body felt leaner, his head, as advertised, was at least twice the size of a normal head and abnormally shaped. His hands, however, were nice, expressive, and very friendly. He told you he had grown up in a place called New Jersey and was hard of hearing and low-vision because of his big head.

He also said he had been looking forward to meeting you for weeks, and this made you like him even more.

"Hey! I'm bored! Talk same time!" Martin signed.

Then Martin did something you didn't even know was possible. He pushed his hands under both yours and Big Head Lawrence's, and suddenly all three of you were in a six-hand, simultaneous Tactile Sign Language conversation.

"See what I mean?" Martin signed. "I honest. Big head, right? Means very smart. Math . . . Big Head Lawrence champ!"

Then Martin turned his body slightly, addressing Big Head Lawrence while your hands listened.

"Arlo's ASL . . . lousy. We must sign slow for him now. Teach him ASL better! Okay?"

For the next thirty minutes the two boys filled your hands with new signs, many of which were sinful and disrespectful, including signs for *pissed off, wiped out (tired), bitch, asshole,* and various ways to sign *oops I got busted.* They also taught you the best way to avoid participating in gym class (mix mustard and water to fake puke), how to get your intervenor to reveal answers to spelling tests (keep acting confused when she signs the word), and which dorm bosses were the most strict and which had other assets worth exploiting.

"Best dorm boss name 'C-A-N-D-Y'!"

Sign CANDY: *Pointer finger twists in a dimple.*

Big Head Lawrence gushed, "Wow! Candy has huge boobs! I pretend with her . . . " He acted out the conversation. " 'Who are you? I don't know,' I say. Then I feel her face, feel her arm, then feel her huge"—he fingerspelled slowly—"B-O-O-B-S. Squeeze. Squeeze. Long time. One, two, then three time she stops me. Wow. Fun!"

Big Head Lawrence's and Martin's bodies exploded in a virtual earthquake of laughter. You laughed as hard, but in truth you didn't know what was so funny. Then, when your own ignorance again became too painful, you tapped the laughing boys on their backs.

"Question?" you signed. "B-O-O-B-S. What mean?"

Martin and Big Head Lawrence engaged in a quick private discussion, then Martin's hands returned to yours.

"If not understand something must ask," Martin signed emphatically. "Don't be pea brain! Here, feel!"

Right in the middle of gym, Martin pulled your hands to his chest and encouraged you to squeeze. Then he made you feel Big Head Lawrence's and your own pectoral muscles. Big Head Lawrence's chest was flat and thin like yours, but Martin's was much rounder and full of fat.

"Understand?" Martin declared. "I have B-O-O-B-S! Titties!"

Sign TITTIES *(slang): Two fists form the breasts on the front of the chest and bounce accordingly.*

"You and Big Head Lawrence have C-H-E-S-T-S! Different!"

"Martin [has] very small boobs compared to Candy's," Big Head Lawrence explained, reminding you that he had firsthand experience. "Candy, her boobs champ! Huge! Why? Because Candy born babies already. Our dog born babies already. Dogs have many, many boobs. Puppies drink milk . . . make many boobs grow quick and B-I-G. Understand? People same."

You had accidentally touched your mama's boobs before. Hers were not very large — only a little larger than Martin's, yet she had given birth to you. Of course, it was unlikely your mother let you drink milk out of her boobs. In fact, your mama said it was a red star sin to touch boobs unless you were married. But Martin still let you touch his boobs several more times.

Suddenly, you realized there was another word you needed. A word you knew Molly would never teach you, if she knew it at all. *The thing between your legs* that Brother Birch said Satan and his demons used to try to coax you to do evil things that you knew were sinful and would lead to the Lake of Fire.

You took Martin's hand and brushed it against your crotch, and simultaneously touched him quickly over his jeans.

"That . . . sign what?"

Martin pointed the tip of his "P" hand to his nose (ASL for *penis*), then fingerspelled the English word "P-E-N-I-S."

Big Head Lawrence explained that you could also sign the same body part with the "D" hand, which meant D-I-C-K.

"Jerk-off feel good!" Big Head Lawrence signed. "But careful!" *Gulp!* "Don't let dorm boss or teacher catch you. Forbidden!"

"I already told him!" Martin added.

As you touched your nose with the letters D and P over and over again, you became curious *why* you were touching your nose.

"Sign for *penis* . . . why?" you asked.

"Because when you jack off P-E-N-I-S becomes hard like nose," Martin told you. "And when you jack off again and again and again"—*his hands make a splatter gesture*—"sticky P-E-E all over like snot from nose. Feels awesome!"

Martin's and Big Head Lawrence's bodies shook with laughter as they joyously slapped their hands on your back and thighs.

Sticky P-E-E? Feels awesome?

"Hey!" You slapped their backs, trying to stop them from laughing. "My penis not make sticky pee. Just water pee. Why?"

"You're signing too big! Shh!" *Gulp!* Martin demanded in his bossy tone. "Follow us. We talk private."

Martin told you to put both your hands on his shoulder, then he put his hands on Big Head Lawrence's shoulder, and then Big Head Lawrence, who had the better vision, pulled out his white cane and, like the engine car of a very small train, began leading the three of you across the gym floor, out a side door, around a corner, and to the dead end of an empty alley.

"Nosy sighted Deaf kids always watch and gossip, gossip, gossip!" Martin signed, now signing large and freely. "Here private place! Now pay attention!"

Martin told you the ins and outs of making sticky pee, and how to hide it from the dorm bosses by only doing it at night or in the shower. Big Head Lawrence warned you to wipe the sticky pee on your sock, because if you did it on the sheets the dorm bosses would get mad. Then Martin and Big Head Lawrence told you all the other things they did at night for F-U-N, like telling stories after lights out and making plans to play dirty tricks on the sighted students.

"Like what?" you asked.

"Like hiding all the soap in the shower room," Big Head Lawrence signed.

"Or stealing syrup from the cafeteria and putting into the shampoo bottles!" Martin added.

They soon admitted they never actually played these tricks, but if they did and they got caught, Martin said he would just laugh, give the middle finger to the sighted students, and run. This made you all laugh so hard that your bodies slid down the brick wall onto the asphalt, a giggling, bouncing pile of boys. Big Head Lawrence's body smelled like crayons and medicine. Martin's wiry buzz cut scratched your face like warm itchy happiness.

"Shhh! Our plans for dirty tricks . . . no one knows," Big Head Lawrence warned. "If sighted kids find out . . . Bam! KO! Must careful! Especially with Deaf Devils!"

"Deaf Devils?" The very name sent chills through your entire body. "You lie?"

"No lie," Martin insisted. "Deaf Devils is gang . . . bad Deaf boys. They hurt everybody, especially disabled and DeafBlind. Once they push Big Head Lawrence into big outside garbage! Very dangerous because if hurt head he maybe will die forever."

Big Head Lawrence debated Martin on that, but he agreed that the Deaf Devils were the worst bullies in the entire school. Martin heard that one of them (a boy whose name-sign indicated he picked his nose a lot) had even demanded a Deaf boy with cerebral palsy turn over his chocolate cupcake dessert. When the boy refused, the bully pushed the boy to the ground.

"Wait! Wait!" Big Head Lawrence interrupted. "Worse! CP boy cried, cried, cried. The Deaf Devil bully pulled off boy's hearing aids and threw them down on hallway floor. Other student overlook the hearing aids . . . crush them under feet!"

Could this be true? Could any bully be that cruel? Your new roommates did not appear to be lying. The fear traveled from your spine into your stomach. Would these Deaf Devil maniacs hurt your roommates? Would they hurt you?

"Last year they hurt Martin!" Big Head Lawrence signed, pushing Martin to the side. "Many times. Deaf Devils steal his cane and hide it. And when Martin sitting cafeteria, dreaming-dreaming, not pay attention . . . Deaf Devils put too much salt on his lunch food. Martin cry, cry, cry."

"But I eat anyway . . ." Martin added.

"Principal punish Deaf Devils—why not?" you ask.

"Because all kids afraid to tell principal or teachers," Martin told you. "If tell, Deaf Devils will lie and hurt worse. Or maybe they make it look like you do something bad. Then principal sends you to Dogwood, and no one ever sees you again!"

"Dogwood?" you asked. "What Dogwood?"

Big Head Lawrence explained that all the students were afraid of Dogwood House. That was the dorm at the back of campus where "special students" with either mental illness or severe disability were housed and kept away from the rest of the students back in the olden days. But someone had told Big Head Lawrence that if a student was very bad, like if he stole something or was found playing sex, then they would send the student to Dogwood House as punishment. Martin added that some of these bad students go to Dogwood House and are never seen again.

"If Deaf Devils very bad boys always," you ask, "why teacher not send to Dogwood already?"

"I don't know!" Martin signed, almost annoyed that you asked. "Because they very sneaky! Just avoid Deaf Devils! And, whatever you do, don't go to Dogwood!"

Martin didn't need to say any more. You were convinced. The Deaf Devils were clearly monsters. But going to Dogwood seemed even worse. You patted your friends' hands to get their attention.

"If Deaf Devils try put me in dumpster or spoil my food . . . I punch!" For emphasis you punched the air and puffed out your chest. "Deaf Devils—I will KO! My old school I beat up bullies many times. I strong. Feel!"

You offered your flexed arm for Martin to squeeze. He did, and then let his fingers meander to your chest and back, which he explored in detail.

"Wow! Strong like Superman," Martin signed. Then he took Big Head Lawrence's hands and showed how your body was firmer and a head taller than them both.

A moment later both boys removed their hands abruptly, and you could tell they were speaking only to each other. Had your lies about beating people up frightened them? Even though you had just met them, your heart ached from being excluded from their private conversation. Just as you were about to tell them the truth about never having hit anyone in your life, Martin's fingers tapped your arm.

"Good news!" he signed. "Me and Big Head Lawrence decided. We three best friends now!"

"Best friends?" you asked, confused.

Sign BEST FRIENDS: *Pointer and middle finger cross, pointing toward sky, palm toward body.*

Martin repeated the sign, thinking you didn't know it. But you did. You just never had cause to use it before. Your only real friend until that moment had been your mama. All the other children you had encountered in your life at the hearing school or at Kingdom Hall had been forced to play with you, if they played with you at all. But now you had two best friends, who could sign better than anyone you had ever met, living in the same room as you! You held your stomach, attempting to trap the feeling of happiness from ever leaving. Martin slapped his hand on your shoulder to get your attention.

"Hey! Pay attention! Understand? Best friends mean you, me, Martin will eat breakfast, lunch, dinner together. At bedtime we tell each other stories. We only DeafBlind kids at school. Must support each other! You big boy. Bigger than all Deaf Devils! Suppose they try bully Martin and me . . . what do? You must"—*punches the air*—"KO! Make Deaf Devils bloody and cry, cry, cry! Pah! Success! Agree?"

Your stomach sank. What had you done? If you told them the truth, that you were just a coward who happened to be tall, they would rescind their offer of best friendship. You had no choice.

"Agree!" you declared. "Will protect!"

"Great!" Martin signed. "Together we will be famous roommates team. You, strong one. Big Head Lawrence, smart one. Me? Most handsome man in the world! We will play best games, fun, enjoy, craziness!"

"Wait! One more thing," Big Head Lawrence interrupted. "Tell Arlo about beds."

"Oh, right. You will need sleep in bed by window. Me? I sleep by door, because I go bathroom a lot. Big Head Lawrence sleeps by back wall, because he scared of ghosts coming in window. Okay?"

Ghosts? The word made your heart leap. You learned at Sunday meeting that demons can take the form of ghosts. To what kind of school had they sent you? Deaf Devil gangs? Nightmare dorms like Dogwood? And now demon ghosts?

"You teasing?" you asked.

Martin patted the side of your arm.

"Not teasing. School have many ghosts. It's okay. If ghost comes to hurt you . . . quick wake up Big Head Lawrence. Why? Because best friend now and he can help. But don't wake me up. I sleep strong."

10

HANNE

After my first day working with Arlo, I needed to decompress before I headed to an early-evening gig at the dental clinic. So I went to the No Filter coffee shop, where my best friend Hanne works. Hanne was an aspiring artist, and used to be an aspiring yoga instructor, and now is an aspiring nursing student in her second year at Dutchess Community College. Whether or not she will actually finish is always in question. Hanne likes to say that yearning for things she doesn't have is her superpower.

Of course one of my favorite things about Hanne, besides her constant curiosity and near-boundless energy, is that she has absolutely nothing to do with interpreting. The last thing I want to do is spend my free time listening to snide comments about this or that fellow interpreter, or complaints about how some agency isn't giving them work. And, of course, most of the interpreters in that area were also friends with my ex, and there's still a lot of judgment coming my way. Who needs that crap? Hanne is my emotional and vocational palate cleanser and talks my ear off about whatever topic most obsesses her. At that moment it was anything and everything to do with nursing school. She loves recounting the grotesqueries of her clinical classes, everything from how to suck out mucus from a tracheostomy to learning how maggots in a wound can actually save flesh from infection. She can be *a lot*, and sometimes that's exactly what I need.

"Cirilje! Cirilje! *Goedendag!*" Hanne shouted from behind the espresso machine, waving a small pitcher of steamed milk like a sexy Flemish mad scientist. "Come in! Come in! I need to tell you something!"

Hanne also has the annoying habit of peppering her sentences with Flemish despite the fact she left Belgium almost twenty-five years ago. I think it's her way of trying to individuate herself from the rest of us who found ourselves stuck in Poughkeepsie.

"Okay," I said hesitantly. "What is it? Whoever it is, I'm not going out with him."

"Ach! It's not about a boy. Last night I was reading my microbiology textbook and there was this chapter about parasites. It's totally going to freak you out!"

"Gross," I said. "No thanks."

From the look in Hanne's eyes I knew there would be no stopping her, even though she was in the middle of making a cappuccino and a customer was waiting.

"So, Cirilje, it turns out there are these worms called blood flukes. Also known as schistosomes—and yes, I practiced the pronunciation. Anyway, you know how you like to go swim in the lake? So clean and beautiful, right? Wrong! Lakes can be filled with blood flukes, which look like teeny-tiny monster worms that burrow right into your urethra!"

"Stop!" I begged, exaggerating my cringing reaction. "I can't—"

Hanne laughed very loudly, the way only a beautiful woman can without everyone thinking she's crazy. (Which, truth be told, Hanne is a little.)

"Wait! Wait! There's more! Then the little blood fluke babies travel up your penis and spend middle school and high school in your bladder. After graduation, if left untreated, they travel to your lungs, liver, and even the brain, causing all sorts of awfulness like enlargement of the liver and bladder cancer. *Verschrikkelijk*, right? Terrible, *ja*?"

Hanne finally handed her customer his cappuccino to go.

"Here you go," she said. "Made with blood-fluke-free water."

Oddly enough the man thanked Hanne for her reassurance and when he was leaving looked back at her in that way straight guys do when they want to carve the memory of a woman's face into their mind.

"Have a nice day!" she called after him, rolling her eyes at his obvious flirtation.

Hanne had been my best friend in Poughkeepsie ever since high school. Her parents had relocated from Bruges when her father got a job at the old IBM plant. Hanne was fifteen years old and stunning with her blond hair and golden skin. A former teen model in Belgium, she was also a genius who spoke four languages and skipped two grades. In our junior year she had a crush on me and asked me out on a date. It turned into my very last attempt at being straight and the first time I ever told someone I was gay. I wept like a baby. She was great about it, hugged me and immediately started telling me all about her gay friends back in Belgium. During our twenty-four-year friendship we have been through hell together, including the whole thing with Bruno, and her marrying a heroin addict named Curtis.

Hanne got sober herself when she was pregnant with her son, Wout, but Curtis has been in and out of rehab over the last seventeen years and hasn't been very good at earning a living. A few years ago she started vowing to leave Curtis as soon as Wout turned eighteen, and then she would move to New York, study oil painting, get a nursing job at a big hospital, and have *mad and wicked affairs*. If we had anything in common, it was that: our dream to get the hell out of Poughkeepsie. But each time one of us got close, something got in the way. We called it our Taconic Vortex of Hell. The Philly job offer looked like my first real chance to make the move.

"By the way," Hanne said, lowering her voice like she had the most delicious secret, "I actually did meet this nice gay guy at the Promises meeting last Saturday. Sort of a bear, which you like, right?"

"You can stop right now," I said, rolling my eyes. "We've talked about this."

"But this one is really cute—I mean, for Poughkeepsie. And he almost has a year sober!"

"I'm good," I said, using my *the discussion is over* voice. "Let's talk more about worms in my penis, okay?"

"Okay, okay. Stay single. You're probably smart. Marriage is a pain in the *achterwerk*. And, by the way, don't worry, there are sadly no blood flukes around Poughkeepsie. Just another way this area is so boring."

"Oh, thank God."

"So, tell me, why do I get to see my little Cyrilje in the middle of the day? You have a job nearby?"

"I do. I started today. It's this crazy temporary-ongoing gig."

Hanne smiled and then shouted over a particularly loud hiss coming from the milk steamer that she had started cleaning out. "Temporary-ongoing?! What's that mean?! Is this not some profound existential question?!"

"In fact, it is!" I shouted back. "Existential questions define the life of a freelance ASL interpreter! The good news is this replaced that gig I lost and it's at the community college so we might be able to meet up on campus!"

"Super!" Hanne shouted before stopping the steamer. "I want all I can get of my little lobster man. Come. Sit up at my bar. Tell me fascinating stories of your life. The boring monsters are trying to eat me here."

Hanne tossed her head toward her store manager, Kenny, the pie-faced twenty-five-year-old Marist student who sat in the small room in the back working on spreadsheets. Other than us the café was completely empty.

"Free cappuccino if you stay and talk to me?" Hanne said, tempting me with a large cup.

"Alas, I really need to go chill out before my next gig."

"Please! Just fifteen minutes. You must save me from literally sticking my hand in the Frappuccino blender just to remind myself I'm alive."

"I think I can do that," I said. "But give me two extra shots. I'm feeling a bit tired for some reason."

Hanne gave me a once-over and raised her eyebrows with a semijudgmental but friendly smirk before she started making me my cappuccino.

"Was my little baby hungover again this morning? Remember, if you ever want to make the visit to one of my 'pottery classes' with me, you are welcome."

Pottery class is Hanne's code word for her AA meetings. My needing to get sober is another one of the million little inside jokes we have with each other.

"Here you go. A triple cap. This will put the red fur on your chest. Now, tell me more about your eternal-ephemeral interpreting job!"

"*Temporary-ongoing*," I corrected. "And it means the gig will last a few months, three hours a day, five days a week. Cha-ching."

"Wonderful," Hanne said. "And you were worried about money, *ja?*"

"Yep. And it pays ten bucks an hour over my usual rate. I'm golden."

"Does this mean . . . ?"

Hanne pushed out her lower lip in an exaggerated sad face.

"That's what I'm hoping," I said, crossing my fingers. "Which is yet another reason you don't need to force strange gay men on me to date, since, come September, it's bye-bye, Poughkeepsie. Of course, I've said that like a dozen times, right?"

"The Taconic Vortex of Hell," Hanne said, nodding.

"Exactly. But I think this time it's actually possible. Unfortunately, the job itself is not gonna be easy. The client is DeafBlind, which is decidedly out of my comfort zone."

"Wait . . . what?" Hanne asked, her eyes widening in rapt fascination. "But how does that work?"

Before I knew it, Hanne was begging me to give her a demonstration of how Tactile ASL worked. I told her to close her eyes and signed "Hello. What's up? This is Tactile interpreting, H-A-N-N-E."

"Oh my God, it tickles!" Hanne laughed, pulling her hands from mine. "I love this. Oh, Cyrilje, it's also kind of sexy, *ja?* But this freaks you out, right?"

"Um, no, I mean, at first I was dreading it. I had this bad experience when I was a baby interpreter, so I never tried again. I guess years more experience helps. But the Tactile thing still takes getting used to. I think it's because I don't fully trust myself yet. The DeafBlind guy is pretty reserved but seems cool enough. Young. My team is another story, ugh. I can't really talk about it."

The first tenet of the Registry of Interpreters for the Deaf's Code of Professional Conduct is about confidentiality. I had already violated that tenet by telling Hanne where I was working. Adding the information that the consumer was a young DeafBlind male at the community college made it way worse. Anything that reveals identifying information about a consumer is considered a violation. But to be absolutely honest, my boundaries with Hanne were sometimes really blurry.

"Oh, come on," Hanne said, rolling her eyes. "I don't even know who this person is. And I always keep your secrets.. *Verdomme.* Just tell me. Please, please, please. Just don't tell me his name."

Keeping it as vague as possible, I told her all about Molly and my first day with "the DeafBlind client," including the tug-of-war with Molly in the hallway. Hanne was leaning so far over the counter she was almost in my lap.

"Can you get her fired?" Hanne asked. "She doesn't seem to be very respectful."

"That's the thing," I said. "She's been with him forever. He obviously likes her. Her skills are good. It could be the whole Jehovah's Witness thing."

Hanne narrowed her gaze, curious as to what I meant. "Jehovah's Witness? Is that a problem? Are they awful?"

"No, not at all," I said, and I meant it. "That's the thing. Most of the JW interpreters I know are really nice. Never had a problem, other than the random attempt to convert me here and there. And, frankly, they are some of the best interpreters around. But this one . . . Jesus. She's rigid and suspicious and looks at me like I smell bad or something. But I need this job. Luckily, I think I'm doing better than I thought with the whole Tactile thing."

"Of course you are. My Cyrilje is the best interpreter."

"Yeah, right. I'm not *that* good. And how would you know, by the way?"

"True, but I sense it."

"Okay, but really I think it's because this DeafBlind guy is just way smarter than people realize, and he's making up for my incompetence."

Just as I was trying to finish my thought, Hanne's eyes widened at something she saw through the window.

"*Verdomme!* That's him, isn't it?"

"Him? Him who?"

"The DeafBlind student. The one you're working with. Does he have an old dog?"

I turned to see whom Hanne was pointing at. Sure enough, Arlo and Snap were standing right outside the coffee shop. His huge yellow I'M DEAF-BLIND button shining in the sun. It was like the RID education committee had sent him as an example of why an interpreter should keep all information confidential. I quickly shrunk down on my stool, feeling guilty as heck.

"Hey, Hanne, chill," I hissed. "Remember? I'm not supposed to have told you anything. Please stop looking at him."

Hanne quickly turned away, then more subtly craned her neck to catch a glance.

"He's different than I imagined," she said. "The old dog is so cute too. Wait, is the skinny woman who just walked over to him that awful Jehovah's Witness you told me about?"

Inconspicuously as possible, I turned my head to look. Yep, it was Molly, my nightmare. I quickly walked behind the counter and pushed Hanne in front of me, using her as a shield.

"Cyrilje? What are you doing?"

"I just don't like running into people I work with when I'm not, you know, prepared. What are they doing in this part of town?"

Hanne turned and pretended to be wiping off the counter and glanced up at Molly and Arlo through the window.

"Careful. Please!" I barked, ducking again. "I just can't deal with her right now."

Hanne looked at me, puzzled.

"You're actually scared of that skinny little woman?"

"It's not that I'm scared. Okay, maybe a little. I just don't want her to know anything about me. I don't trust her."

When I looked toward the window again, Molly was placing Arlo's hand on the windowpane, anchoring him there so he had some sense of where he was. Then she walked off. Arlo turned his face toward the café and for a moment it looked like he was staring directly at us. Hanne checked to see where Molly had gone.

"She just went into the deli on the corner," Hanne said, sighing. "She reminds me of this old woman I knew when I was little back in Belgium. Her name was Hildegard. Hildegard's husband died when she was still young, so she joined this lay religious order in the middle of Bruges, famous for making lace. All day, when she wasn't praying, Hildegard would make lace. Her fingers going so fast it was incredible. But she always looked so tense and unhappy. It didn't matter how beautiful the lace was, Hildegard always looked like she was holding the biggest shit inside her ass. Like she didn't want to surrender it. Like it was all she had. Your new coworker looks the same, like she's afraid of letting go of her shit."

"That pretty much sums her up," I said, finally letting a small laugh relieve my tension.

Hanne walked straight up to the windowpane, just inches from Arlo's face, and stared directly into his eyes. The hairs on my neck jumped to attention.

"Hanne, I know he can't see but . . . be careful. Okay?"

"I will."

Hanne pressed her pointer finger on the windowpane, and as if she were measuring out some future portrait, she outlined Arlo's face, eyes, nose, and mouth. The accompanying squeak sounded like a small out-of-tune violin.

"You didn't tell me he looked like that," she whispered. "He's like a beautiful sad broken doll with wandering eyes—like he's searching for God."

"Um . . . Hanne?" I warned, nervous. "Molly could come back any minute."

Hanne stepped back from the window, but kept staring at Arlo intently, as if she were in the process of painting him.

"He needs different clothes. And that hair . . . ugh! *Verschrikkelijk*. Get rid of the bangs. You should fix him up, Cyrilje. You gay boys love that sort of thing, *ja*? He could be quite handsome, in my opinion."

Hanne crossed back to the window and quickly kissed the pane of glass right in front of Arlo's mouth, fogging it. Just then Arlo's dog looked up to the right and barked, like she was warning me, and there was Molly approaching with a bag of groceries.

"Hanne!" I whispered harshly.

Hanne quickly moved away from the window and joined me hovering behind the coffee bar. The whole time she kept her eyes on Arlo.

"See? It's all okay. Can you be honest with me about something, Cyrilje?"

"Always."

"So when you and the student talk with your fingers to each other, aren't you just a little attracted to him?"

I shook my head and groaned. "No. As a matter of fact, I'm not. For one, as you know, he's not my type. And more importantly, I would never hook up with a client. I won't even become close friends with someone Deaf if I know I'll be working with them all the time. It causes too many ethical problems. My job is just to be the voices in the room. That's it."

Hanne looked at me mockingly.

"Just the voices in the room?" she repeated. "That's such a sterile and pat answer."

"We have to have rules," I said. "If we want to stay sane and not inadvertently cause a mess."

"I see," she said, suddenly turning somber. "So if you save enough money this summer, when would you move to Philadelphia?"

"September. After the gig is done, and I pay off some bills. Maybe mid-September."

Hanne forced a smile and muttered how great that was. Five seconds later she started wiping down the espresso machine, looking annoyed. Hanne has never been good at hiding her emotions, and I've become used to her artistic mood swings. Though I wasn't sure if at that moment she was angry or sad. I walked to the counter and grabbed her hand.

"You know, Hanneje, you could always come with me."

"Who knows," she said. "Maybe I will. There are a lot of hospitals in Philadelphia. I'll be a famous nurse-slash-artist and you'll be a famous red-headed sign language interpreter."

"Perfect. But what will you do with Wout and Curtis?"

Hanne grimaced. I might as well have asked her about a boil she needed to lance.

"Ach . . . them. Must we? Let's see, in a few years my brilliant Wout will most likely be a computer game designer or perhaps an international assassin, and Curtis, my lost and messy husband? Hmm. He will hopefully have run off with his rehab counselor."

We both laughed really hard. But at a certain point our laughing stopped, and Hanne and I looked into each other's eyes. It was that thing that has always been there between us: our deep kinship as outsiders living lives we hadn't planned or necessarily wanted, our mutual hope that someday we might be able to free ourselves from the Taconic Vortex of Hell, and our fear that neither of us ever would.

11

WHAT IS THE GRASS?

Professor Lavinia Bahr finished writing the assignment on the whiteboard and turned to the class. She looked even more fabulous than usual, wearing an embroidered red-black-green-yellow dashiki blouse over a long black skirt with her head wrapped in a matching silk scarf. From her ears dangled large golden hoops featuring a pair of beaded bumblebees chasing each other around the gilded circles. Professor Bahr, the queen bee of summertime, the empress of the thesis sentence.

Professor Bahr winked at Molly and me. It had become her signal that she was ready to begin. After two weeks of classes, despite my gentle clarification, she was still under the assumption that we ASL interpreters were like her co-teachers. (Sadly, a common misunderstanding.)

"Ladies and gentlemen!" Professor Bahr announced, as her golden bees bounced excitedly at her earlobes. "It's time to begin your first response paper. Five pages, typed neatly, double-spaced. Worth twenty-five points. As you can see from the handout, each prompt involves a famous poem or section of a poem and an idea for you to think about. The point of this is to get you to think and to write personally about your thoughts. This is not a research paper! It's a response paper. Include your own life experiences. Do you all understand? Now let's take a look at the poems."

I caught Molly's attention and rolled my eyes, mouthing the word *poetry*. She, in return, looked to heaven (or wherever JWs look to) and shook her head. If any struggle could unite ASL interpreters, it was being told we'd have to interpret a poem without any preparation. It was not just the linguistic challenge of turning English into ASL. We also had to interpret the poem—as in analyze and comprehend the meaning of it and then turn it into ASL—the whole time adjusting for whether the Deaf person may or may not have any understanding of sound, meter, rhyme, or most of the hearing-centered metaphors. To do this well on the spot was nearly impossible, and I hated it. There was only one thing worse.

"Can someone volunteer to read the first stanza of the Keats poem aloud?" Professor Bahr announced.

And *that* was what I hated more: having to interpret a poem recited badly by some mush-mouthed hearing student who read too fast, too quietly, and in a monotone. Of course, I suddenly had to do this in Tactile ASL, which took twice as long given my inexperience. I wanted to die.

The student, a Peruvian ESL speaker, stammered quietly through the stanza:

> Ah, *what can ail thee, wretched wight,*
> *Alone and palely loitering;*
> *The sedge is withered from the lake,*
> *And no birds sing.*

Did he say "white"? I glanced at Arlo's large print-copy of the poem and the word was "wight." *Okay, what the fuck is a "wight"?* Then I remembered *Game of Thrones. Zombies? Was he writing about zombies? Maybe he meant a ghost.* I used the sign for *spirit. But what in the hell did he mean by "sedge"?* There wasn't time to google it, and Molly couldn't help, since she was equally clueless. I fingerspelled the unknown words and then roughed my way through the rest. It was a disaster. "Palely loitering" I interpreted as "spirit very white. Standing in same place for a long time. Waiting." My signs felt devoid of meaning, like I might as well just have wiggled my fingers in the air. Of course, most interpreters would have quickly fallen into a lame word-by-word transliteration of the poem. So a metaphor like "a storm within my heart," which probably could be interpreted as "within myself, emotions, confusion, chaos," might end up being interpreted by the stressed-out ASL interpreter as: "Rain and wind inside my heart." Thus, the metaphorical becomes meteorological. And the interpreter ends up staring at the disengaged face of a Deaf or DeafBlind student and vows never to interpret another class that might include poetry.

I felt utterly inept.

"The student had a really thick accent," I signed to Arlo, explaining the disaster. "Very old language. It's just so different. Next time I'll ask the teacher to give us the poems beforehand so we can be better prepared."

"Other students understand poem?" he asked.

I looked around at the other vacant faces, some sneaking peeks at their smartphones or staring out the window.

"I can't say for sure, but I doubt it."

"Okay," Arlo signed, shrugging

Arlo had grown used to not understanding, or just to the mediocrity of most poetry interpretations. I looked back at Molly, hoping for another blast of interpreter simpatico. But she quickly looked back down at her copy of The Watchtower. That previous glimmer of Nice Molly was clearly an aberration.

The students were given time to look over the poems and prompts to make a choice. Arlo pulled out his big magnifying glass and stared at his handout like he was examining a rare blue butterfly. After what had to be a good ten minutes, Arlo said he had chosen to do Walt Whitman's Leaves of Grass, section 6. I wondered why he chose it. It wasn't as bad as Keats's, but still not as straightforward as I had hoped.

"Are you sure this is the one you want to do?" Molly asked, probably thinking the same thing as me. "There are other poems that would be easier."

I interjected that there were more contemporary poets on the list that might be more relatable, like Sylvia Plath or Langston Hughes. But Molly quickly snatched Arlo's hands back from me.

"I don't think either of them are appropriate," Molly grumbled. "Both, I believe, are very depressing. And Whitman is too hard. What about this poem by Wallace Stevens: 'The Snow Man'? That sounds nice."

Molly knew enough to steer Arlo clear of poems by gay Black men and suicidal feminists, but apparently wasn't privy to Stevens's complexity or Big Ol' Homo Bear Walt's passionate proclivities. Arlo furrowed his brow. I expected he'd second-guess his choice and cave to one of our suggestions, which neither of us should have been offering. But he didn't. He tapped the paper and fingerspelled W-A-L-T. No other explanation to either of us. I was proud of him.

It was still hard to figure Arlo out. Other than his comment about the ADA that first day, and his mentioning of his two former best friends, Martin and Big Head Lawrence, he barely talked about himself. Sometimes when there was downtime Arlo would simply stare off into that nothing place. Once in a while, I'd see his eyebrows knit with the slightest look of anguish on his face, as if he were angry at someone inside his head.

"Class is over. It's time to go," Molly signed, waking him from his daydream.

"Can Cyril stay few minutes? Interpret poem and assignment for me? Okay?"

Without even asking me, Molly told him that she doubted the Disability Office would pay for any extra time.

"We'll meet at your house later," Molly signed. "No need to involve Cyril."

"Thank you," Arlo responded, measuring his words carefully. "But . . . if you don't mind, I want Cyril to interpret poem. Okay? Molly, you interpret about God and heaven. Expert! But Cyril interprets poetry—wow! Champion!"

I imagined a small explosion of jealousy going off in Molly's head. I broke out in a smile. It wasn't so much that Arlo was choosing me over Molly, but rather that my disaster at interpreting Keats didn't sour Arlo on me.

"Don't worry, Molly," I signed, grabbing up Arlo's hands to interpret. "Mrs. Shuster won't mind if I add a little time to the invoice. Arlo, let's meet in the cafeteria in about thirty minutes, so I can prepare, okay?"

As I left I gave Molly a little salute but didn't wait for a response.

◊ ◊ ◊

When I finished prepping, I found Arlo sitting by himself in the cafeteria at a huge empty table with Snap asleep at his feet, one of her big paws resting on his sneaker. All around the room hearing-sighted students chatted away, eating sandwiches or working on their laptops. It was like Arlo had been banished to some lonely DeafBlind desert island. I could also tell he was having another one of those internal arguments. With whom was the big question. I touched his arm to get his attention, and his body jerked violently in shock. *Hadn't he been expecting me?* Leaning back, he squinted and scanned the space where I stood. Then I reached out and fingerspelled my name in his hands. He smiled and suddenly looked relaxed in a way I hadn't seen him around Molly or Mrs. Shuster. After I sat next to him, Arlo immediately pointed to a large-font printout of the assignment next to a magnifying glass.

"Poem, L-E-A-V-E-S *of Grass*. Wow! Good poem! But, honest . . . a little confused."

"Poetry can be challenging," I signed. "I'm curious. This poem, why'd you pick it?"

Arlo crunched his forehead and considered my question for an unusually long time, as if it were a test.

"I like grass," he finally answered.

"Okay," I signed, chuckling to myself. "That's as good a reason as any."

"Can you interpret poem for me?"

"Sure. I'll give it a try."

I rolled up my sleeves and began my stab at interpreting the text. As poems go, it wasn't as hard as I feared. There was a little struggle over how to sign "hieroglyphics," "Kanuck," and "Cuff," but then, just two lines later, Whitman writes, "Tenderly will I use you curling grass," and then describes the grass growing from the "breasts of young men."

After my first attempt at an interpretation, Arlo paused to look through his magnifying glass at his copy, focusing on the line:

It may be you transpire from the breasts of young men.

"*T-R-A-N-S-P-I-R-E* means?" Arlo asked. "Like bus or train?"

"No," I signed. "You're thinking *transportation.*"

(I had seen other Deaf readers—the ones who struggled with English— mix up words with similar shapes. I had often wondered whether they looked at words as pictures rather than collections of sounds.)

"Transpire here means to *arise from* or *happen*. That *happened* and then this *happened*. But it could also be signed 'pop up' or even 'grow,' depending on the context."

Arlo nodded and repeated my definition verbatim. But I could tell he wasn't getting it.

"Actually," I signed, "I could express this entire passage like this . . ."

I created the graveyard in front of Arlo, showing that it was filled with young soldiers' dead bodies. Whitman's physicality lent itself beautifully to ASL. I mimed the grass growing from one of the bodies. Then the old poet lay down on the graves and imagined the grass being both the extension of the beautiful and noble dead young men and their reincarnated bodies.

Arlo nodded again and started to smile. His expressions gently shifted with each line of Whitman's stanza, as if he was actually seeing it in his mind. His reaction encouraged me, and suddenly it was as if my fingers were on fire. I was momentarily the King of All Interpreters.

When I finally finished, I felt utterly spent, but also so satisfied. Arlo

effused at how clear I had made the poem, and then asked if I could interpret the essay prompt for him. After reading it over I did a basic Englishy
interpretation.

"Section 6 of *Leaves of Grass* by Walt Whitman. Discuss the ideas and
images of death and the sublime contained in Whitman's poem excerpt.
REMEMBER, I want to also hear your own reflections on what the poem
means to you. What is your relationship to death? What is your relationship to the sublime?"

Arlo didn't get it and asked me to sign it again, and then again. Each
time when I fingerspelled "the sublime" he would look confused. Finally,
he stopped me.

"Word: the S-U-B-L-I-M-E? Don't understand. ASL what?"

Shit. I had hoped fingerspelling of the word would be enough. I really
couldn't think of any proper ASL sign for *the sublime* in this context. I
would have normally interpreted *sublime* with the signs for *amazing* and/
or *beautiful*. I might have added chills shooting up my arm, but, if I was to
be honest with myself, that wasn't correct. The prompt said the expression
was "*the* sublime." It was a noun, not an adjective. The professor meant
something more. Something I didn't understand myself.

"Hold on a minute," I signed. "I'm a little confused too. I need to google something."

After a quick search I found something on the internet.

"'The sublime is primarily characterized by its ability to evoke powerful feelings.'"

"Powerful feelings?" he asked. "Like car engine power?"

"No. Bigger. More spiritual."

"Like Jesus or Jehovah God?"

"Maybe—no—different, I think. Let's keep reading."

I interpreted more about the sublime from the website, clarifying
words and concepts for the both of us. It turned out that the Romantic
poets of the nineteenth century believed that when one was awe-inspired

by beauty in nature, one was transported beyond oneself and could obtain enlightenment—but only briefly.

"A-W-E?" Arlo asked. "Meaning?"

I sighed, frustrated with myself. Explaining the sublime to Arlo was like peeling an ontological onion. I told him that *awe* was like seeing something so huge and beautiful that you were both inspired and fearful. I then read him the part of a Wiki where Wordsworth explained the sublime by saying that the "mind [tries] to grasp at something towards which it can make approaches but which it is incapable of attaining."

"Like when we look out the window here and see all those big, beautiful Taconic Mountains!"

As soon as the signs came out of my fingers I felt like an ass. Was I referring to things he had never seen? Was I being patronizing and making assumptions? My fingers did the Tactile equivalent of stammering.

"Long time ago, I see very big mountains," Arlo finally signed, clearly reading my awkwardness. "I remember. I very young. We drive to Catskills for JW conference . . ."

He aimed his eyes up and gestured a shape he saw in his mind.

"Like giant piles of green laundry. So big. Scary. Beautiful. I love mountains!"

"Well, there," I signed. "Maybe you experienced the sublime then."

"I don't think so," he signed. "I wish I could see mountains again clear. See S-U-B-L-I-M-E. But my eyes getting worse. Mountains only inside my brain. Anyway . . . good memory."

Before I could divine some pablum to ease my own uncomfortable hearing-sighted conscience, Arlo started talking more about his childhood trip to the Catskills. He told me about seeing rocky cliffs with waterfalls, a real log cabin, and how his mother bought him rock candy that looked like ice on a stick. When he spoke about his mother, his eyes grew misty. He explained that she didn't know ASL, but instead communicated via home sign—limited gestures they developed between them.

"If can't see mountains . . . means can't see S-U-B-L-I-M-E?" Arlo asked.

"No, no. Lots of things can cause the sublime," I declared, then listed things he might have experienced. "Sunsets, the ocean . . ."

"Ocean . . . never see. Too far away. Hudson River, I saw. Big lakes, swimming pool—I saw. See S-U-B-L-I-M-E? Never."

He waited. The smile vanished from his face. I was losing him again.

"You don't *see* sublime," I signed. "The sublime is more like a feeling. The sublime is those big questions you want to ask about the world, but you can't put them into words. The sublime is bigger than words. Have you felt that? You wanted to tell someone about some very important experience, but the event was just too big, amazing, and beautiful to talk about? And maybe it made you feel very, very happy but also—at the same time—a little sad and scared. The sublime feels like being overwhelmed by the hugeness of something that makes you feel both joy and fear simultaneously. That's why the Romantic poets would use the word when describing things of great beauty in nature, you know, like a mountain or the ocean or . . . Sometimes the sublime can even make a person cry because it shows us what's possible in our hearts, but it's so huge we can't really explain it, like . . . um . . . It's like . . . like . . ."

I ran out of metaphors, bankrupt of analogies. Arlo just stared ahead, his hands atop mine, waiting, wanting something more. I could think of nothing that might cause a sense of the sublime that was still (or ever) accessible to him. I pulled my hands from his, and my mind became saturated in a sense of pity. And pity was such a cowardly and useless response to offer Arlo. What if someone had pitied me for my red hair, or the psoriasis scars I sometimes got on my elbows, or the fact that I was a middle-aged, single gay man living in a one-bedroom apartment in Poughkeepsie? Did I want pity because the only person I had ever really loved dumped me and then died without ever wanting to see me again? No. We are who we are, and we understand the world based on our experiences, circumstances, and senses. Pity was just an emotional excuse. It wasn't what *Arlo* didn't know; it was what *I* didn't know. It was not *his* limits as a DeafBlind man; it was *my* limits as both an unimaginative human and a less-than-brilliant interpreter.

I suddenly felt so angry.

How did I find myself in this position? It was not my job to make Arlo understand the concept of the sublime. I was not his teacher! Certainly an educated Deaf person could explain it far better than I could. So what if I couldn't make a concept clear? There was no reason every DeafBlind man on the planet needed to understand the full meaning of every word. Arlo could just continue, like the rest of humanity, to use words willy-nilly simply because others used them, or because he loved their shape. After all, the vast majority of humanity only has the most casual of relationships with the meanings of words. Linguistic one-night stands. *Fuck it*, I thought. *Arlo has the right to do the same!*

Then I saw Arlo had been trying to get my attention, smiling and excitedly waving at me.

"Cyril! S-U-B-L-I-M-E means what? I think I understand!"

"Okay . . . go on."

"S-U-B-L-I-M-E . . . like when you love something, cherish something. When you feel like inside your chest . . . wow! Will explode! Happy, but same time sad. Long time ago . . . I remember, when little kid. I can see perfect. See almost everything. I lie next to Mama on grass. She not sick yet. Big blue sky. Clouds. Smell flowers. Beautiful day. Not too hot. Not cold. Mama hug me and kiss me and I stare in the sky and very, very happy. Mama starts to cry. I ask: *What's wrong?* But Mama says nothing. At first . . . confused, because she likes pretty sky, she likes smell of flowers, she loves me. Sad—what for?" *Snaps fingers.* "Then I understand! Mama cries . . . why? Because the world so beautiful, and we so happy, but all will disappear at Judgment Day. Both happy and sad? Right?"

Before I could respond, Arlo turned his head to the right, almost like he was trying to feel if anyone else was around.

"Cyril . . . shh . . . just between you and me, okay? Long time ago, high school, I love someone so much. For many years. Shh. Can't tell you who. Forbidden. But with this person I feel very happy. First time in my life. But then, because I want that person with me forever . . . inside my chest it feels . . . huge but confusing. I also both very, very happy and very, very sad same time. That means S-U-B-L-I-M-E, right?"

His hands reached for my response, but I was speechless. Who was this person he was talking about? Why wasn't he allowed to tell me? There was so much he and I didn't know about each other and would never know. *Very, very happy and very, very sad at the same time.*

Suddenly my mind connected to something in my own past: that autumn day Bruno and I drove up to Niagara Falls for the kitsch of it. It was chilly out and we had gone to the end of that tunnel that opens up underneath the falls. My mouth ached from all the kissing we had just done. That hard kind of kissing where it seemed the mouth was truly trying to devour the soul of the other person. He had only told me about his illness two weeks prior and had left it up to me whether to stay or go. He was so vulnerable, standing there, leaving it all up to me. Arlo's words had made me remember it so clearly: that full-body melancholy I felt as I held the man I wanted to spend my entire life with, but at the same time knowing that a lifetime might be incredibly short. *Very, very happy and very, very sad at the same time.*

"Yes!" I told Arlo. "Exactly! You got it! Perfect! Brilliant, in fact! That is the sublime!"

A pink flush of pleasure ran across Arlo's face as he started to joyously rock his body backward and forward. I asked him if he could think of a better sign for the concept of the sublime rather than our fingerspelling it each time. Arlo suggested combining several signs. He used one gesture that could be best described as "seeing stars," one that indicated goose bumps or hair standing up on your arm, and finally the sign that meant "a touched heart."

"Hmmm," I signed. "That's a bit long. Could you condense that to just the touch of the heart and the sign for *chills*?"

Arlo shook his head.

"Not enough. I need to think. Just fingerspell word for now."

"Okay. Do you need anything else?" I asked as I stood up, ready to leave. Arlo, like some DeafBlind ninja, grabbed my wrist, stopping me.

"Wait!" he demanded. "I think Walt Whitman didn't need see big mountain, big ocean to feel the S-U-B-L-I-M-E. Not everybody rich and can travel to ocean and mountain. Not everybody sees good or hears good. Maybe Walt Whitman writes the poem for those people. Poem means: Look! Look everywhere! See, down on ground! Grass! Little. Not important. Even grass can cause you feel the S-U-B-L-I-M-E. You just need look for a long time and then understand and . . . chills . . . wow . . . beautiful. Connected . . . connected to grass . . . to grave . . . to dead soldier . . . to old dead people. See grass . . . think S-U-B-L-I-M-E . . . think dead people not gone. Wow! Walt Whitman very expert poet!"

Suddenly, it was I who was feeling awe—for Arlo. I considered just tossing it all and letting myself cry, but instead, I drummed my hands on the table and stomped my feet, letting Arlo feel the vibration of my excitement.

"That!" I shouted in both voice and sign. "Yes! That! I'm not supposed to tell you what to write your response paper about, but what you just said sounds great to me! You should write that down!"

Arlo opened up his laptop to make notes. Then I said I'd see him Monday and gathered my things to leave. He stopped me again.

"Cyril, ask you other question. You know stairway have banister?"

"Yes, I know."

"At the end of old banisters, sometime have . . ."

Arlo mimed the shape of a large knoblike ornamentation at the bottom of an old staircase railing.

"That thing . . . that have word? Name what?"

"That's a funny question," I signed, chuckling to myself. "Yeah. Pretty much everything has a name. The post itself is called a N-E-W-E-L P-O-S-T. As for that thing on top . . . Wait a minute, let me think. I once interpreted an architecture class over at Marist College. Oh right. I remember. That little decorative bit at the top is called a F-I-N-I-A-L or newel cap. Either of those will work. But don't worry, almost nobody knows what they're called. Thank goodness for the internet."

Arlo removed his hands from mine and placed them back on the keyboard. I saw him type the words *finial* and *newel cap*. I waited a second to see if he had any other questions about obscure architectural decoration, but he had disappeared inside his head again. It was a look I was starting to recognize. Maybe he was thinking about that sad-happy person he loved, or maybe he was lost amid the vast, secret mountain range of his mind. Somewhere sublime.

12

GHOST CHILD

You have been sitting at your bedroom desk writing your assignment for Professor Lavinia Bahr's class. The words and ideas about the sublime and how you think and feel about Walt Whitman's poem *Leaves of Grass* (section 6) have made your mind tired but excited. You wrote about your mama, and that sunny day you were small, when you could still see well, and Mama let you lie down inside a pile of scratchy-but-soft leaves. Then she raked more leaves on top of you until you were buried, which made you laugh. You lay there for a long time, smelling twigs, moist ground, grass, a fire burning somewhere. You looked up and saw the sun shining through all the leaves, like a stained glass window of yellow, gold, orange, and red. *The sublime.*

You lift your fingers from the keyboard and your mind attaches to something else. A forbidden thought. You fall inside the memory.

You were sixteen and a half years old.

It was near the beginning of September. Yet already so chilly. Smell of cold. Smell of damp wood. Smell of blankets and someone's breath. Three years already at the Rose Garden School. Alone in your bed. Your dorm room was pitch black. You were supposed to be asleep.

"Hello? Martin? I know you stand there!"

It was the second time it happened that week. Awakened in the middle of the night by the presence of someone standing over your bed. You thought it might be one of your roommates, Martin or Big Head Lawrence, who liked to play such games. But each time it happened, you got up and found your best friends asleep in their beds, both breathing slowly. *Could it have been the dorm boss?* They did random bed checks at night, but this mysterious body that had just hovered over you, breathing on you, seemed smaller and slight. You knew the dorm boss's breath, and you had memorized her heavy stomp coming down the hallway. No. This was someone you didn't know.

During the summer break your body changed. Last year your head was just above your mama's shoulder. By August, just before you went back to school, you could rest your chin on her head. Wiry hair had grown in your armpits, and on your legs and around your groin. There were even little soft hairs that had grown in the valley between your chest muscles and on your cheeks and chin.

Brother Birch spoke of the sin of masturbation during one Public Talk, and you knew he must be speaking about you. That first semester of school Big Head Lawrence taught you how to jack off with your pillow. You knew it was a sin, but it felt so good you couldn't stop yourself. Had your mama seen you doing it over the summer? Did she find that you had made sticky pee every morning and night and stained your pillowcase? Did she tell Brother Birch? Was that why your face felt hot with embarrassment when the congregation prayed for the sinners?

The day you returned to school, you informed Martin and Big Head Lawrence they must stop jacking off and making sticky pee or they would face the Lake of Fire and forgo any opportunity to join the Great Crowd on Judgment Day. Big Head Lawrence said he didn't believe in the Lake of Fire, so you told him he had to be careful, because not believing made it even worse. You told him that if he became spiritually strong and stopped jacking off, in heaven he would have a normal-sized head. You then told Martin that if he too accepted Christ and followed the narrow path, he would have real eyes instead of the glass ones his mother promised him.

Excited by the prospect, both your friends promised they would stop jacking off and pray to God. But, after that, none of you talked about it again, and none of you stopped jacking off. And each time you finished the sinful act you grew sad and guilty and you imagined your body burning in the Lake of Fire.

Had the nighttime intruder watched you?

If the nighttime intruder wasn't Martin, Big Head Lawrence, or the dorm boss, then who was it? You knew it must have been around two in the morning because you felt the radiator still rattling and the room temperature was not yet popsicle-cold like it was between three and five. The body stood over you, breathing, moving their face closer. So close you could feel the warmth of their face and smell their spicy-sweet breath.

"Why watch me?" you signed into the blackness. "Tell me who? Why not tell?"

You tried to catch hold of the mysterious trickster. But, fast and small, they quickly escaped your attack. The floor gently shook ahead of you. Whomever or whatever it was, you thought, must have very strong vision.

"Stop! Finish!" you signed ferociously. "You will wake up Martin and Big Head Lawrence! Go! I sleep now!"

Which of the sighted students would play such tricks? Could it be one of the Deaf Devils? Those infamous bullies had played some mean tricks on both Big Head Lawrence and Martin over the years but always spared you. It could have been because of your size, or perhaps they were just waiting. Still, the body of the nighttime intruder weighed very little and the Deaf Devil's breath would not smell so sweet. Nor would one of the bullies linger over you the way they did. Standing so still. Like a *ghost*?

Big Head Lawrence used to tell stories from a large-print book called *Ghost Stories*. Before coming to the Rose Garden School, you had never heard much about ghosts or spirits. When you had asked Molly about ghosts, she reminded you that ghosts could be demons, and JWs believed that demons were real. Ghost stories became yet another thing you had to add to the ever-growing category known as "forbidden things for Jehovah's Witnesses." Martin talked extensively about ghosts too. Real ghosts, not like the ones in Big Head Lawrence's book. Martin's stories horrified you, but also made you excited. You squirmed and shook at each turn of the tale, then pleaded with Martin "no, no, stop," then a moment later begged him to tell the story again.

"Some ghosts at Rose Garden School," Martin signed, very slowly until his fingers would speed up to scare you, "they dead Deaf children! Murdered in Dogwood House!"

"Stop! You playing! Finish you!" you shouted, convinced Martin was just trying to scare you again, knowing how you hated when anyone spoke of Dogwood House, that scary old dorm at the back of the campus where all the troublesome and mentally deranged children were allegedly sent.

"No! Truth!" Big Head Lawrence confirmed. "Long ago, children die in Dogwood House. Then ghosts of dead children sometimes visit live students. They beg for help!"

"Please, please, please," Martin signed shakily and slow, acting as if he were the ghost of a dead Deaf child. "Help me escape from Dogwood House!"

You laughed at Martin's impersonation even though it also gave you chills.

Your friends explained that these Dogwood ghost children didn't know they were dead. Then, after a quick private conference with Big Head Lawrence, Martin told you about the worst ghost of all: Angry John.

"Big Head Lawrence doesn't want me tell story. He scared baby! But I tell you. Angry John looks same as you. But only Deaf, not low-vision. Long long time ago Angry John sent to Dogwood House because he very bad boy. The mean dorm boss at Dogwood House have big teeth and claws and she sat on Angry John so long he couldn't breathe. Angry John scream help help, but everyone ignores because he bad Deaf boy. And then . . . dead. Dorm boss scared. Why? Because she thinks they will blame her. So she digs hole in wall of Dogwood House and puts Angry John's dead body inside. Then uses cement and make it look like regular wall. Ever since, the ghost of Angry John flies around the Rose Garden School at night asking live Deaf children to help get his body out of wall. Sometimes children wake up with bloody fingernails because he makes them dig at cement wall with hands. Dorm bosses thinks it's wind or bad kids playing. Deaf kids don't hear because they deaf. But many see him! Feel him sometimes. Sometimes smell him."

"Angry John smell bad!" Big Head Lawrence added.

"Shut up!" Martin chided. "I tell story! One time Angry John tried to wake Big Head Lawrence when he sleeping. He tries to convince Big Head Lawrence to help him dig wall! Why? Because inside wall at Dogwood House his body all shriveled and smell like big garbage cans with bad food in back of cafeteria!"

Three years later, as you lay in your bed, Martin's old story still gave you goose bumps even though you were so much older. You ran your hand across the tiny, raised follicles on your skin like it was flesh braille. Was that a message from a ghost? Was the mysterious trickster with the sweet-smelling breath who kept sneaking into your room, standing over your body, Angry John? You pulled the covers and a pillow over your face. If Angry John was going to kill you, there was no point in making it easy for him.

After two nights of no nightly visitor, you figured Angry John (or whatever ghost child it was) had decided to haunt someone else. Finally, you could sleep in peace. But then, the very next night, you felt those same small feet walk across the floor. You felt the sweet breath, the face coming closer, you felt the warmth of skin, and then, for the first time, the ghost's small fingers pressed themselves into your cheek.

That does it. You yanked off the blankets and grabbed for the ghost child, but again the small assailant was too fast, and you felt the feet scamper across the floor again. *Wait. Do ghosts have feet?* You jumped out of your bed. The cold tiled floor stung your bare feet. Sensing whoever it was had headed for Martin's bed, you stumbled across the room. Martin's body still slept undisturbed. But then you felt something coming from the floor under Martin's bed. Hot breath was blowing on your toes. You kicked your foot under the bed and the ghost child scurried out between your legs, across the floor, and then jumped into your bed. That was it. You were furious. Murderous ghost or not, you ran back to your bed and leaped, pressing your whole weight upon the wriggling culprit. The body was slight and half your size, solid and so warm it was clearly made of flesh and bone. You straddled the squirming small frame, trapping it tightly between your knees.

"I know you play with me!" you signed furiously into the darkness. "I know not Angry John! Who?! Why you in my bed?"

You grabbed for the imposter ghost child's thrashing hands, hoping they would speak to you. But, instead, they yanked the pillow over their face. You felt the warm, small body wriggle between your legs. Suddenly you found yourself growing stiff in your pajamas. Embarrassed at your body's reaction, you lifted your crotch off the wiggling small body so as not to accidentally commit a red star sin. Whoever it was, they were definitely not any kind of threat. They weren't even seriously trying to escape anymore. Was this all a game?

"Don't sneak around," you signed after removing the pillow from their face. "If you want play, you must sign Tactile with me. Now tell me who?"

When they didn't answer you reached down to explore their face, which had very soft skin and small features. Then you felt the mound of long hair on their head, the narrow neck the width of your forearm, their skinny shoulder, which you stroked, letting them know you were no longer angry. It wasn't until you touched their chest that you noticed something truly peculiar. It was a thin body, but, like Martin, it had . . . breasts?

"Sorry!" you signed after leaping to the other side of the bed. "I didn't know you girl. Very sorry."

Your hands reached out and this time the small hands entered yours.

They were the most beautiful hands you had ever felt. She slowly stroked two letters on the inside of your palm.

"H-I."

"Hi," you signed back. "Name?"

But she didn't answer. Instead, she pulled your palm to her face and sniffed your skin, then stroked the inside of your arm gently with her fingers. Your mother had stroked your arms before you went to sleep at night, but the ghost child girl's touch was a different kind of warm, a different kind of good.

"Why you come here?"

Again you reached out your hands, hoping for words. But the ghost child girl tickled the insides of your palms with nonsense signs, as if her hands were trying to approximate Tactile Sign Language.

"You not blind?" you asked. "You just Deaf?"

You wanted to feel more of her hands, even though you knew it was a sin to be alone with a girl, especially now that you were a young man. Brother Birch said the only girls you were allowed to be alone with were your mama and Molly. If you were with other girls, you needed to have someone else with you. But you wanted to feel the girl's hands again. You rationalized with yourself: If she really were a ghost then you wouldn't be committing a sin, or at least none you knew about. The ghost child's hands reached for you, but this time they continued up to your chest and along your neck and suddenly they were stroking your face. She pulled your head into her neck and you breathed in the smell of her thicket of hair. Burning leaves and jasmine flowers. You let your hands run along her arms and again across her T-shirt to the softness of her chest. Your sinful penis pressed hard against the cotton of your pajamas, so you grabbed the pillow and shoved it between your bodies for protection. She stroked the back of your neck; you felt her heart rattling like a drum against your hand. You leaned back again so you could feel her eyelids, feel the marblelike roundness beneath, and the thick paintbrush-like eyelashes. Her face lifted and came closer to yours and you smelled the breath, spicy-sweet, turmeric and coriander. You faintly remembered a similar scent from years before, that first day when you arrived at school. Was it the same girl? How many times had she been around you?

"Please tell me. Who?"

Then the girl did something no one had ever done before. She placed her mouth on yours, breathed in your breath, and let the wetness of her mouth drain into yours. Suddenly there was a feeling of such joy fluttering around your heart, and at the same time you felt an overwhelming sense of melancholy at the thought that the kiss would end. It was the most beautiful pain you had ever felt.

"My name A-R-L-O . . . Name-sign: A . . ."

The ghost child pressed her perfect fingers into your palms. "I know your name."

Then she signed your name-sign like she had always known it.

Before you could ask her name, she kissed you again. That time it was even deeper and hungrier. You pressed your body against hers. There was a desperation to your hands and lips. Suddenly she was a locked room you needed to enter. Your hands wandered to the sinful places of her body, but she pushed you away and leaped off the bed.

"What's wrong?" you signed into the darkness. "I sorry. Come back. Please."

A second later you felt the vibration of her small feet run out of the room. A soul sickness overwhelmed you. You felt sadder than you had ever felt, but not because you had committed a terrible sin. Because you could still taste the ghost child's lips on your mouth and understood there was no guarantee you would ever meet her again.

13

LUNCHTIME EPIPHANIES

Molly had a broken molar and was outside the classroom trying to call for an emergency dental appointment. All morning Arlo had barely said a word to me, which surprised me considering his openness the previous Friday.

"Did you have a nice weekend?" I asked. "Molly is still in the hallway."

I wondered if it was Molly's presence that caused his restraint. But after tossing out a brief *okay*, he returned his hands to his lap. I wasn't ready to give up.

"Did you finish writing the Whitman response paper? That was such a great idea you had."

He merely shook his head no. Had I offended him? After our conversation about awe and the sublime on Friday, the sudden chill felt a little like being ghosted after a fantastic first date. I was dumbfounded. Professor Bahr finally returned and handed out a flyer about a field trip to Albany set to happen at the end of July, and reminded the students that there would be no extensions for their response papers that would soon be due. As the students were leaving, Molly pushed her way back into the room, holding her inflamed cheek with a look of mild agony.

"I hate to do this," she began. "The only appointment my dentist has this week is in twenty minutes. Could you help Arlo get his lunch in the cafeteria?"

"Sure. I have to kill some time anyway. Good luck with the tooth."

"I don't believe in luck," she said in the most Mollyish of ways. "Just seat him at an empty table at the front. He'll give you exact change for the lunch. It costs $4.75. He always has the same thing: a baloney and American cheese sandwich. White bread, lettuce, tomato, mayonnaise. No mustard. He hates mustard. Bring it to his table and then you can leave."

Molly looked at Arlo and then at me. Beneath her tooth pain, I perceived a different concern.

"Don't worry," I said. "Go. I got it covered."

"Just do us a favor," Molly said, lowering her voice. "Please no more extracurricular discussions about religion or anything of that sort. Brother Birch doesn't like it, and it makes Arlo uncomfortable."

"Excuse me?" I said, utterly confused. "I never . . ."

Before I could ask her what the hell she was talking about she was out the door. I scanned my mind for anything I might have said that could be perceived as religious. I came up blank until I remembered the sublime. Was that it? Had I totally misread Arlo's reaction? I felt like an idiot. *Oh well*, I thought, *you're damned if you do and, well—in my case—just damned.*

I tapped Arlo on the shoulder.

"Lunch?"

◊ ◊ ◊

The cafeteria was packed. Hordes of summer students were cramming into the lunch line and filling the tables.

As we dodged the hurrying, hungry bodies, Arlo took my elbow and walked a step behind me as though he and Snap were my nervous prom dates. A blind person taking your arm in this manner is pretty standard, but still, for some reason, the intimacy made me uncomfortable at first. It had been years since another person had held my arm in public. Then I noticed some frat boy type staring at us, snickering and muttering what I assumed were homophobic comments to his friends. You'd have thought the guide dog might have given him a clue. *Asshole*.

I found Arlo and Snap an available table near the front. The old guide dog lay down at her boss's feet. I turned to go get the baloney sandwich like Molly had told me, but when I glanced around, I saw how all the tables were filled with young people talking and laughing. I looked back at Arlo sitting completely alone, abandoned on his DeafBlind island. I returned and tapped him on the shoulder.

"Hey. Molly said I'm supposed to go get your sandwich, but I was wondering if you'd like to come up and order it yourself?"

Arlo looked almost surprised, like I had just suggested we go smoke some crack or something.

"You mean, we stand in cafeteria line together? Allowed?"

"Of course," I signed. "No law against it. Come on."

Arlo turned his head to the side, as if he were looking for some invisible person to give him the thumbs-up. A second later he and Snap got up and we headed for the lunch line. Snap, usually the epitome of canine cool, started wagging her tail, hungrily inhaling the greasy air with her wet, pink nose.

"Snap sure enjoys the smells!" I signed.

"Ha ha," he signed, yanking the harness. "Snap first time in line too. Smells good, right, Snap?"

Arlo smiled broadly; his earlier indifference toward me had vanished.

There were only three people in the lunch line ahead of us. When they saw Snap and Arlo, they motioned for us to go ahead. Soon enough we were face-to-face with Doris and Bitsy, the guardians of the goulash. Both women were in their middle years, squeezed into gravy-stained white uniforms, and both wore the boiled expressions of having labored far too long over the heat of the steam table. They held their serving spoons aloft, like graveyard shovels, across the metal coffins of the day's offerings. Bitsy, the taller of the two, recognized Arlo.

"Aaaoh," she said with her cigarette-ravaged, South Jersey–transplant rasp. "Isn't that the blind-and-mute kid who sits all alone out by them soda machines? Name's *Arno*, right? He don't need to come up for his sandwich hisself, poor thing. Usually his other caretaker—the skinny lady—comes up."

Immediately I had to suppress my agitation with Bitsy's insensitivities regarding Deafness as well as the interpreting profession. I usually would just let the Deaf person take the lead on educating the hearing about what was appropriate. But when it was clear Arlo wasn't going to, I smiled at Bitsy and did my best not to sound smug.

"Actually, his name is Arlo, and DeafBlind is the proper term, and that thin older woman and I are called *interpreters*, not *caretakers*."

As soon as I said it, Bitsy gave Doris a *Get a load of who thinks he's so special* look.

"He's having his usual, right?" Bitsy asked, clearly feeling affectionate toward Arlo despite whatever she was feeling toward me.

I turned to Arlo and started signing fairly broadly, mostly to demonstrate that someone with deaf-blindness could answer for himself.

"You want the usual baloney and American cheese sandwich with mayo, lettuce, and tomato, right? Molly said baloney is your favorite."

Arlo paused. Once again, being asked a basic question seemed alien to him, and he looked confused by it. At the same time, from the corner of my eye, I could see that Bitsy was already slathering the slices of white bread with gobs of mayonnaise.

"Baloney and American coming right up!" she called out. "Who's next?"

"Hey, Bitsy," I interrupted. "Do you mind holding a minute, please? I'm not sure he wants baloney. Just one sec."

I turned back to Arlo.

"Is there something else you would like?"

Arlo stood there thinking for a good fifteen seconds, like it was the $100,000 question on *Who Wants to Be a Millionaire*. Bitsy, meanwhile, nodded toward the line, which was growing longer behind us.

"I wish cafeteria cook other good food for students too," Arlo finally signed. "Not fair. Cook good food for teachers. Students only allow sand-wiches."

"What?"

When I pursued it further, it turned out that since Molly had never offered Arlo anything other than his usual baloney sandwich, he was under the impression that students were limited to buying sandwiches, while the cafeteria's hot food was the exclusive purview of teachers and administrators.

"Other good food, can eat?" he asked.

"Well, I mean, cafeteria food is rarely good, but there are lots of other choices. Let's see. They have spaghetti and meatballs pretty much every day, pizza—which is pretty horrendous. They also have hamburgers, some old-looking salads. And . . . umm . . . chicken M-A-R-S-A-L-A with mush-rooms. That's the special."

Suddenly, Arlo's brow furrowed.

"What?" he signed, exasperated. "Spaghetti and meatballs? Have? Every day have?"

"I think so . . . yes, it's painted permanently on the board, so yes, every day."

Arlo's eyes widened, followed by another long bout of silent thinking. The line behind us was getting uncomfortably long.

"Come on! Hurry up!" a male voice shouted. "What the hell is taking so long?"

"Sorry!" I yelled back as pleasantly as possible.

"Cool your jets," Bitsy snapped at the impatient student. "Ever think of looking before you speak?"

Then Bitsy tossed her head toward Arlo and Snap, clearly hoping the SOB would feel guilty for rushing a DeafBlind guy.

"I think I want spaghetti and meatballs," Arlo finally signed.

I breathed a sigh of relief, ready to put in the order when he started signing again.

"Wait . . . what means chicken M-A-R-S-A-L-A? Why label *special*? Means very very delicious?"

"Um, no, *special* just means this food isn't on the regular menu."

Arlo looked confused. I told some people to go ahead of us while I explained the menu.

"So chicken M-A-R-S-A-L-A is chicken covered in flour and S-A-U-T-E-E-D"—suddenly, despite having interpreted a half dozen chef trainings, I forgot the sign for *sauté*. Fuck it—"means cooked. Fried"—that's it!—"rather, in a kind of red wine sauce. Though I doubt they use real wine here. It also has mushrooms and butter. It can be delicious, but in this cafeteria, who knows? 'Special' in this circumstance means it's a special food that they cook rarely. Also, it comes with a free dessert, which looks like pudding or something."

Upon hearing about the pudding, Arlo started rocking his torso, smiling.

"Now understand *special*. Free dessert. Cool!"

"Specials are something most restaurants and cafeterias have," I signed. "But they don't always come with a free dessert. Anyway, we need to order fast. We're holding up the line, and the lunch women look like they are about to throw knives at me."

Arlo looked down for another moment, considering his final order. But by that time Bitsy could see the line was getting out of hand.

"Okay, time's up, Red," she said. "We got a major traffic clog. Arno's gonna need to decide pronto."

"Arlo!" I snapped. "We just need a min—"

"Christ, ladies!" a male voice cried out, followed by a flurry of snickers.

I turned and looked behind us. It was the homophobic frat boy and his friends from earlier. He was in his midtwenties, prematurely balding, with a polo that was a size too small for his paunchy body.

"Why don't you take your boyfriend to Olive Garden or something?"

Frat Boy said, exaggerating the sibilant "s" sound. "It's lunch, not freaking rocket science!"

He followed the comment with a flourish of effeminate fake sign language, causing his buddies to laugh.

That was it. I lost it. My face pulsed with blood. I grabbed the food tray and slammed it down.

"Excuse me, ladies and gentlemen!" I shouted, my angry tone sharpened with sarcasm. "Bitsy, Doris! All you fine people in line! Arlo and I apologize for the delay! For some of us it can take a little longer to order lunch!" I glared at the homophobic frat boy, and then lowered my eyes toward his jelly gut. "By the look of some of you, it's pretty obvious you won't starve! So, would you all do me the kind favor of being a little more patient and BACK THE FUCK OFF!"

When I finally stopped screaming, Bitsy and Doris looked downright frightened, while everyone behind us in line, including the frat boys, was staring at the crazy redheaded interpreter, checking to see whether he had a gun or not. Poor Snap was scratching her paw on my leg, whining, trying to get me to calm down.

"Don't worry, Snap. It's okay," I whispered to her.

That's when I realized I hadn't been interpreting anything that was happening for Arlo, but he could feel my body quaking.

"Something wrong?" he finally asked.

"Nothing," I lied, not wanting to take up even more time. "I think we should order now."

"Okay. I know what I want."

"Great!" I said, loud enough for everyone to hear. "Look, Doris, Bitsy, I'm sorry I exploded, and, well, he's ready to order!"

Then to Arlo: "What's it going to be?"

"I want *special* chicken food M . . . (then Arlo wiggled his fingers to indicate he had no idea how to spell the rest of the word *marsala*) with free special dessert."

"Okay," I said, thinking he had finished. But he hadn't.

"And I also want spaghetti and meatballs . . . extra meatballs . . . and french fries!"

"Um, that's a lot of food . . ."

"I know. I have nine dollars and seventy-five cents in wallet. Various dishes—must try today. Why? So later I will know what I want to order. Many many years baloney sandwich lunch every day. Same same same. Fed up. I want something new. Thank you."

Arlo pulled out his wallet and felt each of the nine dollar bills and then dug into the change pocket for three quarters, placing all of it in my hand. Then he smiled, like he had just placed an order for a Rolls-Royce when he could only afford a Ford Fiesta. I looked at Bitsy, who, despite everything, had once again picked up the white bread and knife full of mayonnaise.

"Put down the knife, Bitsy!" I said. "No baloney and cheese today!"

Then, without signing to Arlo, since I wanted it to be a surprise, I told her to get ready to give us all the entrées they had available on the line. I was gonna go sit Arlo down at the table then come back to get the food. She and Doris looked at me again like I was crazy.

"*All* the food?" Doris asked. "Are you shittin' me? That'll be over thirty bucks, ya know?"

"Yep. The spaghetti and meatballs, the special, everything! And you know something, also make him a BLT, which happens to be my favorite sandwich. It's time we all lived a little around here, right?"

Doris looked to Bitsy, deferring to the taller woman for the go-ahead. Bitsy placed her mayonnaise knife down and picked up her serving spoon and grinned like a devilish conspirator.

"Let's give the kid what he wants, for chrissakes!"

◊ ◊ ◊

You wait for Cyril to bring you the delicious food you ordered. It will cost almost two days' worth of lunch money, but you are very excited to try the new food. Waiting, waiting, waiting. Suddenly, as if your body is possessed by a demon, your fingers try to remember how to spell the name. S-H-H-A? S-A-H-S? S-I-H-H-A? You remember her name-sign, but the spoken name was like how people spell the sound the mouth makes when a person says "shhh" plus other letters.

A-H-S-S? S-A-S-H?

Someone taps you on the shoulder and you jump from fear.

"Hey, sorry, I didn't mean to frighten you," Cyril signs into your hands. "You were spelling something to yourself?"

"Doesn't matter," you lie. "Just trying to remember something for essay." Red star.

Cyril then moves two trays of food in front of you, and you are overwhelmed by the smells. You push all the sinful memories back down into the bad part of your brain. You are starving.

"I hope you are hungry!" Cyril says. "You have a lot of choices."

You breathe in the fragrant spicy spaghetti sauce and the "special" chicken dish . . . but, wait, there is even more than what you remember. Sniff. Does the "special" chicken dish have bacon? Sniff. What is that flowery smell in the meatballs? You lower your head like a bloodhound, trying to locate the source of each luscious scent.

"Can eat now?" you ask.

"Sure, sure! Go ahead! Dig in!"

After you make your way around the sumptuous spaghetti and meatballs, the dark and surprising "special" chicken, you discover that the interpreter has brought you even more food than you ordered. French fries, pizza, and a sandwich you have never tried before. You bite into it. The harsh crunch of the toasted bread itches your lips. But then your senses are ravaged as the cool tomato chills your teeth, the wet lettuce snaps and whips against the inside of your cheek, and finally the warm mayonnaise and the salty-sweet crunch of the bacon!

Cyril taps your shoulder.

"You like it?"

"Yes!" you say. "Delicious!"

Sign DELICIOUS: *The middle finger and thumb touch each other as they meet your lips, then they pull outward as the thumb curls against the middle finger, which draws down to the palm, as if it's pulling a sumptuous string from your mouth.*

"Sandwich name, what?" you ask.

"It's called a B-L-T. Its initials. It stands for bacon, lettuce, and tomato."

Because he is doing Tactile Sign Language with you, the interpreter's hands now have mayonnaise on them too.

You take turns eating from each plate in front of you. One more bite of BLT, then spaghetti and meatballs, then special chicken and back again. Snap's big head slides warmly into your lap. She is hoping something juicy will fall from your hands, unnoticed. Even guide dogs take advantage of the DeafBlind sometimes. But this time it's okay. There is enough food for everyone. You feel for a meatball in your spaghetti plate and sneak it down to Snap, who gobbles it down, almost nibbling off your fingers.

"Snap! Down!" you sign like you are angry, but you're not.

Snap lowers down while you clean your hands with sanitizer. You can feel from how her body is shivering that she's as excited as you are about the new lunch. For the next twenty-five minutes you say nothing to Cyril or Snap until you're too full of delicious new food to eat any more. Only a meatball and a few strands of spaghetti remain on your plate. You pretend to accidentally drop the other meatball on the floor for Snap, who gobbles it down, then licks your ankle to say thank you.

"Cyril? Are you still here?"

He is.

"Are you still hungry?" Cyril asks jokingly.

"Ha ha. No. I'm full now. Thanks for helping me get new food to try.

Special food is delicious too. I have again tomorrow . . . but not all at same time."

"Okay," Cyril says. "I'm going now. Oh, hey. The lunch ladies decided to give you a big discount today. So here's your money back."

Cyril puts nine dollar bills in your hand. For a moment you hold the money in your palm, surprised that the lunch ladies would be so nice. You put the money back in your wallet.

"Do you know your way back to the library?" Cyril asks.

You do know your way back, but really you want to say, I am lonely, please stay so I have someone to talk to. I will give you the nine dollars back if you just stay. *You want to tell him that you trust him, and then tell him secrets the way you used to tell Martin and Big Head Lawrence. You want to tell him about your mother, and about S and what happened. But he is just your interpreter, not your friend, so you say, "Yes. I know where library. Thank you. See you tomorrow."*

14

HANNE MEETS ARLO

After Arlo's class the following Wednesday I met Hanne at the community college for a coffee and catch-up. She had just gotten off work and changed from her barista outfit into her nursing scrubs for her clinical class. It was one of those rare midsummer days where the temperature was only in the high seventies, so we sat outside on the grass in front of Hudson Hall enjoying the weather. Hanne had swept her hair up in an old-fashioned French twist and, as always, garnered some lingering stares from the male students, which she ignored as if they were as common as the gnats that flitted about the lawn.

Before I could even ask her how school was going or if Curtis and Wout were doing okay, Hanne immediately began peppering me with questions about "that extraordinary DeafBlind boy," as she called him. It was like I was working with her favorite rock star. I told myself I wasn't breaking the confidentiality clause of the RID Code of Professional Conduct, because I never actually said Arlo's name and tried to speak in what I thought were generalities. But, being that he was basically my only client in the dead of summer, Hanne knew good and well to whom I was referring. (I'm not proud of this.) I just needed someone to talk to about it, because the more I worked with Arlo, the more mystery seemed to surround him.

"I'm telling you there's something there. I feel it," I told Hanne.

"Are all Deaf people so withholding about their personal lives?" she asked.

I laughed and almost snorted my iced coffee onto the grass.

"Hell no! Most Deaf I know reveal way too much. You ask them where they bought a sweater and you end up hearing about how their aunt just left her husband for the milkman. It's another reason why I love the Deaf community. This student's different, though. I barely know anything about him."

"I thought you said he was opening up more?"

"He did, I guess," I said, plucking a blade of grass from the lawn. "But it's like the door slammed shut again. But I know there's something there. Something he's dying to say. I saw him having this private conversation with himself—or rather with someone inside his head. The look on his face—it was so desperate. Heartbroken even. When I tapped him to get his attention, he jumped an inch off his chair like I had caught him in the act of committing a crime. He looked terrified."

Hanne squinted and scratched her chin like she was some gorgeous Belgian nurse-detective.

"Interesting," she said. "A secret lover?"

I shook my head, despite the fact Arlo had indeed told me his vague secret of loving someone a long time ago; that was not something I'd ever reveal to Hanne or anyone. I had promised. And I knew that if he was currently seeing someone, he probably would have hinted at it in that moment.

"No. I doubt it," I said. "I get a strong feeling he's still a virgin, anyway."

"Impossible," Hanne protested. "With that beautiful face?"

"Um, he's also a Jehovah's Witness. Besides, from what I can tell, he's barely ever alone outside his home unless he's studying at the library or waiting for a bus. He usually has his interpreter or guardian around. But who knows?"

Hanne's brow knitted, and then the spark of another idea flashed in her eyes.

"Cyrilje, I hope this isn't a rude question, but what is someone Deaf-Blind attracted to anyway? Sexually? Romantically? What part of a person do they fall in love with? Like for me, I'm drawn to a man's hands or thick muscular legs, or the sound of a good low voice. What does someone who can't see or hear find attractive?"

I shrugged.

"It obviously depends on the individual," I said. "Just like anyone else, I imagine. And remember, this student still sees a little, but not much. When he was small, he could see pretty well. But if someone was deaf and blind from birth? Or what this consumer eroticizes now that his vision is gone? Honestly, I haven't a clue. Maybe the feel of the body? The smell?"

"Fascinating!" Hanne's eyes glowed with curiosity. "Could you ask him?"

I laughed.

"Sure, I'll go right ahead and do that," I said sarcastically. *"Hey, buddy, what turns you on? While you're at it, tell me, what deep dark secret are you hiding? You secretly sleeping with Ariana Grande? My friend Hanne is really curious . . . Oh, and by the way, she wants to know if you're a virgin?* I'd be fired by the end of the day. Besides, he and I are rarely alone. I just wonder—"

Hanne's eyes widened as she pointed toward Hudson Hall.

"Verdomme!" Hanne whispered. "There he is again. It's like he's following us."

Sure enough, there was Arlo having just sat down on the bench at his Able-Ride pickup spot.

"That's weird," I said. "It's almost four p.m. I wonder why he's here so late."

I looked around and saw no sign of Molly. Hanne sat up and started pushing in any loose hairs from her French twist, like she was ready to walk over to him.

"Could you introduce me?" she asked.

"I'm not sure that's a great idea," I said. "He seems pretty shy."

"Oh, come on, just a quick introduction. What could it hurt?"

"Yeah, but . . ."

The truth was Hanne could be very unpredictable sometimes. There was also the confidentiality issue. And to be honest, I felt very protective of the relationship I had already built with Arlo, and I worried Hanne might say something about me that could put it at risk.

"If you don't feel comfortable, then I won't," Hanne said, practically reading my mind. "I just really want to say hi to him, and I'm sure if he's as lonely as you say, he probably would like to say hi to other people too, right?"

Hanne wasn't wrong. Also, if I had run into a sighted Deaf consumer, while I wouldn't reveal that we worked together, I would say hello and introduce them to whomever I was with. To not do the same for Arlo felt unfair. If Arlo had taught me anything, it was that DeafBlind people wanted to know all they could about what was happening around them.

"Okay," I said. "We can say hi. But just don't say anything controversial, okay?"

"Ach! Of course not," she said, rolling her eyes.

We walked over to Arlo, but before I could even get his attention, Hanne made kissing sounds toward Snap, causing the obdurate old mutt to squirm out from under the bench, blinking her sleepy eyes and wagging her tail wildly. Hanne started scratching Snap on her withers, inciting the pooch to close her eyes and lift her snout to the sky in forbidden ecstasy.

"Oh, hey," I warned Hanne, pointing to Snap's orange vest. "See, it says 'Do Not Pet.' It distracts her from her duties."

"Sorry, doggie," Hanne said with a pouty face before pulling her hands from Snap's neck.

I tapped Arlo on the shoulder and put my name into his hand.

"I'm here with my friend H-A-N-N-E," I signed. "She's a nursing student here at the community college, and also works at a café on Main Street. She wants to say hi."

Arlo moved his head around, attempting to catch Hanne's image in his field of vision. When he finally did, he introduced himself and then offered his hand. Hanne grabbed it in both of hers and held on.

"So his name is Arlo. Such a beautiful name. Does he want to feel my face?" Hanne whispered. "I don't mind if he does."

"Hanne. Chill. I don't imagine DeafBlind people go around feeling the faces of every Tom, Dick, and Harry they meet on the street. Just shake his hand, say hi, and let's be on our way. His ride should be here any minute."

I tried to motivate Hanne's exit by making a move to leave myself, but she stood there, her hand in his.

"He's not letting go," she said, happily trapped. "What can I do?"

Arlo was smiling and appeared to be curious about who Hanne was, so he slowly started feeling her wrist, squeezing it, then moving farther up her forearm and then back to her hand. He appeared to be checking her out. At that point I just wanted the uncomfortable collision of my two worlds to end.

"Okay, then," I said, the anxiety showing in my voice. "He probably wants to focus on schoolwork or something, so . . ."

Hanne then gently released Arlo's hand.

"Cyrilje, I'm curious about something. Suppose I ran into a DeafBlind person at the coffee shop and they wanted to talk with me. How would I do it without an interpreter?"

I interpreted Hanne's comment to Arlo, and much to my chagrin, he enthusiastically started explaining to her about his notebook, magnifying glass, and the black Magic Marker he used so non-signing people could write back and forth with him. Then he explained how for longer conversations he had an old piece of equipment called a screen braille communicator.

"It's called an SBC for short," Arlo said via my voicing. "It writes braille automatically. Suppose there is no interpreter around and a sighted-hearing person wants to have a long chat. Going back and forth with the Magic Marker and paper gets boring and can give me a headache if my eye starts to hurt. With the SBC I can talk for a long time. It works this way: the sighted person just types on the keyboard and their words instantly become braille. Then I will type back and my words appear on a little screen for the hearing-sighted person."

"That's very cool!" Hanne exclaimed. "Could we try?"

"Hanne," I said, interpreting simultaneously. "Arlo has his ride home coming, and besides, it's not like he'd be carrying it around with him—"

"Not true," Arlo interrupted. "I have SBC in backpack. Always. Also, van won't come long time. Always thirty or forty minutes late. If she wants, I can show now."

"Yay!" Hanne clapped. "Yes please! I really want to try."

"Um," I stammered, realizing there was no way out. Then, without signing, I said through my teeth: "Hanne, please remember he comes from a really conservative family and this is making me really nervous."

Hanne looked at me in that way she does, like she was seeing inside me.

"Cyrilje," she said, in a voice an enlightened mother uses with her child who is having a tantrum. "I completely understand, and we can absolutely go if you really think that's the right thing to do, but didn't you once tell me about how some interpreters can act like babysitters around Deaf people? And didn't you once say how your job is to just interpret the message accurately so the Deaf person can make their own choice?"

"Yeah," I said. "Maybe I am being a little paternalistic, but . . ."

"Also," Hanne added, "aren't you supposed to be interpreting everything that's being said in front of him?"

Infuriating as it was, Hanne was right again.

I gently pushed Hanne out of the way so I could interpret, but I gave her a warning look that said *Don't say anything stupid*. Without voicing for Hanne, I told Arlo everything Hanne had just said, including the part about Hanne wanting him to feel her face, and her saying I was acting like a babysitter and even her calling me out about not interpreting. Arlo laughed, which made me feel a little better. I then described Hanne's appearance, explaining that she was very smart and pretty and could be a little flirty and crazy. When I told him that Hanne thought he was handsome, the briefest of blushes tinted his face. Again, Arlo strained to locate Hanne's face.

"I have an idea," Arlo signed. "Maybe we three can go cafeteria? Sit and chat? Typing on table with SBC more comfortable. Maybe Hanne and me talk, you can read my essay? Tell me if good?"

"What did he say?" Hanne asked.

Before I could even tell her, Arlo started walking back toward Hudson Hall and waved for us to follow him.

"He wants us to go to the cafeteria to show you the SBC and talk," I said, shaking my head. "But please, let's just keep it short and sweet, okay?"

◊ ◊ ◊

You sit in the college cafeteria with Cyril's friend named Hanne. From the texture and thickness of her skin, you can tell she's not really a girl but a woman. She must be younger than Molly, but still older than you. Cyril says she has hair that is dark blond, gray-green eyes, a thin build, pretty. But her hands are not very beautiful. The flesh of her knuckles bunches under your touch, the bones protrude obscenely on her thumb, her cuticles are bitten and rough. When Cyril says "pretty," he means her face. To you, who can barely see the shape of a face anymore, a head has become an abstract object of mere bone and flesh. An ill-shaped bowling ball in a soft leather bag. You suspect she is a sinful woman, and if someone from church saw you, you'd get in trouble. But talking to a sinful woman excites you, so you teach her how to use the SBC and ask Cyril to read your essay so you can be alone.

Red star.

Hanne tells you she's a painter and was born in a country called Belgium. She also says she studies nursing at the community college. She is married and has a child, but, despite this, her knee bumps into your leg under the table every so often when you are typing. Maybe she doesn't like her husband anymore, maybe her child has grown and gone away. Maybe she's very lonely like you.

You feel the braille bumps of Hanne's words leap beneath your fingertips like a millipede running across the refreshable display. Hanne tells you a secret, that she doesn't like living in Poughkeepsie, and that she's not sure she wants to become a nurse, and that she would prefer to go to New York City to make art. You like hearing this other person's dreams. It is the first time in a very long time you had another person talk to you like this. When she asks you your dream, you say it is to become a pioneer at the Kingdom Hall and go to a very far-away country called Ecuador to preach to Deaf and Deaf-Blind people and teach them about Jesus and Jehovah God. To offer them eternal salvation. She types, "That's interesting," but you sense she can see on your face that you aren't telling the whole truth. Out of nowhere she asks you if there is anyone you are in love with. This is a very personal question, and maybe this is what Cyril meant about her being "a little crazy." But you don't want her to stop talking with you, so you type:

"No. You in love?"

"Yes," *she types.* **"With my husband and my son, of course."**

Then she asks an even more personal and private question, about if you're a virgin or not. This makes your face feel hot, and you feel a strange kind of nervousness, which isn't entirely unpleasant. You don't type anything for a while, but something about this woman makes you trust her even though you know you shouldn't. The thought suddenly occurs to you that Hanne may be a witch or sorceress. JWs believe in witches. The Bible teaches us that we must be on the lookout and avoid them. A witch could force you to reveal all your secrets. You clench your hands in a fist in front of the keyboard. You think of Jesus, and of your desire to go to heaven someday. You must resist the witch. Then you type:

"I not virgin. Shh. Secret. Please no tell. Shh. Please."

"Don't worry," *she says.* **"I won't say anything. I promise."**

◇　◇　◇

For twenty-five minutes, while Arlo and Hanne typed back and forth on his unusually old-looking SBC equipment, I read over the rough draft of his essay. I immediately recognized the familiar grammatical errors of a Deaf person who struggles with English: tenses a mess, incorrect use of prepositions, defaulting to ASL structure, etc. It is pretty common for Deaf folks who didn't have access to proper sign language (or any language) until they started school. But still, his ideas were great, and it was obvious he yearned to do a good job. Even though it is definitely *not* the responsibility of the terp to correct a student's paper—*ethically wrong, in fact*—I still made some notes about errors he might want to check with the teacher, writing them large enough that he might be able to see them with his magnifying glass. Every few minutes I craned my neck, hoping to catch a glimpse of the SBC screen to see what they were discussing, but it was useless. So I pretended to go to the bathroom, walking behind Hanne to get a clear view of the display. I was only able to see two sentences on the screen:

Arlo: Never.

Hanne: Never? You're kidding me!

I hovered for a moment more, waiting, but Hanne gave me a dirty look and positioned her shoulders so I couldn't see the screen. Whatever they were discussing, Arlo didn't seem to mind. After a rather long exchange where they both typed back and forth several times, I saw Hanne suddenly look overcome with emotion. She typed something back, causing Arlo to appear both sad and disturbed. I left to continue my false toilet run but wanted to get back to them as soon as possible.

◊ ◊ ◊

Hanne stops typing for a long time, like she's thinking. Then she asks:

"The person who you made love to? Do you still love them?"

You type **"no."** *This is a lie? No. This isn't a lie. Because you can't love something that's not there anymore. Something that's gone. You can love Jehovah God and Jesus, who are both invisible, but Jehovah God and Jesus are invisible for a reason. So, we can use our faith to believe in Them. The reason the unmentionable person is invisible is because of their sin. Besides, what you thought you were in love with was a lie. The person you loved never existed and never will exist again. Finish. Gone. Forgotten.*

Then the Hanne person asks if you are sad at never having been in love.
You say, yes you are sad, and that's the truth, even though you are still half
lying about you-know-who. Again this witchlike person uses her power to
make you say something you have never told anyone. You explain that you
are lonely, and that you would like a girlfriend, because you lied a minute
ago, that yes, once, a long time ago, you were in love with someone. But that
person is gone. And you explain how difficult it is to find someone since you
have Usher syndrome. Most people can't even talk to you. Some of the hear-
ing girls at church do, but you doubt they would date you—or you would
want to date them. The few Deaf Jehovah's Witness girls you've met live far
away, and they might not want to be with a Deaf man who will be totally
blind someday. And if they would, you need to be spiritually strong, because
Jehovah's Witness girls like a man who is spiritually strong. And the way to
prove you are spiritually strong is to get baptized, become a pioneer, and go
on missions and bring as many goats to Jehovah as possible. You ask Hanne,
a possible witch, not to tell anyone what you said about you having been in
love before. It's a secret. She promises. You promise to keep her secrets too.

◇ ◇ ◇

I couldn't bear Hanne and Arlo's private SBC conversation any longer.
When I looked out the window and saw the Able-Ride van waiting downstairs, I leaped to my feet.

"Hey, time to go!" I told Arlo, emphasizing the urgency. "The van is
outside. Hurry, before he leaves!"

"Can you tell him to wait?" Arlo asked.

"Sure," I signed, though I hesitated to leave them alone again, signaling to Hanne to wrap it up.

After running downstairs and telling the van driver that Arlo was on his
way, I sprinted back up to the cafeteria. When I stepped through the door,
I saw Arlo hugging Hanne goodbye. Both her hands were rubbing Arlo's
back, like she was comforting him.

"Gotta go now!" I called out.

"Cyrilje, please tell him if he emails me I will write him back, and that I look forward to seeing him again."

"You gave him your email?" I said, an obvious chill in my voice.

"Was that wrong?" Hanne asked.

"It's just not . . . whatever," I stammered.

"Cyrilje, why are you making that ridiculous serious face? We just had a very good talk, like friends. That's all."

Without saying another word, nor interpreting what Hanne said, I started walking Arlo to the elevator.

Hanne shouted after us as the elevator door closed.

"Please tell Arlo not to worry! I'm good at keeping secrets!"

I wanted to rip her Belgian head off.

◊ ◊ ◊

Later that night, after drinking a bit too much, I called Hanne.

"So," I said, the booze removing any caution I might have felt. "Everything. I want to hear every single thing you two said to each other. Don't lie to me."

For a moment she didn't say anything and all I could hear was her breathing.

"We were just introducing ourselves, Cyrilje," Hanne finally said. There was a weariness in her voice. "I told him about my art and nursing school, he told me about wanting to go on some mission. We connected. The funny thing is, it actually felt like we had a lot in common, really."

Hanne's voice cracked, and it almost sounded like she was sniffling.

"What is it?" I asked. "Hanne, are you okay?"

"Oh, Cyrilje, I can't stop thinking about that extraordinary boy. He really brings out the mommy bear in me. I asked him about his friends, and he said he hasn't really had any since high school and that you and that Molly person are the only people he really talks to outside his home and church. The rest of the time he's just all alone. What kind of life is that?"

I stuttered through some pathetic suggestion that we shouldn't judge his happiness based on our values, and that maybe he wasn't lonely. But I knew that Hanne was probably right. And just as I was about to forgive Hanne for overstepping in her conversation with Arlo, she added, "I even wondered if there might be something else going on, like he might be gay or something, but he said no."

"Wait—what?!" I shouted loud enough into the phone to hear the echo of my own voice. "You actually asked Arlo if he was gay?"

"So, what's wrong with that?"

"Jesus Christ, Hanne, he's a fucking Jehovah's Witness. Great, now I'm gonna totally get in trouble. You can be so smart, Hanne, until you do something so stupid. Okay, now tell me, what else did you say?"

Hanne said nothing for a long time. I could sense she was pissed.

"Cyril, you are unbelievable. You're managing to simultaneously be both drama queen and self-hating homosexual. *Godverdomme*. He was just so nervous when I talked about anything to do with relationships, so I thought it meant he might be gay. You used to act the same way: turn the conversation back to me, evade questions. So I just asked. It's not an unreasonable question."

"But what if he says something to his uncle or Molly?"

"Cyrilje, he's not going to say anything to anyone."

"What were you talking about at the elevator?"

"I don't understand—"

"At the elevator, what secret did he tell you?"

Hanne took a breath and I thought she was going to respond, but instead she made up some excuse about having to study for her microbiology test. Then she hung up. I called back three times, but she didn't answer.

15

CRAZY CHARLES

The next day I saw Arlo waiting for the Able-Ride outside Hudson Hall. I apologized if Hanne had asked anything too personal. Arlo said he didn't mind and that he liked talking with her. I kept fishing for him to tell me the secret he told Hanne, but instead he started asking me how long I had known Hanne, and how old she was when she came over from Belgium, and had I met her husband and kid, and even whether she was a Christian or not. His questioning was a curious mix of earnest interest and suspicion.

"Before, high school—you two sweethearts?"

"No," I signed with a laugh. I had become an ace at giving vague answers to consumers' personal questions. "She's not my type. We were just best friends."

"Best friends—most important," Arlo signed, grinning broadly. It appeared that me having a best friend surprised him a little. *The interpreter is human after all.*

"Yeah. Having someone like Hanne as a best friend has been pretty fun. Everyone in high school thought it was cool that she was from Belgium. She was really popular, which made things easier for me since it shielded me from a lot of bullying."

"Bully you?" Arlo asked with disbelief. "Really?"

"Sometimes. Not as bad as some of the other kids. But there was always some asshole that wanted to tease me because of my red hair, or other stupid reasons."

Arlo got that familiar look he gets just before he zones out. But that time he didn't disappear inside his head. Instead, he just smiled and asked me the time. I told him, and he said the van would, hopefully, be coming in twenty minutes, and did I want to hear his story about a bully.

"Sure," I signed, eagerly wanting any biographical crumb that might illuminate the riddle that was Arlo Dilly. "I'd like to hear it."

"But shhh," he signed, pressing his finger to his lips. "Secret. Just between you and me, okay?"

"Sure."

And he told me . . .

◊ ◊ ◊

Mid-October of your junior year. You had just gotten back to the Rose Garden School after spending a weekend at home, since Brother Birch was helping to organize a three-day conference and wanted you and Molly to participate and to inspire. Your mama didn't come to the conference because she had a bad cold, but still you got to see her in the morning and at night before bed. It was hard leaving your mama, but you were excited to be back at school with friends who spoke your language.

One day you walked into your dorm room and found Big Head Lawrence crying on his bed. Martin explained how one of the sighted students told Big Head Lawrence that there was a new older boy at school who had joined the Deaf Devils, and he was meaner and bigger than all the rest. His name was Crazy Charles ("C" hand turns around the ear to indicate craziness) and he was already eighteen and only in tenth grade because he had gotten held back at his old school, where he was kicked out—or that's what the rumor said.

"Crazy Charles brain messed up," Martin signed. "That's reason he picks on weaker kids. His ASL—the worst! Not learn sign until age twelve.

Can't sign. Can't read words. Can't read lips. Nothing. Now, when someone signs something, if Crazy Charles not understand . . . he punches hard. Now Deaf Devils even more dangerous!"

Then Martin explained how that afternoon the Deaf Devils and Crazy Charles had drawn mean cartoons of Big Head Lawrence all over the bathroom walls and library desks. Under the drawings they wrote: Big Head Lawrence, Monster Boy. *Big Head Lawrence was certain Crazy Charles would be looking to hurt him.*

Even though you and Martin tried to comfort him, Big Head Lawrence could not be consoled.

"Will not leave room until I graduate," Big Head Lawrence insisted.

If only your vision had been stronger you would have forced this bully Crazy Charles to clean up all the mean drawings. You felt helpless.

"From now on we three must stay together all the time," Martin signed. "Then Crazy Charles can't bother us."

So you did stay together as best you could. Weeks passed without incident, but then, on the very last day of the month, you and your roommates were waiting in the lunch line and the other kids started pushing so hard that all three of you became separated. You expected to find each other a few minutes later, safely at your usual lunch table. But then a crush of anxious bodies shoved past you. You worried that there might be a fire, so you followed the rushing crowd. Suddenly you ran into the backs of a huge circle of students all watching something. This meant only one thing: someone was fighting. You began to panic and tried to force your way through the wall of cheering sighted-Deaf students, but it was no use since so many others were elbowing in to get a better view, while you could barely make out the back of the person's head in front of you. The fight seemed to go on forever. When the teachers finally arrived, the bullies had run off and there were both Martin and Big Head Lawrence on the ground, bleeding.

Big Head Lawrence was too embarrassed to tell the teachers what happened, but later he told you everything. The new bully, Crazy Charles, had dragged Big Head Lawrence out of the lunch line and swung him into a group of three girls. The girls jumped back, causing Big Head Lawrence to fall and smash his head on the ground. This was very dangerous for someone with a head like Lawrence's, so he got scared and started to cry. No one helped him up for fear that Crazy Charles or one of the Deaf Devils would get mad at them. The big circle of students formed around Crazy Charles and Big Head Lawrence. Unfortunately, not blind enough, Big Head Lawrence was able to make out the faces of the Deaf Devil gang, along with three girls, staring down at him on the floor, laughing and signing things like disgusting, ugly, monster.

Then Crazy Charles threw a small, hard plastic dish of creamed corn at Big Head Lawrence's head and said it was monster cum. He said if the girls touched or talked to Big Head Lawrence they would have monster babies.

When someone told Martin that Big Head Lawrence was getting beaten up, he started screaming for help. The Deaf Devils grabbed Martin's cane from him and started pushing him back and forth between the gang members. When Martin told you this part of the story, every inch of your body filled with rage. Being pushed around was bad enough but being pushed around when you can't see anything at all is the worst thing ever. Then one of the Deaf Devils held Martin's arms behind him while another boy covered Martin's mouth. Then Crazy Charles started stabbing Martin's thigh over and over again with what he later learned was a safety pin. On top of that, Martin also learned that Crazy Charles and the Deaf Devils said many racist things the whole time. Martin started crying, and also had trouble breathing because the boy's hand was over his mouth to muffle his screams.

One of the Deaf Devils signed into Martin's hand, "You DeafBlind asshole. Snitch teacher? Crazy Charles will revenge."

Martin did not stop shaking through the whole story. Big Head Lawrence covered himself with his pillows because he was crying again and felt embarrassed. That's when you decided something had to be done about Crazy Charles.

◇ ◇ ◇

You waited until it was the middle of gym class on Friday morning. You asked Molly to take you to the locker room because you needed to go pee before it was time to do your sit-ups. (Despite your age, you still avoided climbing the rope, which you were convinced would be certain death.) Molly wouldn't go into the locker room with you since she would see boys naked and that was a sin. This would give you the time you needed.

The locker room was too dim for you to see anything. So you stood stone-still, feeling for the vibrations of footsteps and the breezes of bodies. To make sure you were alone, you swung your cane around your body, slashing the air.

The coast was clear.

Romans 12:17 says, "Return evil for evil to no one." You learned that the summer before in Bible study. That meant if Crazy Charles bullied you or your friends, Jehovah God said to ignore it, and The Watchtower *advises to either make a joke to calm the situation or report it to a teacher. Which were good suggestions until a sighted bully stuck a safety pin in the leg of one of your best friends.*

You took a deep breath and walked to the first row of lockers next to the showers—Big Head Lawrence had snooped around and found out where the right one was. You counted six bottom lockers in from the end and felt for the raised metal number: 117. This was Crazy Charles's locker. You pulled at the lock to see if it had been left open. It hadn't. Then you felt for the slats of the metal door that lets the lockers breathe so gym clothes don't get moldy. You sniffed the locker and could tell it was full of whatever Crazy Charles kept in there, most likely school clothes, shoes, and a book bag. You pulled down your pants and aimed the tip of your penis through the slats of the locker. All morning you had been drinking water and holding it. Your piss was as strong as the water from a hose, and it sprayed everywhere inside his locker. The smell was thick and disgusting. The whole time you thought about what he had done to Martin and Big Head Lawrence.

Fuck you, bullies!

Red star.

Empty. You quickly zipped up your pants and rushed back out to the gym, hoping no one saw you come out of the locker room. Molly tapped you on your arm.

"What took you so long? The others are doing the rope climb. Do you want to do sit-ups?"

"I will rope climb today!" you signed excitedly, the thrill of revenge swirling in your veins.

"But you've always said the rope climb was too dangerous—"

"Change my mind!"

You handed Molly your cane and Gym Teacher quickly handed you the thick scratchy rope. You imagined how Crazy Charles and all the Deaf Devils would be watching you: the poor low-vision boy. Your hands reached up and held the rope tight, pulling your body off the floor. You were much stronger than you had been three years before. But not only that, it was as if an invisible hand had grabbed your shirt collar and was dragging you toward the ceiling, past the third knot, and the fourth and the fifth, escaping everything and everyone that was below. Up, up, up. You could tell you were getting close to the ceiling because of the stuffy smell of the dusty tiles, and the air getting warmer. You entwined your legs around the rope and kept hold with one hand, and with your free hand you reached up and slapped the ceiling very hard. Pah! Success! For a split second you thought, What if I never came down?

After two minutes you felt the rope jiggle, which you sensed was the signal from Gym Teacher to come down. You had no choice. You reversed the climb, hand under hand, gravity assisting. When you hit the soft mat, Molly hugged you and told you that you had terrified her, but also that all the other students were clapping. Gym Teacher told you that you went higher and faster than any other student in class. He called you Spider-Man.

"Why are you smiling so much today, Spider-Man?" he signed. "You smiled all the way up and all the way down."

Smiling? I'm smiling? Stop smiling. If you smile too much, they will know it was you who pissed in Crazy Charles's locker.

You commanded the corners of your mouth to lower themselves. They refused. You curled your lips inward. Without lips you couldn't smile. If you didn't smile or do anything out of the ordinary, no one would suspect a DeafBlind Jehovah's Witness of doing anything bad. You went to your locker and changed your clothes. Immediately you could tell something was wrong. Bodies were rushing through the locker room. The vibrations of angry feet stomped on the floor. You caught a sighted boy by the arm and asked him what was happening.

"Someone toilet in Crazy Charles locker," he signed, laughing. "Ooooh! Stink bad! Crazy Charles explode! Punch lockers! Other kids are laughing! Clothes, shoes, backpack all covered with toilet! Stink! All ruin!"

You shook your head, curled in your lips, and made your eyebrows dip toward the middle so you looked concerned. Without taking a shower you quickly dressed and left.

Later, in your private place outside the cafeteria, Martin told you he heard gossip about how Crazy Charles had to wear pee-covered clothes to walk back to his dorm room to change and everyone was making fun of him.

Then Big Head Lawrence told you, "I hear Crazy Charles cry so much. Why? Because his shoes new. Also, his family very poor. He get big trouble!"

A wave of sympathy momentarily washed over you for the impoverished Crazy Charles. You thought about him weeping, and how bad his ASL was and how maybe Jehovah God would want you to forgive him and admit your wrong, but then you remembered what he did to your friends and the pins in Martin's leg and Big Head Lawrence possibly dying when he hit his head.

"I don't care," you told them. "Crazy Charles stupid asshole! He probably toilet in own pants anyway!"

And then you started laughing very hard, which made Martin laugh, *and that caused Big Head Lawrence to laugh. Suddenly, all three of you, with your hands entwined, became a giant, six-legged, three-headed laughing monster.*

◇ ◇ ◇

"That's a very funny story," Cyril tells you. "You are a very good storyteller!" You ask Cyril if he wants to hear the rest of the story. He tells you he does. But you are worried that telling him the rest of the story is a sin, because you promised Jehovah God and Brother Birch that you would let it go and forget. But there is a strange surging power inside of you, and maybe because of Hanne's magic spell on you, you are compelled to tell it. So you do.

◇ ◇ ◇

In the middle of laughing with Martin and Big Head Lawrence, two hands grabbed you by your backpack, yanking you away from your friends. The hands started flinging you around in a circle until they let go, and because of your bad balance you were flung violently to the asphalt. Pain shot through your skull and right wrist. You wanted to run away, but you lost your cane and didn't know which way you were facing, or if the attacker would strike again. Then a foot kicked you in the back of your knees and you went down again. Next, they tore your backpack, filled with all your expensive accessibility equipment, from your back. What seemed like several sets of fists attacked you all at once, punching you on all parts of your body. One fist landed on the side of your head, another punched you in the stomach, a third pulled your legs out from under you, and again you were on the ground. That's when one of the Deaf Devils sat on your legs while another sat on your chest. It was hard to breathe. The boy on your chest dug his knees very hard into your arms so you couldn't fight back. Then a boy stood over you. You squinted your eyes, trying to find a face. You caught pieces of eyes, a nose, a mouth. It didn't matter. You knew who it was. Crazy Charles squatted down over you and started writing something on your face. The crisp chemical smell of the Magic Marker mingled with the scent of your blood. You felt the stab and stink of a wet marker tip pressing unknown words into the flesh of your forehead and your cheeks. This was followed by another deluge of punches to your stomach and face, over and over. You thought you might die.

After several minutes the punching suddenly stopped, and you felt the boys' bodies being pulled off yours. Your eyes were filled with blood, so you could see less than nothing.

You raised your bruised body to its feet and found your way to the wall, to anchor to something. Without your cane, without any vision at all, without someone to guide you, you were lost. You wanted to run, but you weren't even sure it was safe to move. You felt footsteps moving in different directions. Most moved away from you, but one person came closer. You wiped your wounded eyes on your shirt, and then someone touched your arm. At first you pulled away, thinking it might be Crazy Charles. But then you recognized the touch, the smell.

(This is the part. This is the part you are not allowed to tell Cyril. This is the part. Do not say it!)

A moment later your cane was back in your hand. You felt someone's hands, smaller, softer, rise up into yours. You were relieved, shocked, and embarrassed. Your vision was blurred from the blood, but there was enough light for you to make out the thick mop of black hair, the beautiful brown skin, the blackest of eyes.

◊ ◊ ◊

"Who was it?" Cyril suddenly asks. "Was this the friend? The one you cared about?"

You don't answer him. You just tell the story.

◊ ◊ ◊

You reached up to touch her face, to make it stick inside your brain. The ghost child nervously pushed your hands down and signed, "Not here. Dangerous, if people see. Don't worry. Bad boys won't bother you again. I bite bullies and kick them and beat them with your cane. I very strong. I tell Crazy Charles I was person who squirt pee in locker with toy water gun. But he won't fight me. Why? Long time ago, we classmates old school. We friends. I only one can understand his terrible sign language. Crazy Charles pea brain—bully. He won't hurt you ever again. I will protect you!"

"Protect me?" you repeated the ghost child's words.

You felt the air from her mouth sting the open wounds on your lip. There was no confusion now. The ghost child was a living, sighted, short-but-strong Deaf girl who just beat up a bully. A girl whose skin smelled like jasmine, turmeric, and coriander. A girl you had already kissed, and who you wanted to kiss again, even with the blood on your face and the ache in your ribs and stomach.

"Will tell me your name now?" you begged. "Please tell me! I want protect you too!"

The girl fingerspelled her spoken name into your palm. You had never felt such a name before. Her last name was longer and contained the letter M and ended in a train of Es. Three more times you asked her how to spell her first name—one time it had twice as many letters since there was a long version and a short version. The longer version, she told you, was the name of her mother's favorite movie star, who drowned in a bathtub. The short version looked like the word shh, a sound you used to practice in speech therapy, a sound someone makes when they press their finger to their lips asking you to keep secrets. You would always remember this. The spelling you wouldn't.

"Name-sign, what?" you finally asked.

She showed you. It was the letter S placed at the side of the eye above the cheek, then twisted up and down like one was pretending to cry. You asked her the reason she was given that particular name-sign.

"Because when I first came school I cry, cry, cry! One week. Two week. Kids gave me name-sign because me like crying baby."

You repeated S's name-sign once on your body, and then a second time on S's body, and then . . .

◊ ◊ ◊

Arlo's hands froze in midair as if some invisible being whispered to him to be silent. A moment before his face had been enraptured, but all of a sudden he looked desperately sad.

"What's wrong?" I signed. "Don't stop. What happened? Did she become your girlfriend? What were the letters you remember of her name?"

And that's when the Able-Ride van arrived. Part of me didn't want to tell him, but I had to. He started gathering his things. I interrupted him.

"Maybe you can finish the story tomorrow?" I asked, a slight pleading to my request. I needed to know. Was this the secret he had told Hanne?

"No!" Arlo signed, almost petulantly. "You always asking, asking, asking . . . enough! Finish! I wrong telling story. Bad story. Sin story. Sorry. Please shhh . . .. don't tell anyone. Okay? Secret. Okay?"

"Okay. Sure," I signed, concerned that I had said something wrong. "Our secret. You better get on the van before it leaves."

Then, as he was boarding the van, he turned around at the last minute.

"Cyril? Tell you more stories . . . I can't. Never again. Okay? Shh. Forget everything. Important. Forget everything."

And that was it.

16

ESSAY CRIT

I woke up thinking about Arlo's story in the middle of the night. Images of Crazy Charles and the mysterious dark-haired ghost child with the pretty fingers floated across my brain. I was certain Hanne knew more, and considered calling her and waking her up, demanding she tell me or I would share no more of my stories of Arlo with her. The story of this DeafBlind man's life had become a bargaining chip. It was all too clear I had become obsessed. I hated not knowing things. It was a good quality in a sign language interpreter, but painful at times nonetheless. I did my best to get back to sleep, but I managed only another three hours because my phone started ringing at 7 a.m. It was Ange from the agency saying she got a call late at night from Clara Shuster at the Abilities Institute asking if I could interpret an 8 a.m. meeting between Professor Bahr and Arlo.

"Um . . . that's in an hour. You know I'm not a morning person. Why isn't Molly doing it? Aren't Jehovah's Witnesses naturally early risers?"

"You were specifically requested," Ange said, clearly happy that one of her interpreters had made a good impression.

"Okay, I'll head right over," I told her.

I assumed Arlo had made the request and wondered if it was a sign that he had changed his mind and was ready to tell me more of his story. But when Professor Bahr opened the door to her office, I saw that Arlo wasn't even there.

"I'm so glad you were able to make it!" Professor Bahr exclaimed. "Come in."

"It's probably better to wait until Arlo gets here," I said, getting an uncomfortable feeling in my gut.

"Don 't be silly," she said, directing me to one of the two chairs facing her desk. "I need to discuss something with you alone. Arlo will be here in about thirty minutes."

And there it was: the reason for my discomfort. I stood at the back of the chairs, puzzling on how to explain the ethical problem she was presenting. Professor Bahr swept herself behind her desk. It was another day of bee earrings and the royal-blue dashiki.

"Um," I said. "Really it's better if I wait for the student."

"Please just sit!" Professor Bahr commanded, only half smiling now.

I did.

The stuffy windowless room was just a bit larger than a cubicle, with shelves of books packed tightly. The limited wall space was filled with photos of Professor Bahr's husband, and what I assumed were other family members, as well as degrees from the City College of New York and Columbia University. There was also a tropical travel poster of Saint Kitts taped to where a window might be. Now that I was seated, Professor Bahr's demeanor shifted to something far more serious. She tapped her pen on Arlo's response essay about Whitman's poem and the sublime. I immediately saw how the white, crisp pages were bloodied with red correction marks. There was a large red D circled at the top. I immediately felt sad and a little defensive.

"I'm afraid we have a grave problem, Mr. Cyril. A grave problem. I need your advice. Arlo's paper is a disaster. His grammar and spelling are unbelievable . . ."

"Hold it just a minute," I interrupted. "If we could—"

"Just look at it! The idea he has about Whitman and the sublime is a good one, a sound idea. And his personal anecdote, if the reader could decipher it, could be moving. But his writing! How to say this politely? Oh, there is no way to say it politely: It is atrocious!"

"If you could just—"

"He writes as if he doesn't know the language! The verb *to be* is missing completely or else misused. And I won't even begin to discuss his butchering of prepositions: on, of, about, in, over, et cetera. It's grammar goulash!"

"Professor, please stop!" I barked, then quickly lowered my voice. "I'm sorry. I guess I wasn't clear. I can't discuss the consumer with you without him present. It's unethical. I'm sorry."

At first Professor Bahr looked offended by my explanation, but soon her ire deflated. Three times she started to say something, but then stopped. Finally, she just tossed Arlo's paper on the desk in front of me and placed her hand over her eyes. With a quick glance I could see Arlo hadn't asked the teacher for help, and had made only a few adjustments from the draft he had shown me. His English was still a mess, filled with his unique mix of ASL transliteration, acquired linguistic quirks, and moments of a convoluted but impressive intellect. Something between a young elementary school student and an Eastern European philosopher who only took two semesters of English. I had seen something similar in the writings of a hundred other Deaf students who suffered language deprivation.

Professor Bahr sighed, frustrated and sad.

"I called you here because I thought you, far more than your colleague, had a yearning to be supportive."

"I do," I said. "And I'm sure she does too, in her way. But the point is, if I'm here without the student's permission, then it's a betrayal of his trust. He needs to know that anything he says to me or in my presence won't be shared with other people, so even finding me here alone with you could shake that trust. You understand, right?"

"Yes, I see what you're saying," Professor Bahr said, still looking despondent. "It's just that I truly want to help Arlo, but I don't think I'm the one. His language problem appears to be far too serious. I think it would be better if he found a more remedial program that helps the learning disabled."

I wanted to scream, and not because I was in jeopardy of losing an entire summer of my escape money. Arlo would be heartbroken. And there it was, one of those moments every interpreter faces. You have knowledge you want to share, but you also have to think about the ethics of sharing it. Ethical rigidity or empathetic advocacy? And as I tended to do, I erred on the side of advocacy, even as I sensed it might come back to bite me in the ass later.

"Look, Professor, let's not talk about Arlo. Let's just talk about my general experience over the years working with the Deaf. And I'm being totally honest with you, this atypical English thing . . . it's pretty common. Sure, there are Deaf who are brilliant writers. DeafBlind as well. There's Helen Keller of course, but also other contemporary Deaf and DeafBlind poets, novelists, and essayists who are truly amazing. Whether a Deaf or Deaf-Blind individual learns to write well depends on any number of things. Most important, at what age they first had access to language. But even for the ones who struggle with writing perfect English, it doesn't mean they are stupid or learning disabled."

"I never said Arlo was stupid," Professor Bahr interjected defensively.

"I know, I know. And remember we're *not* talking about Arlo, and I don't teach the Deaf. I'm just an interpreter, explaining what I've seen and heard over the years. What I'm saying is that even with that kind of grammar, it doesn't mean the Deaf person can't read or comprehend or learn. I've worked with people whose writing wasn't that much better than Arlo's. Yet they've managed to find their right vocation and have thrived. The thing is this: learning to write for the Deaf isn't the same as a hearing person learning another spoken language. The hearing learner gets to listen to the cadence of the language from birth; the Deaf never do. Sure, they might be able to learn the rules, but it's not quite the same. ASL, in fact, is structurally more like Chinese than English. There are no tenses. There aren't pronouns the way we use them. And now I'm gonna break my own rule and speak about Arlo specifically. When Arlo chooses to really express himself in ASL, he is fluent and very articulate."

I could see that Professor Bahr was on the edge of convincing, but not yet there.

I picked up Arlo's paper and read the opening paragraph while Professor Bahr watched me. Again, I was convinced that Arlo had accomplished something really special that Professor Bahr was missing.

"I have a question," I said, becoming even more animated. "When you read his paper, did you understand his thesis?"

Professor Bahr nodded. "I did. And, as I said, it was a first-rate thesis. That's why I was confused with how badly he wrote it. To be honest, I wondered if . . ."

Her voice trailed off, and I saw a faint glimmer of distrust in her eyes. Immediately she became embarrassed.

"You thought maybe someone else gave him the idea?" I asked. "Let me be clear, the idea was all his. I shouldn't be saying any of this, but the fact that you comprehended Arlo's fairly complicated thesis is proof of how smart he really is. And proof that your class is making a difference."

Professor Bahr raised her dagger eyebrows. I had hit a mark.

"But I'm just not sure where to begin," she said. "I'm curious as to whether Arlo's parents even read to him as a child."

"You'll need to ask him," I said. "But I do know something like eighty-eight percent of hearing parents with Deaf children never even learn sign language. If they communicate with their child at all it's via homemade gesture, or they hope their kid lipreads enough to get basic information. Great lipreaders are few and far between."

"You're telling me Arlo's parents didn't even speak to him in his own language growing up?" Professor Bahr was aghast.

"Again, I can't talk about Arlo specifically, you'll need to ask him."

"Not speaking to your child is unforgivable!" Professor Bahr pounded on her desk. Her earring bees raged. "It's abuse! They should be jailed!"

"Then you'd be jailing the vast majority of those parents. I read it's something like sixty percent of Deaf kids who won't learn sign language until they start school, which is way too late. It's called language deprivation. So learning a second language like English becomes even harder. But when a Deaf child does have early access to sign language, it can make a huge difference. The best Deaf writers usually come from either parents who were Deaf or hearing parents who learned ASL right when the Deaf child was born. Also, I've noticed—and this is just my own anecdotal opinion—that these kids are also way more emotionally intelligent. But I wanna be clear: I'm not saying there isn't hope that a Deaf student can improve. And I want to repeat myself: There are genius Deaf writers out there who can write as good or better than most hearing writers. But there're also a whole lot of Deaf folks like Arlo who find writing English very challenging, and in my opinion it's wrong to assume they are learning disabled, because they aren't."

At that point I picked up Arlo's paper again and read some more. Then I jumped to his concluding paragraph.

Yes, yes, yes! Whitman very good, smart poet with many beautiful words, and very touch my heart ideas. The sublime was very important feeling for me. If not sublime, life empty. Life feels flat like cold black tar road. My long time ago best friend make me understand the sublime. Doesn't matter Deaf and low-vision! Experience awe I CAN! Also experience with mama who die six years ago. Even though mama gone, best friends gone, things gone, but also still maybe here like metaphor. Like Walt Whitman important poet say at end of section 6 of Leaves of Grass:

All goes onward and outward, nothing collapses, / And to die is different from what any one / supposed, and luckier.

After reading the paragraph I had to stop myself from screaming with joy. All of that held inside Arlo's head, and almost no one had gotten the chance to see it. And there it was on the paper in front of us. At the same time, I felt incredibly angry that what Arlo was capable of was being hidden because society wasn't willing to look.

"What you read in Arlo's paper was an ASL transliteration into English," I said. "With his own attempts to translate that into what he thought was good English structure. Trust me, I have no doubt Arlo worked very hard on this paper. And as far as whether he's gaining anything from your class, just look at this. He probably never would have even attempted to express that before. And I've seen it in his emails to me. His English grammar is improving. Sure, it may never be Strunk-and-White perfect, but it's better than before. And he's expressing . . ."

My voice cracked. So much for being able to control my emotions.

"I'm sorry," I said. "I've just broken about a dozen interpreting rules. Please just forget about it."

Professor Bahr averted her gaze to the floor. I wasn't sure whether she was moved or annoyed. When she looked up, she had a curious look on her face.

"Cyril, I admire you. It's good to care about your work. Sometimes we get so beaten down, it's hard to maintain. Had you always wanted to be an interpreter?"

"Huh?" I asked, trying to pull myself together. What did any of that have to do with Arlo staying in her class? But then again, I was relieved we were no longer talking about Arlo.

"Not really. Interpreting was kind of an accident. I had originally wanted to be a teacher and maybe a writer, but you know, it was one of those plan B things. You aim for one thing and then end up doing something totally off course, but sometimes it ends up being a good thing. I definitely consider myself lucky, falling into this. I love Deaf people, and they seem okay with me, so, you know, it beats being an assistant manager at the Home Depot."

Professor Bahr laughed.

"You would be a terrible assistant manager. I agree. But I totally understand what you mean. I myself had hoped to be an actress when I was younger. I wanted to be one of Charlie's Angels. But growing up, there were no parts for women who looked like me. I was always voluptuous. My family emigrated from Saint Kitts to Westchester in the 1970s, when I was only twelve. When I was fifteen, I got brave enough to audition at the local community theater. I was devastated when they didn't offer me the role of Laurie in *Oklahoma!* Later, in graduate school, I fell in love with writing poetry and then with a poet who became my husband. But poetry never paid the bills, nor did my husband. And then one thing, then another, and so I am an adjunct professor."

"As Arlo said, you're a great teacher."

Professor Bahr smiled, half-sad, half-proud.

"Am I?"

At that moment there was a knock at the door, and by the awkward sound of it, I knew it was Arlo. Professor Bahr invited him and Snap to sit and relax while she reread his essay. I described Professor Bahr's expression as she was reading, her head shakes, nods, grimaces, as well as the red marks on the page, and the bad grade. Arlo looked disappointed but also like he expected as much. I also filled him in on everything I had discussed with Professor Bahr.

"Sorry if I overstepped my role as your interpreter," I signed. "I guess I just wanted her to know what I thought. But it wasn't appropriate for me to do that."

"It's okay," he signed, barely blinking an eye that I had broken his confidentiality.

Professor Bahr, finally finished, circled a sentence in Arlo's essay several times, then lifted her head.

"So I've decided," she announced, "that you have a lot to learn about English grammar, Mr. Dilly. However—and this is important—many of your mistakes are consistent, which will make it easier to address them. Upon rereading I see now that your ideas and passion are truly outstanding. So I'm adjusting your grade."

Professor Bahr scribbled out the D and wrote a large C+ on the top of his page. Upon hearing this, Arlo started to smile and rock back and forth. I tapped him on the leg to let him know Professor Bahr wasn't finished.

"You will improve your English, Mr. Dilly. I am certain of that. As your poet Walt Whitman once said: 'Urge, urge, urge!' You have inspired me! I have something for you!"

Professor Bahr spun her chair around and pulled an old hardback volume from the shelf.

"I'm giving you a copy of Whitman's *Leaves of Grass*. You might enjoy reading it. Just return it by the end of the summer. I assume you can use that magnifier with it?"

Arlo nodded, beaming. He lifted the hardcover to his nose and sniffed it. Both Professor Bahr and I smiled at his gesture.

"I too love the smell of books!" she said with a laugh. "You know something, I have an idea. Instead of the other response paper assignment, I want you to try something else. Sometimes when we write out our personal stories, it reveals our true voice. So I want you to write a short informal essay about a very important day in your life. A happy moment, sad moment, it doesn't matter. It just needs to be something vital, something you might tell someone on your deathbed. Understand? No footnotes or citations required. It won't be due until after the July Fourth break."

The smile that had been on Arlo's face a moment before disappeared.

"Story about me? Private story? Deathbed?"

Professor Bahr laughed and reached across to pat Arlo on the shoulder.

"Don't be nervous. I just mean it needs *gravitas*. It will be a chance to improve your grammar and for us to learn who you are. But pick one of the most important days of your life. Not some trifling nothing. Your *worst day*. A *day that changed everything!* We all have them."

17

THE ONE WHO STAYS BEHIND

You sit at your computer in the basement of Brother Birch's house. It is a very hot day and the dryer is running, and there is sweat pouring down your temples, and it's a little hard to breathe. You are thinking about what Professor Lavinia Bahr has asked you to do: write a story about an important day in your life, a day that changed everything. But your skull is pressing in on your brain, maybe because of the heat, maybe because Jehovah God wants to keep all the sinful memories inside your head. You know the day you should write about, but it is the day you are forbidden to ever mention. For five long years you have worked hard to erase its memory.

Forget that day, forget that day, forget that day.

A different memory finally floats across your brain. It was November, not long after you had learned S's name. S, who had been visiting your room every night, suddenly stopped showing up. You were confused and worried. Every night you waited up late for her, but she didn't come.

Then one day you were sitting in your braille class, exhausted from no sleep, working on Grade 2 contractions. Martin and Big Head Lawrence were nearby. Molly had left the room for fifteen minutes and when she returned, she tapped you gently on your shoulder and you knew something was wrong.

"Come with me," she signed. Her hands were colder than usual, and you could tell she was anxious. "We need to go to the principal's office right away. Something has happened . . . I'm so sorry."

"What?"

"The principal will tell you."

Did they already discover that you were the one who peed in Crazy Charles's locker? Had someone seen you kissing S in your room? Was that the reason S was not visiting you? Your mind performed all sorts of calculations. You took the square root of Molly's silence multiplied by the slower-than-usual walk, divided by the way she signed "sorry." You started to realize this wasn't about what happened with Crazy Charles or with S. Molly was being too gentle, too serious.

When you arrived at the principal's office, Molly sat you down in front of his desk. You had never met the principal before, but his power was legendary. Your face felt hot. Your stomach tightened. You wanted to pee. In a moment the principal would be explaining your sin and your punishment. There were so many red star sins you had committed. Your mind filled with images of Judgment Day, a swirling vision of lava and fire, the Great Crowd looking down upon you, huddled with the sinners and goats, all screaming and begging to be saved. Just as you were about to confess everything you had ever done, Molly started interpreting.

"Arlo," the principal said. "We have some very sad news. It's about your mother."

Mama? Why would they bring your mama into this? Were you being kicked out of school? Was your mama there in the room?

"Mama here?"

"No, no. Your mother is not here. Your uncle Jonathan called us this morning."

Jonathan was the other name for Brother Birch. It was a name you never used for him, but it was what other people who were not in the Kingdom Hall called him. You waited for what the principal had to say next, but he appeared to take a long time, or Molly was just listening first and then would interpret his words when she understood his whole point. Again, Molly's hands felt different. She was scared or sad or both.

"When you first came here your mother knew she was sick. That's one of the reasons you were sent here. She was hoping she was going to get well again, but . . . I'm very sorry. She went into the hospital this past week and passed away sometime early this morning."

Molly used the sign *passed away*.

Sign PASSED AWAY: *The hand facing up, fingers splayed upward as if offering something up to heaven, then descends backward through the "C"-shaped hole of the other hand. As the splayed fingers pass through the hole, they close and shrink like a withered flower.*

But you misunderstood the sign. It could also mean "missing" or "disappear" or any number of words that indicated something was here and now it's not.

"Missing?" you asked. Your heart started pounding in your chest. "Missing, why? I help! We go find her!"

Molly grabbed your hands and then, with Deaf directness, she signed, "Dead. Your mama is dead. I'm so sorry."

Then Molly hugged you as hard as she could, but there was little comfort. You could barely feel it. Your mind traced the word *dead* from your hand, up your arm, into your head. Suddenly you felt like you were being pushed under water. You gasped for air. Something had to be stuck inside your throat, your heart, your lungs. Why couldn't you breathe? You pushed Molly away to try to get space. A moment later you started signing violently into the blur.

"Before . . . why not tell me Mama dying?" your hands shouted. "Not take me see her, why? Wait wait long time! Now too late! Now she . . ."

Gone. There would be no fixing this. Your mama was not one of the chosen ones. She didn't lead a spiritually strong life the way Brother Birch had. She loved you too much. She didn't spend enough time at the mall or going door-to-door. She would be one of the masses of sinners who would need to wait until Judgment Day. When would you see her again? Tomorrow or in a thousand years? And what if *your* sins could not be forgiven?

You weren't crying. You should have been crying. You wanted to cry, if only to let more air inside. But you couldn't. You could barely breathe, much less cry.

Instead, you vomited all over Principal's carpet.

Over the next few days other students, strangers even, came up to you and patted you on the back in that way that said: *You are the saddest boy in the world. Thank God this didn't happen to me.* One day at lunch, Big Head Lawrence told you he would ask his mother if you could come live with his family. Molly told him that was impossible. That's when you learned that you would be living with Brother Birch from then on.

"He is your guardian now," Molly signed. "That means Brother Birch is like your father now."

"Long time ago my father disappear," you signed.

"Yes. I know," she replied. "But Brother Birch will watch over you and take care of you like a father."

For the first time in your life, you felt lucky to be going blind. Your blindness allowed you to make people disappear when you wanted, placing them in the blurry unreal place in your peripheral vision. You reserved the small clear spot for a blank wall or the floor. A completely empty world. That was true. That was real.

The night before you were to go home to Poughkeepsie for your mother's funeral, five nights after she had already died, someone walked into your room at two in the morning. You knew the smell of the body; you knew the feel of the breath. When her hand reached out to touch you, you slapped it away and leaped from the bed, flailing your hands.

"Not visit me long time, why?!" you screamed. "Leave me alone, why?! Before you promise will protect me! My mama dead! I hate you! I hate you! Fuck you! Go away! Never come back! I want you die!"

Your body fell back onto your bed, shivering with rage and embarrassment. Something broke inside you, dislodging what had been deeply stuck. Finally tears gushed from your eyes, snot from your nose. S stroked your hair with one hand while the other rode the weeping earthquake of your back. When your sobs grew stronger, S climbed into your bed, weaving her body into a protective web of arms and legs. After your crying subsided, you felt the cold chill on your wet face, the clog of your nose, the salt-stuck eyelids that were so exhausted from squeezing themselves dry.

S pressed her perfect fingers into your palms.

"Sorry. I not come long time. Why? Because dorm boss catch me sneaking out late night. *You bad! You bad!*' They bawl me out many times. Later, I hear your mama die. So sad! I say, *I must see Arlo! I don't care if punish!* I sneak, try visit you! But nighttime dorm boss catch me and lock my door. Visit you . . . impossible. But tonight, I wait until late, then climb out window. Window locked? Not. Ha ha! Stupid dorm boss. Tonight, I will stay with you. I'm sorry. I'm sorry. I won't leave you alone again. Never!"

You pushed yourself halfway out of S's net of limbs. Suddenly you wanted—you needed—for S to understand about the wound you felt. You wanted to explain that there would be no more summer vacations where your mama would sit out on the grass with you and tickle your nose and eyelids with a twig or leaf. There would never be another autumn where your mama would let you jump in the leaf piles at the Kingdom Hall. You would never smell her orange blossom perfume again or get to rub your face into the cotton of her dress or eat her thick peanut butter and strawberry jam sandwiches or get to feel her soft fingers awkwardly sign *bad boy, good boy, hamburger, love you*. But the only thing you were able to sign to S was:

"Me? What do? What do? No family. No mama. I will alone forever."

Then you fell into S's arms again and the turbulence of your sobbing made the bed rumble. After what seemed like thirty minutes of uninterrupted weeping, S pressed her finger to your lips like the S-H-H of her forgotten name.

"Shh. Shh. Careful," she signed. "Will wake up roommates. If dorm boss catch us, will trouble."

S slid off the bed to leave, but you grabbed her arm.

"Please. Don't leave. Please stay."

"Don't worry. I not leave. Never leave. Follow me. I know secret hiding place."

You took S's arm. The world you had known a few days ago had vanished. You needed to trust someone. Slowly, carefully, S guided you across the floor to the door. After checking outside to make sure no one was around, she led you down the hall to the janitor's closet by the bathrooms. The flat soles of your bare feet flapped on the freezing hard floor. Even though you were already six foot, S treated you like you were smaller than her, and she pushed you into the cramped supply closet and told you to sit on the floor.

"Wait here. Back one minute."

The door closed. You were alone. The stench of old moldy mops, bottles of cleaning supplies, and soiled rags filled your nostrils. You lifted your arm to cover your nose, and S's spicy-sweet smell still clung to the fabric of your pajama sleeve. It soothed you. Two minutes later S returned with a blanket from your room. Sitting on the cold closet floor next to you, she covered both your bodies with the blanket. This made you tell S the story of how your mama would let a smaller you climb under the covers of her bed on winter mornings and you would pretend you were living in a very warm cave deep under the earth. And your mama would sometimes pretend that she was a monster attacking the cave from outside the blanket. The memory of the blanket cave caused you to cry again. S hugged you tightly. You should have been embarrassed to cry in front of S, but you weren't. You let your tears flow for several minutes straight into S's thick hair. Her beating heart merged with your own. The thought occurred to you: *Sorrow has edges. The pain will end.* You pulled your arm free from S's embrace and stroked her soft, elusive face. A face, you imagined, that must be the most beautiful face on earth. You needed S to know you more deeply. The more S knew you, the more real S became. The more real you became.

"Can I tell you long story?" you signed.

"Yes! Tell me very long story. Stay here all night."

An avalanche of words released from your fingers. You told S everything, about how you cried too when you first came to school; about not knowing who your father was; about hating your uncle; about Martin and Big Head Lawrence being your first real friends; about getting so sad when S stopped visiting. You told secret upon secret, never concerned about Jehovah God's watchful eye.

"You . . . how old?" you asked.

"Sixteen," she signed.

"Impossible," you joked. "You so short! Ha ha!"

"Not short! You are too big! Like a cow! You are half cow, half boy. You are Cow-Boy!" she teased.

You both fell into each other's arms laughing, letting your bodies slowly settle, until there were only aftershocks and, finally, stillness and breath.

"Question," you ask. "From now on, you and me best friends and sweethearts? Okay?"

S caressed your face and pressed her soft lips against yours, holding them there for a long time.

"Okay," S signed into your hands while simultaneously kissing you. "We will sweethearts! Also . . . now, we family. I am mama, papa, sister, brother, auntie, uncle. I all your family!"

Then, after she moved her head away from yours, she signed something you had never been told before."

"You so beautiful."

"Finish you! You tease?"

"No. True! Your face and body . . . beautiful. Handsome like movie star. When you bawling tears? Doesn't matter. Still most beautiful boy in school."

S's words made the ceiling open up and the sky poured soft warm clouds all over your heartbroken body.

"You beautiful too," you signed.

"Can you see me?"

"Not now . . . too dark. But before, after you beat up Crazy Charles, I saw a little. But can also feel."

You touched S's face, tracing the outlines of her nose, cheeks, eyes, lips. You needed to carve it into your brain, locking in every detail, before S disappeared into the darkness, like your mother had. Like everything would.

18

THE GREAT TRIBULATION

Writing class is off today for the Fourth of July break. It is another holiday that JWs do not celebrate. Instead of going to a picnic like other people, you sit alone in your hot room, in front of your computer, thinking about the assignment you are supposed to finish by Friday, the one about the Day That Changed Everything. Snakes of discomfort squirm in your stomach.

To write the essay, Professor Lavinia Bahr says, means becoming a better writer.

To write the essay means opening the gates of your brain to all the sad monsters you've been trying to forget for the last five and a half years.

To write the essay could mean letting them live somewhere else (inside your computer) instead of only in your brain.

To write the essay means breaking your promise to Brother Birch, Molly, Jehovah God, and yourself.

You stare at the blank screen. The giant white cursor blinks impatiently, like a tapping toe, waiting for you to write. So you type the letters R-E-M-E-M-B-E-R and stare at them. Then you zoom in even tighter on the word, making the letters grow like a monster, until the whole word cannot fit on the screen in one piece. So instead of *remember*, the screen is filled with the word *EMBER*. *Ember* means *a small piece of burning or glowing coal or wood in a dying fire*. This makes you think of the Lake of Fire. So you delete it.

Write. You need to write. Write.

You don't.

Get up and stretch.

Scratch Snap behind her ears.

Think about your new friend Hanne and wonder if being a nurse is as hard as writing a personal essay about something you're supposed to have forgotten about.

Think about whether Hanne is practicing sorcery every day or just sometimes. Is it safe for a nurse to also be a witch?

Think about that "special" lunch chicken marsala, and plan to ask Molly if they have it the next time you eat lunch in the cafeteria.

Think about bacon, lettuce, and tomato sandwiches.

Think about how, earlier in the day, a strange woman walked you to the Able-Ride stop. You held her on her naked upper arm and felt the softness of her skin.

Red star.

You close the MS Word window and open the browser window. You open the JW.org website. These giant white letters on the homepage are familiar to you.

Jehovah's Witnesses—Who Are We?

You scan the list of available articles and back issues of *The Watchtower*. The first three: "Enlightening Visions of the Spirit Realm" or "Dr. Marlene Rippelmeyer: A Podiatrist Explains Her Faith" or "Bible Questions Answered: What Is the Great Tribulation?"

Currently your great tribulation is writing this personal essay about a day that changed everything. But the "Tribulation" that JW.org is talking about is different.

The Great Tribulation will occur during the end times when false religion will be destroyed by Jehovah God utilizing the countries represented by the United Nations. During that time there will be an attack on the true religion by a coalition of bad nations that Ezekiel mentioned in his vision and called "Gog of the land of Magog." Where is Magog? Is Gog a person? You can't remember. Did the sinful people from Magog have to write personal essays? You know from JW.org that at the end of the Great Tribulation Gog and his hordes in Magog will be destroyed whether they've written their secret stories or not.

The Great Tribulation is when Judgment Day will happen. Judgment Day is not really a "day" but really one thousand years. You are not sure why the Bible doesn't just say this, unless because one thousand years just sounds too complicated, or maybe—to the infinite Jehovah God—one thousand years equals just one of His days. What does that mean if Jehovah God needs to do His laundry every seven days? Is that once every seven thousand years? Does Jehovah God smell?

Red star.

The best part of Judgment Day is that even the unrighteous sinner who dies a nonbeliever will have a chance to be saved. That means one thousand years to change your mind and behavior. Unlike regular people, Jehovah God is very fair. Cyril and Hanne will still have a chance to be saved. So will Martin and Big Head Lawrence, and so will . . . *stop*. Think of Judgment Day. Think of the throngs of people. Think of Cyril, Hanne, Martin, and Big Head Lawrence, all facing the *embers* of the Lake of Fire, and needing to make a decision: a decision between eternal salvation and eternal death; a decision about being godly sheep or goats; a decision about writing this essay or not writing this essay.

You do another search on JW.org and you find this: "Will All Be Resurrected?" The answer is no. In Luke 12:5 the Bible talks about a place called Gehenna. Gehenna was the name of a garbage dump on the outskirts of ancient Jerusalem. That's where they threw the dead bodies that were unworthy of burial and resurrection. "So Gehenna is a fitting symbol of everlasting destruction. He will never resurrect those whom He judges to be wicked and unwilling to change."

Gehenna is Jehovah God's version of Dogwood.

This part of the story of the Great Tribulation always makes your head hurt. JW.org says *everyone* will be resurrected, the *righteous* and the *unrighteous*, but then it also says not everyone will be resurrected . . . if they are one of the *wicked*. How does one know if someone is so wicked that they cannot even get a second chance?

Is Cyril one of the wicked? Is Hanne? Is Martin? Is Big Head Lawrence? Was S one of the wicked? You type into the search engine at the top of the page: *Who are the wicked?* A list of Bible verses, but none answer the question. It doesn't seem fair that they aren't specific. It doesn't seem fair that some sinners get one thousand years to figure it out and some don't. Your eye starts to ache from looking at the screen.

You close JW.org.

You open up MS Word again and stare again into the blackness of the screen of eternal death, where the brightness of the gigantic white cursor . . . curser . . . curses at you: WRITE YOUR FUCKING ESSAY, YOU DEAFBLIND DUMMY!

Red star.

Maybe if you had a thousand years, instead of one week, you would have enough time to write this essay. Or maybe you'd have time to figure out a way to escape this assignment.

You try again. You type: *The Day That Changed Everything is . . . was . . . was? . . . is? Were? WAS?*

You stare at the glow around the three towering letters filling the black screen: W-A-S. Giant white word ghosts; each letter vibrating with the story it wants to tell: *that* story.

Just as you are about to continue, you feel Brother Birch tap your shoulder and you nearly jump out of your seat.

"Come," he signs.

You are clearly in trouble. But you haven't even written anything yet. The only things you can remember doing wrong recently are things you've done inside your head. Can Brother Birch read minds? (It's a sin to read minds.) You and Snap follow Brother Birch up to the living room. Snap walks slowly because she knows something is wrong too.

As soon as you arrive in the living room, you smell Molly's familiar scent. Brother Birch called her here to tell you something he is unable to sign himself, something complicated. To prepare yourself for bad news, you tighten your stomach and that area between your anus and balls.

"Why were you talking to a strange woman on your SBC the other day?" Brother Birch asks via Molly's interpreting. "In the college cafeteria?"

Shit. He means Hanne. It's a sin for a man to be alone with a woman unless she is a family member or an interpreter. (It's even worse if that woman may or may not be a witch.) You need an excuse. Think, think, think.

"Woman?" you say, squinching your brow, as if the word *woman* meant *flying hamster*. "I don't think so. Again, what day?"

"Please, Arlo," Brother Birch says. "You mustn't lie. One of the elders saw you, and the woman wasn't Molly and wasn't a member of the fellowship. Please tell me who it was?"

How to answer? That you didn't think women older than you counted? That you forgot about the rule even though you are reminded at least once a week at Public Talk? That if Hanne is a witch, she's probably a nice witch? What you really want to say is: *It isn't fair that someone with vision and hearing can spy on a DeafBlind man, but the DeafBlind man can never spy on them.* Still, you are in a panic. Desperation fills your fingers.

"What about you and Molly?" you ask, back-talking to an elder, which is also a sin. "Molly single. Last week, when your wife at convention, you and Molly alone together. Remember? Not fair—!"

Molly grabs your wrists, signaling for you to stop talking. Is it Brother Birch who is angry or Molly or both?

"Shame on you!" Brother Birch yells. Molly's hands are shaking. "You know the only reason Molly and I are alone together is so we can help you, so you can stop that filthy talk. Now, tell me the truth, who was that woman and what were you doing with her?"

"She not woman!" you say, defensively. Your signing grows more intense, as if by sheer muscle power you will convince them. "She artist! Goes to college! Same as me! Will become nurse! She nice!"

Why are you screaming? Can they see the lie on your face? Does it burn red and hot?

You can't make Brother Birch your enemy. Unlike when you first left the Rose Garden School, he trusts you now. This was one of the main reasons Molly was able to talk him into letting you study writing at the community college. You need to keep Brother Birch on your side.

"Sorry," you sign more humbly now. "Blow up at you . . . I wrong. Sorry. But, honest, I not do sin. That woman, I talk to her, why? Try pull her to Jesus. I preach about Jehovah God and give her pamphlet."

For a moment there is silence. It means Brother Birch and Molly are talking secretly.

"You were witnessing?" Brother Birch asks. "Honest?"

"Yes," you say, almost believing the lie yourself.

"Witnessing for Jesus is good. But you know you're not supposed to be spending time alone with any woman who is not a member of your family . . . or Molly, of course."

Worried that Brother Birch might still punish you, you switch your approach. You bow your head and shake it back and forth, like you're very sad. Then you clasp your hands for a moment in a prayerful pose, suddenly slapping your forehead very hard three times.

"I should know better! I disappoint God! I sin! So sorry. You right! Sin to talk to woman alone. I think because cafeteria . . . crowded people . . . it okay to talk to woman alone. Sorry. I stupid! I pea brain!"

You hit yourself again, again, again.

It works. Brother Birch himself grabs your arms to stop you from hurting yourself. Then he himself signs, awkwardly but kindly, in his basic, choppy ASL:

"It—is—okay, Arlo. I—AM—not mad no more. Stop hitting you. It—

is—okay. All JW people D-O bad part-time. Pray and ask Jehovah God T-O . . . forgive us. We . . ."

You try to keep your face looking humble and sad, but it's taking forever for Brother Birch to finish his sentence. He is incredibly slow and rarely signs anything more than two or three words at a time. Molly moves back into the interpreter position.

"Just don't do it again, okay?" Brother Birch says via Molly. "You are a great messenger for Jehovah God, but Satan will try to test you. Now, I need you to tell me the truth about something else. Was it Cyril Brewster who introduced you to this artist-nurse woman?"

"Yes. She and Cyril—best friends. Name: H-A-N-N-E. Born where? Belgium. She very sad woman. Hard life. Need help to find Jehovah God."

You say everything Brother Birch would want to hear, explaining that Hanne is a broken woman in an unhappy marriage with a child and who may be desperate to find God.

"Okay. Now I understand," Brother Birch says. "Your interpreter Cyril was wrong. He shouldn't be introducing you to any strange women. He's just there to help Molly interpret for you. He's not your friend."

You try to defend Cyril, taking the blame for talking to Hanne, but Brother Birch will not listen.

"I told you. I forgive you," Brother Birch says. "Jehovah God forgives you. But I need to explain something to you. Molly has heard bad things about Cyril. He is . . . he's not a good Christian, not a normal man. He is known to commit very serious sins, and most likely will face oblivion if he doesn't change his ways. There's no way around just saying it. Cyril is a gay. H-O-M-O-S-E-X-U-A-L. Do you understand what that means?"

G-A-Y? You have seen the word a hundred times at Public Talk. At least two members of the Kingdom Hall have been reprimanded over the last year for homosexual desire. Then there were rumors about Miss Sybil at the Rose Garden School, and one or two substitute interpreters over the years. *Homosexual* means having S-E-X with people of the same sex.

Martin and some of the other boys at school used to play S-E-X games. But they were children. Only adults can be homosexual. But is Cyril homosexual? Nothing Cyril said would indicate G-A-Y. In fact, he's told you nothing personal about his life. You think of his touch. Did he linger? Did he touch you in a way that was more G-A-Y than not G-A-Y? What do you know about Cyril? You know he's a good interpreter. You know he has red hair and is just a little shorter than you. You know he is smart and knows how to explain poetry to you. But that is all.

"Yes. I know meaning G-A-Y," you tell Brother Birch. "G-A-Y bad sin."

"Did you know that Cyril is gay?"

"Not really."

"What does that mean?"

"Cyril never tell me G-A-Y or straight. But I think Cyril not G-A-Y. Cyril just interpreter."

Again Brother Birch talks secretly with Molly.

Why does it matter if Cyril is or is not a homosexual? You didn't make him a homosexual. But you know doing any kind of sexual activity is a serious sin. If Cyril was really your friend, he would have told you if he was G-A-Y. Perhaps Brother Birch is right again. Cyril is not your friend.

"I think we should ask to find a different interpreter," Brother Birch says. "Someone who is a better match for you. It doesn't matter if it costs the college more money. Perhaps that friend of Molly's who was originally supposed to do the job."

You stop paying attention as Brother Birch talks about this possible replacement for Cyril. A wave of anger heaves itself against the inside of your chest. *Molly is trying to get rid of Cyril. Why? Because she's jealous that Cyril knows more English words than her and is smarter about the world. Or maybe Molly's worried that people will find out that she's the one committing very serious sins? That's why Molly has invented this story of Cyril being a G-A-Y. She's trying to make people look at him instead of her.* You shove Molly's hands away and begin to pummel the air with your anger:

"No! I don't want different interpreter!" You are screaming again. "I want Cyril! He great interpreter! Not fair! Get rid Molly not Cyril! Molly lie! Molly bad interpreter!"

When Molly tries to engage you again, you pull your hands away and shove them into your armpits, refusing to listen. After a few more attempts on Molly's part, Brother Birch yanks your arms out and shoves his own thick hairy hands back into your palms.

"Stop!" he signs. "Bad boy! Pay attention! You talk mean words A-T Molly! Bad boy! Bad boy!"

When Molly's hands return to yours, they feel limp. Your comments have bruised her, and you sense she is struggling to focus on her interpretation.

"Do you know how much Molly has done for you in your life?" Brother Birch says. "Do you know she worked for years at a lower pay rate than she would have earned if she worked somewhere else? Do you realize she even moved down here to Poughkeepsie to continue to work with you? She loves you like I love you! She's the one who taught me to sign so I could communicate with you. Molly is the one who convinced me of your potential, and how you can become a very important preacher. But you speak to her like that? Do you know how much you've hurt her?"

Brother Birch is right. The fury that whirled around your heart has sunk to your stomach in a sickening blob of guilt. Molly's hands, fragile and old, rest in the air under yours. What is that you feel? Is she crying? You are suddenly repulsed at your own ability to crush someone's soul. Molly is imperfect, yes, but she has been your eyes, ears, and voice for ten years. You have nothing without her. True, Cyril has given you more freedom to learn, but Molly was there at the beginning, giving you the words to ask for that freedom. No matter her offense toward Cyril, no matter the threat to your friendship with Hanne, you should never treat Molly so unkindly.

"Molly. Sorry. I just want Cyril stay interpreter. He good interpreter.

I want both you and Cyril. Best interpreters. From now on will respect. Promise."

You hug Molly's bony little body. Then Brother Birch and Molly return to their secret discussion. It goes on for at least ten minutes as you stand there, shifting your weight from one leg to the other. Finally, you feel the tap on your shoulders.

"Okay," Brother Birch says. "Molly convinced me to allow Cyril to stay for now. But no more talking to this Hanne woman. You are to go to school and then come home. Remember, you need to do a lot of studying so we're ready for Ecuador at the end of summer. No more spending time alone with Cyril. That's forbidden. Do you understand me? If we are to do this mission trip together, you need to show me that you're spiritually strong. Are we clear?"

You nod, surprised that Molly stood up for Cyril. You hate the limits that have been set, but you did commit a sin and it's better than nothing. You have survived another day to wait for the Great Tribulation.

"Okay," Brother Birch says. "You and Snap can go back to your room and finish that homework you were working on."

You shake Brother Birch's hand and kiss Molly on the cheek. Molly does love you, and you love her. You return to your room and the black screen and the giant angry cursor. Your stomach feels uneasy. You want to scratch the skin off your arms. The giant angry cursor begins laughing at you: *You can't. You can't. You can't.* You squeeze your head between your hands, stuffing any memories that might have leaked out back inside. Not today. Back to *forget.* The Great Tribulation will need to be postponed. You will need to think of a lie to tell the professor.

19

MY SECRETS/YOUR SECRETS

It was Tuesday morning, and despite having a bit too much to drink the night before, I couldn't sleep. So, I went to the college an hour early with the intention of enjoying a few cups of coffee in the cafeteria, reading the news, and letting myself get into a mild rage at the sorrows of the world. But as I stepped into the dining room, I saw Arlo sitting alone in the nearly empty cafeteria, looking anxious and signing to himself. Snap immediately began slapping her tail on the floor when she saw me, so I walked over and tapped Arlo on the arm, which, as usual, startled him.

"Cyril here," I signed. "Sorry to scare you. Is everything okay? You looked like something was bothering you."

Arlo shook his head, dropping his hands to his lap, like he was trying to silence them. Then, as he often does, he looked out just past me as if he were searching for something in a parallel universe that only he could see.

"Are you sure?" I asked.

Arlo looked hesitant. "We alone?"

"The cafeteria is empty except for Bitsy and Doris in the kitchen," I signed. "Tell me what's up."

"Okay. Shh. Secret. Last night, I email professor. I told her: write personal essay—too hard! Can't. Sorry. But professor say, *you must try*. I ask, can write other hard essay about poem? Professor say: *no, you must try!* Not fair!"

Arlo ran his fingers through his hair and groaned in frustration. I, however, was glad that Professor Bahr was encouraging him to try. Of course, that was partly for my own selfish curiosity.

"I get it," I signed. "Writing is hard. But you took this class to improve, right? It's not my place to say, but the professor seems like a pretty smart person. But again, it's up to you."

Not liking my response, Arlo rolled his eyes in the most sarcastic of ways, causing me to laugh. I had never seen him make that expression. For that moment he was just like any twenty-three-year-old reacting to the pestering of some middle-aged person incapable of understanding the difficulty of writing a personal essay. I decided to drop it but kept him talking.

"I'm curious about your trip to Ecuador," I signed. "What will you do there? I hear there are volcanos, and the G-A-L-Á-P-A-G-O-S Islands. Have you heard about those?"

Arlo nodded. I started yammering on about everything I knew about sea turtles and birds and how the islands were almost untouched. Just when I was about to talk about a *National Geographic* video I saw about iguanas, he stopped me.

"Go Ecuador for vacation? Not! What for? I will preach Bible and Jehovah God to Deaf Ecuador poor people."

"Ah, I see. Is Snap going with you?"

A wave of frustration and sadness rushed across Arlo's face. He squeezed his hands together and then reached down to scratch Snap between her shoulder blades. Rather than give in to it as she usually did, Snap looked up at Arlo, her ears pricked up, her little white eyebrows looking curious and concerned as if she knew what we were talking about.

"No," Arlo signed smaller, not wanting Snap to see. "Too dangerous. Dogs forbidden to go."

Snap released a sigh, before lowering her head sadly onto her paws. Of course, this was my own anthropomorphic interpretation. Snap, at eight and a half, was nearing retirement. That the two would be separated for the yearlong mission meant that they were probably only a matter of weeks away from the end of their working relationship.

"But what will happen to her?" I asked, as dark visions of Snap's fate flooded my mind.

"Snap will okay," Arlo answered, like it was something he had practiced telling himself. "Snap will live where she trained as a puppy. She will help teach other guide dogs. Future, when back, me and Snap will live together again forever. Brother Birch promise."

"I see," I signed, trying to shake off my doubt. "That sounds great. I'm sure she'll be happy there, and a year goes by fast anyway."

Again, Arlo looked disturbed, and did that thing where he squeezed his fist and eyes, like he had a momentary fight with someone in his head.

"Ecuador very far," Arlo signed suddenly, clearly no longer wanting to talk about Snap. "Sitting on plane for seven hours and forty-five minutes. Wow. Very long time. So boring."

"True," I signed, joining him in changing the subject. "I'm curious, what's Ecuadorian sign language like?"

"Not sure yet. But will learn. JWs learn other languages—champion! Our friend already live there. She expert Ecuadorian sign language. Work Deaf school. New sign language, I will learn fast."

"Oh, wow. Cool. I'd give anything to get out of Poughkeepsie for a long trip."

"You don't like Poughkeepsie?"

"It's fine. It's just that I've lived here all my life. The farthest I've ever traveled has been a trip to Miami when I was twelve and a trip to Toronto. I used to have this close friend. We always talked about traveling all over the world together, but it never happened."

"Why?" Arlo asked.

"Well, he and I . . . we stopped being friends," I signed, appropriately vague. "I just never got around to doing it on my own. Too busy, I suppose. Kept putting it off. Things happen that way sometimes. The good news is, I might move to Philadelphia in September and work there. I have to see. It just would be nice to have a change, you know?"

Arlo nodded and then laughed. It was the first time he had smiled since I sat down.

"Yes. I know. Feel the same. I grew up here too. Then went away to Rose Garden School but have to come back."

"The Rose Garden School? That's way up near the Canadian border, right? Wow . . . did you like it?"

"Beats here," he signed, using the sign that can mean *conquer*. "Pough-keepsie very, very boring."

"I agree. So boring! But I guess if you have to be stuck somewhere, Poughkeepsie isn't the worst place to be stuck. I mean, the nature is nice. And New York City isn't that far."

"New York City—I never touch."

"Are you serious?" I signed, a little more surprised than I should have been. "It's only an hour and a half away!"

Arlo shook his head.

"Two times touch Albany, many times touch Rome, Rochester, other places. Not much to do for DeafBlind man in Poughkeepsie. No friends here. Back at school I have best friends, Martin and Big Head Lawrence."

"You mentioned them before," I signed, leaning in, hoping Arlo would tell me more. "I'm curious, why exactly did they give him that name-sign, Big Head Lawrence?"

"Because . . . big head."

I laughed. Sometimes it was hard to know if Arlo understood that what he signed was funny. But other times I was certain he did. He has that terrific mix of innocence and brilliance.

"Okay," I signed, playing along. "That makes sense."

"Long time ago, Martin, me, and Big Head Lawrence do everything together. All night long chat chat chat. F-U-N. And also . . . other friends too. But I curious, I wanted to ask you . . ."

He stops. What? What does he want to know? I feared I might lose the opportunity so I pressed him to talk.

"Do you ever see them? Martin, Big Head Lawrence, or any other friends from school?"

"No. No. Far away. Long time ago."

"You don't email them?"

Just like that, he did his disappearing-inside-his-head thing. I tapped his arm and repeated myself, not wanting another situation where he just let everything drop.

"Hey, why did you lose contact with them?"

"Long story. Where they live? Where work? Last name? I don't know. I know nothing! Before . . . many friends! Here . . . no friends. Only interpreters. Hanne almost friend. But talk to Hanne more—forbidden. No way!"

My stomach tightened. Was Hanne the invisible person he had been arguing with minutes before? Was Hanne the reason for Arlo's retreat?

"Hey, tell me the truth," I signed. "Did Hanne do or say something stupid that day I introduced you? I told you she can act a little crazy."

"No, no. Hanne not crazy. Not do anything bad. Hanne very nice woman."

Again, he begged my secrecy. I wondered whether his paranoia about people sharing his secrets was just specific to him or something shared by other DeafBlind folks. Did a lack of access precede a lack of trust? Of course, whether or not I was to be trusted was something I started to doubt, given my propensity to share Arlo's story with Hanne. She, it was turning out, appeared to be a better confidante than me. Still, I vowed my secrecy.

"I honest," Arlo signed. "What happen? Brother Birch angry, blew up. JW elder saw me with Hanne . . . talk private, alone. Understand? JW not allowed talk with strange woman in private. Red star."

"Um . . . red star?"

"Sorry. Red star mean sin. When I small and I do sin, I get red star sticker next to my name on board at Sunday school. Too many red stars and punished. Must sit alone in room and pray long time. Or sometimes spanking and sitting. Sitting alone worse than spanking. I always many red stars."

Arlo laughed. But all I could think was *What a fucked-up thing to do to a kid.* Arlo went on to explain how the elder who saw him talking to Hanne went on to tell Molly. Then Molly told Brother Birch. Then Brother Birch made Arlo promise never to talk to Hanne again. *Fucking Molly! What kind of interpreter rats out their clients?*

"I'm so sorry," I signed. "That's my fault. I never should have introduced you to Hanne. That was really stupid of me."

"No. New people . . . I enjoy talking. Hanne very interesting, but question . . ."

Arlo appeared uncertain whether his question might offend and hesitated.

"Go ahead," I signed. "What's your question?"

Arlo asked me to be certain no one was watching, and I assured him we were totally alone except for some older teacher reading a stack of papers.

"Tell me truth. Hanne—she witch or S-O-R-C-E-R-E-S-S?"

I waited for him to sign something like "ha ha" and tell me he was joking, but he didn't. I stifled my own laughter before putting my hands into his.

"No. Hanne isn't any kind of witch or sorceress. She can barely brew coffee. Hanne's a brilliant and kind person, with strong opinions and crappy boundaries. She can also be a little too impulsive sometimes. But why would you think she's a witch?"

Arlo knitted his brow and signed small and cautiously.

"When we talk, Hanne influence me. She make me tell secrets even when I don't want to. I think she use magic."

"Ha ha," I signed. "Magic?"

Arlo could feel the laughter I could no longer hold back. He smiled at my reaction, but he was trying not to.

"No. Not joke. Magic real! Bible says so!"

"Yeah, okay. But don't worry. Hanne is definitely not a witch. And if you saw her messy house, you'd know she has a serious fear of brooms."

Arlo finally laughed in earnest, but I could tell he wasn't 100 percent convinced. I told him I understood how Hanne might be mistaken for a witch, and I had seen her ability to get people to confess their secrets. I had done it myself. What I didn't go into with him was that besides being the first person I told about being gay, she was also the first person I told about falling in love with Bruno and the first person I told about the breakup and what happened after. Hanne was a beautiful hurricane into which you could scream all your deepest secrets—or most of them.

"Hey, hey. Cyril," Arlo signed, clearly feeling more comfortable with me now that we'd had a laugh. "Ask you something else private, okay? This about you. Okay?"

"Depends on how personal," I signed jokingly. "But I can tell you right now, I'm not a witch either. Ha ha."

Arlo didn't laugh this time.

"Still alone?" he asked, his head turning toward the door.

"Yes," I signed. "But remember we have to go to class in about fifteen minutes."

"Okay, okay. Question. Long time ago, you become interpreter . . . Why? Molly became interpreter to teach Deaf people become JW. Why you? Parents Deaf?"

This is the most common question Deaf folks ask, but usually when they first meet you. Why he waited so long I had no idea.

"No," I signed. "No one in my family was Deaf. To be honest, becoming an interpreter just happened by accident. I met this Deaf man in college who was teaching an ASL class. I took the class. We became best friends and hung out a lot. I was good at ASL, and I liked Deaf people, so one thing led to another and the next thing you know . . . I've been an interpreter ever since."

Of course, my answer was only adjacent to the truth, but it wasn't the time or place to get into all the gory details.

"You like Deaf better than hearing?" Arlo asked.

I laughed. "Um . . . often. Yes."

"Why? Why you like Deaf better?"

Suddenly the formerly silent, opaque Arlo had turned into a Deaf-Blind talk-show host.

"You have a lot of questions. The Deaf people I've met have been a lot more honest and direct. Hearing people can be pretty phony, not saying what they mean, pretending to feel one way when they really feel another. Deaf people tell it like it is. It's even inherent in ASL. No passive voice. Difficult to be vague without appearing to outright lie. I guess I just feel safer around Deaf people."

"But Deaf always gossip!"

"Okay. Sure. I'm not saying Deaf people are perfect. They aren't. Maybe it just feels safer hanging in a world that isn't my own? An outsider being more comfortable with other outsiders."

"Outsider?" he asked. "Means what?"

I explained the term, but then suddenly was overcome with a queasy feeling. I was stepping into an area of intimacy I had been trying to avoid. I patted Arlo's hand in a way to say the conversation was over.

"Hey, I probably should go to the bathroom before it gets time for the class to start," I signed. "We can talk another time, and maybe you can tell me more about you. It's not fair if only one person talks."

"Wait!" he signed, a look of desperation on his face. "I will tell you something before you go toilet. Before Molly arrives."

He began to pummel the air with words.

"My mother died long time ago when I in Rose Garden School. Because cancer. Father left when I was born. Mama tell me because he bad, drunk man. Not like JW, not believe Jehovah God, but . . . then why not try see me? Confuse. Brother Birch knows truth but tell me nothing. Mama say Father not come back because JW shun him. He bad man. Sinner. Mama and Brother Birch, whole congregation, never talk to Father again. Disfellowshipped. Because Mama die, I must live with Brother Birch and his wife. Why? Brother Birch my mama's uncle. I very lonely. Same as Molly. She lonely too. Now she lonelier. Why? Because she must be more careful with Brother Birch. That's why she upset today."

Arlo stopped, then reached in front of him to make sure I was still there, listening. A flush of humiliation reddened his face.

I reached into his hands, letting him know I hadn't left. I knew there was something more Arlo wanted to tell me.

"I talk too much. Sorry. Go to toilet. Sorry."

"It's okay. Go on."

Arlo took a deep breath, weighing the right way of saying whatever he was about to tell me. He leaned in. I was prepared for him to answer all the questions that had been dogging me since we met. The mystery would finally be solved.

"Hey! Shh! Very secret, okay?"

"Yes. Promise."

"I know something," he began. He looked like whatever he was about to tell me was causing him great pain. "Shh. Secret. Shh. I know you G-A-Y."

I didn't know what to say. He had turned the spotlight back onto me, and I suddenly felt tricked. His minor revelation about his mother dying was just a ploy to get me to confess something. I felt naked in front of him and it angered me. It was not how I liked to feel in front of someone I worked with. I prided myself on my anonymity and professionalism. How had he come to the conclusion about my sexuality? Did I sign like I was gay? Was it because I indicated I was an outsider? No. The answer was obvious: Molly, that puritanical, prudish JW snake, was trying to turn him against me. Whether she had succeeded or not was still in question.

"Look," I signed. "That's too personal of a question."

Arlo pulled his hands away, sat up in his chair, and suddenly took on the look of the good social worker counseling a problem child.

"I understand," he signed. "You embarrass. Not want to tell. Because they say G-A-Y people will disappear forever on Judgment Day. G-A-Y means not saved. Brother Birch want fire you for G-A-Y. If you G-A-Y I don't care. Doesn't matter. Shh. Secret. My old friend from Rose Garden School, Martin, I think he become G-A-Y when grow up. But I don't care. He best friend. So maybe he also will disappear on Judgment Day if not say sorry to Jehovah God. Big Head Lawrence not G-A-Y. But he still maybe die forever because he not believe in God. But I don't care. You be G-A-Y, it's okay. Just not *do* G-A-Y and ask Jehovah God for forgive then all good."

What was I supposed to say? *Thank you for your instructions on how to save my queer soul, but I'll try my chances with eternal damnation if I can still fuck another man?* I shifted in my seat, begging whatever gods existed to please find a way to get me out of the conversation before I said something that would definitely make me lose the job.

"Okay. I'm heading to the toilet. Molly should be here any minute."

When I stood up, I could see from Arlo's expression that he knew he had crossed a line.

"Okay, okay," he signed. "I understand. G-A-Y personal. Private. Okay. Okay. Sorry. We not talk anymore about you G-A-Y. I wrong ask personal. I sorry. But can talk more later? You angry? Cyril?"

Arlo reached his hands out again, fearful that I had already left. I paused briefly, my own petulance getting the better of me. *Let him think I've left!* I stood there for ten seconds, cruelly watching the desperation on his face. I finally shoved my hands back into his. My better angel wanting to assuage his fears, my worse angel seeing his contrition as an opportunity.

"Okay. Fine. We can talk more, but I have a question for you. I'm curious. I saw you once alone in the cafeteria, trying to spell what I think was someone's name. You looked upset. It was S-something. Was that the person that made you feel *happy and sad* at the same time? The one who protected you from Crazy Charles?"

And just like that, Arlo retreated back inside his head, gathering all his secrets, shoving them back in and slamming the door.

"Hey, don't just ignore me," I demanded. "You know, if you search the internet, I bet you could probably find all your old friends. People do that all the time. You could get their emails or contact your old school."

Arlo suddenly looked enraged and with both fists pounded the table very hard. The teacher across the room looked up.

"No!" Arlo signed, punching the air with his signs. "Forbidden!"

"*Forbidden?* What is forbidden? Forbidden to contact the school or your old friends?"

Arlo yanked his hands from mine and turned the interrogation light back onto me.

"No! You!" he shouted, his rare fury reaching new heights. "I already tell you many private stories. Finish! Enough! Now talk about you. Question! The Deaf ASL teacher friend? Is he your G-A-Y sweetheart?"

I grabbed Arlo's wrists and angrily shoved my hands into his.

"That's not your business. We are not talking about the G-A-Y thing anymore. That's my private life. Not up for discussion. You understand that I'm not your friend, right? I'm your interpreter. There's a difference!"

Arlo pulled his hands from mine and I could tell I had reacted too aggressively. I gently reached for his hands.

"Hey, I'm sorry," I signed. "I didn't mean to grab you like that. I'm so sorry."

Arlo's hands listened limply; his expression proved he was somewhere else.

"I'm sorry," I repeated. "I'm not angry. It's just . . . if we continue to work together, it's best we keep it professional. Understand?"

"Class start soon," Arlo signed, his face blank. "I want alone now. Okay?"

Then Arlo folded his arms, shoving his hands into his armpits. Conversation over.

20

EMAIL TO HANNE

Dear Hanne Van Steenkiste:

I am Arlo Dilly. DEAFBLIND boy you meet with interpreter CYRIL
BREWSTER. It have nice was to MEET you. You NICE friendly
woman and ask lots of questions. Thank you. I send LINK to
JW.org website show INFORMATION about Jehovah God and
Jesus. Thank YOU. Read if WANT BE saved. (SMILE)

OKAY?

Is 2:30 a.m. in morning. Snap asleep, but I CANNOT. Too many
words and stories in brain.

I tell you other SECRET. SHH. You ask me if I want meet GIRL
to marry. YES! I want meet SOMEDAY JW girl marry and DATE.
But NOT EASY for DEAFBLIND man and girl have THE SUBLIME
relationship. Deaf girls not want talk on me. Girls SIGHTED and
HEARING not interest DEAFBLIND man. Maybe when I moving
to ECUADOR because become JW PIONEER I meeting DEAF-
BLIND ECUADOR JW WOMAN with beautiful hands and SMART.
Smooth skin. Smell nice. Soft warm body. Tell STORIES to me!
Maybe falling in LOVE will TRANSPIRE! Feeling THE SUBLIME!
Feeling AWE! HA HA. Dreaming. (SMILE) BEFORE I hoping will

meet DEAFBLIND girl here. But not likely when LOOK AT STATIS-
TICS find on internet:

PEOPLE WHO I (Arlo Dilly) CAN LOVE AND DATE

IF:

7.8 billion people live Earth

332.2 million in America

19.3 million in New York State

6.6 million people live in upstate New York

30,669 in Poughkeepsie where I live with Brother Birch

(I ask Molly. She guess Molly) 100 people that know sign language in downtown Poughkeepsie

(This also GUESS) 50 can sign language so good can have
long conversation (More Deaf and JW can do sign language in
Rome, New York)

(How many CAN/WILL DO TACTILE ASL IN POUGHKEEP-
SIE?????)

GUESS: 12 that have was spoke to DeafBlind person before
and CAN Tactile ASL

8 of them WOMAN (maybe) that CAN DO TACTILE ASL

(FACT) ONLY 6 woman that live close and has was ACTUALLY
talk with me in TACTILE SIGN

4 who TALK TO ME every month regular

ONLY 3 ARE JW (Forbidden marry NON-JW)

1 = MOLLY, my ongoing SSP/Interpreter (She old, besides not
my taste.)

So I ask you HONEST: WILL ANY of those ONLY 2 GIRLS
LOVE ME? Or me attraction at them? Them attraction at me? NO!!!
because I AM ALONE like DEAFBLIND UGLY MONSTER. (HA HA
I NOT crying. Just SHAKING MY HEAD.) I think I have was TIRED.

SHH. I telling you OTHER Secret. I was LIED before. REMEM-
BER Girl I did sex with first time? I was LOVING her. But she was

NOT JW girl. Was not CHRISTIAN. Shh. Big SECRET. SHH. Gone forever. THEY bad. Sinner. Not allow SPEAK ON SINNER PERSON. Shh. (CRYING) Please no tell. Shhh.

Sorry. Honest. I not allow talking to you no more because you not JW Christian woman. But we still WILL email . . . okay? Or you become JW and we can talking about Jehovah God?!!

Even people practice WITCHCRAFT and SORCERY can SAVED if ask Jehovah God FORGIVENESS!

But if not be SAVED we STILL can secret friends. But Shh. Don't tell. Secret. Please delete after read.

HUGS,
Arlo Dilly

21

THE FIRST TIME

You finish writing the email to Cyril's friend Hanne. You press Send and the email disappears into the computer and flies through the clouds into her computer. She could be reading it now, your secrets becoming her secrets. Witchcraft. Red star. Shh. Shh. Your heart is pounding. Too many sins. Turn off the computer. Climb into bed. You had hoped the voices and stories in your head would stop by writing the note to Hanne, but it's the opposite. A dozen memories wrestle one another to get to the front of your brain.

You were seventeen and a half years old.

It was September again and you could already smell the earth outside your window starting to cool. Your growing muscles pushed against the buttons of your shirts. Hair grew thicker on your face and arms. At lunchtime you ate a minimum of two baloney sandwiches and drank a carton of chocolate milk every day, and still you were always hungry. Arms and ankles felt unfamiliar breezes after being abandoned by too-short shirtsleeves and pant legs. Crazy Charles and the Deaf Devils still picked on weak students, but they didn't bother you or your friends anymore. This was because of what S said to him, but you hoped it was also because you had grown more scary looking.

Other things were changing too.

Usually the Deaf-sighted students avoided talking too much with the

DeafBlind, but suddenly two girls in your class, Marla and Em, started talking to you every day during lunchtime, giving you parts of their lunches they didn't want to eat. One day Em brought you your own extra peanut butter and grape jelly sandwich. The next day Marla brought you two, but with strawberry jam, which you liked better. Both girls let you feel their bodies jiggle when you signed a joke that even you knew wasn't funny.

Martin told you that a lot of the girls in school were gossiping about how you had turned into a *handsome* man over the summer. S once called you *beautiful*. You asked Martin what the difference was between *handsome* and *beautiful*. He said the words meant the same thing, and then he asked to touch your face.

"Your face feels same all faces," Martin signed. "Except for Big Head Lawrence's. His face different. Those girls stupid. You not handsome. I handsome and beautiful!"

Then Martin checked your chest and arms to see if they had changed.

"Okay, okay," Martin signed. "I understand! Your body changed. More muscles. Now very handsome and beautiful. But your face too scratchy and with too many bones!"

But then Big Head Lawrence, who had better working vision than you, argued that your face could indeed be called handsome, since unlike his, it was symmetrical and a normal size.

"Girls call you handsome . . . why?" Big Head Lawrence explained. "Means they want hold your hand or call you sweetheart or kiss you all over. You lucky! I wish I handsome too!"

The next lunchtime you tried to get a better look at Em and Marla. You told Martin that, from *what you could see*, they were pretty. This was a lie. Because the *what you could see* part continued to worsen. Just before the end of summer the doctor had told Brother Birch that he suspected the little vision you had left would probably disappear completely. Maybe soon, maybe later. When he said this, you clenched your fists and squeezed your eyes so you wouldn't cry.

When you got back to school, you used the big magnifying machine they had in the Rose Garden School library to enlarge photographs. The machine had a switch that removed all the color and turned the photograph into a black-and-white negative, making it easier to see the shape of an eye, the curve of a chin, the outlines of hair and a face. You searched across an old photo of your mother like it was a map of the world, focusing in on the ocean of her eyes, the mountain of her nose, the soft valley of her mouth. You puzzled her face together, then carved it into your brain to save forever.

One day, after making certain no one was around, you brought a small photo that S had given you, placed it on the machine, and adjusted the size and contrast. Because the photo was taken from far away it was hard to make out her face. *Yes, that is an eye, that a mouth . . . or wait . . . is that the bottom of S's nose?* Unlike your mama's, you had never seen S's face in its entirety. This made it impossible to puzzle it together. Your memory of S's visual appearance would always be fragmented, as it was with everyone else you met after you lost your ability to see clearly. Still, you knew S was beautiful. You knew it from her smell, her taste, the feel of her hands and the beautiful stories she would tell you in the middle of the night. You removed the small photo of S from the magnifier tray and sniffed it as if the photo paper might contain her essence.

◊ ◊ ◊

One day Marla followed you into the giant cement pipe on the playground and sat next to you. Then, without warning, she kissed you and shoved your hand under her shirt, letting you feel her body. Other than Martin, Big Head Lawrence, and S, this was the first time you felt the nakedness of another person. Where S's chest had slight, soft mounds, Marla's breasts were even bigger than Martin's. Despite knowing it was wrong, you squeezed them and smelled them and felt Marla's body shiver.

Red star.

Soon, your body became too overwhelmed by what Brother Birch had called *Satan's trap of sexual immorality* and before you could stop, Satan made you sticky-pee all over the inside of your underwear. Disgust and guilt rushed through every cell of your body. Marla, still filled with Satanic temptation, signed "What do? What do?" into your hands, then demanded you keep touching her breasts. But Jehovah God, by his grace, had taken away any desire you had for Marla. After apologizing profusely to her, you quickly crawled out of the tunnel and went to wash your hands. Satan or no Satan, how could you have betrayed S like that? Every time S had visited you in the middle of the night and kissed you and told you stories until you fell asleep, she risked being sent to Dogwood. Your entire body felt sick with the weight of the secret. If you told her, you might never see her again. So you said nothing.

◇ ◇ ◇

Two nights later you sprang awake when two small fists started punching you.

"Why you do it?!" S screamed into your hands. "Why?! I hate you! I hate you!"

"Stop!" you begged between her blows. "Finish! Finish! What do?! What do?!"

Then S told you how she heard what had happened in the cement pipe on the playground.

"I go to Marla's room! She much taller than me! I don't care! I make her tell the truth. Then I punched her in her fat chest and pulled her hair. Stupid white girl!"

Then S punched you in the shoulder very hard.

"Finish! Before, what happened in pipe, nothing important."

"Tell me truth," S demanded. "You like Marla better than me? She kiss you better? She tell you stories better? She protect you better than me?"

Your hands went cold, afraid what S might say next.

"No!" you shouted.

S pulled her hands from yours and turned her back. You felt her shoulders shake with the rage of her tears. You hugged her until the tremors grew smaller, then you turned her around and apologized for not telling her yourself. You thought about telling her about Satan's trap, but you decided not to. The next thing you knew S was crying again, but now her tears were sad and not angry.

"What's wrong?" you asked.

"You heard dirty gossip?" S asked. "That's why, right?"

"Gossip? Meaning?"

"About me and Crazy Charles. That reason you no more my sweetheart and hook up with bitch Marla, because you hate me now. But I kiss Crazy Charles, why? Because protect you! Promise. I don't want him! I want you!"

"You kiss Crazy Charles?"

Your heart broke into a hundred pieces, all falling into the bubbling cauldron of your jealous stomach. You didn't know what to do. Had everything you felt for each other been a lie? You wanted to push S from the bed, and at the same time pull her closer. Confused, you shoved your hands into your armpits, shutting her out. S tapped at your shoulder with her fingers, then tapped harder, then she beat on your back with the flats of her hands, and finally pried your fingers open with her small strong fingers.

"Pay attention!" she demanded through her tears. "Not fair! I didn't kiss him because I like Crazy Charles!"

"You supposed to be my girlfriend!" you yelled.

"I am!" S yelled back. "You not understand! I must kiss Crazy Charles! Why? Because that day he and Deaf Devils beat on you. Remember? I stop them . . . how? Because I beat on him? No! He stronger than me. He stop—why? Remember, I tell you, long time ago, at old school, I only one can understand Crazy Charles? Then happen: Crazy Charles fall in love with me. I say, *Go away, I don't like you*. But he very sad boy. Can't talk. Can't sign. Can't express. Nothing. His family very mean. Sometimes he arrive school and all over his body: bruises. I feel so sorry. So one time I let him kiss me. Why? I know soon I will transfer to Rose Garden School and Crazy Charles stay at old school far away. But then last year he move to Rose Garden School too. Still wants to kiss me. I say, *Go away, you disgusting*. But then that day when you peed in his locker . . . he say he will kill you. How stop him? So I make promise . . ."

S suddenly stopped signing. Her hands vibrated with the words she was afraid to express.

"Promise what?"

"I promise: if he and Deaf Devils not kill you, then I will meet Crazy Charles behind gym and let him kiss me again. He agree. So I go. He kiss long time. Disgusting. Other kids saw and laugh. I tell Crazy Charles, *Finish, finish. No more!* He say, *Okay, okay*. He agree, from then on, we will just friends, no more kissing, and will never hurt you again. Promise finish."

S started to cry again, and you wanted to cry too. Not because Crazy Charles kissed S, but because your diminishing eyesight was the reason S had to both fight for you and kiss Crazy Charles. She was able to protect you, but could you protect her?

"Okay, okay," you told S. "Don't cry. Okay. Now we equal. I kiss and touch Marla. You kiss and touch Crazy Charles. Finish. Finish. Never again."

"But you kiss and touch Marla because you want her, not because protect."

"Yes. Sorry, sorry. I very wrong. Sorry. Both promise no more kissing other people, okay? But I can fight for myself, okay? No more fight for me, okay? Promise?"

"Promise," S signed, her hands soggy with tears.

Then you lay in each other's arms for a long time, until all the fear of losing each other evaporated from your entwined bodies. Despite causing each other so much pain, you still were able to forgive and suddenly that precious thing you thought you had lost you found more deeply.

Your fingers caressed S's face, feeling the salty stickiness of S's tears in the corner of her eyelashes. You spelled the words *I love you* slowly onto her chest. Then S kissed you hard on the mouth before sliding down and blowing tickle vibrations into the skin of your belly. Then, with gentle teeth tugs, she pulled the new little hairs on your chest. This made you laugh even though it hurt. S quickly pressed her fingers against your lips, silencing you.

"Shh!" she signed. "Dorm boss have special powerful ears—like giant hearing aids. Shh. Must quiet like caterpillar."

"Okay, okay. I will quiet like caterpillar."

Both of you made the sign for *caterpillar* then let your caterpillars wrestle each other, then S's caterpillar finger walked across your chest and down to your belly. Then S made her caterpillar turn into a butterfly and the butterfly flew all around your body and landed on your nose, before slowly pulling her hands from your body.

"Please continue talking to me," you begged. "Talk to me forever until I will sleep."

So S, her soft hands in yours, recounted more about what happened with Marla, but then you laughed, thinking how brave S was to confront someone almost twice her size, like David and Goliath. And then S told you stories about growing up in Queens, New York, and about how much she loved her mother and her aunties, and how she enjoyed playing soccer and making a sweet dessert called coconut ladoo for a holiday called Diwali. You asked S more questions, but you only half listened. Really you just wanted to feel S's fingers making word-birds on your body. Then, snuggling under the covers, S nuzzled her nose into your fuzzy armpits, making you beg her to stop because you were laughing too hard. Quieter, S blew breath onto your eyelashes like they were the white fluffy seeds of dandelions. Then a kiss on the lips, a tumble-around with the tongue, more cuddles, twisting your body into knots, more kisses until your mouths hurt. Instead of satisfying you, each kiss only made you both hungrier. For the first time S pulled your hand inside her pajama bottoms and down to that mysterious, sinful part of her body. Your fingers pressed into the soft warm wetness, while S caressed that aching part of you straining to be free. Seconds later, hands and feet, both yours and hers, pushed pajama bottoms around ankles like soft cotton shackles. Smells of spit, piss, blood, and skin all intermingled in your nose. You knew the sin you were about to commit could not be stopped. One breath. Two breaths. Three breaths.

"Please," S begged into your hand, grinding her pelvis against you. "Want now. Please."

"No! Stop! Maybe sin. Maybe Jehovah God angry. Maybe very, very wrong."

S held your hands to quiet them, and then the same soft warm fingers signed, "Shh. Shh. Not sin. We love each other. Not sin."

In the blind darkness you saw a thousand red stars coming over the horizon, but you couldn't stop. You pushed Jehovah God from your mind. *Not here, not now. No red stars.* Your tongues went so deep into each other's mouths you became one inseparable thing, two halves of chewing gum crushed between teeth. *Still not close enough. Never enough.* You wanted to be inside. You needed to be inside. S's naked legs lifted around your waist. Your hips, hypnotized by the demon, rubbed your hardness against S's soft wet opening. You felt yourself leak, and worried you had already sticky-peed on S, but S wouldn't let you pull away. Instead, S guided you inside her. Your hearts beat together, both your bodies shook. Your cheek trembled with the vibration coming from S's lungs and throat. You moved farther inside. Cool tears slipped down the side of your face. *S's tears? Why is S crying?* You started to pull out, but S wouldn't allow it. You felt the heat and liquid of S's insides grip you as you began to thrust hard, then harder. It. Felt. So. Good. You could not control yourself any longer. One more thrust, and your body convulsed into a wave of shivers as a stream of sticky pee flooded deep inside. Breathing in unison. One breath, two breaths, three breaths.

You both lay together for a long time with your sweaty, sticky bodies clinging to each other. Jehovah God tried to creep back into your head, but you wouldn't let Him. Not at that moment. There was only enough room for you and S. Then, with her nose pressed into your cheek, you could feel S's tiny sleepy snores blow bubbles into the remains of her tears.

◊ ◊ ◊

In the morning, after you came back from your shower, the dorm boss was waiting for you in your room.

"There's blood on your sheets," the dorm boss signed. "Did you cut yourself?"

Blood? Your stomach tightened, and your face flushed hot. Without warning, the dorm boss yanked the towel from your waist and examined your naked grown-up body as if you were a little child.

"I can't see anything," she signed.

Where could the blood have come from? You were too worried to even be embarrassed that the dorm boss was still looking at your nakedness. Suddenly, you remembered S's tears, and your hungry embrace. *I did hurt her! Why didn't she say anything?* You lied to the dorm boss about forgetting you had a nosebleed the previous night. She told you to gather your sheets and take them to the laundry room. When she had gone, you took out your magnifying glass and searched the sheets until you located the dark red-brown patch of S's blood. You pressed your nose into the stain and breathed in the smell of blood, sticky pee, spit, sweat, and human. It was hard to distinguish what was S and what was you. You pulled the bloody sheets up against your body and rubbed them onto your chest, arms, face, and hair. S loved you so much that she spilled her blood for you. You wanted it with you forever.

22

THE GIVEBACK

It was Friday morning when my phone rang at 6 a.m. I immediately recognized the familiar rasp on the other end. It was Ange from the agency.

"Hey there, Cy! How's it going?"

"Jesus, Ange, why are you calling this early? Why's your number blocked?"

"Sorry. Calling from my weekend house in Hudson. I just got a call for an emergency Tactile interpreting gig in Rochester at noon today. Important conference. The scheduled terp—a real fuck-twat—called out last-minute. Pays seventy per hour emergency rate. Will be a total of sixteen hours over the weekend and includes transportation. We're talking at least sixteen hundred. I need an answer now."

Ugh, I thought, and remembered how much I could use the money for my move to Philly in September. Still, something else was tugging at me.

"Sorry, Ange. You know I have my ongoing gig with Arlo until noon today."

"Of course. That's the thing. By some miracle I found someone who will cover for you. It's just one day, so no one will mind you're gone."

"Jesus. Thanks, Ange," I said, annoyed that she thought Arlo wouldn't care. "But you know how it is, we've already developed certain class-specific signs the new person wouldn't know. Let the sub you've found do it."

"Unfortunately, this terp won't do platform work. Besides, you're my best. Please, Cy, I really need you to do this for me. They are desperate. Mindy-who-used-to-live-here called me. She'd be your team. You know how good she is. *And* she requested you."

"Mindy Ames asked for me specifically?"

A warm flush filled my chest. Having *the* Mindy Ames, celebrity interpreter, request me was a big deal.

"Yes! She remembered you. I told her you've been working with Arlo and doing Tactile now, and she got really excited. She said you'd be teamed with two of the East Coast's best Tactile interpreters and would learn a ton. The DeafBlind client is a PhD and heads the Laura Bridgman Center. Remember how you didn't even want to do this Tactile job, and now you're rocking it? Think how you could use this experience to do a better job with Arlo!"

Ange knows me well. I've always been the sort of interpreter who hates doing a half-assed job. To actually watch some top-rated Tactile interpreters in action and work with another DeafBlind client—someone professional—was a huge learning opportunity for me. But then I imagined Arlo meeting the substitute terp. What if it was some hot young woman who Arlo found attractive? Or some straight Jehovah's Witness guy who Arlo related to way more than me? I wanted the money and I wanted the experience, but I knew that if Arlo liked the new person, Molly would try to persuade Arlo to replace me. It was a completely irrational fear, but it was bugging me nonetheless.

"I'm gonna pass, Ange. I'm just not sure it's the right thing to do."

"Look, Cy, I know you feel guilty leaving the kid with some stranger. But remember, Molly's there, and this is a great opportunity for everybody."

Ange was partially right. What she missed was that I was also being paranoid and selfish. I was acting like I owned the job—a job I hadn't even wanted in the first place. I told myself: *You should want Arlo to have the best interpreter. You should also want to be the best interpreter for Arlo. And you need the money!* And if interpreting had taught me anything, it's that no gig was permanent. I would not be working with Arlo forever. It was best not to hold on too tight.

"Ange," I said into the phone, my voice almost like a pleading child's. "You promise you found someone good to sub for me? And not fucking Justin?"

"Cy, babe, you know confidentiality prevents me from saying who is doing the job, but I swear to friggin' G-O-D I found someone that will do just fine for one goddamned day!"

Before I could say anything more, Ange jumped in with, "Great! I'll email the deets. Now get your ass in gear!"

◊ ◊ ◊

After hitting the shower, I threw my interpreter essentials in my travel bag: two black shirts, black pants, black jacket, black tie. The contents of my suitcase looked like I was a funeral director. Within a short time I was on I-90 headed north, and five hours later I saw the top of the Xerox Tower rising in the distance.

I have a love-hate relationship with Rochester, having had both my favorite moments and the worst moments of my life take place there. The best moment was when I met and fell in love with Bruno twenty years ago. The worst moments? They include one or two fights with him on the corner of University and Beacon, then being dumped by him via pay phone at the Bachelor Forum bar while I was drunk and eating a bag of cheese puffs. My pleading tears laced with greasy orange dust pouring down my chin. And then there was . . . I felt my stomach tighten, and that familiar cloudy feeling inside my head returned. My mind flashed to things I didn't actually see but only imagined for years: Bruno lying in his hospital bed, his thin body unrecognizable, his poor mother sitting in that chair . . .

Nope. No time to go there. Not today. It was stupid to think about the past when I needed to get all my mental energy on the job. *And the fact is you weren't even lovers with Bruno when all that happened. You weren't even talking. You're romanticizing a past that didn't really exist.*

I suddenly remembered what Arlo had said about the sublime and about loving someone and losing them. What must it be like to have such a beautiful feeling toward loss?

I began to romanticize what Arlo felt when he thought about his old friends at the Rose Garden School. I knew something hugely important happened for him there. *Love? It had to be love.* I wished I could just get a direct answer. *What happened, my friend? What happened at that school?*

Then I started worrying about how things had gone in the classroom. Was the sub good enough? Did everything go smoothly? At a stoplight on East Main Street I checked my cell phone to see if Molly or Ange had sent me any urgent texts. Nothing.

"Snap out of it," I yelled at myself. "Arlo Dilly survived twenty-three years without you. Now get it together so you can focus. You've got a show to do!"

23

ROMEO AND JULIET

As you lie in bed, the Blue Devil God passes across your brain. It has been a long time since he visited you, but your recent thoughts about S have caused him to awaken. You pray to Jehovah God to remove the demon from your mind. But when Jehovah God finally erases the Blue Devil God, He replaces him with the remaining pieces of S's face that had been etched into your brain: the small nose; the beautiful dark skin; the hair, thick and black like a horse's mane; her dark wet eyes.

Big Head Lawrence, with his better vision, once said that S had eyes that were larger than other people's. Martin thought larger eyes meant that S's eyesight was keener than normal. Big Head Lawrence told you S was also the most beautiful and strongest girl in school. You didn't need to be told. All that was unimportant compared to the beauty of S's hands and brain. For hours after you made love, S's perfect fingers would stroke your face and tell you more stories of growing up in New York City. Or how she went to India when she was eleven for her grandmother's funeral, and how her aunties and uncles stood around gossiping, poking the fire, discussing how to make the body burn faster. After her grandmother's body had become ashes, the whole family went to a big room and ate delicious foods, including desserts that filled an entire table. S promised that when you lived together someday, she would cook something called

gulab jamun and jalebi. Then S told of all the other gods her family wor-
shiped, including an elephant-faced god, and that Blue God who could
be both mean and kind. (That god that still haunts you as the Blue Devil
God.)

When S spoke of her gods you grew silent for a long time.

"What what?" she asked. "You angry, why?"

"You must become Christian JW!" you yelled. "If you not believe in
Jesus, Jehovah God . . . what will happen? Future, in heaven, we will not
together! Elephant God and Blue God evil! If you continue worshiping
them, you will die and disappear forever!"

After S calmed you down, she promised to consider believing in Jesus
and Jehovah God but only if she could still worship both the elephant-faced
god and the Blue God as well.

"Lord Krishna and Ganesh will accept your god. They accept all
gods."

You didn't talk about it after that. You just thought to yourself, *Later,
later you will convince her. Later you will save S's soul.*

It was late September of your senior year when you felt the footsteps
of the dorm boss that one night and S had to drop down on the side of the
bed and hide underneath until the coast was clear.

"Was someone else in your room last night?" the dorm boss asked you
the next day.

After that, you decided you needed to be more careful. Martin told
you about a private place called the Secret Forest. It wasn't really a forest. It was the long thick row of forsythia bushes that formed a tunnel of
branches along the back wall of Forsythia House—the only building at
the Rose Garden School that actually had the plants for which the dorm
was named. Inside the Secret Forest, generations of Deaf students had dug
holes in the dirt, which they covered with old salvaged plywood. These
small subterranean cubbyholes were where the students could smoke cig-

arettes, cut class, play sex games, and do other sinful things away from the eyes of adults.

Martin, who had taken other boys back there, told you that you could only go to the Secret Forest at night to be safe.

"Last week, during daytime, Deaf Devils catch kids doing sex in Secret Forest and beat them. Kids don't tell about beating . . . Why? Because Crazy Charles will tell Principal about secret, dirty sex and then send kids to Dogwood. But nighttime you and S will be okay. Mean Deaf boys too afraid of ghost Angry John to look in holes at night."

Big Head Lawrence had never gone into the Secret Forest because it wasn't safe, and also because no one wanted to play with him in that way. Big Head Lawrence pretended he didn't care, but you knew he did. You told him that someday he would meet a girl who didn't mind about his head, because Big Head Lawrence had a good strong body, was excellent in math, and had handsome hands that said smart and funny things.

"Girls do not do sex with Big Head Lawrence because mean girls say he ugly," S told you later. "Not fair some boys pretty like you, and some ugly like Big Head Lawrence."

You wanted to tell S about how well you understood the unfairness of life. Crazy Charles picking on weaker students was not fair. Sighted-hearing people withholding information was not fair. Having to live with Brother Birch and his wife was not fair. Your mother dying was not fair. Going blind was not fair. It was also unfair that Jehovah God would send a person you loved to eternal death just because of what they believed or didn't believe. This felt like the most unfair thing of all at that moment. But you just shook your head sadly and agreed with S because even thinking about all that made your head hurt.

Your mind jumps.

The last whole day you spent with S:

It was a Saturday? Sunday? You were lying with S under a pile of dried leaves like you used to when you were a child. The shimmering sunlight and S's warm body made the chill bearable. Twigs and leaves tickled you. You smelled fires burning, earth, and S's smooth dark skin. You and S pressed your bodies closer, melting together like two unwrapped candy bars left in your pocket on a hot day. Where did S's body begin? Where did yours end? Your tongue tasted S's spit and played with her rubbery ears and soft sweet nipples, which you kissed. Your hand slipped into S's jeans and made her body quiver. You lifted your fingers to your nose and mouth. You wanted S's scent and taste inside you, the way you put yourself inside S.

"I want hold your hand in cafeteria," you told S. "Why you not let me?"

"Deaf always gossip," she explained. "Suppose Crazy Charles tells family and his family tell my family? Then I would be in big trouble, and my auntie would tell school to send me to Dogwood. And we would never see each other again."

You knew S was right. It would be a disaster if Brother Birch or Molly found out. You had already committed unforgivable sins with S. Red star sins. Brother Birch, being an elder at the Kingdom Hall, might shun you. Where would you live in the summertime? Who would help you when you graduated? No, neither S's family nor yours could know you were together. It was like that story you had learned about in English class called *Romeo and Juliet*. Molly had left out some of the best parts, but Big Head Lawrence told you the whole story later, with lots of good description. *Romeo and Juliet* was a story about a boy and girl who fell in love, but they were from families that hated each other. They got married anyway and had sex. But then when they planned to run away together they made very stupid mistakes. The girl pretended she was dead until the boy got back but forgot to tell the boy she was faking. The boy thought the girl was really dead and got so sad that he killed himself. Then the girl woke up and saw the boy was really dead, so she killed herself. It was the saddest story you ever heard. Would you and S end up like Romeo and Juliet? Just like them, your families would hate each other. That was why you and S had to be sneaky quiet in the Secret Forest and make sure you never ended up killing yourselves.

"Important," S signed. "Always communicate with each other—must! No lies. No secrets. Agree?"

"Agree."

24

RAINSTORM

It has been a very frustrating Friday. Cyril didn't show up at your English Comp class today because he had to take an emergency job in Rochester. You are left with Molly and a substitute interpreter named Justin. When Justin spells his name in your hand, he fumbles nervously, and you can already tell he has never done Tactile ASL before and isn't even a good signer. Molly asks Justin why no one told him that he was supposed to wear a solid black shirt, instead of the light-colored shirt that is close to his skin tone. She explains to him that it will be hard for you to locate his hands without the contrast in color.

You are very very annoyed but try not to show it.

When it's Justin's turn to interpret, his hands are shaking, and he pulls them away from you every chance he gets. Despite Molly's instruction, he signs so big that he drags your hands around like it's a Tactile rodeo. Your head aches. Your arms ache. When the professor asks you a question, you can't answer since you haven't understood anything Justin has interpreted.

Molly finally shoves Justin out of the way and takes over.

"So, Mr. Dilly," the professor repeats, angrily. "I asked, have you made any progress with your next assignment?"

You tell the professor that you haven't started the assignment. This is a lie, because you have started it. You tell the professor that you will get it to her by next week. This is also a lie. You will never turn in the assignment. Red star.

When the professor returns to talking to the whole class, Molly quickly asks you what assignment the professor is talking about. You lie to her too. Lying has become very easy.

"Like last assignment. Read poem. Respond. Same."

Luckily, Molly is so bothered by Justin's bad interpreting that she doesn't ask more questions. To make it less awful for you, Molly changes the amount of time they take turns interpreting. Molly goes for twenty minutes, and then lets Justin interpret for just five minutes to give Molly a break. Despite your previous anger at Molly's betrayal of Cyril, you are grateful to her. Molly has always been there for you in times like this. Now you are mad at Cyril. Besides prying into your personal business without sharing anything of himself, he was very wrong to take another job and leave you alone at the hands of an incompetent interpreter.

At the end of the class, Justin runs out of the room without even saying goodbye.

Good.

"I'm sorry," Molly says. "I promise he won't be back. I'll let the agency know. I can't believe Cyril canceled at the last minute like this. For what? To take another job. It's completely irresponsible and selfish. I'm sorry. I shouldn't say anything."

You thank Molly for saving you and jumping in to interpret for you. Molly is right. Cyril is irresponsible and selfish. You can tell Molly's hands are aching. When you were younger, she once had to wear a brace on her wrist and go to physical therapy because she hurt herself interpreting for you. Working with the DeafBlind is harder on an interpreter's body because of pressure from the weight of a DeafBlind person's hands. Now you feel guilty times three. Guilty from maybe hurting Molly, and guilty from maybe getting Cyril into more trouble, and guilty for promising the professor that you would turn something in that you have no intention of turning in, but still writing something you were not supposed to write, which is also betraying Jehovah God and Brother Birch . . . so that's times four . . . or five?

Red star. Red star. Red star. Red star. Red star.

"I'm going to rest," Molly says. "Would you like me to take you to the Able-Ride stop?"

You tell Molly there is no need, you have asked for a later pickup so you can work on your homework in the library. This is another lie. Before Molly leaves, she gives you one of her hesitant, bony hugs and says, "You know I only told your uncle what I know about Cyril because I care about you, right? You are a very important person to me, and I don't want to see you hurt again."

The words that make up Molly's statement seem loving and simple, but they are not. Sometimes words are like old sticky candy left in your pocket. They have so many things stuck to them, like old stories and lint, that they have a different taste from the one they are supposed to have. But you don't say that. You say, "I understand. See you tomorrow."

A little while later you are sitting alone in the library staring at the computer screen. Even though you are supposed to be working on your personal essay that you have no intention of turning in, that's not the real reason you have come to the library today. You came to try to find your old friends Martin and Big Head Lawrence on the internet. You couldn't do this at home, since it's a sin and Brother Birch might tell you that it's the Devil working in your heart. And maybe it is. But when Cyril mentioned finding friends on the internet, it made you curious. Before Jehovah God can come into your heart, you quickly type the word M-A-R-T-I-N and the word DeafBlind into the Google search box and hit Enter.

There are a billion Martins, and even with the words DeafBlind or Deaf-Blind or deaf and blind, there are still too many to read. So you try L-A-W-R-E-N-C-E, which is hard to spell. Then you type big and head. Press Enter. Nothing comes up with the name Big Head Lawrence, or at least not all the words together right next to each other.

But with the internet, even when you don't find what you are looking for, you discover other interesting things. You learn that there are many famous people and things named Lawrence. For example, Lawrence of Arabia is really someone named T. E. Lawrence who was a famous Englishman with many skills, including writing and *diplomacy* (a word you look up), who helped fight the Ottomans—you learn these are people from Turkey but a long time ago—during World War I. Lawrence of Arabia, despite doing all these amazing things, died after a motorcycle crash back home in England. There is also a place called Lawrence, Kansas, which is the sixth-largest city in the state of Kansas and has a population of 100,205 people, making it over three times the size of Poughkeepsie, but a lot smaller than Manhattan. The writers Langston Hughes and William S. Burroughs spent some time in Lawrence, Kansas. There is also a famous writer named D. H. Lawrence who wrote so many books you can't count, and whose books were banned for many years in the United States, including one called *Lady Chatterley's Lover*, which was considered *obscene* (another new word!). You write the name of this book down to see if it's available to read at a later date. You wish you could tell Big Head Lawrence how many amazing things are associated with his name. Then you type in the name *Martin* again, and that leads somewhere which leads somewhere which leads somewhere until suddenly . . .

It's 4:50 p.m., twenty minutes past the time you were supposed to meet your Able-Ride driver, and you panic. You gather your things: your laptop, your SBC, your notepad, your cane, stuffing them away willy-nilly, and you rush out of the library with Snap at your side. You walk as fast as possible through the halls to the elevator and down to the front of the building. Then Snap has to pee. *Hurry up, Snap!* The air feels strange, heavy, moist. The wind is beginning to blow stronger. You smell a thunderstorm coming. You better hurry or you may get stuck in it. You trip over a curb since you aren't paying attention and fall down. Snap licks your face to make sure you're okay. You get up and scratch her head. Then you rush to the pickup spot and check your watch. It's 5 p.m.

The Able-Ride van has left.

This is bad. Really bad. You don't have any Wi-Fi on your laptop to contact the van. Worse, if it starts to rain, all your technology equipment could be ruined. You will have to go all the way back to the library to use the Wi-Fi, but the library closes at five in the summer, so there won't be time to go back to the library. But if you go back, you won't get caught in the rain. But what if the ride comes back for you while you are gone? That happened once and you got in trouble. Brother Birch said if you miss rides too many times, they will stop coming. So you stay where you are, but you are feeling very frustrated, because you are hungry and Snap is hungry, and now you are very, very angry because it isn't fair that you don't have an iPhone on which you can contact the ride service or your uncle or someone to help you. If someone was there, you could ask them to call for you. You take out one of your laminated assistance cards and hold it up in front of you. The card says:

PLEASE HELP ME! I AM DEAFBLIND!

You hold the card up in front of your chest, then next to your ear so people can see it from the front and back. Then you also wave your hand and say "Hey" in all directions, hoping someone is there, but no one is there. You use your voice and shout:

"Hello! Hello! I need help!"

Someone once told you that when you yell you sound like a seal barking, but it's all you can do at the moment.

You wait.

Nothing.

The wind gets stronger. You feel a drop of rain.

So you sit on the bench with your laminated HELP card and wait some more. No driver. The raindrops increase. One hits your cheek. One hits your forehead. Your shoulder. You hide your backpack under the bench, hoping it will protect it from the rain. Then you get up and you are pacing and angry. Snap tries to calm you by licking your hand with her big, wet tongue. But it doesn't help because the storm clouds have made the sky dark, and now you can't see anything. The rain begins to fall in earnest now. The panic gets worse. Then you do something stupid. You take your cane and wallet out of your back pocket and place them on the bench next to you with the intention of returning them to your backpack safe and dry under the bench. But because you didn't put things back in their right place you get distracted and start angrily rearranging things to their proper place. When you reach for your wallet and cane they are no longer on the bench next to you. They must have fallen off or been stolen. You can't go around without your cane. You are no one without your wallet and ID. You crawl on the wet ground and swing your arms, searching for your precious things. You're breathing really fast, and your heart is pounding. You ask Snap to help you find your lost things, but Snap doesn't understand, and keeps trying to get you to calm yourself, but you can't be calm because you still can't find your cane and wallet. And you know Brother Birch and Mrs. Brother Birch are doing mission work at the mall tonight, so they will have no idea you need help. They would have left your peanut butter and grape jelly sandwich in the refrigerator. But you can't eat it because you are left alone on the street, without a ride, without a cane, without a wallet, money, ID, and you are getting soaked and maybe all your equipment in your backpack is getting wet and being destroyed. This isn't fair. It's just not fair. You sit on your ass on the street, hug your legs, and scream.

"Hello! Hello! I need help!"

Snap, soaking wet, squeezes her body next to you, as the rain gushes down.

After fifteen minutes you are both shivering. Your arms have grown too tired to hold up the laminated HELP card any longer. You hug your wet old dog who is now licking your face and you wonder if you and Snap are going to die. Your dark brain imagines an alternate communication card: I AM DEAFBLIND AND MISSED MY ABLE-RIDE. IF YOU FIND OUR DEAD BODIES PLEASE DELIVER THEM TO THIS ADDRESS . . .

Then Snap gets up and wags her entire body like she's happy. Someone is approaching. Narrow fingers tap your back. They are a woman's hands, but you are not sure which woman. Then the wet fingers, inexperienced at sign language, press the letters H-A-N-N-E into your palm.

You smile, because someone has come to your rescue, but at the same time you are both cautious and embarrassed. This is Hanne after all, the possible sorceress, who has the ability to yank secrets from your heart like an open box of Kleenex. Hanne, the one you are forbidden to see.

Before you can find a reason to object, Hanne grabs your backpack and guides you and Snap to her car. She puts Snap in the back seat and you in the front. You are shivering harder than you were before, and Hanne hands you an old sweatshirt of hers and you dry your face and hands. Then she drives the car for ten minutes until she parks. Then Hanne leads you and Snap into the café where she works. Only you can tell the place is closed because it's completely dark when she first brings you inside and sits you at a table. You pull out your SBC and luckily it still works, and you ask Hanne why she was at the college in the first place. She types that she had just finished taking a class called Nursing Science IV and was walking to her car when she saw you. You sense that you are totally alone with her in the café and this makes you panic. Your hands still shaking, you type to her:

"Sorry. I NOT ALLOW be alone and talk at you. Can get someone HELP? I loss CANE and wallet. I wait outside."

After a moment Hanne types back:

"You will drown outside! We'll just stay here until the rain calms down. Then I'll take you right home. Don't think of me as a woman. Think of me as just a friend, okay? And I think your family will understand this is an emergency."

You sit there frozen with your hands on the SBC, waiting for Jehovah God to inspire you for your next right move. Your body is shivering. After several seconds you feel the bumps on the display come alive. Hanne is typing again.

"I'm gonna go back and look for your things," she types. **"Just wait here and stay warm. Here are paper towels so you can dry your dog."**

Then Hanne leaves you alone in the empty coffee shop with the roll of paper towels. You dry Snap as best you can. Her wet fur stinks. With the remaining paper towels you dab at your soaking wet clothes, but it doesn't help. Then thunder makes the room rumble. Now you, Snap, and the room are all shivering for different reasons.

You pray to Jehovah God, but as you pray a blurry image appears in your mind. It's her photograph, the one that you held in your pocket for so long. Then another face appears. This one is blue. It's S's god. The Blue God.

25

TABITHA

The conference center was massive, but within a few minutes I was able to find the hall and locate Mindy, my old colleague from Poughkeepsie, along with a whole gaggle of other interpreters. Interpreters are never hard to spot in a room thanks to their unflashy, solid-colored, skin-contrasting clothes, their usually obtrusive stance at the front of a room, and their quintessential *interpreter faces,* which say: Yes, *you see us in this space, but we reside in a liminal world between you and the reason you are here, so don't ask us questions.*

Mindy looked different from when we worked together years ago. She had gone full-on glamour butch with short hair and a tailored black suit. She greeted me with a hug and then introduced me to the two other interpreters who were part of the consumer's regular team. By the way they dressed and their just-bored-enough demeanor, it was easy to tell they both came from New York City. There was Liz, an olive-skinned woman in her late twenties with long dyed-blond hair. She was a Certified Deaf Interpreter (CDI), which means she's Deaf herself and excels at working with atypical language users (Deaf folks who don't use standard ASL or might be foreign born and have limited language) as well as the DeafBlind. I always felt like I hit paydirt when I got teamed with a good CDI, since I'd get to see how a native signer would make a difficult concept breathtakingly clear.

The other interpreter was Zach, a hearing guy in his midthirties who wore edgy earlobe plugs and had a military buzz cut, giving him a bit of a covert leather-man look. Zach was kind of hot and instantly flirty with me, which I might have reciprocated if I weren't so nervous. I soon found out that the four of us would be responsible for interpreting only for our consumer, who was the main speaker. A second team of interpreters, two hearing and two CDIs, would be responsible for voicing/ASL interpreting for the Deaf and hearing audience Q and A. Add to all of us a whole boat-load of Tactile ASL interpreters and SSPs who would be working with any DeafBlind folks sitting in the audience. Then there were the captioners who would make sure those audience members who didn't hear and didn't know sign language could read along. *This is real access,* I thought. *Why can't it always be like this?*

"So, our boss, Tabitha, will present for about thirty minutes," Mindy explained in ASL. (If you're a sign language user in a Deaf space it's expected that you will always be signing.) "You'll love her. Brilliant and super easy to understand. You and I will take turns interpreting TSL and voicing onstage. Meanwhile Zach and Liz here will be doing Haptics stuff on Tabitha's back. Even though she lost the bulk of her vision just last year, she's very Protactile, so be aware."

Haptics? Protactile? I had no idea what Mindy was talking about, but I was too nervous about working with big-city interpreters and didn't want to seem stupid, so I just nodded.

"You don't know what Protactile and Haptics are, do you?" Mindy asked, smiling. "Relax, we're here to help."

"I don't exactly have a poker face, do I?"

"Cy, you've always had the face of a human mood ring. Which is why Deaf folks love you. Don't worry. You'll dig Protactile and Haptics. I promise."

Mindy briefly went over how Haptics (developed by hearing researchers in Norway) and Protactile (developed by the DeafBlind community in Seattle) are two very different things that Tabitha would not only be lecturing about but also employing during her talk. Haptics is not a language, but more like a set of touch signals used in addition to Tactile ASL as a way to get more environmental cues and information to the DeafBlind.

"Now Protactile, hmm, how to explain this quickly and concisely?" Mindy asked herself, signaling the complexity of the subject. "Fact is: I can't. Fundamentally, Protactile is a new language that has developed organically between DeafBlind speakers in Seattle and elsewhere. Where ASL depends on visual space, Protactile works with the tactile space, using both bodies to form words and communication. Instead of being a two-handed language, Protactile depends on four hands."

Mindy went on to explain how Protactile isn't only a language but an entire DeafBlind way of life, which includes politics, philosophy, attitudes, and ways of engagement. One tenet is that the DeafBlind and their interlocutors are *always* touching each other—whether they are the signer or the listener. *Constant touch*, Mindy called it. This allows the DeafBlind to become immersed in the other person's physical presence as well as their emotions, the environment, and getting to experience those vital little bits of information sighted-hearing people take for granted: smiles, frowns, looks of confusion, head nods, and "mmm-hmms" that signal to the speaker that understanding is happening. This is called backchanneling.

"Interesting, right?" Mindy asked. "Now notice what you just did right there. You bit your lower lip and nodded. Imagine speaking or signing to someone and not getting any of that. You don't know if your listener understands, cares, or even walked out of the room, leaving you to talk to the air. That's a pretty big deal."

I started thinking about how often Arlo would check in and ask if I was still there. Or all the times I would feel a need to shove my hands into his to sign "I understand," which would disrupt his flow and sometimes make him lose his train of thought. So Mindy showed me how to use the flat of the hand gently tapping on the arm or leg of a DeafBlind person, which is the equivalent of a nod or saying "mmm-hmm," while the other person is speaking, and how a closed fist tapping means *yes*.

"Why didn't my team or my DeafBlind client tell me about this?" I asked, already in awe at the possibilities Arlo, Molly, and I had been missing.

"Are they involved in the DeafBlind community?" she asked.

"Not at all. Not even really the Deaf community anymore," I signed.

"They probably just don't know about it. You know how this community works. It's all about access. This stuff is relatively new. And while the Protactile language and way of life are becoming more widely known, lots of DeafBlind people are left out of the loop. That's why Tabitha is doing today's talk."

Mindy emphasized that all terps working with the DeafBlind needed to learn about Protactile and Haptics in order to provide the DeafBlind consumers with options. I was hungry to know more. One of the best parts of being an interpreter is constantly learning new things. Not that there's much choice since the ways of working, modalities of communication, and even the signs themselves are constantly evolving.

"So what's Haptics, then?" I asked.

"That's completely different," Mindy said. "And let me warn you, a lot of Protactile adherents hate it, feeling it's yet another thing the hearing world is forcing on them. But Tabitha uses both. Haptics is a way for the interpreter to give the DeafBlind real-time information like, in Tabitha's case, showing her the audience's reaction, expressing laughter, sorrow, excitement, movement, and so much more. It's almost like the difference between reading just the dialogue of a screenplay and actually seeing the movie—in IMAX 5-D!"

Zach, who had been listening, smiled and jumped in.

"First time working with the DeafBlind, huh?"

"No," I signed defensively. "Okay, yeah. Kind of. I did it once before . . . really badly. But now I'm working a lot with one DeafBlind guy in particular. A twenty-three-year-old taking a college writing class. Down in Poughkeepsie."

Zach grimaced as if I had said I lived in a ditch. Mindy punched him in the arm.

"Don't be a dick, Zach," she growled.

"Sorry," Zach signed, earnestly apologizing. "I'm a city boy. How do you like working with the DeafBlind?"

"To be honest," I signed, "I freaked out at first. I didn't think I could do it. But now I guess I kind of love it. The client is really amazing. I mean, he comprehends way more than I thought possible. It's mind-blowing."

Mindy and Zach nodded, which immediately made me think of how a DeafBlind person might miss out on that information without the Protactile arm tap.

"Looks like we have a convert," Zach signed.

"Always happens," Mindy added. "The DeafBlind are fucking incredible people. Well, not all, but most of the DB peeps we work with are off-the-charts brilliant. Tabitha, of course, is in a realm all by herself. Get ready to be dazzled. Speaking of which . . ."

Mindy pointed across the room to an attractive woman with wavy long blond hair holding a white cane and being led by a swarthy "hot daddy" type, who turned out to be her sighted-hearing husband. When Tabitha reached the stage, I saw her pull out a load of top-level, brand-new equipment, including a communication device that looked generations newer than Arlo's old SBC. She also had something that looked like a small label-making machine that she attached to her iPhone. It allowed any words that appeared on the phone's screen to be instantly translated into braille.

"My client back home doesn't have any of that equipment," I signed with frustration. "Except some really old-looking SBC. He doesn't even have a cell phone."

Zach and Mindy looked at each other and shook their heads.

"No iPhone? Seriously?" Mindy asked. "Can he read and write?"

"Yeah," I signed.

Liz, the CDI who had been watching our signed conversation from a few yards away, suddenly walked over.

"What the fuck?" Liz signed and spoke at the same time. "Your consumer definitely should have an iPhone and a braille reader. How the fuck does he communicate when he's out of range of a computer?"

I suddenly felt ganged up on, like they were blaming me for Arlo not having the newest and best equipment.

"Actually, I just started working with him in June," I signed. "Is it possible the case manager is just really clueless?"

Mindy and Zach shook their heads, puzzled, while Liz looked outraged.

"Bullshit," Liz signed. "In my opinion somebody in Poughkeepsie is either lazy as fuck or they just don't want your client to have access for some reason."

"Well," Mindy signed, trying to move the conversation back to the task at hand, and to a more positive note, "I guess this is the reason Tabitha's going around the country doing these talks. And with that, the show is about to start. Let's go meet Tabitha and get set up. Oh, heads up, Tabitha will want you to do Protactile with her."

"Wait . . . what?" My stomach heaved with a wave of nerves. "I can't, I barely know—"

"Relax," Mindy signed. "You're aren't expected to know Protactile for the presentation. Just when you talk to her privately. Follow her lead."

My heart was pounding as we introduced ourselves. Tabitha's name-sign was the sign for *shiny* but made from the corner of her crystalline blue eyes, which were slightly askew like Arlo's. She was even more beautiful up close. When Tabitha signed to me she insisted that instead of me just using my eyes to watch her as I did with any Deaf or DeafBlind person, I was to keep my hands on hers while she signed, as if I were Deaf-Blind as well. Tabitha sensed my nervousness and told me I was doing great, promising not to bite "yet," and broke out in a charming, boisterous laugh that instantly put me at ease. Then Tabitha went over the parameters of how she liked her interpreters to work and used my chest as the physical representation of the stage. Suddenly, I too was experiencing the back-channeling, the nodding fist on my chest, the tapping hand, the grabbing laughter on my upper arm. At certain moments she used my forearm or hand as the base for a few of her signs the Protactile way. It was incredible, but the close proximity and constant touch made it harder to see what she was signing, so I had to partially depend on feeling to clarify the words.

"You will get it. Don't worry. Just watch my regulars," Tabitha signed, winking. "Wow! Those three: champs!"

Five minutes later the lecture began. Liz and I sat on chairs to the side of the stage while Zach and Mindy took the first twenty-minute turn. I couldn't take my eyes off them. Mindy was definitely one of the best interpreters I'd ever seen—a hundred times better than I was—and Zach was working at Tabitha's back like a puppeteer on amphetamines. All three together looked like they were performing some outrageous modern dance. Zach's hands drew squares, circles, and lines. His fingers swished up and across her shoulder blades. I understood that he was describing the room, the people asking questions, their facial expressions and location in the room. Tabitha was totally engaged in the question-and-answer session, clearly knowing where the person asking the question was standing. Her answers and reactions were a perfect fit to the mood of the audience. Mindy was incredible, and I noticed how for certain signs that the terp would normally put on their own body, Mindy was using Tabitha's body to make the sign just as Tabitha had done with me. When an audience member told the story of an accident that involved climbing a tree, Mindy, instead of using her own forearm to make the sign for tree, used Tabitha's and thus Tabitha got to *feel* the person climbing the trunk (her forearm) and then falling from the branches (her fingers).

A Deaf-sighted audience member raised their hand, and asked nervously, "When they do all that Haptic stuff on your back, doesn't it distract you from what your regular interpreter is signing to you?"

"That's a fair question," Tabitha answered via Mindy's voicing. "Did that person who just walked by you to go to the bathroom distract you? I know you look surprised right now. My interpreter just showed me both the person walking across the front of the room to head toward the bathroom and the look on your face. Did that person's move cause you to lose concentration? Does the hum of the air conditioner, or the hundred people in the room, or the smell of the chicken parmigiana waiting in the dining room next door? Okay, maybe that is distracting me. I'm hungry. But seriously, sighted-hearing people get a massive amount of information into their eyes and ears every second. So they pay attention to it or ignore it. Now, of course, some DeafBlind don't like touch signals at all. But me? I want to devour every single aspect of life. I want it all. That's one of the main things about Protactile. It's about our right to access. Our right to be part of the world."

Before I knew it, it was my turn to take over the Tactile interpreting with Liz doing the Haptics on Tabitha's back. I was incredibly nervous, but also excited. When I voiced for Tabitha, my tone lightened. It wasn't an imitation of a woman, but I was trying to express Tabitha's specific kind of charm. Tabitha told how her parents, who knew she had Usher syndrome 1, hid the fact that she might go blind until she was nearly twenty. When she found out, she was furious.

"If only I knew earlier," she signed, "I would have looked at everything more deeply. I would have taken it all in . . . everything. I would have eaten life with my eyes. But I missed so much . . . the Grand Canyon, Hawaii, Paris. The hearing-sighted often try to control our access to the world. Either like my parents did, by not telling me I was going blind, or the way our government does by not giving all DeafBlind free access to SSPs or requiring that all parents of Deaf and DeafBlind babies learn sign language immediately, so they have a common language with their child. In my opinion, without mandated access, the world is being stolen from us."

Then a middle-aged hearing man with a salt-and-pepper beard raised his hand. He identified himself as a writer and ASL interpreter from New York. He was writing something about deaf-blindness and wanted to know how Protactile had affected Tabitha's life.

Tabitha took an extra-deep breath.

"My night blindness started in my teens, but as recently as two years ago my vision was still good enough to drive," she explained. "And any day of the week I was doing twenty things at once. Traveling around the country, going to conferences and Deaf advocacy groups, swimming, running. My husband called me the Tasmanian devil of multitasking. But then, almost overnight, my vision got so bad I was designated legally blind. Then it got worse. I couldn't go to Bloomingdale's on my own anymore. I couldn't take dance class or go to the museum without help. Forget about chatting for hours with friends on the videophone. I had lost so many things that made my life meaningful."

Tabitha wiped a tear from her cheek, then gathered herself and smiled.

"I know what you're probably thinking: *Tabitha, you work in the field of disability. You know lots of DeafBlind who can do lots of things independently*. Yes. True. But they weren't *me*. I sunk into the worst depression of my life, and I wasn't sure I was going to be able to get out of it. I would wake up every morning, see the dark fog in front of my eyes, and remember I was blind. Then I'd run to the toilet and vomit. I hate saying this, but, for the first time in my life, I wanted to die. Then one day, six months after my depression started, my husband and a DeafBlind mentor of mine staged an intervention and basically bawled me out. They said, 'Tabitha, this isn't who you are. You're a strong woman. You can't just sit around with nothing to do.' And they were right. So, despite my depression, I finally went back to work. And the next thing I knew, my supervisor at the Bridgman Center sent me on that trip to Seattle where I met those two awesome DeafBlind women who taught me about Protactile. And let me tell you, it was like the great DeafBlind God in the sky reached down and lifted the chains from my soul. The Protactile way of life made me feel like I was brought back to Earth. I was back inside the room again. Here. With you, and you, and you."

Tabitha pointed to different places in the room that Liz had previously described via touch signals on her back.

"With the three women sitting in the front row, with the one on the right wearing a frilly salmon-colored blouse, and you, the handsome man who I'm told looks a little like George Clooney, who is nodding his head as I speak, and . . . are your eyes tearing up? Mine too. Protactile put me back into life again . . . and I need it. I need it so badly. I also need my interpreters and my SSPs—some places are calling them co-navigators now. Whatever you call them, they let me know what's happening in the environment around me. I can be independent and still need other people to get access to information. Everyone, sighted-hearing, able-bodied or not—we all use tools to live. That's why the ADA law needs to be amended so every DeafBlind person can have access to the world, including orientation and mobility training, Protactile training, and the right to co-navigator services every week. Access must be considered a human right. We're not going to get these things overnight. But like the wise person who taught me how to navigate the world with a cane once said, 'You swing right, you swing left, you steer clear of obstacles, and one step at a time you can make your way across a continent.'"

Tabitha signed "finished" with a flick of her open hands. The audience, in various states of "wrecked," leaped to their feet, stomping the floor and wiggling their raised fingers in the sign for *applause*. Liz drummed her flat hands on Tabitha's back in matching Protactile applause. I joined in. Tabitha absorbed the joyous strumming on her body, with happy tears rolling down her cheeks. She was there in the room. Completely there.

26

RAINSTORM (PART 2)

Hanne types onto your SBC and her words rise into your fingertips.

"Sorry I took so long. Now I'm as wet as you! I found your cane and wallet! Why were you staying so late at school?"

"I was MUST to finish story for class. Instead I search internet. Get very distract."

"What kind of story?"

"Secret story about most Important sad day of my life."

"Secret stories are the best stories! Can I read it?"

"Not allowed tell story. Forbidden. I will get bad grade instead."

"Don't be silly! Cyril says you write wonderful things! I can help you if you want. I'm always helping my son. Wait here. I'm going to dry your wallet on top of the espresso machine. We need to dry your clothes before you catch cold. Then I can look at your story."

You need to get away from Hanne. The chills you feel may not be just because you are cold. They could also be the presence of the Devil trying to tempt you. Maybe this is why thoughts of the Blue God have been haunting you. When Hanne returns you type:

"I go now. You point me bus stop. I wait there."

"If you really want to, you can. But the street is flooding and there is lightning. It's not safe out there. We won't tell anyone we talked. It's only you and me here anyway. After we dry off, I'll drive you home. I promise."

You could insist she call Brother Birch or Molly. But you don't.

"**Okay,**" you type. "**But when rain stops must go home.**"

"**Perfect!**" Hanne types. "**Take your shirt off and I'll throw it in the dryer in the back. I'll also get you a towel to dry off.**"

You will not let the Devil have his way. You want to type "no," but Hanne has already removed your outside shirt and is tugging your wet T-shirt over your head. For a matter of seconds you can't breathe until the shirt is off. You have never been shirtless in front of an adult woman except your mama, female nurses, and the dorm boss at school. Your cold body shakes as if you are having a small seizure. Hanne throws a dry towel around you and rubs your chest and back very hard, warming you. You smell her breath, her hair, her wet clothes. When she finishes, her one hand is resting in the little hairs at the center of your naked chest. Your heart pounds against her palm. She quickly removes her hand. Then she pats your chest muscles and pulls someone else's dry T-shirt over your head. It smells like a new shirt, and you wonder where she got it. The shirt makes you feel safer.

After that, Hanne dries herself and gives Snap water and some oatmeal cookies. She gives you a hot chocolate and a delicious doughnut and cinnamon roll. You explain that you don't have any money with you, but Hanne says it's free for you because you are friends. Then you remind her that you're not allowed to be alone with a grown woman who isn't a relative or your interpreter.

Hanne types:

"**Okay. I totally understand. Do you want to give me your family's phone number? I can call them now. I'll just say I'm a stranger and then they can pick you up. Would that work?**"

You sit there, uncertain what to do. You wish Hanne hadn't given you that choice. *The Devil is very powerful.*

"**No. It OK. LATER drive me home. But shh. Secret. OK?**"

"**Okay, definitely our secret. Maybe you can just tell them Cyril drove you home?**"

Then you explain that Molly told Brother Birch bad things about Cyril, so that is also not a good idea.

"Molly said this because Cyril is gay?" Hanne asks. **"Is this why he's not allowed to drive you home?"**

"He not Christian man."

"True, but he's a very, very good man."

Hanne is Cyril's real friend. That's why she is defending him. Maybe with his real friends Cyril isn't so selfish and closed off. After a moment you type to Hanne:

"Cyril just interpreter. Not my friend. He keeping his secrets. OK. I understanding. Private. SHH. But later I tell Cyril some of my secret, but Cyril say NO! I will NOT TOLD ARLO private life. Not fair. Rule: If I told secrets You told too. Right?"

Hanne thinks for a long time. Then she types:

"Maybe Cyril thought, because of your religion, he needed to be careful. Maybe he was afraid you would think he's a bad man because he's gay?"

"No. Jesus loving everyone! JW loving everyone. Jesus loving gay people just like regular people. But GAY SEX meaning BAD SIN. Jesus say IF no doing gay sex then OK. Fine. No problem. Jehovah God saying GAY people was OK! Can will be save and maybe goes to heaven. Just NOT DO GAY SEX."

Hanne doesn't even think before typing back:

"Do you really believe gay sex is a sin? Aren't there things you do that are sinful? Is that why you're afraid to finish your story?"

Your hands reach to type a response. You could lie or tell the truth. If you lie, you might bring Hanne closer to Jehovah and salvation. If you tell the truth, you might bring yourself closer to Hanne—the sorceress. *What do you really want?* You type:

"Yes. I honest. I doing sin. Bad sin. I told you before. Long time ago. I was loving someone. I doing sex with someone but no married. Bad

things happen. Heartbreak. But I stopping sin. Later I baptize. I asking Jehovah God forgiveness. I pure now. Action pure."

"Really? Only pure?"

Again, it must be sorcery and the Devil, because without thinking your hands type almost automatically:

"OK, that lying too. I still do sin. But not worse sin. Not like Cyril sin. He force me telling him secrets then he not telling me secrets! Unfair!"

Hanne types:

"Cyril makes me really angry sometimes. In fact, we had a big fight a couple of weeks ago. But now I'm not mad at him anymore. I'll tell you a secret about Cyril: He doesn't like to open up to people. It took him a long time to tell me any of his secrets."

"Cyril wrong! He so selfish!"

"I don't know. He doesn't think of himself as selfish. He thinks he's just being professional. Instead of selfish, I think he's more afraid to let anyone get to know him. He's lonely too. It's hard to be gay in Poughkeepsie. It's hard to be anyone in Poughkeepsie! Ha ha!"

"I know. Ha ha. But September Cyril moving to Philadelphia. Will happy there."

"Ha ha! Cyril won't move. He is always talking about leaving Poughkeepsie, but he never does."

"I don't understand."

"Cyril always says he's going to take this class or that class or go to graduate school or start his own interpreting agency or take a trip to Europe. Now he says he's moving to Philadelphia for a job offer. He won't. We've been over this many times together. At least I am going to nursing school. Cyril is just so stuck, and he's angry at himself about it. But I understand. It's hard to change things when you are older after life has disappointed you. You become more afraid."

You think about Cyril and the story of him being afraid. You assumed Cyril, like all hearing-sighted people, had an easy life, where things like work and relationships were just a matter of picking one, like the minia-ture toy chests in your old doctor's office: just reach inside and grab. But Cyril's life is different than you imagined. When the class is over and you go to Ecuador, he won't be going to Philadelphia. Even though it is a sin, you wish Cyril could meet another nice gay man and stop being stuck and lonely.

You type to Hanne:

"OK OK. You was RIGHT! I not mad at Cyril anymore for keeping se-cret. I not mad he leaved me alone today with bad interpreter. Cyril good man, good interpreter. I sorry."

Hanne reaches over and ruffles her fingers through your wet hair like you're a little kid and she's your mother. You reach up to feel Hanne's wrist and hand. She lets you linger. Her wrist feels nice, but her fingers are knobby like you remember. Hanne takes her hand away, but lets it slide through your hand slowly. This makes you nervous, excited, and confused.

Hanne types:

"Can you do me a favor?"

"What?"

"Can you at least try to finish your story? If we keep things inside too tightly, they can destroy us. Trust me."

"Will bad trouble."

"Okay. It's up to you. But, if you won't show me your story, how about before I get you home, you let me cut your hair?"

"No thank you. Brother Birch cutting my hair last week."

"Ugh! To be honest, it looks like someone cut it with a bowl. You would look much more handsome if you let me cut it. I'm very good at cutting hair."

You don't want to look like someone cut your hair with a bowl. But if you let Hanne cut your hair, then she might tell you more secrets, and let you touch her in the way she just did, and then things might get more dangerous. You definitely should not let Hanne cut your hair.

"Yes. You can haircutting."

A few minutes later Hanne leads you and Snap into the back room of the café and sits you in a chair. The back room is much warmer than the front. Suddenly, Hanne pulls off the new dry T-shirt and again you are half-naked in front of a woman who is not your mother or the nurse in your doctor's office. Then she takes scissors out and starts cutting your hair. As she clips, she pushes your head and hair around. Her fingers slide along the back of your neck and it makes your skin leap to attention. Are Hanne's face and body beautiful, like Cyril said? Hanne blows on your face to remove pieces of hair that have stuck on your cheeks and eyelids. Her breath smells like coffee and oranges. Her armpits smell like deodorant. When she stands on her tiptoes to cut the hair on top of your head she presses her pelvis against your hand and her breasts lean into your ear. There is a clear demarcation between the scratchiness of her bra and the softness of her flesh. You smell her skin.

The Devil makes your penis strain against the material of your still-wet pants and underwear. What you want to do with Hanne is a very bad sin. But you are lonely. You have not been touched in a long time. You reach up to feel her wrist again. Red star red star red star.

27

PROTACTILE

Monday morning. Cyril is back to work and all excited about something called Protactile. You aren't exactly sure what he's talking about, but he doesn't stop touching you even when you are signing. One part of Protactile, other than always touching you, is tapping your arm, which is supposed to be like someone narrowing their eyes and nodding thoughtfully. At first it is distracting, but then you start liking it. It lets you know people are listening and makes you feel like you're more part of what's going on. Halfway into his demonstration Cyril notices that your hair is cut and that your shirt is not buttoned all the way to the neck.

"What happened to you?" Cyril asks like he is surprised. "Who cut your hair?"

"You didn't do this?" Molly asks suspiciously, which Cyril (who is interpreting) emphasizes by describing her expression.

"No," Cyril says. "Not me. I just got back last night."

"I see," Molly says, but you know she doesn't believe him.

"Well, you look great," Cyril says, tousling your hair. "You look like a real college man now. So tell us, who cut it?"

You are nervous and worried that your face might give you away, so to change the subject (and also because you are still very curious) you ask Cyril to show you and Molly more about Protactile. Your trick works because Cyril gets so excited his hands are almost shaking when he explains the philosophy behind it. Like how you are always touching the person you're talking to *(constant touch)* and that Protactile was invented completely by the DeafBlind. Then Cyril tells you other things he learned, something called Haptics that could help with interpreting.

"Let me show you guys an example!" Cyril says.

Then Cyril asks Molly to interpret while he sits in a chair behind you. Then he asks you to lean forward a bit and takes his fingers and draws a square on your back and explains that this square represents the room in which you are sitting. Then he draws the desks across the front of the room and three small circles behind each desk. He says these are the heads of the students that just came into the room and sat down next to you. Then he shows you how he would point to the different heads and show if they were laughing, crying, or walking out the door.

"This is fascinating," Molly tells Cyril, which is not something she has ever said to him before. "Could you show us more? This could be very useful."

"Sure," Cyril says, clearly happy that Molly is being nice to him for a change. Then he asks you, "Do you like it, Arlo? Or is it confusing?"

"I like it," you say. "But still confusing."

Cyril continues to do the touch signals on your body, and you begin to connect them with what is happening around you. More students come in and sit down. One of the students in the back leaves to go to the bathroom. Instead of using the space in the air you can't see, Cyril tells Molly to use your chest to walk the student across the room. Molly and Cyril never take their hands from you the whole time. Electricity ignites all over your brain, causing the hair follicles on your arms and the back of your neck to vibrate. Suddenly you are a DeafBlind spaceman who left a very quiet planet a long time ago and are just arriving back on Earth, in a classroom, surrounded by a crowd of noisy people.

"Now I understand!" you say excitedly. "Wow! Protactile very cool!"

For the time you are learning about Protactile and Haptics you don't even think about what you did with Hanne and what will happen if Molly and Brother Birch find out. Now, all you want to do is learn more of what Cyril has learned.

"Conference, interesting things . . . what else?"

Cyril tells you how every summer there are special camps in Maryland and Washington State where hundreds of DeafBlind people go, and where you could go too. He also tells you that Seattle is the best city in the country for the DeafBlind, because they have lots of DeafBlind people who know about their rights, and it is where Protactile was developed. Cyril also says there are places in New York State where you could get training to become more independent and maybe live on your own someday. When he says this, Molly's signing becomes more hesitant, like Cyril is saying something she is worried can hurt you.

"Conference show new tech equipment?" you ask, changing the subject.

Again Cyril gets excited and describes a very small refreshable braille display—much smaller than your SBC—and explains how DeafBlind people can just plug it into their iPhone and be able to read the news or books or send and receive emails and text messages while they are walking around. You've already read about such equipment on the internet a long time ago, but because Cyril is so excited you say:

"That! I crave! I wish have iPhone too!"

"Why don't you?" Cyril asks, as though he is asking both you and Molly. "You should talk to the Abilities Institute. It's a pretty key piece of equipment for the Deaf and DeafBlind. There's even an organization called iCanConnect that helps DeafBlind people pay for equipment. I found the website online. I'm sure something could be worked out. Right, Molly?"

You wish Cyril hadn't said that. Now he has made Molly very uncomfortable, because she has already advocated for you with Brother Birch and the Abilities Institute about the new cell phone and new portable keyboard.

Brother Birch told Molly and Mrs. Shuster no. Brother Birch said the sub-
sidies wouldn't pay for all of it and more importantly, he worried that it
could lead you astray and put you in danger because of what's happened
before. Maybe Molly explains this to Cyril, or maybe she says something
else. You can feel in Cyril's hands that whatever Molly said has bothered
him. This is another thing about the *constant touch* thing: it lets you feel
that there are secrets inside someone's body.

"Anyway," Cyril says, moving to the front of you to sign for himself, and
changes the subject. "The main speaker at the conference was a DeafBlind
woman named Tabitha and she was brilliant."

Molly tries to do the Haptics on your back, but she's not as good as
Cyril and you ask her to stop. Then Cyril tells you more about the Deaf-
Blind Tabitha woman. How she works at a place called the Laura Bridgman Center, where they have lots of trainings for the DeafBlind to make
their lives better. He tells you how Tabitha is fighting for SSPs to be mandated by law for all DeafBlind people so they can have more access to the
world. Tabitha is also fighting so all parents of Deaf babies will learn sign
language. You wonder what it would have been like for your mother to
have really known sign language so you could have talked to her before
she died. Would you have grown closer? Or would you have learned things
that made you grow distant?

"I wish you could have met her," Cyril says, which confuses you at
first since you are thinking about your mother. "Tabitha is the head of the
whole center. The top boss!"

"Top boss?" you ask in disbelief. "DeafBlind?"

Cyril's words don't make sense. The only bosses you have ever known
are hearing and sighted. None of the elders at your Kingdom Hall have
been DeafBlind. You had Deaf teachers, but never any who were Deaf-
Blind. *DeafBlind people can't be bosses.*

"Tabitha say hearing workers follow her orders? Really? Ha ha! Lie!"
Cyril laughs like you made a joke.

"No," Cyril says. "Not a lie. Honest. Really."

Then you think you've figured out the trick in Cyril's story.

"Tabitha full DeafBlind or just low-vision?"

"She's *completely* deaf and blind," Cyril says.

You try to imagine this DeafBlind superhuman bossing people around, but you can't.

"Future . . . I will meet Tabitha maybe?"

"Maybe you can," Cyril says.

Then he speaks nervously and quickly, maybe because he knows Molly doesn't trust him.

"I mean, there's always the chance you could visit the Laura Bridgman Center where Tabitha works. She's not the only DeafBlind boss. The two women that introduced Protactile to the world are also DeafBlind bosses. DeafBlind people can do a lot with the right technology and access. You know, DeafBlind people from all over go to the Bridgman Center for training."

That's when Molly abruptly takes your hands away from Cyril and says: "We can talk more about this later. The class is starting."

But you want to know more about Tabitha, and what Cyril has learned about DeafBlind bosses, and about the Protactile stuff that DeafBlind people invented.

"Protactile and Haptics, continue during class, can?" you ask.

"Another time. It might disturb the class," Molly says.

Before you can ask again, Molly and Cyril stop the Protactile and aren't signing anything to you for almost a minute—which is unethical! You sit and wait, and wonder if they're having an argument. Then Cyril moves behind you while Molly sits in the interpreter's chair.

"We'll try it," Molly signs, but then adds, "but just for a minute."

Using his hands and fingers across your back and shoulders, Cyril shows the professor entering the room. He draws a face with a straight line across for the mouth. This means the professor is not smiling or frowning.

Then Cyril's fingers show the professor is moving back and forth in front of the blackboard. She writes something, which Molly has interpreted into your hands as *the difference between the words* its *and* it's. Then Cyril draws the professor's face again. This time she's frowning and walks very slowly to the edge of the desk.

Your body starts to rock with excitement, and Molly reminds you not to do that.

The professor starts her lesson, but then she stops talking. Cyril draws her face again. This is the worst one yet. Her frown is very deep, and the inside part of her eyebrows dive downward. She's angry. She walks toward your desk.

"Can someone tell me what's going on?" the professor asks Cyril and Molly.

Cyril's hands pull away from your back. The professor wants him to explain what he is doing. He quickly explains Protactile, which still takes a long time. The professor continues looking bothered and confused. The way Molly interprets for Cyril makes it seem as if he's nervous.

"It's new," Cyril says. "Let me show you . . ."

Cyril takes more time to explain Haptics. The professor tells Cyril they can continue with what they are doing, but now Molly is annoyed.

"I think we should stop," she says. "I told you it would disrupt the class. It's all very fascinating, but the classroom is not the place to practice. It's distracting Arlo."

"Do you want me to stop?" Cyril asks you. "Is it making it hard to concentrate on the class?"

You are caught in the middle. If you say for him to continue, Molly will be upset. But Molly was already upset because of the haircut, and maybe because she suspects what you did with Hanne. You tell Cyril, "No. I like Protactile and touching my back. Very interesting. Continue, if Molly says okay."

Molly's hands grow tense. You feel the gust of an angry sigh from her mouth. This means she is going to let Cyril continue but she is not going to be nice for the rest of the day. A moment later the professor tells the class:

"Now, before we move on, I want to remind everyone that a week from this Friday we will be having our travel essay field trip to Albany! Remember to dress comfortably and bring that extra money for lunch! Also, certain people owe me assignments."

When the professor says the word *assignments*, all the excitement you had been feeling about Protactile suddenly seeps out of your body onto the floor. You remember the promise you broke to Jehovah God and Brother Birch. You want to believe the professor is talking to the other students, but Cyril's fingers draw the professor walking over to your desk. Now you wish Cyril would turn off the touch signals.

Something has made Molly go silent. When Molly starts to interpret, the professor's words come out of her fingers with Molly's own bitterness.

"So, Mr. Dilly, hopefully whatever your interpreters are up to is not making you forget to do your homework. Do you have that personal essay for me?"

"What is the professor talking about?" Molly asks you privately. "You never told me about any personal essay."

You say nothing to Molly. Cyril draws the professor's face on your back: a circle, with her two black arched eyebrows puzzling themselves. *So where is the personal essay?* Then Cyril draws Molly's angry face. The muscles of your back and shoulders tighten. Can Cyril feel it? Does Professor Bahr know how impossible it was for you to complete this assignment? You wish Hanne were here with you, to share the blame. Does Molly even imagine you'd be brave enough to betray Brother Birch and Jehovah God and write the story of the saddest, most important day of your life?

You can't breathe.

28

THE ARGUMENT

Arlo just sat there, ignoring Professor Bahr's request for his assignment. Like Mindy had taught me, I used my two fingers like a paintbrush, drawing Professor Bahr's expression of anticipation on his back, a straight line for her mouth (not happy, not sad) and her dramatically arched eyebrows.

"Did you or did you not do the assignment, Mr. Dilly?" Professor Bahr asked sternly.

I drew a big question mark on Arlo's back to emphasize the teacher was waiting for him. *Come on, come on!* I thought. *Either hand in your assignment or just admit you didn't do it.* My stomach clenched in anticipation of bad news, and I longed for it to be over with. But, instead, Arlo reached into his backpack and pulled out a thick pile of papers. Twenty pages? Thirty pages? It was far longer than Professor Bahr had required. All of us were shocked. Arlo held the stack out toward Professor Bahr, turning his head slightly away, as if he was disavowing what he had written. Molly stared intently at the dangling document, attempting to capture what might be printed beneath the cover page.

"My, my, my, Mr. Dilly," Professor Bahr said, smiling and taking the stack from Arlo's hands. "You have outdone yourself! You only had to do seven pages, but this is practically a dissertation!"

Professor Bahr flipped through the pages with an expression of both pleasure and disbelief. Molly glared at me as if I had just done something unforgivable, her lips squeezed into thin slits, her eyes absurdly wide, as if she had telekinesis and was attempting to make my head explode. She signed to me without voicing or interpreting to Arlo:

"What was that? What did he just give her?"

"I have no idea," I signed back. "I guess just his homework. What's wrong? The professor was just trying to get him to open up with a personal essay and find his voice. Nobody expected him to write that much. It's awesome!"

Molly dismissed me with gritted teeth, then craned her neck to see Professor Bahr perusing Arlo's essay. I immediately fantasized about Molly trying to snatch the essay back and me wrestling her to the ground, rescuing the document and getting it back into Professor Bahr's hands. Although in my fantasy I also got a chance to read it first. Truth be told, I was as curious as Molly. What had Arlo written? And why had he not shown me? The professor closed the essay and set it on her desk. I quickly stood up under the pretense of stretching and was able to glance at the title page: "Mine Very Sad True (AND SUBLIME) Love Story by Arlo Dilly."

I started smiling so hard I was on the brink of rocking my body the way Arlo did when he was happy. At that same moment Molly, who had also seen the title page, placed her hands back into Arlo's.

"Did your uncle approve?"

Before Arlo could respond, Professor Bahr held up his essay like it was some holy document and addressed him loudly enough for the whole class to hear.

"Well done, Mr. Dilly! I'm already engrossed. I look forward to reading this from cover to cover. Perhaps we can read some of it to the whole class?"

Molly's eyes fixed on the pages in Professor Bahr's hand. She was no longer interpreting, lost in some thought. Arlo was waiting. I leaped out of my chair and tapped Molly on the shoulder.

"My turn," I signed. "Take the back . . . or take a break."

I nudged Molly out of the seat before she could refuse, and then interpreted what Professor Bahr had recently said about reading the story out loud in front of the class. Arlo went pale and started shaking his head rapidly.

"No, no!" he signed anxiously. "Very personal story. Please don't read for whole class. Okay? Please."

Professor Bahr nodded her head in understanding.

"The best writing is the most personal, Mr. Dilly," she said, "even when we need to work on possessive pronouns! But I shall respect your wishes, of course. Class, and I'm speaking to all of you, not just to the brilliant Mr. Dilly. When we share with others the secrets hidden inside us, this—THIS—is what saves us!"

Professor Bahr mimed holding a knife in her hand. She was always a little dramatic, but suddenly she was really pouring it on.

"We must take the dagger that is our pens, our pencils, our computer keyboards, and we must slice open our chest and spill the blood onto the page that gushes from our pulsing hearts! Do you understand, class?"

All the hearing-sighted students stared at Professor Bahr silently. Perhaps they were wondering if she had finally gone mad from all their misplaced apostrophes. Arlo, however, rocked excitedly, nodding his head.

Professor Bahr smiled at him and then began explaining how all the great writers drained their own lives for their masterpieces: Melville, Fitzgerald, Joyce.

"And Helen Keller!" she finally shouted. "A genius who could neither hear nor see, like Mr. Dilly here. I've been rereading her lately. Keller wrote twelve books—that's right, twelve. Most were based on her own life. Our lives are our gold, students! Now, ladies and gentlemen, if you will excuse me, I need to run to the office to make copies. Please just stare at your smartphones like zombies for a few minutes until I return."

When I finished interpreting Professor Bahr's final comment, I looked up and found Molly had left her seat. Looking through the glass of the door, I saw her in the hallway, angrily jabbing the keys on her cell phone. I was grateful for the moment alone with Arlo.

"Hey, Molly left the room," I signed to him. "I wanted to tell you something. I hope you don't mind but I mentioned to Tabitha that you would like to get in touch with your old Deaf school friends. She suggested checking the DeafBlind Facebook groups. She says people from all over the country stay in touch there."

Arlo asked what I meant by the sign—the initials F-B—that I had used for Facebook. I tried the various other signs I had seen for the social networking website. Finally, I just fingerspelled it. He still didn't know what I was talking about.

"Okay," I signed. "Facebook is like this place on the internet where you can connect with friends from all over the world, and usually try to make them think your life is way better than it really is. Also, you can post photos of your cat, or dog, or write things about how much you hate people from other political parties."

I added *ha ha*, but the joke was lost on Arlo.

"Anyway, Facebook also has specific groups just for the DeafBlind. There's a good chance you'd be able to find out about your friends from school. It's totally free to join."

Just then I heard a loud, purposeful cough. I turned to look at the door, and there was Molly glaring at me again. Then, in the harshest of whispers, she pointed to the hallway and said, "Outside. Now."

After Arlo gave me a concerned "Okay," I slipped out into the hallway and shut the door behind me, staring into Molly's face, red and pinched, like she couldn't breathe.

"I see what you're doing!" she hissed. "The essay? The new haircut? Giving him money to buy lunches? Your stories about that DeafBlind woman and getting new gadgets. Facebook? You think we're stupid?"

"Excuse me, Molly," I said calmly, squeezing out a condescending smile. "I told you I had nothing to do with his haircut or the essay. That's all him. The last time I saw him, I was with you. And what's the big deal? He looks a hell of a lot better."

Her eyes narrowed and she shook her head with disgust.

"You're a liar and I know it. We've seen what you've been trying to do."

"*Trying to do?* Molly, I have no idea what you're talking about."

"Oh, please!" her voice exploded. She immediately lowered her voice again, but the anger remained. "Let me explain something to you, Mr. Brewster. Arlo can't just go to some other school or buy all the high-tech equipment you're telling him about. He's barely able to survive on his disability payments without help from his uncle. Also, both Brother Birch and Arlo have worked very hard in building a trusting relationship with each other, and you're sowing distrust!"

"I am doing nothing of the kind," I protested.

"You're not? Mr. Birch is a spiritually strong man, and he adores Arlo like his son. But Mr. Birch also has a wife he needs to care for, and service work, and only has time for a part-time job. He doesn't have extra money for extravagances. Trust me, sir, Mr. Birch makes sure Arlo gets everything he truly needs. How you could insinuate . . ."

Looking pained, Molly pressed her fingers into her forehead and temple. Having a fit did not come naturally to her.

Again, I tried my best to modulate my tone, hoping to get back to some sense of sanity.

"Look, Molly, we really need to get back in there so Arlo isn't stuck there alone. But before we do, let me just say that I'm not trying to cause problems for Arlo's uncle or you. I'm trying to help. The Laura Bridgman Center and the new tech equipment are things he can get financial help with—at least in part. There are a lot of resources available for people with disabilities. Maybe not for everything, but more than Arlo has at the moment. I mean, why shouldn't Arlo have all the assistance he can get? It's not fair to deny him."

I immediately saw that I had crossed another line. Molly pointed her finger at me, sputtering like I had accused her of murder.

"How dare you. You have no idea."

My forced calmness had run its course. I could feel the veins pulse on my forehead as I snapped.

"Okay, *Ms. Clinch*, time to chill the fuck out! Maybe I have a better idea than you. Ever consider that? And since we're laying our cards on the table, let's just go for it. Arlo's uncle has allowed Arlo the bare minimum in services and training. It could almost be called neglect. Arlo's equipment is so damn outdated it's a wonder he can still get parts to fix it. With everything that's out there, someone as smart as Arlo would have a good chance of being independent. At least partially. He may not even need to live with his uncle. Does he even know he has a choice?"

"That's enough!" Molly screeched so loudly it echoed down the hallway. She flung her opened hand in front of my face, silencing me.

"Cyril Brewster," she said, a bitter smile stretched across her thin lips, "the World-Renowned Expert on DeafBlind Accessibility. Hallelujah! He has arrived in the land of the poor, pitiful, starving DeafBlind. Hallelujah! The second coming of Annie Sullivan. How *did* we all function before you arrived?"

It was like she had lost her mind. I shook my head and lowered my voice, gesturing toward the classroom.

"Jesus. We have to get back in there," I whispered harshly. "He's been alone since—"

"No!" Again Molly's banshee-level squeal cut me off. "You don't get to talk anymore. You think you're the first interpreter who's made some snap judgment about how Brother Birch and I have cared for Arlo? You're not. Just like you, they all swoop in, try to disrupt poor Arlo's life, and then suddenly disappear when some less complicated, better-paying job comes along."

"You know nothing about me," I responded, far too defensively.

"Admit it. You took this job for the money. Not because you give a hoot about the DeafBlind. It's summertime and work was thin, right?"

"Maybe at first—"

"But you care now?" she mocked. "Then what happened on Friday? You care so much that you'd bail on Arlo last-minute, leaving him with that horrible Justin?"

"Justin?" I said, my anger suddenly tripping over a huge lump of remorse. "But Ange gave me her word she wouldn't send Justin."

"Have you ever seen me cancel for another job?" Molly barked.

"No, but—"

"No! I'm there every single day, unless I'm dying with the flu, and then I make sure there's a competent sub. Does Brother Birch tell Arlo, *Sorry, I can't be your guardian today?* You have no idea what that man has sacrificed for that boy!"

What was going on? Why was Molly defending Arlo's uncle so vociferously?

"Molly, let's get honest here. His uncle is not exactly nurturing. If anything, he's limiting Arlo's access—"

"Arlo's uncle is a great man I have known for many, many years. When Arlo's mother died there was no father around to step in. Arlo's uncle, a man who had his own life, his own family, his own work, had to suddenly take a troubled DeafBlind teenager into his house. Do you know the strain that put on Brother Birch? On his own relationships?"

Molly's voice cracked with feeling.

"Molly, I'm just trying to help Arlo."

"But you don't have any idea what that poor boy has been through. You just make assumptions. When I started working with Arlo ten years ago, he was horrified when he arrived at school. His language skills were terrible, and he barely understood the basics of how to care for himself. But I was there for all his training. I practically introduced him to the world. Me! Not you. Me! I earn a fraction of what you do, but I work with Arlo because

I actually care. I love that boy. I was the one who had to tell him when his mother died, I was the one who had to pick up the pieces when he was kicked out of school and tell him that his friend—"

Molly clapped her hand over her mouth, stopping herself. I wasn't sure whether it was because of emotion or not wanting to say more. Removing her hand, she attempted to steady her voice in a low, hoarse whisper.

"I gave up everything for that boy. We were like *a family.* I even moved to Poughkeepsie for him. And you accuse me and Brother Birch of *neglect*? Of taking advantage of him? We aren't the ones using him as some little experiment to feel good about ourselves. Or dragging him around and introducing him to sluts like he's a show-and-tell toy!"

My face flushed lobster red with guilt. Had it been Hanne who was responsible for the haircut thing? The dressing him differently? The essay? A sick feeling overcame me. If he was hanging around Hanne, what else might have happened?

"First, you can stop calling my friends sluts," I said defensively. "Hanne's a good person. And maybe I shouldn't have been introducing him around, but—"

"And for your information," Molly hissed through gritted teeth, "there are good reasons to keep Arlo away from his old school friends. Putting him in contact could be dangerous. Brother Birch did everything to bring that boy back from where he was five and a half years ago. No, I don't agree with everything Brother Birch has done. But you encouraging Arlo to write that essay, making him remember all those terrible things, could cause him to have a mental breakdown again. Is that what you want? I can't believe I defended you!"

"Defended me?!" I was screaming again, my voice bouncing off the hallway walls. "From what?! And for your information, I had no idea Arlo had any kind of mental breakdown, and I wasn't trying to encourage anything. And could someone please tell me what exactly happened at that fucking school?!"

Molly's expression suddenly turned from rage to shock. She nodded to something behind me. It was Professor Bahr, commanding us with her eyes to be silent.

"If you please," she whispered angrily. "Those of us in this school who are *not* deaf can hear everything you have just said. However, Arlo—your sole purpose for being here—is sitting all alone in that room, unable to understand what's happening around him while you two . . ."

Professor Bahr inhaled through her nose, shaking her head in disappointment. I felt disgusted with myself. Molly wiped the remaining tears from her eyes as we followed Professor Bahr back into the classroom. Everyone in the room except Arlo must've heard us. Arlo sat there looking distraught, reaching out to see if we had returned. I hurried to him and told him we were back.

"What happened?" he asked. "Emergency? Something wrong?"

I lied. I told him it was nothing, just a little disagreement between Molly and me, but he knew it was something more.

"Please tell Molly I'm sorry," he pleaded. "I do wrong. I'm sorry."

29

TOP SECRET

I spent half the afternoon fantasizing about things I might have said to Molly during our argument, and the other half disgusted with myself for blowing up the way I did. I had expected a reprimand from the agency, but I heard nothing by the end of the day. Then, just as I was headed to bed, I received an email from Arlo.

Dear Cyril Brewster, Interpreter:

Hello. Sorry because TROUBLE today in writing class. Molly mad at me and you. She was scare because other JW WATCH her, and because I do SIN. If bad things happening Elders blame her. ALSO, so many years Molly take care about me like her own small child. (FROWNING.) I not small child! She love me and scare. Understand? She trying good Christian JW lady. (She also do sin things too BEFORE, but ask JH GOD forgiving . . . SHH secret.) Molly good interpreter and SSP. Help me lot, so much. WOW. Think many time she helping me. (ALMOST CRY!) But she not on purpose behave ANGRY bitch person. Because her very hard time life. (All of us having hard time life. I know!) But Molly and Brother Birch think YOUR FAULT cut my hair and write SECRET private essay-story for classroom homework and other SIN things. I telling Brother Birch NOT TRUE. My fault. My idea writing forbidden essay and other SIN. Also they don't like you still do GAY and maybe will future die eternal death forever. (FROWNING.)

But I still you SUPPORT. I am wanting you still interpreter. Do not worry: all TOP SECRET. Not telling NOBODY.

Now I ask you very SECRET PERSONAL QUESTION.

Long time ago I home from school on summer break. Mrs. Brother Birch catch me search on dirty SIN website called porn-fiesta21.com. (Gasp! Gulp! EMBARRASS FACE!) Brother Birch very angry. He not talking at me for long time. So disappoint! Then later during Public Talk at Church he telling all congregation about SIN how I was jerk off with hands and looking at NAKED SIN PIC-TURES WOMEN and being willful young man who JH God should punished. Doesn't matter disabled or not. Brother Birch NOT say my name, but I know everyone look at me anyway. They know I sinner. Later I promising BROTHER BIRCH I never do sin on pornfiesta21.com again. But still not trust me. He was say: I know young men, and I know Devil. After that he put special program on computer to restrict sinful websites. I only supposed look JW.org unless special permission. Brother Birch have secret SNEAKY way to check to see if I was be cheating.

So ask SPECIAL FAVOR: Can you helping me join FACE-BOOKS special website and DeafBlind GROUP on internet? I need find old friend Martin and Big Head Lawrence long time not see and have questions. At library, I try set up FACEBOOKS myself but FAILING. Website not easy to enlarge and understand TOO COMPLICATED AND MANY ADVERTISEMENT. Can not see how to make profile for find friends. Please help?

But SHHHHH secret. Shhhhh. Must not TELL anyone. (VERY
SERIOUS FACE.) Big Trouble. Please DELETE email after read.

HUGS,

Arlo Dilly

I stared at the email, longing to reach through the screen and give Arlo
a hug with one hand and choke his uncle with the other. But his request
put me in an impossible position. It was like one of the ethical questions
one might see on the written part of the RID interpreter certification test:

*Interpreter Question 164. If there is no physical or sexual abuse,
should an interpreter get involved in a complicated conflict between
the client, his family, and his ongoing interpreter?*
A. *Yes. Always.*
B. *Sometimes. Depending on the situation.*
C. *Rarely. Only if the client isn't getting to use the internet the way
he wants.*
D. *NO! ARE YOU FUCKING KIDDING ME, YOU STUPID
UNETHICAL FUCK-FACE?!*

My job was not to set up social media profiles, nor to enlighten the
student about the unfairness of their situation, nor to tell the client their
religion is full of shit and everybody jerks off. My job was to relay the
message between the hearing consumer and deaf consumer clearly and
accurately. Molly was right: I was not Arlo's savior. I reread his email
one more time before I deleted it. As I lay in bed unable to sleep, I
couldn't stop thinking about that one sentence: (All of us having hard
time life. I know!) Why a parenthetical? All? I assumed he was talking

about DeafBlind people and Molly, but then I started to wonder if he meant me too.

After thirty-five more minutes of pointless restlessness, I got out of bed, typed Facebook into the browser, and clicked the big green button that said Create an Account.

I just needed to get a photo of him.

30

TRUTH-TELLING

The next day I asked Hanne to meet me for coffee before work at the Dunkin' Donuts near Main and Lewis. I needed someone to talk to about everything that was happening, but also wanted to find out if Hanne had met with Arlo while I was gone. *Was she behind Arlo's little makeover?*

I expected Hanne to be late as usual, but when I walked into the store, I saw her sitting at a table against the bright orange wall, sipping a large black coffee. She was wearing a yellow sundress and her giant Euro-looking sunglasses with her hair swept up in a very 1960s do.

"You okay?" I asked. "You look like a very somber, latter-day Jackie Kennedy."

"It's my mood," she said, removing her movie-star sunglasses to reveal red, tired eyes. "Curtis is back in rehab and I have to meet his counselor today. I don't want to look like the cause of his addiction. So I'm trying for the long-suffering-yet-beautiful-wife look."

"Suits you," I said. Neither of us managed a laugh.

After some awkward silence, hoping she might tell me what was really going on, I caught her up on the details of my life. Then, to follow up on my hunch, I mentioned how good Arlo looked with his new haircut. I searched her face for some sort of reaction but there was nothing. She simply stared at her coffee, barely even nodding. I figured my assumption was wrong. Then as I started talking about Arlo's desire for a Facebook profile and needing a photo, Hanne's eyes started to dampen. I reached for her hand but she quickly pulled it away. The gesture angered me.

"What the fuck, Hanne? If you have something going on, just tell me. Are you worried Curtis isn't serious about getting sober again?"

Hanne shook her head and wrapped her arms tightly around her middle like she had a stomachache. She turned her eyes toward the shelves of frosted doughnuts behind the counter, and tears dripped from the angle of her jaw and splatted onto her yellow dress.

"Is it Wout?" I asked.

"No, no. Everyone is fine," she said, still looking away from me. "Curtis says he's serious about rehab. And Wout is doing some camping thing up at Bear Mountain with friends. It's just . . ."

She went silent, like she was trying to avoid words that might make her cry. Her eyes stayed fixed on the rows of colorful frosted doughnuts.

"Those doughnuts, the ones in the middle with all the . . . what's it called? I'm suddenly forgetting the word. Confetti?"

"I always call them jimmies, but some people say sprinkles. It's one of those words that depends on where you live."

"Jimmies? Well, I love them. They're beautiful. I want to paint a painting filled with those jimmy doughnuts. Dozens of beautiful multicolored pop-art pastries, but then in the middle of them—the empty part—I want to paint the darkest black with little scenes of hell and suffering. Just chaos . . . chaos and darkness."

"I prefer plain cake doughnuts myself," I said.

Hanne briefly smiled at my joke, then fell into another bout of silent tears, leaving me feeling helpless. The counter staff started staring at me, as if I were some lover who had just jilted the pretty lady in the yellow dress.

"Hanne," I finally said, feigning hurt annoyance. "If you're not going to tell me what's going on, then there's no point in me being here. I came here because I need some support from you!"

I pushed my seat out for extra effect. The chair squealed against the

Formica floor, causing the Dunkin' ladies to sneer at me. Hanne wiped her eyes and laughed as she took a sip of coffee.

"Ugh. You are such the drama queen, Cyrilje."

"Me? Drama queen? I'm not the one using doughnuts as existential metaphors."

This caused Hanne to snort coffee out of her nose, which in turn made me laugh, and then next thing you know, we were holding hands over the café table and the staff were shaking their heads, smiling, assuming we had made up.

"Are you okay now?" I asked.

"Yes. I'm fine. But Cyrilje, I need to tell you something. While you were away at your conference, Arlo and I spent some time together."

I tried to listen without judgment as she also admitted to giving Arlo the new haircut, and to telling him to wear his clothes differently. Part of me was relieved that my instincts were still intact, but the other part was furious and began to suspect the worst.

"Did you tell him anything about me?" I said as calmly as I could.

"No," Hanne said. "I mean, not details. He obviously already knows you're gay. He's deaf and blind . . . not stupid."

"Funny," I said, not even smiling. "What else did you say?"

"I just said you hadn't had a boyfriend in a long time and that was one of the reasons you were so uptight."

I sat there stone-faced, hating the fact that I had no control over what might have happened.

"Don't worry, we didn't talk anything more about you. Such an ego-maniac you are."

"So what else happened?" I asked matter-of-factly, hoping to draw out the truth.

Hanne closed her eyes, more tears flowed, and the guilty expression on her face seemed to be the confession I feared the most. I felt my chest tighten. I pictured Hanne seducing Arlo, sending that poor confused kid over the edge, betraying his trust, betraying *my* trust. My fists pounded hard on the table; hot coffee leaped up and splattered my hand.

"What the fuck, Hanne?!" I snapped. "You're pathological, you know that?"

Again the counter staff was staring at us, smiles gone. I could feel the burn of the coffee on my hands. Hanne grabbed some napkins to help. I shoved her hands away.

"He's disabled, for chrissakes," I hissed. "You are unbelievable. He's sixteen years younger than you. You are such a . . ."

"*Whore?*" she asked coldly. "Is that what you want to call me, Cyrilje?"

Hanne's wet eyes glared at me. I shook my head in disgust. I was waiting for her to either break down in tears again or at least offer the apology she owed me. Instead she just rolled her eyes like she was both angered and bored with the conversation.

"Oh, please," she groaned. "So I'm a whore? Fuck you, you sexist little hypocrite. And, by the way, Arlo is not some fragile broken little boy. He's a man. He has passion and hunger. I hate to surprise you like this, Cyrilje, but Arlo likes sex! Bwah! You are as bad as those Jehovah's Witnesses. You're not his mommy."

I felt choked by rage.

"You . . . you . . ." I sputtered, searching but failing to find a cutting retort. "That's— You have no right! You know I could get fired!"

Hanne snorted a bitter laugh.

"Ach, *mijn* God! Wah, wah, wah," she mocked. "*Maak daar toch niet zo'n scene van!*"

I threw a napkin at her. "And stop with the Flemish bullshit! You've lived in Poughkeepsie for almost a quarter of a century!"

Hanne leaned in like she wanted to tell me a secret. Her voice purred in exaggerated sensuousness.

"Are you jealous? Is that it, Cyrilje? Huh? Are you upset that I fucked the handsome DeafBlind boy? Or is it that you wanted to fuck him yourself?"

Hanne's eyes locked onto mine, as if I was the one under interrogation now.

"Fuck you," I said, lowering my voice to a whisper. "You know me better than that."

As soon as I responded, I somehow still felt guilty. Intellectually I knew I was telling the truth, but at the same time I was also lying to myself about something. Was she right? Had I been suppressing an attraction to Arlo? Was that why I had become so invested in him? No. That wasn't it. And all of a sudden it was like a hidden chamber in my brain opened up, and I suddenly had a foggy sense of some deeper truth I hadn't acknowledged. No, I didn't want to have sex with Arlo. I wanted to save him—or was it someone else I wanted to save?

"I just want Arlo to have a chance," I said. "What's happening to him is just not fair. I think that's why I've gotten in way over my head."

Hanne took my hand. Her eyes softened, and all her anger and sarcasm disappeared.

"I'm sorry, Cy," she said. "Ach, I'm a stupid bitch. I know you're not like that. I was obviously projecting. Forgive me?"

"I want to. I really do. But you shouldn't have fucked him, Hanne. What if he develops feelings for you? He's already struggling with so much."

Hanne briefly covered her face with her hand. I couldn't tell if she was about to cry again or laugh.

"Cyrilje, I have an even worse confession," she whispered. "A real one this time. I didn't fuck him."

"Didn't . . . like did *not*?"

Hanne nodded. She was telling the truth. I was so relieved I burst into laughter. Hanne joined in, but her laugh was smaller, almost melancholy.

"Oh my God, you totally had me there," I said with a laughing sigh. "I hate you for doing that but thank you very much for not trying to have sex with my consumer."

Hanne's eyes, dampening, did a coquettish circle and she bit her lower lip.

"You know me better than that, Cyrilje," she said. "Bwah! Of course I wanted to have sex with him. I practically sat on his face, but . . ."

Hanne took a deep breath and then covered her face with her hand again like a child trying to hide. I wanted to be furious at her, but I couldn't. Hanne was Hanne. She would never try to take advantage of someone. After a moment she gathered herself.

"So I was cutting his hair, and he reached up and held my wrist for a moment, following my movements so intensely. It was one of the most sensual things I've ever felt. I assumed he was hitting on me. I didn't know what to do. I mean, I felt like his mother, but also . . . I mean, he's so attractive, and I thought, *Should I be treating him any differently?* We're both adults, and you know, it's been six months since Curtis and I . . . whatever. Anyway, I started to respond a little. Flirting. You know, letting my hips and chest graze against him as I used the scissors and comb. Then he kissed me, and so I kissed him back. And it got a little heavier. So I unbuttoned my shirt, and we were touching each other, just sweetly, exploring each other's bodies, but then he . . ."

Hanne looked around the store to make sure the counter staff weren't listening. Then with a pained expression on her face, she gestured toward her lap.

"He lost it . . . you know what I mean? Everything just stopped. And when I looked up into his eyes, oh, Cy, he was crying. I felt so embarrassed and disgusted with myself, and I thought: *What the fuck am I doing?* So we both got our clothes back in order, and I finished cutting his hair. I tried to act like it was all nothing. Stupid, vain slut that I am, I thought he had cried because of not being able to perform. But then he got out that communication-keyboard thing he uses and we typed back and forth and back and forth."

Hanne took a sip of her coffee. Blew her nose.

"Well," I said. "What did he say?"

"A lot. *Mijn* God! For someone who struggles with English he has a lot to say. But the problem is I promised him I'd never tell anyone what happened. And I've already said too much. But, I guess my point is, I just completely misunderstood him. I thought maybe it was his religion that had messed him up in the head. Or he was just too innocent or something. But it was none of that, it was . . ."

She wiped her eyes and did her best to control her emotions.

"I think he thought he wanted to have casual sex, but when it came down to it, he realized he didn't—at least not with me. He wanted something deeper that I couldn't offer. I'm so used to straight men, you know, automatically responding to me in a physical way. For a moment I thought, *Is something wrong with me on the inside?* Like is my soul ugly? Ugh, I sound like an egomaniac. Of course, he apologized profusely. Poor thing. He felt so guilty. He did the whole DeafBlind version of the 'Let's just be friends' bullshit. Ha! Rejected by a boy who can't even see or hear me?"

Hanne snorted a tearful laugh.

"What do DeafBlind guys know?" I joked, reaching for her hand.

"It's not funny, Cyrilje," she said, in gentle reprimand. "Anyway, then Arlo types about how 'Cyril says you're very smart and beautiful and a good friend,' and he thanked me for 'thinking he was handsome,' and all sorts of other sweet things. But then, and this is the really weird part, out of nowhere Arlo asks me . . ."

Hanne started to laugh quietly to herself, recalling a memory.

"What?"

"He asked me if I did *sorcery*."

I snorted a laugh, surprised he actually asked her, but refrained from telling her he'd long suspected her witchery.

"Can you imagine?" she said. "He doesn't explain why, and then just continues saying all these other nice things about how easy I am to talk to, and how he hasn't had a real friend in a very long time, and the next thing you know, I'm telling him about Wout's ADHD, and Curtis's addiction, and how I got sober, and about becoming a nurse because of my lack of faith in myself as an artist, and blah blah blah. Then I'm crying again and he feels the tears on my face, and he strokes my hand. He types: 'No, no, you good artist, you good person.' And then says all these other things about my character, and my ability to perceive things, and how I'm probably a really great artist. And I think, *What the fuck is this? The DeafBlind boy rejects me and now is trying to make the middle-aged woman feel better about her life?* And you know what's really, really crazy? That's exactly what he ended up doing."

Hanne stopped as a knot of emotion filled her throat. After a few seconds she looked at me with her bloodshot eyes.

"Then he showed me his story on the laptop."

"Wait, what? He actually showed you the assignment for his class?"

Hanne nodded and lowered her voice even more.

"He said he was afraid to show it to anyone because it was supposed to be a secret, and he could get in trouble. He made me promise never to tell anyone."

"Was the story about S?"

"Yes. It was so devastating . . . heartbreaking. He asked me to help him fix the grammar and spelling, make sure he wasn't using 'is,' 'was,' or 'have' wrong. I said I would try. So we made our plan for the next day. He would tell his uncle he was working on a special research paper at the college library, and I would pick him up in the parking lot there each morning and then drop him back there in the evening to catch the van home. We worked all weekend at the café. On breaks I told him how to dress better and comb his hair and we chatted about our lives. Unfortunately, we didn't get through the whole essay, but he said he'd try and finish on his own—even though he still wasn't sure if he'd hand it in. His English is a mess, but there was still something so beautiful and poetic about it. He had this one sentence: *heart hurting so bad, must pushing down hurt or can't think.*"

Hanne grabbed my hand. That time it was my eyes filling up. I was suddenly so glad Hanne had stepped over the line. Arlo was right. Hanne is a witch.

"He needs your help, Cyrilje," Hanne said, squeezing my hand. "He wants to find his other friends from school. Not S . . . two boys. If you could help him with a Facebook profile—"

"So you're the one who told him to ask me?"

Hanne bit her lip, looking sheepish.

"Yes. I might have suggested that. But, Cyrilje, there's no one else he can turn to. You can speak sign language. He needs you. Wait, I have something you can use . . ."

Hanne pulled out her cell phone and texted me a great photo of Arlo she had taken just after she cut his hair. He could have been a slightly cross-eyed college catalogue model with a perplexed look on his face. Hanne and I held hands and looked at the photo as if it were of our long-lost son.

"You will help him, Cyrilje?" Hanne whispered.

I took a moment. I didn't want it to sound like a threat.

"I know you promised not to say anything. But before we move ahead, I need to know. Who was S? What happened?"

31

THE DAY THAT CHANGED EVERYTHING

The Day That Changed Everything was five and a half years ago.

It was November.

Two weeks until you were supposed to go home for fall recess. (The goats call it Thanksgiving.) It was the middle of the night, and it was very cold out. It smelled like snow was coming and somewhere wood fireplaces were burning. S guided you through the darkness. When you ducked your head to walk beneath the forsythia bushes, the branches felt like long, skinny, cold fingers scratching and tickling you on the back of your neck, sexy and scary.

Your favorite spot in the Secret Forest was toward the end of the tunnel of forsythia bushes, a deep cubbyhole that was big enough for you both to lie down on two blankets S would bring from her dorm. After tucking you under the blankets, S pulled the piece of old plywood over the top of the hole as extra protection from anyone seeing. Just as always, you kissed, signed stories, pulled down your clothes to make love. Afterward, you snuggled tight to stay warm and then played your favorite story game: *What will we do in the future?*

"Next year, you and me will graduate," you signed. "Then what do? We will get jobs, get married, and then rent big house with Martin and Big Head Lawrence. All four will live together forever."

"Yes! Yes!" S signed, her body shaking with laughter. "Martin and Big Head Lawrence like our children!"

"Ha ha! Yes! I father, you mother, and Molly will our full-time inter-preter and SSP. She will do whatever we tell her."

S kissed you on your smiling mouth, and your teeth clacked together. Then you kissed S on her eyes. Her eyelashes fluttered against your lips. Then S grew serious.

"Promise me again," she begged, as she often would. "Please, promise we will together forever."

"Okay. Okay. I promise, we will together forever!"

You finished your vow by making the sign for *promise* by combining one of S's hands with one of your own. "Promise!"

You attempted to pull S's body even closer, though there was no "closer" without being inside each other. Making space again to sign, S whispered with her fingers:

"Kiss me very long time. Kiss me until our mouths hurt."

Soon you were inside S again and everything in front of you was warm, while the back of you shivered from the cold wind that blew through the gap between the warped plywood and the earth. A home was supposed to be warm. S was your home.

How could Jehovah God make you love someone that much only to take them from you on Judgment Day? It was the first time you considered the possibility that Brother Birch and the JW elders did not know every-thing that Jehovah God believed. Red star. You let the confusing, sinful thought slip out of your brain, and you squeezed S closer, inhaling the smell of her hair, breath, and skin until you both fell asleep.

But.

Then.

S's hands shook you awake.

"I see people's shadows!" she signed, her desperate fingers entreating you to run. "Get up! Maybe Deaf Devils searching for me! Hurry!"

"What for? Deaf Devils won't bother us. You friends with Crazy Charles now, right?"

"Hurry!" S demanded. "Later will explain. Now I will make them chase me! You—run to dorm. We meet there later, okay?"

"I will stay and protect you," you signed. "I bigger! I stronger! I beat them—can!"

S grabbed your hands, silencing you.

"No!" S demanded. "Pay attention! Too dark here! If can't see, can't fight! Stop talk stupid! Follow what I say!"

There was no time to argue. You tried to kiss S one more time, but she pushed you away.

"They coming! No time! Ready?"

Sign READY: *Both hands shape the letter R and point up toward one shoulder, then like a person signaling a race car they quickly swoop across until they are pointing to the opposite shoulder.*

Ready was the last thing S would ever sign to you.

Telling what happened next is like trying to see something in the distance on a foggy day. You remember helping S shove the plywood and leaping from the hole. S's body left yours. Just darkness and the sting of forsythia branches, the wind of bodies, your heart pounding. Instead of running back to the dorm as you promised, you swung at the air in front of you, hoping they might attack you instead of S. But no one came. Were they already chasing S? You pulled out your cane and felt for the wall of the building to guide you back to the dorm. Two steps. Three steps. Thick hands pushed you as hard as they could until your body flew forward. The entirety of Forsythia House slammed directly into your head. A sharp, hot, heavy hurt consumed you.

And that was the last thing you remembered until the next day. How much time had passed? Hours? Days? Weeks? You woke up in a bed that wasn't yours. Your head still ached. A crust of snot, salt tears, and what you later learned was dried blood covered your face. You sniffed the air and it smelled like paper, concrete, coffee, cigarettes. A moan vibrated in your chest and throat. You needed to find out what happened to S. You scanned the room for illumination, discovering the shapes of two bodies moving in and out of your field of vision.

"Hey! Hey!" You waved your arms.

The two men moved closer. Their smells were unfamiliar. One held something in front of you. You reached for it: a wallet with a cold metal badge inside. *Police detectives?* Something bad had happened. *They found out about us, and now we're in trouble. Did someone tell the principal? Was S sent to Dogwood? Am I in Dogwood already? Did the Deaf Devils hurt her?*

"S where?" you pleaded, signing and using your out-of-tune saxophone voice. "S hurt? Tell me! Don't take S to Dogwood! My fault. I force her do sin!"

Mistaking your signing for aggression, the two detectives grabbed your arms. You struggled to free yourself so you could speak. One of the detectives hit you on the side of the face. The other detective punched you in the stomach, causing the air to leave your lungs. Before you could do anything, they strapped your legs and arms to the bed. Totally silenced.

Another day passed. Another night passed.

It was morning and the straps had been taken from your body. The scent of eggs and toast sat on a tray in front of you. But you had no desire to eat, since you still could only think of S. *Maybe S didn't go to Dogwood. Maybe S ran away and was waiting for you somewhere.*

A short while later you were taken to another room, this one much brighter, with several people you did not recognize. They sat you in a hard wooden chair. A moment later a woman tapped your forearm and began to sign into your hands.

"My name is T-I-N-A," she signed. "I (pause) am (pause) interpreter."

Someone who signs! Finally! For a moment you felt relief. But then, in terrible, halting sign language, the interpreter explained that you were in a place called (she fingerspelled) J-U-V-E-N-I-L-E (pause) F-E-T-E-N-T-I-O-N. *Fetention?* While you had grown used to bad interpreters in your life, Tina wasn't really an interpreter at all, and she definitely had never worked with someone who was blind or low-vision. She punched her amateurish signs into your palms as if the sheer physical force would fix her consistent errors. When she fingerspelled (which was the bulk of her signing), she consistently mistook the letter F for the letter D.

"A-R-L-O, you . . . W-I-L-L . . . talk . . . to . . . *the* . . . F-E-T-E-C-T-I-V-E . . . now."

What? What?!

With every mistake she would shake her ugly, sweaty hands, blame them for the fault of her brain. Her breath smelled like sour milk.

"Please sign again," you begged, hoping if you signed slowly that she might understand.

"Okay," she signed. "*The* F-E-T-E-C-T-I-V-E . . . wants . . . to . . . think [she means *know*] why . . . you . . . R-A-K-C-E . . . *the* . . . tiny . . . [*unintelligible*] . . ."

After a dozen attempts, you became familiar with her errors, and began to decode. R-A . . . she used the letter K but maybe she meant P. R-A-P . . . she tended to sign E like a C . . . R-A-P-E. *Rape? What rape? Had the Deaf Devils raped S?* Lightning bolts of rage erupted inside your heart.

"Where S?!" you screamed, pounding on the table. "I want real interpreter!"

But it was no use. Tina either didn't understand or was refusing to interpret your message. She came at you with another of the "fetective's" questions.

"Are . . . you . . . A . . . G-A-N-G?"

What was she talking about? You asked her to repeat her signs over and over. When you finally understood, you punched your signs violently in front of you, hoping they might hit the terrible interpreter in the face and silence her.

"No! No! No!"

But your angry answer just prompted more indecipherable signing.

"You . . . express (or was that the sign for *poem*?) . . . you . . . sin . . . bad . . . boy . . . other kid . . . R-O-O-F . . . September/Autumn . . . D-O-W-N . . . break . . . Bad. Sin sin sin . . . S-H . . ."

Then she spelled out a name—the name you still can't remember—and signed: "You know, Indian girl?"

Your heart started thrashing inside your chest. Something terrible must have happened to S.

"Please," you signed as slowly as possible in Signed English. "Where is S?! When . . . can . . . I . . . see H-E-R?! Please!"

No answer came. Instead, they put a piece of paper under your hands and gave you a pen with which to sign it. And you did. You were too exhausted to complain about the impossibly small print, and you thought maybe the paper might help you to see S again. After that they brought you back to your room and you fell asleep for a very long time.

◊ ◊ ◊

It was Molly's hands that shook you awake. You reached up to hug her, but she pushed you away.

"Come on," she signed angrily, coldly. "Let's go. Your uncle is here."

You explained about the bad interpreter and how the detectives punched you, and you begged Molly to take you to S as soon as possible.

"Stop!" Molly commanded. "No more talk. You are going home to your uncle's house now. You are never allowed back at the Rose Garden School. Finished."

You raged and pleaded, but it didn't matter. On the car ride home you sat alone in the back, staring at the flickering light-dark of the shadows out the window, feeling the cool of the glass against your cheek, the ache of the bruise next to your eye, the wet of your nose, which dripped tearful snot. When you left the school, why did Molly not even say goodbye to you? Why did Brother Birch not offer his usual handshake when he met you at the car? You tried to puzzle together what must have happened in the Secret Forest, to S, to Crazy Charles, to you. But too many pieces were missing.

◊ ◊ ◊

When you got back to Brother Birch's house, he forced you to kneel on the hardwood floor and ask Jehovah God's forgiveness for an hour. The pain in your knees felt like fire. At the end of your prayer session, Brother Birch lifted you up by the nape of your neck to make you stand up. When you were a child you imagined Brother Birch was the tallest man in the world, with hands capable of crushing your whole body with ease. But that day you noticed how short he had become, and how his hands had become shriveled and creased with thick ropy veins, like someone had pulled the plug from his body and let most of the water drain out.

The smaller, withered Brother Birch shoved you into a seat at the kitchen table. A moment later, Molly, who you hadn't seen since the detention center, put her hands under yours, telling you Brother Birch called her to Poughkeepsie because he needed to have a serious talk with you.

"Okay," you signed, grateful that you'd be able to ask some questions. "Okay. But, first, where S? What happen to S?"

She didn't respond. Was it her not telling you? Was it Brother Birch? Then Brother Birch said, via Molly's interpreting, "Did the other boys force you to commit that sin? Did you hurt anyone else?"

Other boys? Hurt? Was he talking about the sins you committed in the Secret Forest with S?

"Forced someone . . . never!" you insisted. "Hurt someone . . . never! Only me and S there. Long time, we love each other. Tell me! S . . . where?! I must see S!"

Molly and Brother Birch started talking to each other without signing to you. Telling secrets. After a very long time Molly's hands returned to yours, and she was finally speaking for herself. She proceeded to tell you a story you'd never heard before. A story about you. She said things like, *"You did this . . . Then you did that . . ."* And the whole time the word *you* didn't make sense because the story about "you" matched nothing in your memory.

Molly's story went like this: You were part of the Deaf Devils gang. You forced the younger and smaller students to go into the Secret Forest and do sex games with you. This is what the detectives meant when they said rape. Another student told a dorm boss that you were part of the gang of boys and you were hurting one of the students. The dorm boss was the one who called the police and sent them to find you in the bushes behind Forsythia House.

"Did you rape S?" Molly asked you directly.

Sign RAPE: *Your two hands, palms down, mime tearing something apart, one hand moves forward, the other backward.*

Just feeling the word in your hands sickened you. You were ready to scream your denial, but then something stopped you. You suddenly remembered that first time you had sex with S. You remembered the blood on the sheet. Had S lied to you? Did the blood mean you had hurt S that first time? Was that "rape"?

You started to cry so hard that it became difficult to breathe.

"Blood mean rape?" you told Molly while you wept. "Yes, yes some blood first time. But I didn't know! We sex each other because love. I love S! S love me! Is S hurt? Please tell me!"

"So you weren't part of the Deaf Devils?" Molly asked, speaking for herself. Her tone was more uncertain, like she was starting to believe you. "You didn't force S to have sex with you?"

"No! Never force! We sweethearts. Me with Deaf Devils? Never! They bad gang. They hurt kids. Someone push me against hard wall. S run away!"

"But you signed the paper at the detention center," Molly signed, her tone frustrated and confused. "It said that you were a gang member and that you raped S."

You began to sob again: "Paper very small print. See can't! Too dark. No magnifying glass. I can't understand interpreter! Confused! I not rape S! I not Deaf Devils! Please, please, tell me where S!"

Molly disappeared into an hourlong secret conversation with Brother Birch. When she returned, her hands were cold and shaking. She started signing much more slowly than before, like she was afraid to speak.

"Sorry. Your uncle and I have some very sad news for you. After what happened in the bushes behind Forsythia House, something else very bad happened. Someone was hurt very badly."

Molly's hands stopped. Was she gathering herself? Was she talking to Brother Birch? Her hands stood still in the air under your own.

A heavy darkness poured into the bottom of your stomach. You considered blocking whatever Molly was about to say from ever making contact with your brain, leaving her words forever stuck in the in-between place of knowing and not knowing.

"After the police found you by Forsythia House, S must have gotten very frightened and started running. She ran to Magnolia House and up the steps to the roof."

Molly's words became a blur of horror that you would try to erase from your mind for the next five and a half years. It is only when you write the essay for Professor Lavinia Bahr's class that you see Molly's story appear again in your mind. It is only with your new friend Hanne that you dare to look at the words chiseled into your brain like the names on old-fashioned tombstones.

S walked to the edge of the roof.

Someone tried to stop her.

S jumped.

No one really knows.

You slammed your head on the table over and over. Molly pulled your shoulders from the table and forced her own quaking hands back into yours.

"The ambulance came and took S to the hospital," she signed, her tears dampening her hands. She didn't want to tell you the story. She had to force herself. "The doctors tried their best. But S's injuries were just too serious. I'm so sorry, but S . . ."

The sign Molly used, the upward-facing five-hand collapsing through the hole of the other hand, was the same sign she used when she told you the sad news about your mother. The sign could still have meant so many other things: *disappear, missing, lost.* But you knew the word she meant.

32

THE FACEBOOK PROFILE

I spent the rest of the day lying in bed staring at the ceiling, re-creating the story of Arlo and S's last day in my head. There was no word in ASL or English that could capture the absolute injustice of it.

After opening a second bottle of red wine, I sat in front of my computer staring at Hanne's photo of Arlo. One of his eyes looked directly at the camera, while the other was slightly crossed. He seemed to be looking at me and beyond me. In this world, but not of this world. At the same time there was something so familiar about him.

All of a sudden it wasn't hard to see the resemblance. I just hadn't wanted to see it before. It wasn't exact, of course. They didn't look like brothers or anything. Bruno was mixed-race and, when we first met, already in his midthirties. He also wasn't blind. But I had to admit, the shape of the eyebrows, the dimples, that inner brilliance that pushed against the eyes, yearning to come out in spite of the world's communication deficiencies, even some of Arlo's sweet deaf chirps and sighs were similar. Both men possessed a powerful and innocent presence that inspired a desire to rescue and be rescued by them.

I switched tabs from Facebook to Google and typed in Bruno's full name. I wanted to see if I could find some old high school or college photo that might have been posted online. I was only twenty-one when Bruno was my ASL instructor up in Rochester. I had always been attracted to older men and didn't remember ever having seen a photo of Bruno in his younger days. What did he look like when he was Arlo's age? My first search revealed nothing, only a dozen other people with the same name. I searched again, adding all the information I knew about him: Deaf, full name, his parents' old address on Alfred Avenue, New York State School for the Deaf, the National Technical Institute for the Deaf, professor, communications, class of 1992. I pressed Search. Because Bruno went to high school in the eighties and had no social media presence later in life, all that came up was his obituary and an entry on the NTID Alumni site for deceased members of his class, under the words "May They Rest in Peace": Bruno James Sipkowski, Class of '92, died January 2011.

That was all I could find.

In December 2010 I drove all the way to Rochester at about six in the morning. Bruno and I had broken up six months before, and I had promised to give him "space." But that morning I knew I had to try one more time. I arrived at his house and looked up at the window of his old room, hoping to see his face look down for me, smiling like he used to do. I sat in my car for at least forty minutes, thinking about that first time we kissed in that room, the first time I had physically been with someone I actually loved. I could have knocked on the door that day, but I didn't. If I did knock, if he did answer, I would have apologized for—what? Not coming sooner? Being afraid? Not being a better boyfriend? Something.

I closed the tabs of my hopeless search and returned to the Facebook Create Profile page. Name: Arlo Dilly. Age: 23. Occupation: Student. High School: The Rose Garden School for the Deaf. College: Dutchess Community College. Hometown: Poughkeepsie, New York. Religion: Jehovah's Witness. Relationship Status: Single. Interested in: Women. I made sure to write enough personal information on his profile that if any of his old friends looked for him, he'd be easy to find. Next, I searched for the DeafBlind Facebook groups Tabitha had suggested, joining the ones with the most members. I read through some of the posts on the wall for DeafBlind Connections NY.

There were a few announcements of DeafBlind get-togethers down in the city. One announcement for guide-dog applications from a place in Rochester. A DeafBlind guy from Mineola, on Long Island, wrote a post about his frustration with applying for housing. I saw a post from the previous week: "Hey, anyone on tonight?! I'm bored and want talk." More than a few other DeafBlind folks chimed in, "Hey! I'm bored too. What's happening?" Suddenly there was a lively group conversation about DeafBlind camps and a lousy co-navigator. Say what you want about the evils of technology, but the internet is definitely one of the greatest advancements in the world of the Deaf and DeafBlind. That is, if the person can both see and read well enough, and isn't prohibited from using the internet.

I started building a network of connections for Arlo, friending a few dozen DeafBlind members on the pages. If hearing-sighted people had six degrees of separation, the Deaf had three degrees, and the DeafBlind maybe one and a half or less. One of those random DeafBlind connections had to know someone from the Rose Garden School. After friending at least fifty DeafBlind group members, I posted the following message on each group's wall:

> Hi. My name is Arlo Dilly, I was a student at the Rose Garden School for the Deaf in Ogdensburg, New York. I'm looking for my good friends Martin and Big Head Lawrence who would have graduated between four and six years ago. I don't know their last names, but I was their roommate. If you know them could you ask them to send me their contact information. I live in Poughkeepsie, New York. I would very much like to hear from them. I miss them very much. Private message me here or you can send an email to . . .

I typed in my own email address. *Look at me*, I thought, *I'm being the Cyrano de Bergerac of the DeafBlind.*

Before I went to bed I checked the board, but there were no responses.

As I was about to shut down my computer, I heard the *ting* of a new message. I quickly opened an email in my *gingerterp69* in-box from someone named Larry Garcia:

> Dear Arlo:
>
> I am very surprised! I thought you was disappeared forever! Yes, I will like to meet and talk long time. I work Philadelphia School for Blind but will staying at Helen Keller Center in Long Island for workshop. I can take train to see you up in Poughkeepsie. I am free Tuesdays and Thursdays. Are you free to meet next week? Just write me email where to meet and I will come. Must talk to you. What for your email called gingerterp69?
>
> Larry "Big Head Lawrence"
Garcia

I quickly forwarded Arlo the email, telling him to respond to Big Head Lawrence as soon as he could via the Gmail account I had set up for the purpose. I was beyond excited. I felt like I had done something truly good for the first time in such a long time. Intoxicated by the wine and the success of the plan, I hunted down Larry "Big Head Lawrence" Garcia's profile in the DeafBlind group. His main photo was just the Guy Fawkes mask, that scary white-faced icon of anarchy that hacker groups tended to use. When I searched through Larry's other photos, I noticed the majority appeared to be of other people, especially women. Then I found a group shot, from what looked like one of those DeafBlind camps Tabitha had told me about. The photo showed about a dozen DeafBlind folks with their white canes and two or three guide dogs. My eyes were suddenly drawn to a shorter person with a hoodie at the edge of the group wearing what I thought at first was a novelty rubber Halloween mask. When I clicked through more of the photos, I found even more of the same masked short boy.

I zoomed in, and quite literally gasped. I finally understood. What I mistook for a boy in a mask was actually a man's face and head covered with small and large tumors. The condition, called NF1 (neurofibromatosis type 1), is often misidentified as the same condition the famous Elephant Man suffered from but is quite different—and more common. The tumors grow along the nerves of the skin. I learned about it years ago when I attended a workshop on medical interpreting. Larry was also much shorter than the other men in the group photo, with a typical-looking young man's body. His huge head composed nearly a third of his entire height. Enlarging the photo further, I looked into Larry's one unobfuscated eye. It was dark and innocent-looking, almost like an anime character's in its openness. Above it was a well-shaped quizzical eyebrow that seemed to be in the midst of asking a question. This was Big Head Lawrence.

33

REUNION

You will be meeting Big Head Lawrence at a specific bench on an inside walkway that goes over the tracks at the Poughkeepsie train station. Cyril met you at the Abilities Institute and secretly drove you to the station. You tell Cyril that Big Head Lawrence most certainly will be traveling with an SSP, or a friend. Even though his vision has always been better than yours, he surely could not get all the way from his home in Philadelphia to the Helen Keller National Center in Long Island and then all the way to Poughkeepsie on his own. Still, Cyril wrote Big Head Lawrence specific directions, pointing out that the bench is between two giant square trash cans.

You finally tell Cyril to leave, because you'd like some time to think before Big Head Lawrence gets there. Cyril keeps saying, "Are you sure you'll be okay?" and doesn't seem like he wants to leave. You tell him you will be fine and that you will meet him at 5 p.m. — right outside the front door like he showed you — so he can take you back to the Abilities Institute where you will catch the Able-Ride back home.

When you are alone on the bench, your heart beats very fast. The vibrations of trains, like thirty-second earthquakes, rock the floor beneath you. People are traveling to all sorts of places. Some are going all the way to Canada or down to Florida. Maybe they too are meeting old best friends. Your hands are sweaty, so you wipe them on Snap's fur. Snap doesn't mind since she likes to be petted, and she knows how nervous you are because you're breaking your promise to Molly, Brother Birch, and Jehovah God.

Red star.

Your intention for this meeting—at least the one you tell yourself and the one you will tell Brother Birch if he finds out—is to reconnect with Big Head Lawrence for the purpose of giving him some JW literature and to talk about Jehovah God. Your backpack is full of brochures, *Watchtowers*, and a large-print copy of the Bible.

Gold star.

If your old friend becomes a JW then maybe he can tell Martin and then he will convert to JW too and then you all can be friends again. Together the three of you can help many Deaf and DeafBlind people come to the light and spend eternity in God's paradise.

Double gold star.

But this is mostly a lie.

Red star.

You really want to see your old friend because you miss him, because you're lonely, because seeing him is like connecting a line from your present life to your past life—a past life you have worked so hard to forget.

Double red star.

Another train going somewhere passes beneath you.

Five and a half years ago, after what happened at the Rose Garden School, there was an investigation by police detectives and social workers. During that year, the brothers and sisters at the Kingdom Hall mostly avoided you. Brother Birch told you that you had gone down a dark road, and you needed to ask Jehovah God for help. But you didn't. You mostly just wanted to disappear. Then, a year later, Brother Birch said that you (as well as the other boys at the Rose Garden School) were *cleared of all charges*. No one had been raped, they admitted. No one would be blamed for S jumping off the building. No one. You asked Brother Birch if you could visit your old friends Martin and Big Head Lawrence. But Brother

Birch said no. *If you want to be happy, you need to let that part of your life go. Promise me you will not mention their names or the name of that school. You may not have committed a crime, but you have committed a grave sin in the eyes of Jehovah God. You need to read the Bible and pray to Jehovah God to heal your soul and help you forget the sinful people Satan brought into your life. The word of Jehovah will drown out the evil memories.* And you tried. You prayed, you read, you tried to forget. But, instead, with every other breath, you thought about S and what happened. You still recalled the smell of S's skin, the touch of S's fingers writing love words on your body. Remembering the good things hurt worse than remembering the bad.

You couldn't concentrate. You barely ate.

The bad dreams started.

In these dreams, you always have excellent vision like when you were small. You can see people's faces clearly, and the bright light doesn't bother your eyes. But with this magical clear vision you can also see S running from some evil unseen person. You chase S up steep stairs to the roof of the building. S stands far across the roof from you and looks over the edge. The wind blows in your hair and face. You too look over the edge and the ground is so far away that the fear causes your testicles to retreat inside you. S turns toward you, looking terrified, and begs: *Please. Don't let me fall. Please.* Suddenly a pair of hands try to force S over the edge. You are desperate to stop the evil person from killing her. But that is when you recognize that the hands—the hands pushing S off the building—are yours. S looks at you with her beautiful, heartbroken eyes. You whisper to her: *I sorry. I bad boy. I love you.* Then you shove S's body as hard as you can off the roof. Her body falls for a very long time, tumbling slowly through the air. Through her eyes, you can see the sky, and the birds, and the tops of the trees, and then the ground moving closer and closer. You see S's beautiful, perfect hands reach out to stop the ground. But the ground won't stop. Just before she hits, you are back outside S's body, watching it all happen. Her body crashes onto the pavement and shatters into a hundred pieces. Body parts and blood are everywhere. You begin to drown in sadness, and you grab at your eyes with their perfect vision and scratch and dig, wanting to be blind again. But, as hard as you try, your eyesight stays strong, and you stare at S's remains, seeing everything forever.

For a year you had dreams like this. You knew you would die if you didn't stop thinking about S. You told yourself: *FACT: S killed herself. FACT: S cannot be saved. FACT: You can save yourself. FACT: You are heartbroken over a person who did not even exist. Satan was trying to trick you into committing sin. That's why you can't forget. It was the ghost child that visited you in the middle of the night. It was the ghost child's idea to commit the sin of sex. The ghost child bled and said nothing. But, worst of all, if Satan sent a doomed Hindu goat to persuade a poor DeafBlind boy to do sinful things and turn his back on the way of Jehovah God and Jesus Christ, Son of God, that means the ghost child just lied about loving you in order to send you to eternal death.*

That means the ghost child never loved you.

You finally felt something toward S you had never felt before: hatred. You promised yourself that you would no longer think of that name unless it was attached to the words *betrayal, sin,* and *Satan.* After you had these realizations you could finally breathe again. Jehovah God had saved you.

One afternoon, almost two years after the Day That Changed Everything, you walked into Brother Birch's living room when Molly was there. You told Brother Birch: *Long time ago I did bad things at school. I disobey Jehovah God and follow Satan. Sorry. Sorry. I wrong. I want Jesus save me! I want become preacher and spread word of Jehovah God and our Lord Jesus Christ our Savior. Please forgive me.*

Brother Birch hugged you, told you he loved you, and said he was proud of you and would help you to be a spiritually strong young man, and he asked Mrs. Brother Birch to give you two pieces of chocolate cake at dinner.

Molly said she was crying because she was happy. She hugged you too. You thought you had finally, really, truly forgotten.

◊ ◊ ◊

But you hadn't. You just became an expert at lying to yourself for the next three years. And then you met Cyril and started to learn about the sublime, and then you met Hanne, who made you be honest, and then you wrote your essay and started to tell the truth. Now you sit on the bench, in the middle of a walkway at Poughkeepsie Amtrak Train Station, waiting for your old friend. Gooseflesh erupts on your neck and upper arms. You are excited and scared. What if this is the key back into that room full of sorrow? What if, this time, you will never get back out?

Your hand rubs against the smooth metal slats that cover the metal bench. It curves to match the shape of a sitting body. You wouldn't mind sitting here for a very long time. All the people traveling on trains make you feel connected to the world somehow. It suddenly occurs to you that maybe a thousand people have sat on the very same bench waiting for their train or their friend to visit. When you are done rubbing the bench, you pull out your hand sanitizer and clean your hands.

Thirty minutes later Snap pulls his leash as someone approaches. You scan the space in front of you, but the light from the window glares in your face and makes it impossible to see. A moment later you can tell someone is in front of you. He taps your shoulder and presses his name into your palm. You do the same. It's him. It's you. You hug each other long and hard. He reaches up to touch your cheek. You caress his head, which is even bigger and more strangely shaped than you remember. But his small body, his smell, the way he signs are all exactly the same. Instantly, you are brought back to those hundreds of nights where you, Martin, and he would huddle your bodies together for warmth and tell stories until two in the morning. You and Big Head Lawrence sit down on the bench so your knees touch, your hands entwine. You soon learn

that Big Head Lawrence didn't come with an SSP or friend. He made the
entire journey alone.

"Wow!" you say. "You train from Philadelphia to Long Island then
New York City and then Poughkeepsie . . . very far. Can't believe it. Yourself? Alone?"

Big Head Lawrence scoffs at your suggestion that he would need a
guide.

"I train alone one thousand times!" he signs. "I already train Chicago,
Orlando, New Orleans. You train alone, never?"

Big Head Lawrence's question embarrasses you. Not only haven't you
taken the train alone, you haven't ever ridden a train at all. You even failed
at taking a bus alone. This, in fact, is the first time you have set foot in
the Poughkeepsie train station. You decide to ignore Big Head Lawrence's
question and get back to important things.

"Wow! Long time never see you," you say. "Curious, after you graduate
high school, then what do? I know zero. Since then: What's up?"

Then Big Head Lawrence starts telling you a very surprising story.
First, he went to college at the Rochester Institute of Technology (RIT),
where he stopped using the name Big Head Lawrence, since it was a mean
name, and started using another name: Larry.

Name-sign LARRY: *The thumb of the "L" hand flicks off the middle
of his forehead the same way the crooked middle finger of the "five"
hand would flick off his forehead for the word* smart *or* brilliant.

After having a lot of fun at college he moved to Philadelphia and started
working at the Pennsylvania School for the Blind in the library as a tech
specialist. He gets a salary and benefits and lives with an annoying roommate in Northeast Philadelphia. He also takes the bus by himself every day
and plays chess on the internet. Because he is an expert in technology for
the DeafBlind, Larry has traveled to thirteen states to teach workshops.

"Next month, I will give a presentation at Gallaudet University conference. I will top technology speaker. You should come!"

You say you wish you could, but maybe next time. Part of you wants to cry because Larry has done so much and you have done so little, and another part wants to cry because you've missed being with someone else who understands what it means to be DeafBlind.

"Wow! Your life!" You make the ASL sign indicating to take off and soar. "What about best friend Martin? Martin live where? College too?"

Larry tells you how Martin moved to Seattle two years after graduating from the Rose Garden School, and now lives with an interpreter named Mel.

Name-sign MEL: *"M" on the bicep because Mel is a bodybuilder as well as an interpreter.*

"Martin and Mel are G-A-Y partners," Larry says. "You know Martin always G-A-Y, right?"

"Yes, I know. My interpreter he also G-A-Y. He help me find you. He my friend. Curious . . . you G-A-Y too?"

"No! Not G-A-Y. I love women! My favorite . . . short woman with big boobs. But no girlfriend now. Single."

Larry doesn't appear to be sad about not having a girlfriend. You remember what S had once told you about how cruel people were to Larry because of his unusual looks. Were you hurting his feelings every time you called him Big Head Lawrence? Before you can ask, Larry continues.

"I had girlfriend for a while—name T-A-R-A. Blind girl, hard of hearing. But broke up. Why? Let me have sex with her . . . very rare. Maybe touch her breast and finger her . . . that's all. D-U-L-L. Kiss once, twice. Nothing! But Tara always wants me buy her everything. Clothes, movies, dinner. Can't afford! Tara too expensive. Fed up! Finish! Done with that! I wait until meet new girl who has own job and likes me kiss her and sex with her ten times every week. Martin, he smartest! Why? His boyfriend very affectionate and helps pay the bills!"

"Martin working too?"

Larry tells you that Martin doesn't have a job at the moment, but lives comfortably on disability and has a nice apartment filled with all the newest technologies. In his free time Martin volunteers for a DeafBlind rights organization and goes to college part-time in hopes of becoming a social worker. Martin is very happy living in Seattle and being gay.

"You know, Seattle best place for DeafBlind!" Larry says. "So many services, DeafBlind housing, get-togethers, parties, F-U-N! Next year I maybe move to Seattle to be roommates with Martin and his boyfriend. They live in big nice supportive housing. Have extra bedroom. Very cheap. Hey, idea! Maybe you can come too. Why not?! We can roommates again. Like old times!"

For a split second you let yourself have the dream. You imagine yourself in that faraway place called Seattle, which appears in your brain like a warm beautiful farm by a lake with friendly horses that would smell like flowers and delicious foods. You would spend all day with your DeafBlind best friends, in your own warm, fully accessible apartment, telling stories, gossiping, and eating whatever you wanted without having to answer to Brother Birch. But soon a cold blanket of reality settles over you. The dream is an impossibility. The law says Brother Birch, your legal guardian, decides what you do and where you live. Yet one more thing you are embarrassed to tell Larry.

"Impossible!" you say. "Will survive, how? Every year, my eyesight gets worse. Without parents or guardian, I stuck. SSI check not enough. Martin's gay boyfriend take care of three DeafBlind? Doubt it. I must stay in Poughkeepsie because Brother Birch takes care of me."

"What for?" Larry laughs. "Not need someone take care of you. We take care of each other. We independent."

"Independent? Impossible! Cook for you . . . who? Arranges rides for you . . . who? Make sure you don't spend too much money . . . who? Talk to Social Security office for you . . . who? What if murderer break in apartment? Live alone? No way! Scared. Forget it!"

You can feel your old friend's hands go silent, yet they still twitch like they are full of words. *Why doesn't he say something? Is he angry about you disregarding his invite?* All of a sudden, a tidal wave of angry words pummels your hands.

"Finish you! You not baby. DeafBlind can! Look, I cook, I clean, I take the bus and train alone. I get O and M training! If need special help, I just contact friends or case manager. No big deal. Sometimes hard? Sure. Some DeafBlind struggle. Sure. I see better than you? Sure. But know what? Martin full blind, vision zero, but he independent!"

You want to crawl under the metal bench. You recall how Cyril had tried to make the same point as Larry, when he came back from that conference and told you about that woman Tabitha, the DeafBlind boss. Why has no one told you about this possibility of independence before? Larry goes on to tell you how both he and Martin are involved in the DeafBlind rights movement, and that both of them had traveled to Washington, DC, with a big group to demand the government provide funding for SSPs, trainings, and free assistive technology for DeafBlind people all over America.

Then your old friend, perhaps feeling he has been too harsh, says, "Sorry. I talk too much . . . blah blah blah. What about you? Still live with uncle? Molly still interpreter?"

You wish you had some long story of a new happy life to tell him, but you don't.

"Yes. Same thing," you say. "Many years."

"Can I ask you private question?" Larry asks in a more serious tone, which makes you nervous. "Long time ago, at school, you ran away and didn't say goodbye to best friends. Why?!"

Larry's signs grow more agitated, while his leg presses against yours, twitching like he is trying to control himself.

"When you disappear everyone very upset! Girls Em and Marla cry, *Why Arlo leave us? Why Arlo not write email to us?* Me and Martin, when not hear from you many weeks, we cry too. You supposed to be our best friend . . . but then disappear . . . no explanation. Recently, when Victor from DeafBlind Facebook group tell me you want contact me, I think: *Fuck Arlo! Fuck Arlo for run away and ignore friends many years!* Then I ask Martin. He says: *Calm down, Larry! You must go and ask Arlo 'Hurt us . . . why? Disappear . . . what for?'* So, now tell me! Why? Why you run away and so cruel?"

Larry's anger confuses you. Didn't they already know? Didn't both he and Martin know how you were charged with a crime? Didn't he understand how S's death impacted you? Did they actually think it was your choice to disappear and not communicate with them?

Your hands pound his palms in fury.

"You crazy? I not run away! I want to say goodbye to best friends. School and uncle force me leave! I want to contact, but uncle forbid! They tell me I must forget. And I hurt so bad . . . hurt so bad for long time. Must forget! Understand? Because of what happened. You know! What happen with sweetheart S!"

You can't do this. Too much remembering. The word *sweetheart* connected to the name S makes the long-ago ache return. Your stomach roils with sick.

"No, no, no," you shout. "Can't talk about that! No!"

You yank your hands from Larry's and sit on them, feeling utterly alone again. After a moment, using the same Protactile method Cyril taught you, Larry "nods his head" on the side of your thigh. He understands. You unleash your hands and lift them to him.

"You still heartbreak?" Larry asks. "So sad about S."

"My heart broken . . . forever."

There it is. The truth.

Again Larry "nods his head" on your thigh, then says, "So many people cry because what happened S. Everyone gossip that S not jump, that S pushed. Very puzzling! No one say truth. But still . . . not fair. Stuck in hospital many years. Can't walk. No school. No work."

Huh? Hospital many years? No school? No work? Larry talks about S as if she is alive. Is he misunderstanding who you are talking about?

"You not pay attention!" you shout, enraged by his ignorance. "I talking about S! My S! Indian girl from Queens, New York. My sweetheart, S! You stupid!"

"What?! Don't call me stupid! I know S!"

"Spell name . . . how?!"

And Larry spells out the letters of S's full name. It is the first time you have seen the actual spelling of S's name in years.

"First name spell, S-H-R-I, last name M-U-K-H-E-R-J-E-E. Pea brain! I know who Shri is!"

That was it! There is no misunderstanding. That was her name, now you recalled the letters, the shape: Shri Mukherjee. Full name: Shridevi Mukherjee!

Your hands stab the awful truth into Larry's ignorant hands.

"Shri dead! Killed herself! Jumped from building! Dead!"

"What?" Larry says. You can feel the confusion in his hands. "You crazy! Shri not dead! Shri only hurt self . . . very bad hurt. Broke spine. Can't walk. Then, after accident, family stick Shri in nursing home somewhere back in New York City. Not good life. Very lonely there."

What? What?! Your body begins to quake. Your heart vibrates inside the liquid of your own confusion. You might vomit. Shri is alive? Shri . . . is alive?! You are lost between truths. Could Larry just have gotten it wrong? He's deaf and blind, after all. Molly and Brother Birch see perfectly, hear perfectly. They are good Christians. Molly told you Shri was dead. Brother Birch told you so too. The investigators? Didn't they tell you Shri was dead? No, they thought you had raped Shri. They said Shri jumped off the building, but they never said the word dead.

"You saw Shri alive? True business?"

"I didn't see, but Em saw. Before they good friends. Two or three years ago, Em visited Shri. Shri lives in a place in Queens. Place like half apartment, half hospital. Em say Shri stuck there like prison. Shri's mother move back to India, and aunts and uncles almost never visit. Not fair. Very sad story. You should visit! I bet Shri still in love with you!"

Is this another bad dream waiting to trick you? You ask Larry to repeat the story three more times. Shri fell (or was pushed) from the roof. The Deaf students saw them take S's living body away. The teachers told the students that Shri was seriously injured but would live. Even Em and Marla visited S in the hospital. Everyone thought you disappeared but would return to rescue S. But you didn't.

Larry is telling the truth. This is not a dream.

Your mind scans that moment Molly told you the terrible news five and a half years before. Her hands were shaking, her tone unreal. Was she shaking because she was upset or because . . .

Molly and Brother Birch lied to you?

You can't breathe. Your body trembles. An explosion of emotion goes off in your brain: buildings crumble, sidewalks crack, bridges collapse. Snap scratches her paw on your thigh, trying to calm you down. But you can't be calm. Your world has been turned right-side up. You are laughing, crying, and in a rage all at the same time. For the first time in five and a half years you let the full, complete idea of Shri back inside your brain. Shri is alive! You start slapping your hands on Larry's body.

"Why hit me?" Larry asks, annoyed. "What for? You epilepsy attack?"

Larry's confusion makes you laugh and cry harder. You take deep breaths and steady yourself. You assure Snap and Larry that you are okay. Then, very slowly, you recount the story of the last five and a half years, repeating the lies Molly and Brother Birch told you. You tell of the promises you made to forget, and all the tricks you had to play on yourself so you wouldn't drown in the quicksand of sadness. Larry shares your anger at

Molly and Brother Birch. He apologizes for thinking the worst of you, and vows to tell Martin and the others the truth.

"Doesn't matter," you tell him. "I must go see Shri now. Help me! Show me where now!"

"Calm down," Larry warns. "Must calm. Remember . . . your uncle and Molly will try and stop you. They liars. Must smart. Must keep secret. Go slowly. We need research problem. Step-by-step."

You know your old friend is right. You take deep breaths. You try to make your pounding heart stay calm, but you know it's no use. Shri is alive.

34

ALONE AGAIN

You wake up and it's a sticky, hot Wednesday morning. You stretch your body, squeezing the sleep from your muscles. Instead of your usual morning sadness, there is another feeling tingling at the top of your skin . . . *Hope? Wait . . . that's right . . . not a dream . . . S is alive!*

Swirls of light and joy whip around your insides. You pummel your bed with your fists and legs, wanting even the room to vibrate with happiness. But then you quiet yourself. Larry warned that you needed a plan. If you let Brother Birch or Molly know, you may never get to S.

But what about the hatred that burns in your belly? Just how many lies did they tell? Was it true how your mother, Alma, died? Was it true how your father left? And what about Jehovah God? Jesus? The 144,000 saved souls who will immediately ascend to heaven while the others need to wait for Judgment Day? When people lie, they take away your ability to make a real decision. They take away your ability to be happy. It is as if, for five and a half years, Molly and Brother Birch rearranged the furniture of your life, and you have constantly been tripping ever since. Worse, they have condemned poor S to be locked away, alone, in some horrible place, thinking you stopped caring.

That! That can never be forgiven!

Your heart pounds with rage. *If only they could feel the pain that's consumed me for the last five and a half years.* But as soon as your mind turns to thoughts of cold revenge, the sunlight of the moment warms you again, causing you to remember that *Shri is alive!*

Very soon you will be able to touch Shri's hand, taste her sweet mouth, smell her turmeric-and-coriander breath. You twist your sheet into a ball and pretend it's Shri's smaller body wrapped up in your long limbs. You linger in the fantasy briefly before you leap from your bed, thinking, *Time to work on a plan.*

After dressing yourself, you put Snap's harness on and give her extra scratches on her favorite spot, where her spine meets the top of her tail. Your head fills with fantasies of escape. You picture Shri, using her keen, lucid vision, leading you on the getaway, as Snap snarls and bites Brother Birch and Molly, who follow close behind. You imagine your enemies throwing Bibles at you, shouting about how you will die an eternal death if you don't follow what they say. You and Shri will laugh at them and say: *Jehovah God is on our side now! As is the Blue God! And the Elephant God!* Then you and Shri will jump on Snap's strong back as if she's a horse and ride off far ahead of Molly and Brother Birch, who will be too out of breath to follow.

You will be free.

Brother Birch sits in the kitchen when you enter. You remove all emotion from your face and say good morning. As Larry said, you must keep everything secret until you have a plan. You say a fake prayer, then eat a piece of white toast with grape jelly.

Brother Birch stops you from eating to sign in his shitty sign language, "Remember, Arlo, Jehovah God . . . see you . . . see, see: Careful! You cannot H-I-D-E."

Why did he say that? Could someone have seen you yesterday and told Brother Birch about you and Larry at the Amtrak station? You force yourself to finish eating. Just as you are leaving your seat, Brother Birch grabs your wrist and pulls you back down.

"I know what you D-I-D!" Brother Birch signs. "I know what you wrote in the E-S-S-A-Y! Not O-B-E-Y me! You lie! You C-O-M-M-I-T-T-E-D bad sin!"

The essay? He's talking about the essay. It's not about Larry. Why is he bringing up the essay again? He still doesn't know what you wrote since you deleted the file from your computer. Only Hanne and the professor have a copy. Did they betray you? You stall, pretending you didn't understand Brother Birch's signs.

"Sorry. Don't understand. Say again."

"You lie!" Brother Birch shouts in his awful signing. "I find the E-S-S-A-Y in the trash F-O-L-D-E-R on the C-O-M-P-U-T-E-R. Bad boy! Bad boy! You try to . . . H-I-D-E . . . E-S-S-A-Y from me! You break P-R-O-M-I-S-E to me and to Jehovah God! I am not happy! Jehovah God is not happy!"

You did not know there was something called a trash folder on the computer. You thought once you deleted a document it was gone forever. Another violation of your trust. Your heart bursts into flames yet again. Is it time to take Brother Birch by the throat and tell him you know he's been lying to you? Is it time to pummel his face until your knuckles feel the bones of his skull? No. Not yet. Larry would tell you to hold it inside. Wait for the right time. For now, pretend to feel confused and sorry. Make your eyebrows, like contortionists, bend themselves into unnatural contrition. Tell Brother Birch that it was the professor's idea to write the essay, and it was for her eyes only, and so you didn't think it would count as disobeying him. Brother Birch grabs your hands, silencing you.

"Stop lying! Jehovah God hates liars! Bible says . . ."

Brother Birch stumbles over the fingerspelling of the biblical characters' names. He is quoting the story he taught once in Bible study about Ananias and Sapphira lying to the Apostle Peter. The lesson was that any time you lie to anyone, you are also lying to the Holy Spirit.

"Arlo! You know that Jehovah God K-I-L-L-E-D them for lying? Now, tell me what else you are H-I-D-I-N-G!"

What else does he know? Can he also look inside the trash folder of your brain? No. He can't.

"I sorry," you sign slowly to him. "I wrote about sinful time. Never again."

Again Brother Birch angrily punches his hands into yours, shouting, "Why do you keep lying to me?!"

The table shakes from his body bouncing up and down. He's disappointed you aren't his good DeafBlind JW miracle boy anymore. The one who will keep the secrets of his own hypocrisy. You aren't useful any longer.

"You break Jehovah God's heart! You break my heart! College bad I-N-F-L-U-E-N-C-E on you. Interpreter C-Y-R-I-L is bad man! Bad man! He help you write E-S-S-A-Y?"

"No, no. Cyril knows nothing. My fault. I use computer at school. Very sorry. I sin. Never do again. Promise!"

You wait a long time for Brother Birch to say something. When he finally does, he doesn't appear to be angry. He is calm and gentle. This scares you more.

"I am sorry," he says. "I am sorry I A-N-G-R-Y. We all C-O-M-M-I-T sins sometimes. I am a sinner too. If we sin, then we ask F-O-R-G-I-V-E-N-E-S-S. Do you ask for F-O-R . . . ?"

Before he can finish spelling the word, you tell him, yes, you ask Jehovah God for forgiveness. But inside, you don't. Next Brother Birch has you take out your SBC so he can write in his own language rather than struggling through yours. He types:

"Good. You are a good boy, Arlo, but the Devil is testing you. So, as your guardian, I will help you commit no more sins. From now on, you are not allowed to submit any more assignments without me or Molly checking them. Understand? Also, you can't go to the Abilities Institute, the Dunkin' Donuts, or anywhere else alone between now and when we leave for Ecuador. Do you understand?"

But how will you go see Shri if you can't find time away from Molly and Brother Birch? You want to confront Brother Birch about his lies and tell him you know about his sins. But, like Larry said, you need to be smarter.

"I understand," you say. "I sorry. I not go anywhere alone. I not write personal story ever again. Promise!"

Then you look up to heaven and fold your hands and pretend to pray.

"Jehovah God, Jesus . . . I sinner. Please forgive me and help me not sin again. Hallelujah!"

"Good boy," Brother Birch signs, waving the *I love you* sign. "You are like"—*he uses the sign for* like, *as in "favoring something," rather than the sign that means* similar—"my O-W-N son. Understand?"

"Yes."

"Molly loves you . . . uh . . . T-O-O. Everything we do is to teach you a G-O-D-L-Y path. Understand?"

"Understand," you say, then, switching into very basic Signed English: "I will try to be spiritually strong man."

Brother Birch pats your hand, and via the SBC he reminds you about your potential for bringing many sinful goats into the flock of Jehovah God. Then he types:

"I already booked the Able-Ride for an hour early for your class trip to Albany on Friday. 8 a.m. pickup with a 6 p.m. return. I'm not going to be around or available that morning, since I'm going down to Tuxedo Park for an important Elders meeting. So, you should email Molly and tell her to meet you here at 7:30 a.m. It sounds like a nice field trip. The night before I'll leave a baloney sandwich in the refrigerator for you to bring. Your favorite!"

And that's when you come up with your plan.

35

SAVIOR SYNDROME

Hanne and I met at Caffe Aurora on Mill Street near the train station. Except for the cashier and some random midsummer tourists, we were the only ones there. While Hanne was finishing reading the final email exchange with Big Head Lawrence, I stared at the huge display of chocolate teddy bears with bulging black-and-white sugar eyeballs. They appeared to be in a state of shock—just like Hanne and me.

"This is not possible," she said.

"I know. When he told me, I thought maybe he was just having some wish-fulfilling fantasy. Christ knows I've had the same daydream about Bruno suddenly coming back to life. But that's what Larry told him. S—Shri Mukherjee—is alive. I even looked into it. I called the Rose Garden School. They wouldn't give me the name, but they confirmed that a student did fall from the roof almost six years ago. There were no deaths."

I could see Hanne's stunned look turn to rage as she came to the same conclusion.

"Those people should be arrested!" she said, banging her fist on the marble table.

"I hear you," I said. "But it's not so simple. I mean, if Brother Birch was hitting Arlo, or starving him, I'd have to do something as a mandated reporter. But lying to someone isn't a crime. And right now Arlo's just excited that he'll see Shri again. And—this is the really weird part—Arlo said he talked it out with his uncle and is able to forgive him. I guess that's his whole religious thing. I would have grabbed a knife."

"Well, I won't forgive them," Hanne growled. "He's going to get to see her, yes?"

"That's the plan. Big Head Lawrence was able to find out where she's living, which unfortunately is this long-term nursing rehab in Queens."

"A nursing home?" Hanne looked alarmed. "How disabled is she?"

"Unclear. Arlo told me he was able to contact the home about visiting. Brother Birch can't take him but told Arlo that if he could find his way there, it was okay for him to go. So Arlo's asked me to take him, which has me a little nervous."

"You have to do it!"

"Are you kidding me? I wouldn't miss it for the world."

Hanne began to clap and stomp her feet, which made the old woman behind the counter look over.

"We're driving down tomorrow since he can't miss his church thing on Saturday. Arlo was supposed to go on that museum field trip to Albany, but he wrote his professor and asked if it would be okay for him to write about visiting Shri instead. Naturally Professor Bahr loved the idea."

"This is perfect!" Hanne gushed. "Tell him I want to read it when he's finished. Can I come too?"

"This isn't a reality show, Hanne. No."

"Does that awful woman get to go?" Hanne grumbled.

"Molly? No. In fact, when he was emailing Professor Bahr and me, Arlo asked us not to say anything to Molly. He's forgiving his uncle but not her. He wrote us that he'll just tell Molly last-minute that the professor said there isn't going to be a lot of interpreting needed on the trip so he's just bringing one interpreter: me. I asked him if he didn't think Molly would naturally try and call his uncle to complain, but Arlo says Birch will be incommunicado because of some JW meeting."

"Pretty cunning that one, huh?"

"It appears so. The nursing facility is about an hour-and-forty-five-minute drive—two hours with traffic. We'll be back by dinnertime. It will give Arlo a good hour or so with Shri. Molly will throw a tantrum when she finds out she wasn't included, but boo-hoo for her. I wouldn't be surprised if her days as his interpreter are numbered."

36

THE FIELD TRIP

By nine in the morning that Friday it was already eighty degrees and steaming hot. I waited at the meeting point behind Hudson Hall for fifteen minutes before Arlo finally walked out the door with Snap. He looked really nervous, with sweat stains in his armpits even though he had been inside the air-conditioning for a while. Considering what we were about to do I expected him to be smiling from ear to ear. I tapped his shoulder gently, but still he nearly leaped out of his shoes.

"Take it easy! Cyril here. Why so anxious?"

"I don't want Molly know. She will very jealous."

"Didn't you already tell her she didn't need to work today?"

Arlo nodded. "Yes. But Molly stubborn. Suppose she comes anyway? Or maybe shows up for another reason. If Molly finds out, will ruin everything!"

"Don't worry. It's going to be fine. And today you'll get to see Shri! So let's get this adventure started."

I gave him my arm and we headed across the upper part of the campus to the parking lot. After helping Arlo and Snap get in and settled, I suddenly realized that chatting with Arlo while driving would be difficult since I'd need to take my eyes off the road and my hands off the wheel. I'm sure there are acrobatic Deaf people with superhero peripheral vision who are capable of this but I wasn't. So I told Arlo that if he needed something to just tap my leg and we could pull over to talk.

"Ready?" I asked.

Arlo's smile grew so large it strained the edges of his face. Moments later we were driving past the dozen or so auto-parts stores, the Abilities Institute, and the Poughkeepsie Rural Cemetery. When we stopped at the next red light, I looked over at Arlo and his smile had disappeared, replaced again by that manic look of worry.

"You doing okay?"

"Nervous. First time touch New York City. Also thinking: Suppose Shri doesn't love me anymore?"

My first instinct was to tell him *Everything will be okay.* But I couldn't. People change. Feelings change. In my own life I had seen people go from loving someone to never wanting to see them again. I didn't want to be another person who told him lies.

"You're right," I signed. "Five and a half years is a long time. And you were both teenagers. Maybe Shri has changed a lot. Maybe you have. Sometimes people fall in love with other people when they've been separated for so long."

"I haven't."

"Okay. Fair enough. But you'll just have to wait and see. I'll be honest with you, things like this don't always work out. But by going to see Shri now, no matter what happens, you won't be spending the rest of your life regretting not ever trying. Right?"

Before Arlo could say anything, the light turned green. There would be no more talking for a long stretch. When we finally got on the Taconic Parkway, I was speeding along nicely for ten miles, but suddenly traffic slowed to a crawl and then to a stop. Arlo kept lifting and dropping his sunglasses from his eyes, attempting to make out why we weren't moving.

"Stop, why?"

"Car accident somewhere up ahead," I told him, signing with only one hand while I held the wheel with the other. "Google Maps says delays for the next twenty-five miles. It's okay. Not a huge deal."

Arlo punched the door. He grimaced with impatience.

"I don't want late! Different road . . . can?"

I googled an alternate route that would take us down a back road through a park. It would be a huge horseshoe back to the Taconic, but we'd bypass the accident. I pulled onto the shoulder and my tires squealed as we backed up to the nearby exit.

Seeing how anxious Arlo was, I drove as fast as I could to make up for lost time. After thirty minutes, we were in the middle of a forest and stopped along the side of the road for a pee break for Arlo and Snap. I assured Arlo he didn't need to worry about time since we were now running ahead of schedule. When they returned from relieving themselves, Arlo said that the air smelled good and asked me to describe what I saw.

"It's beautiful out here. Lots of big mountains. A long, gray, quiet asphalt road that curves around the next bend. There's a small stream—they also call it a B-R-O-O-K—along the side of the road. The water makes little falls when it pours over the rocks. Old rotten logs make bridges over it. There's a gorgeous big oak tree right in front of the car. It's covered in moss on one side of the trunk. Here! Feel it?"

I guided Arlo and Snap to the tree and Arlo reached out and touched the moss, then reached his hands out to measure the width of the tree.

"The sunlight makes the green at the top glow and sparkle in places where it shines through. There are some rock formations that stick out the side of the hill . . . gray rock with bits of white and black. Granite, I imagine. A dragonfly is skirting across the brook. Some birds are flying above us. I see a squirrel . . . two squirrels . . ."

After I recounted every single thing I saw to Arlo, he took a deep breath.

"Feel the sublime?" he asked.

"Ha ha. Sure. Kind of."

We again found ourselves considering alternate ways to sign *the sublime*.

"No. Not right," Arlo signed to each attempt, claiming that none contained the right sense of power, beauty, or A-W-E.

"Must also heartbreaking," he signed. "Don't worry. Later I will figure it out."

Then, out of nowhere, he said he wanted to ask me something personal. My shoulders tightened—I've never been a fan of questions that start that way.

"Um . . . sure. Go ahead."

Arlo turned his head toward me, but his giant sunglasses made it hard to see if he was actually looking at me. His signs were low and smaller than usual, as if he thought someone might have been watching.

"Long time ago you fall in love, right?"

So we're finally getting to it, I thought. I couldn't help but smile.

"I know Hanne talked to you about me," I signed.

Arlo's face flushed beneath the rim of his sunglasses.

"I know. Very private. Sorry."

"It's okay," I signed. "We can talk about it. Yeah, I was in love. A long time ago when I was your age. Remember I told you about that Deaf teacher I followed into his sign language class during college?"

Arlo nodded and leaned forward as if he had been waiting for this moment. Suddenly I found myself telling him all about Bruno. How he had been my ASL teacher at RIT. How he was older than me and how one night our friendship became something more. I realized it was the first time I had told the story in years. I had been avoiding it, hoping it would lose its power. It hadn't. Suddenly I could see Bruno's face in my mind. The green eyes, the animated face with its peekaboo dimple, the funny way he would lazily sign the letter K like a P. I could see his room, smell his cologne, imagine his bed with the neatly folded blue knitted afghan.

"One night we were in his living room practicing ASL with each other and our knees touched, and neither of us jumped away; in fact, we both just sat there, attached, letting that warm feeling flow between us. I figured I might be imagining it until . . . you know . . . we . . . um . . . kissed."

Arlo smiled broadly and gave one big rock back and forth.

"I know that feeling," Arlo signed excitedly. "Me and Shri . . . same. Our bodies touch and inside heart . . . " *Snaps fingers.* "We know! Not need talk talk talk. Hands know, fingers know . . . knees know. Ha ha."

I signaled my own laughter—in the Protactile way—by gently grabbing Arlo's shoulder with the tips of my fingers in quick, repeated motions.

"Question?" Arlo asked, looking puzzled. "When you know you love someone—you feel like you want protect sweetheart and they want protect you?"

I suddenly felt an odd sensation rise in my chest. Then pressure grew behind my eyes, and I had to inhale several times in order to contain myself.

"Yes. I think we wanted to protect each other," I finally signed, grateful that sign language was not like a voice, vulnerable to failure when overcome with emotion. "I know I wanted to protect him, and I think he wanted to protect me. I loved him so much. When he broke up with me I was heartbroken, though not surprised. To be honest, I couldn't believe someone that handsome and smart could ever be in love with me anyway."

Arlo's brows curved downward, bemused by my statement. "You also handsome."

Suddenly I remembered poor Hanne worried whether Arlo thought she was beautiful or not. Now it was me feeling ridiculous.

"No offense," I signed. "But can you see me well enough to know that? I might very well be hideous-looking."

"Ha ha! I know you are handsome . . . how? Because how other people describe you. You . . . freckles and red hair. Skinny, but not like bones. Your hands: good strong hands, smart hands. Good heart. Handsome heart. What about your sweetheart? Bruno expert ASL? Beautiful hands?"

THE SIGN FOR HOME ◊ 295

"Bruno's ASL was breathtaking. A poet. But I don't really recall the details of his hands, other than being fairly strong. I'm sorry."

Arlo looked perplexed by my inability to remember Bruno's hands, but then he smiled mischievously, his mind jumping to another topic.

"Hey, I tell you secret. Shh. Just between you and me, okay? I think Molly also in love with someone."

"Really?" I signed. "Molly? Does she even know what sex is?"

Arlo turned red and did his best not to laugh.

"I'm sorry," I quickly added. "I shouldn't have said that. Why do you think she's in love?"

"Two weeks ago at Public Talk. Elders lecture about sin of adultery. Wow! Trouble. They didn't say what happened? No. Just warning to congregation. But then afterward"—snaps fingers—"Molly no longer going Ecuador. Punished. Elders say she has to stay in Poughkeepsie. Now both Snap and Molly must wait one year to see me. Ha ha. Snap, I will miss. Break heart. Molly miss? No way."

"Ha ha," I signed. Though I was far more curious than amused. "But who is going to interpret for you in Ecuador?"

"Other JW interpreter already lives in Ecuador," Arlo signed. "She will okay. Certified. This moment, I don't care. But still, I curious: Molly adultery with who? Then I realize: Molly not come into house anymore. Waits outside. She never secret talks anymore with Brother Birch. I wonder— was adultery talk about Molly and Brother Birch?"

I burst out laughing.

"You are very funny. Sick sense of humor!"

"No. True business," Arlo signed, biting his lip, growing more agitated as he made his case. "Think. Many times Molly and Brother Birch talk secret. Sometimes I walk into living room . . . Molly and Brother Birch alone together! When? Always when Mrs. Brother Birch not home. JW say forbidden! Adultery very bad sin. They get caught. That's why Molly and Brother Birch not allowed alone with each other, and now Molly forbidden to go to Ecuador. Now Molly can't concentrate, depressed. Sometimes I feel wet on her hands. Crying. Why? Because break up with Brother Birch."

"Anything is possible," I signed, suspecting Arlo was mostly having a revenge fantasy. "But what do you say we head out now?"

Arlo's demeanor shifted again. He clearly wanted to say something.

"Hey, last question: Where did your Deaf sweetheart go? Maybe he will love you again? You better person now. You more friendly, open mind. Should email him. Not have email address? Maybe Larry can help! Finding lost people—Larry champion!"

"I'm afraid it's too long of a sad story," I signed. "We don't want to get too far behind schedule. Aren't you excited to see Shri?"

Arlo checked his braille watch. "Yes. Of course. But you said we have enough time, right? We talk five minutes more, then speed! Okay? I already tell you my two very big secrets. Not fair if you not tell. We friends. Tell me long sad story fast. Bruno stop loving you . . . why?"

Arlo's hands waited in the air in front of me. My own felt like they weighed a hundred pounds.

"To be totally honest with you, I was drinking a lot during that time. And I felt frustrated with my life. I kept telling Bruno that I wanted to leave Poughkeepsie, and blamed him for our being stuck there, which wasn't true. The real reason . . . I mean the *real*, real reason, about a year into our relationship, we found out Bruno was very, very sick. And because there were no dependable interpreters around where he was getting medical care, I had to interpret for him. In fact, I was the one who told him—as if I were the doctor, coldly, calmly—that he was probably going to die."

Arlo removed his hands from mine. For a moment I thought he wanted me to stop the story.

"Sorry," he signed. "Hands shaking, what for? You don't have to tell me story."

"No. I'm okay," I signed. "I want to tell you. I do. Anyway, after eight months of hoping for the best, pretending like I was brave, interpreting every doctor's appointment, something broke inside me. I started fighting with him about stupid things. *He didn't eat enough. He wasn't taking his medicine right. He wasn't trying hard enough to live.* My drinking started getting worse and the fights got worse. It was the cancer I wanted to be fighting, but I couldn't, so I kept harping on the fact that I needed to get out of Poughkeepsie and move out west. Finally, Bruno got fed up. He told me he didn't want to spend the last years of his life with a drunk, crazy hearing man. So he moved back with his Deaf family in Rochester. The funny thing is I didn't blame him. I would have left myself if I could."

"He didn't want see you again? Never?"

While Arlo waited for my response, I felt like I had left my body. I noted the difference between the coolness of the sweat pouring from my temples and the sun frying my skin pink. Could I answer Arlo's question?

"I don't know. I got a letter from him shortly before he died. A paper letter. It just said, 'I forgive you.' The thing is, it might have meant he wanted to see me. By that time I knew he was already in the hospital and close to dying. Something terrified me about seeing him. I mean, if he had called me maybe I would have gone. But, you know, he never called me."

Arlo turned his head and looked like he saw something just beyond my head.

"Too late, right?" he asked.

I couldn't even answer. Arlo suddenly pulled me into a tight hug, patting me on the back like I was three years old. When he finally let go, after I pulled myself together, he signed:

"It's okay. Before, you were younger. You confuse . . . like you asleep. I understand. You woke up. It's okay. Honest with you, I think later your friend forgive you. He just didn't have time. Now must hurry. Must drive very fast to see Shri! We talk more tomorrow. Or next day. Now we friends forever."

"Ha ha. Yes. You're right. We have to get going fast. No more stops, okay? Next stop: Shri!"

As we got back in the car, I opened my phone to check the maps app and saw a parade of message alerts. Some were from Molly, two from Professor Bahr, and then a number I didn't recognize. After reading the first few frantic texts, I grabbed for Arlo's hands.

"Did you lie to me?"

37

NEW PLAN

Arlo never had his uncle's permission like he said. Nor had he alerted the nursing facility. He hadn't even told Shri he was coming. It was all a lie. As we neared Poughkeepsie, I pulled the car into the parking area of a gas station. Arlo was silent the entire trip back and didn't even notice I had stopped the car. Snap squeezed her head between the front seats and licked Arlo's ear and cheek. Then she gave me that admonishing side-eye of hers, seeming to say: *Fer god sakes, Cy, now isn't the time.*

But I wasn't going to allow that wet-nosed emotional manipulator to sway me again.

"Your uncle is very pissed off and so is Professor Bahr," I signed, my hands filled with anger. "They're waiting for us now at the college. You know, by lying to everyone, you put us both in a very fucked-up situation!"

Arlo turned toward me, his face obscured by his sunglasses.

"Question," he signed. "Before, suppose I tell you: *Hey, Cyril, nursing home never respond to my emails . . . oh, and Brother Birch forbid me see Shri . . .* You will still drive me?"

"No. Of course not," I signed back, still furious at him.

"Reason I lie?" Arlo angrily pointed to that place in the air where our hands had just been attached, the place where I had refused him. "That!"

"You don't understand!" I signed, matching his intensity. "We were supposed to be friends. You don't lie to friends!"

Arlo removed his sunglasses. For a few seconds his eyes locked onto mine with a look of hatred.

"Bullshit!" Arlo punched his words into the air. "I fed up! Brother Birch lie! Molly lie! Mama lie! Hearing people always lying! But Deaf-Blind allowed to lie? No! DeafBlind must good boy all the time! Fuck that! ADA law says equality—must! So, if hearing-sighted can lie, then I can lie! And you say: 'But we friends . . .' Ha ha! You worst liar! You say: 'I care about Deaf and DeafBlind.' Lie! Before, Molly say you just take advantage of Deaf for money!"

As soon as Arlo finished eviscerating me, he folded his arms to prevent me from responding. I tried to contain my hurt and anger, but it was no use. I tapped his arm over and over, but he pretzeled himself tighter. Finally, I forced his arms open and pressed my hands back into his.

"Are you fucking serious?!" I shouted. "Can't you see how I've been risking my job for you? Yes, you're right, hearing-sighted people lie! Everybody lies. Yes, I am an interpreter, but I've stupidly also become your friend. And that's the problem. I can't be both anymore!"

Arlo let his limp hands drop as a wounded look filled his face. I had gone too far in my screaming. Snap again confronted me with her disapproving eyes: *Asshole*, they said. I jimmied my hands back into Arlo's.

"Look," I signed, calming my tone. "Let's stop fighting. I'm sorry if I was too rough with you. I was wrong. And what Molly and Brother Birch did to you was awful. Unforgivable. But if you want to see Shri sooner rather than later, you're going to need to play Brother Birch's game for now. So chill. Understand?"

I hoped Arlo would tell me he understood, but he didn't. So we drove on in silence. When we arrived in the parking lot of the college, there were three people waiting for us: Molly, Professor Bahr (who obviously had to bail on the field trip), and a man I figured had to be Brother Birch. He was shorter than I had expected, thick, with a salt-and-pepper military buzz cut, wearing a white shirt and tie. His severe face was covered in a perma-

nent five-o'clock shadow, with thin red lips like an angry stab wound above
his chin. He had a sort of punishing-father sexiness, like the host of one of
those 1960s educational videos about the dangers of syphilis.

For what seemed like a very long time, the three just stared at Arlo and
me sitting in the car from twenty feet away. It was a bit like one of those
long pauses before a shoot-out begins in an old Hollywood western. Professor Bahr said something to Birch, who then shook her hand. As she walked
back into Hudson Hall, she turned back and shot an accusing, hate-filled
look in my direction. I desperately wanted to chase after her and explain
that I had nothing to do with Arlo's lie. But then Birch started walking toward the car, stopping at the edge of the hood, staring at me. His eyes were
the coldest blue I had ever seen.

I stepped out of the car, leaving the air-conditioning on for Arlo and
Snap, who remained inside. It was then that I first noticed the middle-aged
woman, short and thick, with blond hair and glasses, sitting in a nearby car,
watching us with her windows down. I approached Brother Birch.

"Look, Mr. Birch, I get that you're upset about what happened. But
I promise you, we are all on the same team. We all want what's best for
Arlo."

"I see," Birch said. His voice was higher pitched than I'd imagined,
with a distinct upstate accent.

"Yes," I said, smiling. "Of course. I mean, I'm really just his interpreter,
but—"

"His interpreter?" Birch interrupted with a snide smile. "Is it the interpreter's job to drive him out of town without permission? Is it the interpreter's job to fill Arlo's head with false ideas that he could somehow live
independently? Is it the interpreter's job to connect him with some older
woman who molested him?"

"Huh? What are you . . . You mean Hanne? She did not molest him,
sir. Hanne is Arlo's friend. And yes, you're right. Those are not an interpreter's responsibilities. And, yes, I was driving him to see Shri, but I was

completely under the impression that both his teacher and you knew. I give you my word on that."

I did my best to keep my cool. My goal was to make Birch understand we were all on the same team. He did appear to earnestly care about his nephew.

"So, you're giving me your word . . ." Birch scoffed bitterly.

"Yes. And if I may add something, sir. I've worked with the Deaf for a very long time, and while I'm new to the whole DeafBlind thing, it's my opinion that Arlo is an extremely smart young man."

"He is," Birch said.

"Exactly," I said, smiling, hoping I was looking less like a madman. "That's why I let Arlo know about the possibilities for independent living, and the various movements and equipment that could help him toward that goal. Arlo can do so much more with his life than you think. And let's all be real, he certainly deserves to make his own decisions about who he can and can't see."

And there it was. I had gone too far. Birch, red faced, moved a step closer. Molly walked up next to him and began to reach for his arm to calm him, but then drew her hand away.

"Mr. Brewster," Birch began, "I've known Arlo since he was born. For seven years I've been his legal guardian. I'm the one who takes him to his doctor's appointments, pays his bills, puts food on his table, and makes sure he's out of harm's way. My nephew is deaf and blind, and his sight is far worse than he lets on. I've worked hard to put in place a life that will keep Arlo safe physically, spiritually, and emotionally, and, to be quite honest, Mr. Brewster, you've threatened that safety by interfering. For what reason, I can't be sure, but I have my suspicions."

The filthy insinuation in his voice was obvious, and my face flushed with both anger and humiliation. I turned to Molly, believing she'd at least defend me from that sort of accusation. While she and I disagreed on most things, she wasn't vicious. Yet when I looked at her for support, she stared at the ground. *Does Molly actually believe him? Or was she the one who had put the idea in his head?*

"You are way of out of line, Mr. Birch." My voice quavered with hurt fury. "I just wanted what was best for Arlo. Why you and Molly chose to find something dirty in that . . . well . . . I don't know. Maybe that's more about what's happening in *your* hearts than mine?"

At that point Molly looked to Brother Birch, a small terror on her face that she quickly tried to hide. There was only the slightest, momentary shift in Birch's steely demeanor, but enough to show I had hit an accurate target. Arlo had been right about them.

"I think we've had enough," Brother Birch finally said, crossing to Arlo's side of the car and opening the door.

Molly guiltily glanced toward the blond woman who had been watching our drama from her car. Molly shook her head at me in disgust.

I lost it.

"What is it, Molly?" I said, raising my voice. "You don't want strangers to hear what you two holier-than-thou Jehovah's Witnesses have been up to? Is that it? Are you and Brother Birch here having a lot of dirty thoughts you don't want anyone to know about? Is that why you try to control Arlo's life?"

"Stop! Please . . ." Molly begged, almost desperately.

That's when I saw Brother Birch putting Arlo and Snap in the back of the blond woman's car. It finally dawned on me: the stranger was Brother Birch's wife.

"I'm sorry," I stammered. "I didn't know—"

"You're a vile, selfish person," Molly said as she walked closer to me, her chin quivering, her voice so quiet there was no way the others could hear. "How can you be so sick and cruel?"

"Me?" I yelled. "What did you tell them I did to Arlo? Tell me!"

"It doesn't matter what I said. Do you know the damage you've already done to that boy?"

I exploded in an angry laugh.

"The damage I've done?" I screamed. "Are you fucking serious?"

Then I crossed over to about ten feet in front of Mrs. Brother Birch's car, and then, going full-on soap opera queen, I shouted loud enough for her and anyone else on the entire campus to hear me.

"Hey, Mrs. Birch, did you know Molly has been grasping onto Arlo with her skinny claws just to try to stay close to your husband? Isn't that right, Molly? If she loses Arlo, she loses her little honey bear here! Her alleged dedication to Arlo was one big fucking attempt to steal your husband, Mrs. Birch! Where does *The Watchtower* say that shit is okay?"

Brother Birch and Molly stood there speechless. Mrs. Brother Birch's face was a heart-wrenching mask of humiliation. I was instantly disgusted with myself. *Did I really have to hurt that innocent woman? And worse: Did I just make things impossible for Arlo?*

Molly lifted her hand to her face, stifling her tears, and ran toward the door of Hudson Hall. Mrs. Brother Birch had lowered her head to the steering wheel. Birch slowly approached me, shaking his head, his voice barely above a whisper.

"I'm not going to let you hurt my family or that boy any further, Mr. Brewster. I am Arlo's legal guardian. I will protect my nephew any way I can. As for you and that nurse-waitress friend of yours . . . stay away from my nephew. May the Lord help you."

38

TERMINATION

The day after the field trip disaster I woke up at 1 p.m. on my couch, hungover and foggy. The worst part was I remembered everything that happened and everything I had said. When I looked at my phone, there were multiple texts from Hanne and a number of voice messages from Ange. When I called back, Ange told me I had been removed from the job, which wasn't a surprise. Molly finally got what she wanted. When I said as much to Ange, she said that it was, in fact, Arlo who had requested I be taken off the job. I told her that was either a mistake or a lie. Arlo wouldn't have fired me. But she said it didn't matter. I was done. Then Ange insisted I go to the Abilities Institute to meet with Clara Shuster in person. I asked what the point was if I was already fired, but Ange said her agency's reputation was on the line, and if I ever wanted to earn another dime interpreting, I had no choice. I needed to convince Clara of my version of events.

I hung up the phone. I wanted to get as far away from Arlo and Poughkeepsie as possible. And it was then that I remembered: without any income for the rest of the summer, my whole plan to move to Philadelphia was finished. Whatever escape money I had saved had suddenly become my emergency fund.

◇ ◇ ◇

On Monday morning I went to the Abilities Institute. As I waited to speak to Clara, I sat in that conference room staring again at the "happy disabled people" photos, thinking about how I would defend myself to Clara, promising myself I wouldn't grovel.

When Clara finally called me into her office, her usual kind-and-compassionate social worker vibe was nowhere to be seen. Without even looking me in the eye, she gestured for me to sit. While she looked intently at the contents of a manila folder, I inventoried everything she had on her meticulously organized desk, which included three neatly stacked files, tape, a stapler, a snow globe featuring a diorama of Waikiki, and a nicely framed photo of people I assumed were her husband and daughter.

"It's very hot outside today," Clara said finally, looking up at me for the first time.

My knee bounced anxiously; my mouth felt like it was filled with ashes. The most important thing was to maintain a calm, contrite tone.

"This is all a complete bullshit lie," I blurted out, my voice leaping an octave. "Arlo would never fire me. It was his uncle . . . or really . . . Molly Clinch! She's been out to get me since day one!"

"Could you please not raise your voice," Clara said, wincing.

Again I tried to reel myself in emotionally.

"Sorry," I said. "My point is, instead of punishing me or Arlo, you should be looking into what's happening in his home. He's a competent adult, Clara. Arlo should have the right to visit whoever he wants."

"Cyril, we're not here to—"

"His accessibility equipment is completely out of date, for chrissakes," I said, my voice once again rising. "They severely limit his access to the internet. They told him Shri was dead! You're supposed to be his advocate! Do your job!"

Clara's eyes grew furious, and she slapped her manicured hand on her desk, causing the photo of her family to fall over.

"Enough! Stop it!" Her voice cracked as she shouted, which was not the sort of thing Clara Shuster ever did. "You have no idea what I do or don't do in my job. And for your information, there was a very good reason why Arlo wasn't allowed . . . Never mind . . . it doesn't matter. It's not your business. Mr. Birch is Arlo's guardian. Not you."

Clara bit her lower lip, but not in that hurt-about-to-cry way. It was more like an *I'm going to fuck you up now* way. She reopened the manila folder, and, like some cold, officious TV prosecutor, began to go down a list of accusations.

"Have you been writing Arlo's essays in class?" she asked, her voice as calm as a glacier.

"What? No! I spent time helping him understand the assignment, and helped him with some definitions here and there, and maybe a little grammar, but he wrote it himself."

She smiled, mockingly.

"A little grammar? You're telling me a DeafBlind twenty-three-year-old, without even a high school diploma, wrote an essay on . . ."

She read from the file:

"The Concept of the Sublime in Walt Whitman's *Leaves of Grass*?"

"Okay. Yeah. I helped him with the title too, but the paper and the ideas are his. He's an extremely bright young man."

"You're not supposed to be writing papers for your consumers."

"I didn't—"

"Or giving them titles or being their getaway driver on illegal escapades. Your job is to interpret, Cyril. Period."

Clara closed her eyes briefly, like she was giving someone the bad news about their impending death.

"Arlo is not just any adult. He's a person the state has deemed needs custodial care, meaning they believe in order to survive he needs a guardian. I shouldn't say this, but did you know there were accusations of sexual assault in Arlo's background? Did you know that he had wandered off several times and almost gotten killed? That he had a breakdown?"

"Breakdown?" I repeated, a desperate fog filling my brain. "No, I didn't know about that, or about the wandering off. But he wrote about the false charge of . . ."

I stopped myself. I had been assuming I knew Arlo better than other people, that he had told me all his secrets. I covered my reddening face with my hand. My torrent of rage shriveled into a pathetic, embarrassed defensiveness.

"I guess I didn't know everything about him. But getting to visit people he loves is not going to put him in any danger."

"You don't know that!" Clara snapped, the tendons of her neck straining against her pearls. She quickly covered her mouth, surprised by the ferocity of her own voice. She jotted a note in Arlo's folder. Her voice settled again into her cold, controlled monotone.

"Cyril, you know what I need to ask you next. God, I hate this."

Clara ran her fingers through her hair like she was in some old Susan Hayward movie and was about to be sent to the electric chair. Only, I was the one who was supposed to confess.

"Clara, I have absolutely no idea what you're talking about."

She pressed her thumb and forefinger onto her eyes and lowered her voice to a barely audible whisper.

"Cyril, did you try to seduce Arlo?"

Clara's words were a fist to the gut.

"What?" I stammered, shocked. My stomach felt sick. All I needed was to say no, but I couldn't speak. My heart began slamming itself against my chest.

Clara's eyes returned to the case file, and in rapid succession her cold voice went down the page reading the rest of the allegations.

"Did you grab Arlo's leg under the table several times during class? Or stroke him on the back and arm in an inappropriate manner?"

"No," I said, finally, forcing the words out. "Of course not. Unless they mean the Protactile, but that's not—"

"Did you enable him to meet a male friend at the train station?"

"That was Big Head Lawrence, his friend. He asked me to—"

"Did you buy him expensive meals from the cafeteria? Did you take him to get his hair cut and advise him on how to dress?"

"Yes, I bought him some food, but what's the big deal? And no, I didn't cut his hair. Molly said all this, didn't she?"

"Did you introduce him to a woman named Hanne Van Steenkiste, who took him back to her workplace to try and have sex with him? And on this secret trip to New York City, did you or did you not attempt to seduce Arlo in your car?"

I shook my head no. Her charges were almost wholly false, except the first part about Hanne, and buying him lunch and my helping him to see Big Head Lawrence and Shri. As her accusations echoed in my head, I found myself once again questioning myself. Was I lying to myself? Did I break the code of ethics because of some subconscious attraction? No. That was not why I had helped Arlo. Still my face grew red. Of course, knowing my face was flushing made it turn a deeper shade of crimson. Clara interpreted this as an admission of guilt.

"Stop looking at me that way!" I begged, the panic causing my voice to rise, and the more I fought to try to sound levelheaded, the more I started to shout. "I'm a redhead! When anything goes wrong, I immediately turn red! This is ridiculous . . . No . . . No! I never, NEVER, hit on Arlo. I've never hit on any consumer. Whoever said all that is a liar. I've been in this business for almost fifteen years and have a spotless record. Ask the agencies. The only time I ever even touched Arlo was when he'd take my arm to guide him or when I was interpreting for him or doing Protactile!"

"Enough!" Clara shouted. "Monitor your tone! While the investigation is going on, it's best if—"

"Holy Christ, there's a fucking investigation?"

"We are mandated reporters. Arlo is a person at risk."

Suddenly I stood up, placed both hands in the center of Clara's desk, and looked her square in the eyes, my voice trembling as I loudly proclaimed:

"I'm only gonna say this once more, Clara! I did not touch him!"

For some reason I thought the sheer volume of my honesty would burn itself into her brain, but instead, I came off like I was totally unhinged. Clara jumped up and immediately grabbed the telephone and put her fingers on the buttons, ready to call for help.

"You're scaring me! Do not threaten me!"

I took my hands from her desk, turned away to take a breath, then turned back, lowering my voice.

"I'm not threatening you, Clara. I'm so sorry. I don't want you to feel like . . . I just can't believe anyone would think I would do something like that. Please, please believe me."

Clara placed the phone back on the receiver and closed the case file on her desk. She wouldn't look at me again.

"You have already been reported to RID. Even if nothing like that happened, your behavior has violated the interpreter's code of professional conduct. RID will make the final decision whether or not you keep your certification, but if the family or I have anything to say about it, you won't. Arlo and his uncle have taken out a restraining order against you, so you may not have any contact with them whatsoever."

"Is there anyone I can talk to about this?" I asked, a quaver in my voice. "A detective or investigator? Can I at least defend myself?"

Clara stepped to the door and opened it. She was done with me.

"Arlo and his family just want this nightmare to be over, which may be lucky for you in the long run. I'm sorry, I have work to do."

A moment later I was standing in the hot sun outside the building.

Inside me there was only fog. The one thing that worked in my life—interpreting—I was on the brink of losing. *What am I if I'm no longer an interpreter?* Then an even more crushing realization laid a hook into my brain: *What if Arlo believes the lies they're telling him? What if he comes to think that everything I've done for him I did for some perverted reason?* I went to my car, sat behind the burning-hot wheel, and started to sob.

39

CONFRONTATION

Brother Birch stopped letting you go to your writing class because of what happened the day of the field trip. He also changed the password for the internet and won't tell you. Now you can't even read JW.org at home. Instead, you take the Able-Ride to the Kingdom Hall and sit in the reading room all day pretending to read the braille Bible. Brother Birch says you won't be able to use the internet until he feels you are free from unholy influences. At least once a day, in his bad sign language, he reminds you how much he cares for you and wants you to be safe. You pretend that you understand, and that you have forgiven Brother Birch for destroying your life, and that you are planning on still going to Ecuador. But you haven't and you aren't.

You know he feels guilty and is suffering, which makes you happy even if it's not enough. *It's not nearly enough.* Mrs. Brother Birch went to stay with her mother for a few days, and now, following church rules, Molly must wait outside, even when she comes to take you to the Kingdom Hall. If Brother Birch wants her to interpret, he has to go there so other people are around. Soon Brother Birch will be in Ecuador, and Molly will be stuck here.

Brother Birch must feel very lonely.

Molly must feel very lonely.

Good.

Your fingertips ride across the bumpy page of the braille Bible. The spaces and rows between the raised dots become escape routes: roads, rivers, train tracks, mountains, valleys, a wilderness of words. You fantasize about carrying Shri over the sublime mountains. Using her strong and perfect eyes, Shri will tell you which way to go, which rocks to avoid, which way cars are coming. Snap will come too.

You will all be *free*.

Your skin vibrates when you think of that beautiful word, *free*. To have no one lying to you, no one controlling you, no one telling you where to be at what time. You would just run and run and run. Just you, Shri, and Snap forever.

Someone taps you on the shoulder, stabbing a pin in your fantasy. It's Molly.

"Sorry to bother you. May I say something?"

"I don't want talk," you say. "Go away."

You jerk your hands from her and immediately sit on them, employing the DeafBlind superpower to instantly make someone disappear. Gone. Nothing. Molly and her lies cannot touch you now.

But then she tries something she has never tried before. She uses that special Protactile technique she learned from Cyril and draws a question mark on your shoulder. In that small, weak gesture you can feel her begging you for your forgiveness. It's not enough. You want to punish her.

"What?" you finally sign, annoyed. "Bother me, what for? Finish! Go away!"

Still she offers her hands. You pay attention only so you can reject her again.

"Please let me explain," she begs. "I need to tell you my side of the story."

"No! You lie! You say Shri dead. You destroy my life! Finish you!"

"We were only trying to do the right thing. Do you understand? The trouble that was happening at school, we were worried for your soul. But I know now that I was wrong. Please, please, forgive me."

You shake your head no and turn away, a hateful look on your face. Molly's pitiful fingers tap you again on the shoulder.

"Please," Molly pleads. "I care about you so much. You know that. We've been friends for so long."

You push Molly's hands away.

"No more!" you yell. "You not my friend. Never again! Cyril and Hanne my best friends! They understand me deep. Why? Because they understand what it means to really cherish someone. Not you!"

Molly reaches for your hands to speak again, but you push her away again and laugh in a very mean way.

"You pea brain, Molly! Ha ha! I know truth! You commit sin with Brother Birch, right? You two sex together, right? You love him. But, because JW, Brother Birch tell you, *Molly, go away!* What happen? You cry cry cry. I know you cry! I feel wet tears all over your fingers at Public Talk. You chase Brother Birch and beg take you back. He refuse. You let him go. You say, *Oh, poor me, poor me, Jehovah God want Molly be alone! Wah wah wah!* You like scared, sad baby. You will never find new love. No. You just accept, accept. Molly will alone, always alone. Knees shaking. Hide yourself in Kingdom Hall. You sad old woman, Molly. You very sad old woman. You will die alone. Me pity you. Pity pity pity. Fuck you!"

You turn away. Your body is shaking. This time Molly doesn't reach out to touch you or beg your forgiveness again. You can feel her body standing there, filling the space like an empty coat rack someone placed where it shouldn't be. A few moments later you feel her small feet walk across the room. She doesn't slam the door. She is too afraid of Jehovah God to slam anything. She is done with you. And you are done with her forever.

40

THE UNEXPECTED VISITOR

It had been two weeks since I lost my job when I woke up around six forty in the morning from a nightmare. In the nightmare I had this old dog, like a smaller version of Snap but male, and even more mangy and pathetic looking. The dog's name was John Wayne—for God knows what reason—and the dog was deaf and blind, which was pretty on the nose. At a certain point, John Wayne the DeafBlind dog slipped out of his harness and ran toward a busy highway, and I started chasing him in utter panic. Tears streamed down my face because I was making no progress. I kept tripping over these objects the size of toaster ovens that kept popping up every ten feet or so. At first, I had no idea what the hell they were. I just kept running and tripping, running and tripping. Finally, I realized the objects were giant, old-fashioned hearing aids emerging from the ground. The earth, it appeared, had hearing loss. I also noticed that all my tripping had injured me, and the blood was seeping through my baggy white linen pants—which were not at all my style. I thought to myself, *I should just let John Wayne run onto the highway and be killed. Perhaps it's for the best. He's old, deaf, and blind. He'll die soon anyway.* Despite this thought, I kept running, weeping and tripping, my pants getting bloodier and bloodier, still desperate to save him.

As I was just about to fall back to sleep, I heard banging on my front door. I figured it had to be Hanne. I had drunk-dialed her the night before and left a rambling, self-pitying message. Hanne could be selfishness personified, but if someone was in trouble she suddenly turned into the Mother Teresa of MILFs. I threw a towel around my naked lower half, tripped over an empty wine bottle, and barked at the door like a weary, hungover seal.

"For fuck's sake! Don't be such an impatient, codependent bitch! It's not even seven in the goddamn morning!"

But when I opened the door, the person standing there, wrapped in a tassel-covered shawl, was none other than Professor Lavinia Bahr. I quickly pushed the door halfway closed to cover my semi-nakedness and wiped the drunk sleep from my face.

"Oh, shit, Professor. I'm sorry . . . Shoot. I thought you were someone else."

"I assumed so," Professor Bahr said. "I'm so sorry for coming at this hour."

I mumbled something about how I didn't usually use misogynistic language, except with my best friend, and then only in an ironic, campy way. Then I noticed that while she was done up in her usual fashion, her eyeliner and contouring, usually Rembrandt-perfect, looked almost haphazard, as though she hadn't been able to pay attention or was in a rush.

"There's something urgent I need to discuss with you," she said, anguish in her voice.

"Okay, yeah, of course. Hey, would you mind if I, you know, got dressed? It will take me just a few minutes. Be right back."

I slammed the door harder than I meant to, then hobbled to the sink and gargled a mouthful of water to get rid of any wine breath. I pulled on sweatpants and a T-shirt. *Why the fuck is she here this early?* I kicked two empty wine bottles under the couch as I skirted back to the door.

"Um . . . okay," I said. "Did you need to come in? Or did you just wanna do it standing there?"

"Do what?" Professor Bahr asked, stepping inside my vestibule. Her eyes widened at the sight of my just-ransacked-by-Visigoths living room, and taking a sniff of my boozy unshowered perfume, she grimaced.

"Jesus, my man. You smell like skid row on Sunday morning."

"Sorry," I mumbled. "I wasn't expecting visitors at sunrise. Also, I haven't been working lately, because, you know, *because*. So, yep, a bit of a mess."

Professor Bahr shook her head sadly. I steeled myself for the impending berating.

"Look, Professor," I said. "I know what Birch and Molly are telling people."

Professor Bahr lifted her hand to silence me.

"Please, I need to tell you something very important." Professor Bahr took a deep, sad breath. "Arlo withdrew from my class."

"He did?"

"Yes. Two weeks ago. I emailed Molly when he didn't show up for a few days, but I got no reply."

I wanted to rage, to tell her there would be no way Arlo would have quit her class, that Molly didn't respond because she and that uncle creep were the reason he wasn't in class. But I didn't. I had to stay out of it. I had to stop caring.

"I'm sorry, but I really can't—"

"Let me finish. When I discovered he'd withdrawn I was devastated. I wrote him emails, left phone messages for his uncle, but still I heard nothing. Then two days ago I received an envelope in the mail with that copy of *Leaves of Grass* I had lent him. There was a letter stuck inside the front cover written very large with a Magic Marker. He told me everything. He told me about what happened to Shri, and about the lies his family told him. He said his uncle has completely cut him off from all communication with the outside world. He's forbidden to write emails or use the internet at all."

I wanted to feel glad that someone else finally understood the truth, but instead I felt angry that she was pulling me back into it.

"Look, Professor, I'm not working with Arlo anymore."

"Can you please stop calling me 'Professor'? I think we're past that. My name is Lavinia."

"Fine," I said, exasperated. "Lavinia, can we please just finish this—"

"But you need to know that Arlo admitted lying to both of us about the field trip. He wrote that he just wanted to get to Shri. I'm sorry I got so angry."

I was ready to explain how I wasn't even supposed to be talking to anyone about Arlo, that all of it was someone else's problem, and to ask her to just leave me the hell alone. But before I could, Lavinia shoved Arlo's letter in front of me, pointing to a section she had circled in red.

"Read it!" she demanded. Foolishly I did.

I do not want Shri to think I don't care again. How you feel if you love someone and they have disappear and never hear words about what haves been happening on you. (CRYING) I'm torture! I'm heartbreak! Please, Professor Lavinia Bahr, help me! Will PLEASE help me to visit my sweetheart?!!

The rest of the letter contained Arlo's attempt to get the professor to persuade me to help him get to Shri. When I finished reading, I looked up and saw Lavinia's moist eyes staring at me, like I might suddenly jump in the closet and change into my superhero-of-the-disabled outfit.

"You see?" she said. "We must help him see Shri! Then he needs to move out of that house! Maybe he could even stay with you for a short time? We'd need to clean it up, of course."

The absurdity of what she said hit me like a bucket of ice water. Clara and Molly were right. Instead of making things better, I made things much worse. Because of me, Arlo had to leave the class and possibly lost his chance of ever seeing Shri again. It was the unseen end of my dream. Instead of saving the DeafBlind dog from running onto the highway, I was the one who chased him under a Mack truck. I folded Arlo's letter and handed it back to Lavinia.

"I'm sorry," I said. "I can't do this. I'm just an interpreter, Lavinia. That's all. If you want to help him out, that's your business. I'm done."

Lavinia held Arlo's letter aloft in front of her as if it were Arlo himself in paper form.

"But how can I help him without you? I don't know the language. I take Ubers, I don't even drive. I . . . I can't."

"I'm sorry," I said, shrugging my shoulders.

Lavinia placed Arlo's letter back in her purse. When she began to speak again, I wasn't sure if she was talking to me or herself.

"I'm a fifty-eight-year-old adjunct professor who lives in a one-bedroom apartment with a neurotic husband who is constantly underfoot. I have to wake up every morning and pray that one of my half-witted students can write one intelligible English sentence. I'm tired. I'm tired and I'm scared. But every once in a while I meet a student who has such light inside them it reminds me of why I do what I do. Arlo is one of those students."

Lavinia's black-brown eyes fixed onto mine, expecting me to be moved. Instead, I became enraged.

"Are you serious? Do you know there's a fucking restraining order against me? I've been forbidden from even being in the same room with Arlo. They're trying to take my certification from me! I might lose everything I've ever . . ."

A giant lump of self-pity choked me, stopping me from finishing my sentence. Lavinia pressed a hand to her mouth.

"Cyril! That's unjust! I had no idea."

"Molly and Birch have been spreading rumors about me. If I lose my certification, I'm completely fucked. So please stop asking me to help."

My voice cracked and I couldn't say anything more. Lavinia turned toward the window so I could no longer see her face. When she began to speak, her voice was softer and tentative.

"About a month ago the dean called me into his office to tell me that Arlo's family was concerned about you."

"Of course," I said, shaking my head with disgust.

"Their suspicions were completely incongruous with the man I saw in the classroom. I begged them not to jump to conclusions."

"Fuck them. I'm sorry. But Molly has been out to get me from the beginning. Anyway, thank you for defending me."

Lavinia lowered her eyelids. Her breathing was heavy.

"That's the thing. I did defend you . . . at first. Cyril, I'm so sorry. When I thought it was you who lied to me about the day of the field trip, I began to doubt everything. Then Brother Birch indicated you were acting like some puppet master, forcing ideas into Arlo's head, not being professional. He implied that you were the one writing Arlo's essays. I was furious."

"That's absurd! Yes, I helped him with a word here and there on the Whitman piece, Hanne helped him with his grammar on his personal essay, but he wrote them himself! Lavinia, Arlo is smarter than anyone even knows. Smarter even than I knew!"

"I believe you now, Cyril! I saw it. It was his letter to me. It was proof. There were mistakes everywhere, but the voice, the vocabulary . . . I am so sorry I doubted Arlo, and I'm so sorry I said . . ."

Lavinia closed her eyes and began to twist a large blue glass cocktail ring on her finger.

"What?" I said. "You're sorry you said what?"

"When I'm angry I can be so stupid. That afternoon, after I met with Mr. Birch, the dean called me and asked me again if I had seen anything unsavory occur during class. And so I told him about how after you returned from the conference you became more physical with Arlo. How you started to do the touching thing on Arlo's back and thighs."

I ran my hands through my hair and walked to the other side of the living room, putting space between me and Lavinia. But still the rage came.

"Are you fucking kidding me? I told you, Lavinia! I told you that was part of interpreting for the DeafBlind! It's called Protactile! Do you know what you might have done to my life? You told them I molested Arlo?!"

Lavinia gently raised her hands toward me, less as a protection and more as an attempt to calm me.

"I never said the word *molest*," she said. "I just described the action and indicated Molly looked suspiciously at you."

"Molly is suspicious of everyone, especially an agnostic homo who challenges her total control over Arlo."

"I'm so sorry, Cyril. I will call the dean first thing Monday. No. I'll go there in person, I promise. I am crushed with guilt, Cyril. Crushed! I will do everything in my power to make it right."

I could feel my nails dig into the palms of my hands. Fearing my rage would make me do or say something stupid, I walked to the front door and opened it.

"Thank you for the apology, and thank you for doing what you can, but it's probably too late at this point. Anyway, I really have to go back to bed until it's a more gentlemanly time to drink myself into oblivion. Um . . . get home safe."

Lavinia exhaled a groan of sorrow.

"I understand, Cyril. And I don't blame you for wanting to wash your hands of all of this. You've been treated abysmally! But here's my problem. Because I've been a teacher and avid reader for so long, I've got all these other voices inside my head screaming! Gandhi, Anne Frank, James Baldwin! Walt Whitman! All of them calling me to action! Insisting I help others! In elementary school, I memorized a quote from Cicero: 'Non nobis solum nati sumus'—*Not for ourselves alone are we born*. I am an educator, Cyril. You are an interpreter and, I'd argue, also an educator, whether you like it or not. Only in tragedies does the hero refuse her call. How will Arlo see Shri without us? They are in love, Cyril! In love! We will suffer if we do nothing to help. It's our duty."

"Our duty or *my* duty?" I said, silencing Lavinia's disquisition. "This isn't *your* career in jeopardy, Lavinia! Do you realize, because of this filthy gossip—gossip you contributed to—I could even end up in jail? Is that what you people want? I've already lost so much in my life. Do you want me to lose everything for this kid?"

I suddenly noticed that as I was shouting, I had also been signing the whole time, as if there were also someone Deaf in the room to whom I had to defend myself. Lavinia crossed to me and laid the flats of her warm hands on my chest, calming me.

"Shh. Shh. There, there. I'm sorry. I'm being stupid and selfish. I just can't bear the unfairness of it all."

"Neither can I. I'm sorry, but I can't help him anymore."

Lavinia nodded sadly, kissed me on the cheek, and left.

41

GONE GONE GONE

August 16

Three days after Lavinia's visit, I received a letter from the Registry of Interpreters for the Deaf stating that I'd been formally reported for "behavior contrary to the code of professional conduct," and I was required to give a statement to investigators in early September. I would need to get others to vouch for me in writing. Lavinia said I could count on her, but as for professional references, I wasn't sure who I could ask without making things worse. Most of the agencies in the area had heard about my situation and wouldn't even talk to me. Not that they could have helped much anyway if Clara, Molly, and Birch stuck to their stories. Arlo could defend me if he was allowed to. But neither Lavinia, Hanne, nor I had any way to contact him. It was like he no longer existed in our world.

◇ ◇ ◇

August 17

I reached out to a JW terp I knew named Serefina to see if she knew the Birches. The JW thing never stopped her from being a totally cool lady. Serefina and I used to go out and get shit-faced together after gigs when I first started interpreting. (Getting blasted once in a while is not necessarily considered a sin, or that's what Serefina told me.) Serefina, who had heard of Brother Birch and Arlo, agreed to do some secret JW reconnaissance for me. After checking with a friend, she said that Birch and all the other "pioneers," including Arlo, would be flying to Ecuador in just eleven days. It was becoming clear that getting to him would be close to impossible.

◊ ◊ ◊

August 18

Just before the whole field trip debacle, I had emailed Tabitha about how Arlo might become more independent. Her email arrived three weeks too late.

Dear Cyril:

It sounds like your DB consumer faces a complicated situation with his uncle. It's not the first time I've heard of family trying to limit the independence of someone who is DeafBlind and capable, but this situation seems even worse. According to my lawyer friend, if the courts have already found that Arlo is not able to make decisions or care for himself and have given guardianship to his uncle then it will be hard to get him emancipated. However, the lawyer also said if he can either appeal the ruling or prove abuse of some sort then the court may reexamine his case. I'll talk to my friend to see if she knows anyone in the upstate New York area. As far as independence goes, yes, indeed, from how you describe Arlo, he definitely can live more independently. That doesn't mean he won't need support. That's why I'm fighting to get mandatory government-funded SSP/co-navigators nationwide. (It's gonna be a tough fight, but it has to happen.) Meanwhile, if his uncle doesn't prevent him, there are some great DeafBlind Independent Living training programs.

Yours,
Tabitha

For the hell of it I forwarded the email to Arlo's old email address, but like every other email I had sent it was returned, indicating the account had been closed. Ten days left until he would be gone. I fantasized about putting on a disguise and sneaking into the Kingdom Hall, hiding the printed email in my palm, along with a letter begging Arlo for his help. After coming to my senses, I deleted Tabitha's email.

◊ ◊ ◊

August 19

After weeks of no work, I finally booked a gig through an out-of-town spoken language interpretation agency. That sort of agency tends to be clueless about sign language interpreting, which for once served my purposes. I told them I wasn't certified in case they checked with RID. That meant getting paid only two-thirds my regular rate. It was a beautician training course with a Deaf Russian woman an hour and a half south in Yonkers. The woman was sweet as hell and tended to mix Russian sign in with her ASL. She asked me to go to lunch with her, but I was too paranoid about the RID investigation, and anxiously snapped that it was "not appropriate to ask interpreters to hang out." The participant didn't come back from lunch, and I never got another gig from that agency.

◊ ◊ ◊

August 20

Hanne called to chat. But just as she had done for the last few weeks, she pretended to start a discussion about nursing school or her family, but then quickly steered the discussion to Arlo. I finally asked her if we could just not talk about him for a while. He was set to leave in just a matter of days, and I was tired of obsessing about it. The next day Hanne didn't call at all.

◊ ◊ ◊

August 27

It was nearly eleven in the morning and I had only just gotten up after another horrific night of sleep. Tabitha had emailed me again the day before, saying she found a lawyer in Albany who would be willing to talk to Arlo. Again, I didn't bother to return her email. Arlo was flying to Ecuador the very next day. And it was time I thought about what I would do if I indeed lost my certification. (And didn't end up in jail.) I pondered all the other things I might do: Grad school for teaching? Not with a restraining order on my record. Get an MBA? Law school? Ugh, the thought made me ill. I pictured myself sitting behind a desk, seeing the same people day in and day out. I felt like I was suffocating.

I headed into the kitchen to grab some coffee and ibuprofen to handle the moderately agonizing hangover I was experiencing. That's when the phone rang. I looked at the screen and immediately wanted to throw my cell phone across the room.

"Why the fuck would Molly Clinch be calling me?" I said to the kitchen before pressing Ignore.

A second later Molly called again, and again, and again.

By her fifth attempt I decided it was time to give that skinny old religious freak another piece of my (very foggy and hungover) mind and tell her everything I thought was wrong with her and her religion.

"Molly Clinch," I said as coldly and sarcastically as possible. "Why in God's name are you calling me? Did you think destroying my life wasn't enough? Careful before someone's house drops on me. I mean, careful I don't drop someone on your house . . . ah . . . fuck it! I'm gonna drop a house on you!"

"I don't understand what you're saying," Molly said, her voice wobbly, as though she had been crying. "Is he with you?"

"Huh?" I said. "Who?"

"Arlo! You know who I meant. Why are you speaking so oddly?"

"None of your business!" I screamed. "And of course Arlo isn't with me. Look, Molly, if you're trying to find more evidence of my alleged crimes . . ."

"Please stop," she begged in a tone I had never heard from her before. "I don't have time to argue. Arlo has disappeared."

42

CONSPIRATORS

I considered that it might be some elaborate setup. But as Molly requested, I immediately picked up Hanne and drove to Caffe Aurora. Molly was already there. So was Lavinia Bahr, which confused me further. The question haunted me: Why would Molly want to enlist the help of *us three*? *Goats? Satan's tools?*

Molly's eyes were red from crying. Either she was the best actress ever or I was completely missing something. She recounted the story she had told me on the phone to Lavinia and Hanne, including all the details. When she got to the end, her voice slowed, as if even repeating the story caused her pain.

"Then Brother Birch texted to confirm what Arlo had told him about meeting me at the Kingdom Hall to pick up some braille *Watchtowers* he had left there. I didn't want to get Arlo in trouble, so I lied and said I had forgotten. But when I went to the Kingdom Hall, Arlo wasn't there. I waited for over an hour. It isn't like him to just disappear."

Molly took a sip of water, clearing the rasp from her voice. Staring at the table, I turned a napkin into confetti. Meanwhile, Hanne, in her nurse scrubs, kept patting my leg like I was some sickly dog. Lavinia, wearing a large-brimmed white hat and her bee earrings, listened intently. Molly continued.

"The Birches were busy packing for tomorrow's flight. Because I was no longer going on the mission, I was asked to drive Arlo up to Albany to drop off Snap at the seeing eye dog rescue for boarding this afternoon. I knew Arlo would be upset about leaving Snap, as well as everything else. He's barely been speaking to me, other than when I have to interpret for him. I wanted a chance to prove to him that I regretted what I had done—make amends before I might never see him again. So I thought, I could just call the guide dog rescue and let them know I'd bring Snap up tomorrow, and instead use the time to drive Arlo down to the city so he could visit Shri."

"Oh, Molly, that would be wonderful!" Lavinia effused.

"Yes," Hanne said, more reserved than Lavinia, but still seeming to buy into Molly's change of heart. "Thank you, Molly."

My hands curled into fists, and I laughed bitterly.

"So you're telling us that you were going to take Arlo to see Shri?" I asked with more than a little sarcasm in my tone. "You were going to defy Brother Birch, risking your standing with him and your church? Spare me the bullshit. What's your game, Molly?"

Molly closed her eyes, steadying herself, like she was expecting my reaction.

"Of course *you* wouldn't believe me," Molly said angrily. "*Molly is a horrible person! Cyril is wonderful! Oh, Cyril knows the sign for everything! Molly is just a pathetic, old, desperate woman!*"

Molly swallowed back tears, her eyes fixed on the table. For a moment I considered the possibility that she might be on the cusp of losing her mind completely. It certainly didn't make sense to me that she could do what she did and then so quickly flip the switch and become some Jehovah's Witness Joan of Arc.

"So why did I do it?" Molly asked, clearing her throat and seemingly getting herself under control. "Why did I stand by and watch what Brother Birch did to that young man, or rather, what we both did—lying to him about what happened to Shri? I suppose I told myself we were doing the best thing for him. Arlo was so heartbroken, after all. And with the police being involved we assumed there would never be a chance he'd be able to see Shri again anyway. And then with Arlo's emotional breakdown, Jonathan felt it was better for Arlo to be rid of that sort of mental entanglement. He felt Arlo's soul was in danger, and . . ."

Molly paused for a moment and took a swig of water from her bottle. She looked paler than she had a moment before. It was like she was reliving whatever happened in that moment she made the decision that would so alter Arlo's life.

"As soon as I told Arlo the lie I knew I had made a terrible mistake," Molly said. "I just thought that once we were all together I'd be able to make it all right. I could help Arlo become a spiritually strong young man. That he would forget his childhood romance like we all must do. That he would fall in love with someone else—someone who was a better fit."

A weak smile quickly vanished from Molly's face. Lavinia covered her mouth with her hand; the charms from her bracelet swung at her wrist. No doubt she was masking the anger, sadness, and pity we all felt. Hanne, on the other hand, could not mask her disdain.

"You know you're a first-class bitch, right?" she said, glaring at the older woman.

"I understand how you feel," Molly said, not looking anyone in the eye. "But you need to believe me, all of you. I know I was wrong. I know that Jehovah God loves that young man, and that Arlo loves Shri. And I know now that this love must be from God as well. I want to fix this. I need to. My only intention today is to find Arlo and make sure he and Shri get to see each other before he leaves. And whenever he comes back from Ecuador, I'll do whatever I can to help them be together if at all possible. But right now I just need your help in finding him before Brother Birch does or before he hurts himself."

That's when Molly crumbled. Lavinia scooched her chair around the table and stroked Molly's back.

"My dear, it's no use berating yourself," she whispered. "It's been less than two hours. I'm sure he'll show up."

Molly pulled herself away from the professor's touch as if Lavinia's hand were on fire.

"No, he won't!" Molly cried out. "You don't understand. I checked everywhere: the college, the Abilities Institute, the Kingdom Hall, the Dunkin' Donuts, and everywhere in between. Arlo only had travel training to go to those specific places. If he goes anywhere else, he takes me, his uncle, or someone else with him. He doesn't know how to go anywhere else on his own."

"Stop saying what Arlo can and can't do!" I barked, ready to let her have it again. "You clearly don't know him very well. If you had—"

"*Godverdomme!*" Hanne shouted, silencing us. "We don't have time for you two to go at each other. We all need to work together. So think. It's obvious Arlo's gone off to find Shri. The question is how."

"Hanne's right," Lavinia said, more calmly. "Is it possible that Arlo just found some other friend who would drive him down to the city?"

"What about Big Head Lawrence?" Hanne asked.

"It's impossible," Molly insisted. "Jonathan cut off Arlo's internet, thinking it had become a threat to his spiritual fitness. Without the internet Arlo has no access to the outside world. He can't even order an Able-Ride on his own. Jonathan truly believed that Arlo's deaf-blindness was a gift from God meant to keep his nephew pure. I know it doesn't make sense to you, but there is evil out there and the world can be so confusing. Jonathan thought he was giving Arlo a clearer and easier path to salvation."

I started to say something, but Hanne shot me a silencing look.

"My point is," Molly continued, "Arlo has no one else in the world except the four of us right now. And there's absolutely no way he could get to Shri on his own."

"Wait," I said suddenly, standing up and grabbing my backpack. "I think I know where we can find him. If it's not too late."

43

TRAVEL TRAINING FOR AN ESCAPE

"Please help to buy one train ticket Queens, New York."

You stand in front of the train station holding up the note you wrote in Magic Marker. It's the same way you got from Brother Birch's house to the station. Costas, your orientation and mobility instructor, once told you that the only things you need to get around are your guide dog Snap, your white cane, your travel cards, a notebook and Magic Marker, and proper training.

Unfortunately, you don't have the proper training for traveling to or in New York City.

But you have everything else.

And if Larry can get to Poughkeepsie on the train, then you can get to Queens, New York, on the train.

Several people pass by without helping. Finally, a nice man who smells like soap takes you and Snap to the place where you buy tickets. You only have $27.70 in your wallet and the Amtrak train to New York City costs $24.30, even with a discount. That would only leave you $3.40 for the rest of the trip. Luckily, the Metro-North train leaving at 1:50 p.m. is only $12.25 because you are disabled.

"One-way or round-trip?" the man who sells tickets writes in your notebook.

"One-way."

You will need some money to take a cab and to buy lunch if you get hungry. You will figure out what to do about that later. Like Costas said, it's one step at a time. To make sure you are going to the right place, you ask the ticket man if this train will stop in Queens. You are glad you asked because he sets you straight and tells you that when you arrive at Grand Central you will then need to take an MTA subway to Queens.

After you have your ticket you write on the travel card: *Please take me to train to New York City so I can take SUBWAY to Queens to find my sweetheart.* You thought this sounded romantic and might make more people want to be nice and help you.

It works. Only five minutes later, a woman who smells like perfume offers you her nice chubby arm like she has walked with blind people before. Snap is nervous because she can feel the trains rumbling underneath the floor. Perfume Woman walks you through the very large room to the edge of what appear to be steps leading down to the train. The woman walks ahead, and you and Snap follow. Thirty steps later you are on the platform and you thank the woman. It's very hot outside and sweat soaks through your shirt. It's twenty-nine minutes until your train. You walk in a very small circle to pass the time. You use both your cane and Snap for extra protection against holes and obstacles. To get rid of nervous energy, you let your foot play with the bumpy rubber safety strips at the edge of the platform so you remember where it becomes dangerous. It takes you almost ten minutes to realize that there are two sides to the platform, and because you have walked in circles you are now uncertain which side of the platform the New York City train will be on. You hold up another note. Finally, another nice man, who is your size and has a little body odor probably because it is so hot, asks to see your ticket and writes to you that you are on the wrong track. *You need to be on track two for the 1:50 train to Grand Central*, he writes. *It is 1:35.* Body Odor Man leaves before you can ask for help. Heart pounding. Breathing heavy. There is only fifteen minutes before the train comes. Snap is getting very anxious too. You write a note. Soon a nice man who is shorter than you with fat wrists and a cigar smell walks you to track two and sets you on the correct side to take the train. You stand there for five minutes without moving. It's 1:45. Finally, just to be safe, you hold up your sign again about taking the 1:50 train to New York City. Someone taps you on the shoulder and writes in your notebook that there was an announcement and the 1:50 train is switching to track four. There are only three minutes left. Your heart wants to break out of your chest. You groan in frustration. A nice man (maybe Cigar Man?) helps you and Snap rush to the correct track. You hold your breath. The windy rumble of the train approaches, which makes Snap anxious. When the train stops, a man who you think is a conductor takes your arm to help you onto the train. But as you follow Snap into the car, your foot falls into a large and dangerous gap between the platform and the train. You scrape your shin and the hot sting means it's going to bleed. Snap is upset and licks your face. Another man helps the conductor pull your foot out. But you are finally on the train and find an empty seat. You are breathing very heavily, sweat is stinging your eyes, and the blood has started to run down your leg. When the conductor taps your shoulder, you give him your ticket and write a note: *Please tap me when get to Grand Central.*

The train starts to vibrate and begins to roll backward. You let your head lean against the glass of the window and Snap lies at your feet. You did it! You and Snap are on the train going to New York City. You are smiling very large and feeling triumphant like the time you climbed the rope in gym class to the top and slapped the ceiling. The cool air from the air conditioner feels icy against your sweaty, hot skin. The wound on your leg lets you know it's there, but the pain isn't so bad. You take out Snap's bowl and fill it with most of your water bottle, which she gulps down. You are thirsty too and drink the last few drops from the bottle, but it's not enough. You make spit in your mouth to keep it wet, and plan to look for a water fountain when you arrive at Grand Central Station. You will rest for the two-hour train ride since you did not sleep last night thinking of your plan. The vibration of the train feels like continuous thunder. Soon you will be with Shri again. Soon you will be happy forever.

44

CHASING ARLO

While the others scoured the train platforms for Arlo, I checked with the ticket booth to ask if anyone had sold a ticket to a DeafBlind man with a yellow guide dog.

"Sure, I remember him," the clerk told me. "About thirty minutes ago. Young mute with the dog. Showed me a handwritten note saying he wanted a one-way ticket to Grand Central. Sold him a ticket for the one fifty. Wrote down directions how to get to Queens from there. I grew up in Elmhurst. Hope he'll be okay. You know, we could have arranged assistance if he planned ahead."

I texted the women and two minutes later, everyone was reunited in the main hall, gasping for breath.

"Yep," I said. "He's on his way to Queens. What are we gonna do?"

"He's going to get hurt," Molly said, doing all she could to prevent herself from crying again. "If only he had waited for me."

Lavinia and Hanne put their arms around Molly. It was as if their touch turned on the spigot to Molly's tears. Lavinia looked up at me, her voice low and calm.

"I think it's best that you tell his uncle as soon as possible."

I nodded in agreement. Birch was his guardian whether I liked it or not. Hanne, her arm still around Molly, scrunched her face like she tasted something sour.

"Bullshit," Hanne growled. "That means Arlo won't get to see Shri for a long time or ever."

I waited for Molly to tell Hanne to mind her own business, or at least push her arm away. But that's not what happened.

"She's right," Molly said, wiping her nose into a tissue. "If Jonathan finds out, he'll immediately head to the nursing home to stop it. We have to buy Arlo a little time."

Lavinia was nodding her head with the other women while I stood there stunned. Finally, I raised my hand, my incredulous expression exaggerated to make a point.

"Are you three going mad? Molly just said it a minute ago. What if Arlo gets hurt? It's New York fucking City!"

"Stop cursing," Molly snapped through her tears. "And stop yelling. There's no need."

Hanne patted Molly's back and then lifted her hand angrily up into my face.

"Also stop mansplaining everything to us, Cyrilje," Hanne barked. "What about this? In two or three hours Molly lets Birch know that Arlo is headed down to the city. Meanwhile we go down and make sure he's safe. After his visit with Shri we can take him home. Good, *ja*?"

Molly dried any remaining wetness from her eyes with a Kleenex, nodded to Hanne, and then, for the first time, looked directly into my eyes.

"Please, Cyril," she said. "Give me a chance to help him."

"I must agree with Hanne," Lavinia said. "Arlo will be okay. He's clearly on the train. A local. If you hurry, you might be able to meet him at the nursing home. Do you have the address?"

"Yeah," I said. "Larry included it in the email, but—"

"I wish I could come," Lavinia interrupted. "But you'll need the space in your car to bring Arlo and his doggie back. If you need me to do something here, just call. I'm at your disposal. It's best you hurry."

The three women started chatting excitedly and hurriedly gathering their things as if my participation were a done deal and they were off on some big adventure.

"Excuse me," I said, my anger growing as they ignored me. Then I exploded: "For fuck's sake! Please listen! I need to say something!"

My voice echoed in the hall. Suddenly it was not only the three women whose attention I had. Faces everywhere were staring at me.

"Are you forgetting Birch has a restraining order against me?" I said in a harsh whisper. "There's no way I can go."

The three women glanced at one another like I was a child who needed to be handled. Molly asked if she could speak to me alone. While the other two walked far enough away, Molly's pale, tired eyes looked into mine as she gathered her thoughts.

"You have to come, Cyril," she said, her voice hoarse with emotion. "Birch doesn't need to know you're involved."

I had had enough.

"What's really going on, Molly?" I asked, folding my arms and lowering my voice. "You suddenly woke up today and decided to be the hero? Did your allegiance to Brother Birch and God suddenly disappear?"

Molly took a deep breath and rolled her shoulders like a boxer ready to spar. She seemed like she had been waiting for me to say what I had just said.

"Cyril, I know you don't respect my faith."

"Oh, please," I groaned.

"Can you fathom the idea that you shouldn't judge an entire religion by the actions of any one person? Especially Brother Birch. He's just as sinful as anybody. Worse, even. The Bible says you know the goodness of a tree by the fruit it produces. So, we should judge people based on their actions. And I'll say it first: Some of my actions have been reprehensible."

"There's an understatement—"

"You're right. But it wasn't because of ill intention. It was ignorance.

Arlo has shown me I was following a false God in my feelings for Brother Birch. You called it out in front of Sister Doris."

"Who?"

"Jonathan's wife. That day of the field trip in the parking lot. It was cruel of you, but it was the truth."

Molly took another breath, looked up at the grand golden tin ceiling of the train station, and then looked at me. Her eyes were damp, but in a way clearer than I had ever seen them.

"Yes, I was in love with Jonathan, or thought I was. It's hard being alone and controlling every urge inside yourself for most of your life. I so stupidly thought something real was happening. I trusted that Jonathan truly cared about me. But look what's actually happened. I've been shunned by the congregation and removed from the Ecuador trip with Arlo. Meanwhile, Jonathan gets a slap on the wrist. When it was decided he could no longer see me without supervision, he didn't even send me an email to say good-bye. That was it. Done. Like I meant nothing. And all the suffering we . . . I . . . caused for that poor boy . . . for what? Because I trusted that man more than my own instincts. How will God ever forgive me unless I help Arlo make things right? How will I forgive myself? Please help me make things right."

I shook my head, clutching to my skepticism, unwilling to be swayed, but finally believing she was telling the truth.

"You know what you're asking me to risk, right? RID might take my certification away, all because of you."

"I'll speak to RID and defend you. I'll be a witness in court about Birch's treatment of Arlo. I'd go find Arlo alone and help him if I could, Cyril. But I can't. Arlo needs you. I need you."

Molly had been twisting her hands anxiously. I stared at the gnarled bumps of arthritis, a familiar by-product of interpreting for too many years and not taking proper care. I stood there frozen, my head in a fog of pity and dwindling rage. A moment later Hanne and Lavinia walked back toward us. Hanne grabbed my shoulders and stared into my eyes like some old-timey war-movie commander confronting a soldier on his certain-death mission.

"Cyrilje, we have to go if we're going to do this."

The three women stared at me, waiting, impatient, asking me to do something that could amplify the destruction of my entire life.

"I'll help you find Arlo," I said bitterly. "But then I'm done."

Once we were out in the parking lot, Hanne sat in the passenger seat while Molly climbed into the back of my Honda. It all seemed like a bizarre dream. Lavinia, sweat pouring down her face, leaned into the driver's-side window, her eyes and voice damp with emotion.

"Cyril, I need you to do me a favor. When you find Arlo—and I know you will—please tell him it was an honor to have him in my class. And even though he missed the last two weeks, he still earned an A-plus—and I never give an A-plus. If he can learn his tenses, he will become a very good writer someday."

Lavinia looked like she wanted to say something else, but whatever emotion she was feeling prevented her. She gave me one last kiss on the cheek and then waved us off.

45

GRAND CENTRAL

You need to pee. You've needed to pee since an hour into the train ride down to New York City. Unsure if they have toilets on the train, you do not move for fear you won't be able to find your way back to your seat. If you aren't in the same seat, the conductor will not be able to tell you when you've reached Grand Central.

The next time the train stops, lots of people pass you by, but the conductor has not come to get you and your bladder is so full it presses hard against the bottom part of your belly. You check your watch and see that you must have already arrived at Grand Central. The conductor forgot about you, and now your need to get to a bathroom has become an emergency. It would be awful to meet Shri for the first time in five and a half years with pee in your pants. So you quickly write in your notebook: *Can you help me off the train and show me where toilet bathroom PLEASE?!!!*

The breezes of bodies rush by and no one helps you. It occurs to you that if you don't get off the train it might leave again and go back to Poughkeepsie. So you stand up and let Snap lead you off the train. The platform air is stone-still, very hot, and smells like dirt, electricity, piss, and shit. You did not expect this from a place called Grand Central. The platform is too dim to see anything.

To stop your bladder from leaking, you squeeze that part between your balls and your ass.

Snap go! Snap Toilet!

Snap, who has never been to Grand Central before either, turns left and you follow her into the hot darkness. Snap, who can only lead you to a toilet once you're in a restroom, is as confused as you are and stops. Just in case someone is around, you wave your laminated sign asking for help. A drop of urine leaks into your underwear. You assume that the direction of the exit must be in the same direction the train was moving when it arrived in the station, so you turn Snap around and hurry toward the right. A large round trash can in the middle of the platform attacks you from your left. But because you have to go to the toilet so bad you don't really notice the pain. Your feet feel the bumpy warning strip on the floor, keeping you from falling on the tracks. Snap can sense your urgency and walks quickly forward. The hard floor changes textures and starts to slope upward. You can feel cooler air coming from somewhere ahead. A hint of light. A change of scent. You pass through a door. You are in a giant room. Another drop of piss leaks out. You hold up your sign, and finally someone (a woman) touches your shoulder. She smells like hairspray and baby powder. You show the woman the note and she leads you and Snap across a very big room, through crowds of people, then down very slippery hard steps into another room that smells like all different kinds of very delicious food. She pulls you in different directions to avoid hitting things and then finally, just after the smell of *hamburger*-hamburgers and onions, you also smell toilets. Because she's a woman she cannot go inside the men's toilet, so she pushes you in the right direction. You enter the large bathroom and immediately bump into a row of sinks. At school the urinals were at the end of the row of sinks, so you use them as a guide. But at the end of the row of sinks is just a wall. The angry liquid inside presses harder and harder, demanding release. You hold your breath and squeeze. But it's too late. Hot piss gushes into your underwear before leaking all the way down your right pant leg, into your sock, your sneaker, and onto the floor.

You want to cry.

You can't go rescue Shri like this, and you don't have a lot of time. Brother Birch will be looking for you. You need to clean yourself. So you remove your belt and put it and your wallet in the front pouch of your backpack, setting it next to a dry area on the floor. Even though there are other people around, you remove all your dirty clothes from the waist down. Your face boils with embarrassment, so you have to be quick. Locating the soap dispenser, you wash your pants, underwear, right sneaker, and right sock as best as you can. You also wash your crotch, legs, and feet. The wind and vibrations of other people's bodies pass by you. Snap leaps toward something.

No! Stay! Stop causing trouble!

You are mad at Snap for being a bad girl when you are having such a difficult time. When everything is finally clean, you pull the sopping-wet clothes onto your sopping-wet body. It feels terrible. At least you won't smell like piss. You feel good about that. But when you reach for your backpack, it's not where you left it. Panic. You and Snap search the floor of the entire bathroom. Under the sinks. On the counter. In the stalls. Signing and using your voice, you ask for help but no one listens, no one understands. Your backpack with your SBC, magnifying glass, travel cards, notebook, laptop, belt, wallet, money, and Shri's address: all gone. A Deaf-Blind man lost and alone with no way to communicate. You are nothing. You start to scream.

46

LOST AND FOUND

The three of us barely said a word to each other the entire drive down to the city. It was as if we worried that the friction of our voices might slow the car down. Molly texted Birch that after leaving Snap at the guide dog rescue, she and Arlo wanted to have a goodbye dinner together, and asked if it would be all right if Arlo got home on the late side. Birch agreed, probably due to whatever guilt he might have about separating Molly from Arlo. Whatever the reason, it bought us a little more time.

None of us knew much about Queens other than that was where New York kept its airports. The highway led us to boulevards that spit us out onto residential roads where we saw a myriad of cultures walking around, from Hasidic Jews in religious garments to South Asian families in saris and hijabs. The architecture was equally diverse, ranging from elegant English Tudor mansions to ugly brick high-rises. Of course, we weren't there to take in the sights.

"Turn here!" Hanne cried out, her eyes locked on the Maps app. "This is the street where the nursing home is."

As we drove slowly down the road, the apartment buildings and row houses were replaced by car repair shops, a White Castle, and a dirty video store called Jezebel's. And suddenly, there it was: New Bridge Gardens Nursing Home and Rehabilitation Center. It definitely is not one of your upscale nursing homes. It sits between two empty lots and has a rocky, unkempt lawn with two untrimmed boxwood bushes. That day, a large green dumpster sat in front with several dirty mattresses peeking out. The building itself is a one-floor cinder-block construction, with light blue paint and a sign out front that reads, WE CARE FOR THE LONG TERM! For some reason it was the exclamation point that creeped me out the most.

"Are you sure you have the right address?" Molly asked, perhaps hoping for something nicer.

"It's the address Larry sent Arlo," I said. "Not exactly the Taj Mahal, huh?"

"Well," Molly said, "let's go see if he got here."

"Wait," Hanne cautioned. "We should call first. We don't want to make them suspicious."

We all agreed. Then, as Hanne spoke to a person on the phone, we focused intently on every detail of Hanne's "mm-hmms" to get clues to what she was finding out about Shri. Her expression looked concerned, and then she hung up.

"Arlo definitely hasn't gotten here yet," Hanne said.

"What's wrong?" I asked, noting something behind Hanne's eyes.

"The receptionist told me Shri's file says you have to get special permission if you want to visit. She hasn't had any visitors in a long time."

All of us looked at one another, not wanting to acknowledge out loud the challenge that might be ahead.

"Where could Arlo be?" Molly asked, her voice cracking with frustration. "I knew he couldn't make it here on his own."

"Maybe he took a cab?" Hanne asked.

"He couldn't afford a cab," Molly explained. "Birch barely gives him any of his SSI money. What if he got lost on the subway or worse, what if he fell?"

Molly covered her face with her hands, attempting to hide her fears while Hanne got up on her knees and swiveled to face Molly in the back.

"There, there," Hanne whispered, taking Molly's hand. "We will find him. He also has Snap with him, and his keyboard typing dingus, the thing he communicates with, right? He's not a stupid man."

"No, he's not," I said, though my own worry began to escalate, not because of Arlo's lack of intelligence, but because New York City in all its Rube Goldberg complexity was hard to navigate even for the able-bodied. For the disabled it was a nightmare. "But maybe it's time to call Birch and the police?"

"Cyrilje! Stop it," Hanne snapped.

"She's right," Molly added from the back. "Once Birch knows, it's done. None of us will be allowed within a mile of Arlo, and he'll never get to see Shri."

"But what if he's lost?" I argued. "What if he's in trouble?"

"Let's just give it a little more time," Hanne pleaded. "Here is my idea: I'll stay here and watch for Arlo. Cyrilje, you take Molly to wait for him at the exit to the subway station nearest to here. Then you take the subway to Grand Central and see if you can find him."

"But what if he's not there?" I asked.

For some reason this set Molly to crying again.

"Cyrilje, you're not helping!" Hanne punched my leg. "Look, if we can't find Arlo in the next two hours then we call Brother Birch, *ja*?"

Before I could even respond, Molly was buckling her seatbelt again.

"Let's get to the subway station," Molly begged. "Hurry!"

◊ ◊ ◊

I left Hanne at a seedy coffee shop across from the nursing home, with a direct view of the front door. Then I parked my car and left Molly at the Jamaica Center subway station. Because the station has multiple exits, we agreed it was better for her to stay on the inbound platform, watching each train for Arlo. I grabbed the next Manhattan-bound E train, transferring at Roosevelt Avenue for a 7 train into Grand Central. The entire trip took me over an hour, and the whole way I was bombarded with catastrophic visions of Arlo and Snap falling off the edge of the subway platforms, or being kidnapped by potential murderers, or just disappearing into the bottomless pot of human stew that is New York City.

By the time I arrived at Grand Central, it was already rush hour and the station was a crush of people pouring into every tunnel and passageway. I found my way to the cavernous Main Concourse with its golden central clock and its dazzling cerulean-blue ceiling filled with the constellations. I figured Arlo would have had to pass through here. Making my way to the information booth, I was horrified by the thought of Arlo and Snap trying to navigate this crowd.

"I'm sorry," I said loudly to the clerk over the din. "I lost my little brother. He's a DeafBlind man, twenty-three, a little taller than me. Walks a little wobbly. He has a pretty scraggly guide dog. Have you seen him?"

The attendant, an older man with a sheen of sweat on his bald head, looked at me, bored and annoyed. He gestured to the throngs of people and smirked sarcastically.

"No. But, at this time of day, if Godzilla came up to me with a neck brace and a bum leg I wouldn't notice him neither. Ask a friggin' cop. Next?"

After muttering a *Fuck you* I made my way to the top of one of the grand staircases that bookend the Main Concourse. Scanning the throng, I quickly spotted a group of MTA cops leaning against the edge of the ticket counter, all with their heads down looking at their phones. I ran back down the steps and calmly handed them the same story about trying to locate my DeafBlind brother. Three of the four shrugged their shoulders. But the fourth, a cute-as-hell shorter, brown-skinned guy, put his phone away and addressed me politely.

"Is he in any kind of danger? You know you don't have to wait twenty-four hours to file a missing persons report. That's a myth."

"No danger," I said. "But thanks for letting me know."

"By the way," the cop added. "If we run into him we can just get a sign language interpreter right on our phones. Cool, right?"

"Yeah, that's great," I said. "Only problem is, that wouldn't work with his vision loss. If you see him, just tap on his arm and he'll give you a marker and notebook. Then, if you can, write as big as you can that Cyril—that's me—is looking for him. Also tell him that I want to take him to see Shri, okay?"

I had to repeat myself a few times before the short cop registered how to spell Shri and understood how someone that was blind could read writing but not see an interpreter on a screen. After that was cleared up, I searched the perimeter of the Main Concourse again, being more methodical this time, thinking that Arlo would attempt to use the wall as a guide. No luck. Then I went down to the platform where the 1:50 train from Poughkeepsie had arrived. I asked two maintenance men emptying the big round garbage cans if they had seen Arlo. They conferred in some kind of French patois.

"Okay," the one who spoke English said. "My friend here says he did see a guy like that. About an hour or so ago. He had messed his pants and was washing himself in the men's restroom downstairs."

"That can't be him. Washing himself?" I clarified. "The man I'm talking about is neat looking, like a college student?"

I was hoping the man had made a mistake, and he conferred again with his coworker.

"Yep," the man told me. "He says the guy looked like you said. Young. White guy. Had the dog. Was on drugs or something. Says he made crazy sounds like Frankenstein's monster and had on a blue button-down shirt. Men's toilet near Shake Shack."

I thanked the men and bolted back up the stairs and back across the Main Concourse, pushing against bodies, sweat blinding me, asking three different people which way to the "men's restroom." The whole time I was thinking: *Why the hell was Arlo naked and washing himself? Why was he screaming? This is my fault! All of this!* My head ached from fear. My armpits, like waterfalls, drenched my shirt. As I was about to head down the stairs to the men's restroom, I heard a shout from behind me.

"Hey! Buddy! Hey!"

It was the cute MTA cop running toward me.

"We found your little brother!" he said. "He's hanging over in the passageway with some homeless kids. He looks freaked out. Didn't offer me no notebook. You better get over there."

The cop pointed to a passageway at the other end of the Main Concourse. Panicking, I aggressively pushed bodies out of my way, wanting to get to Arlo.

"Yo, Red!" one hulking specimen said, refusing to be moved. "What's your fucking hurry? You just nearly knocked me over!"

"Don't fucking call me Red, buffalo boy!" I shouted back at the towering man, shoving him so hard he stumbled back into the crowd. The insane look on my face probably made him too afraid to challenge me. New Yorkers are tough, but not as tough as an ASL interpreter who is trying to find his DeafBlind consumer.

Within twenty feet of the passageway, I saw the heads of the three other cops looking down at the floor along the wall. There was Arlo, looking a mess, sitting next to several homeless-looking goth kids with dirty clothes and piercings in every flap of skin. Snap was patiently allowing a pit bull puppy to chew on her ear. The puppy's owner was a young woman with wilted pink hair and a homemade tattoo across her cheeks that said *bitch please*. Arlo looked utterly despondent, with a sweaty, filthy face and wearing sopping-wet pants. He only needed some tattoos, a wild haircut, and piercings to completely fit in with his compatriots on the floor.

"Arlo! Snap!" I screamed.

Snap leaped up and began wagging her tail and nudging Arlo with her nose. It was the happiest she had ever been to see me. Arlo began to reach around anxiously. The girl with pink hair looked up at me suspiciously.

"Is Prince Charming here your kid?"

"Yeah," I said.

"Billy found him in the bathroom. He was a mess. He got some bad stuff, I think."

"Thanks for helping him out," I said.

"Can we have five bucks for dinner?" she asked.

I handed Pink Hair Girl a twenty and tapped Arlo on the shoulder, fingerspelled my name. He sat up anxiously.

"Let's go! I'm taking you to see Shri!"

47

THE RESCUERS

Arlo barely thanked me for finding him, since *if hearing people hadn't sto-len his stuff in the first place he wouldn't have needed my help.*

"Hearing people always mess up everything!" Arlo signed bitterly. "Fed up!"

Then, as we were riding the subway back to Queens, I alerted him to the fact that Molly would be waiting for us when we got off. That's when he had a complete meltdown: desperate vocalizing, hands flying. I had to assure the other passengers that I was not, in fact, kidnapping him. Once he calmed down, I tried to get him to believe that Molly was on our side, and how this was her idea and that she had called us all together and lied to Birch. Still Arlo didn't trust her, nor me, it appeared. He was, however, glad that Hanne was waiting for us. After that he refused to talk to me any-more and just sat nervously, lost inside his head, his hands twitching with half-formed signs. One minute he was smiling, probably imagining the moment he would get to touch Shri, and the next, telling off some demon inside his head. *Was it Molly? Birch? Me? All of us?*

When we stepped off the subway car, Molly ran down the platform and hugged Arlo like he was some long-lost soldier back from the war. He just stood there, limp, not returning her embrace. As we drove back to get Hanne, Arlo sat in the back seat with Molly, his hands folded furiously in his armpits. Molly looked so wounded.

"Molly, for what it's worth, he hasn't signed a word to me for the last forty minutes. We're interpreters non grata at the moment."

Molly smiled weakly.

"He used to do this to me when I first started working with him," she said. "If I didn't know a particular sign or word, he would get so angry. He'd accuse me of lying and then wouldn't talk to me for the rest of the day. He played my emotions like a game of guilt Ping-Pong. It's the one thing he got from his uncle."

Molly closed her eyes and pinched her forehead like she had a headache. What she had to be feeling! In only a matter of weeks she had lost her lover, gotten kicked off the Ecuador mission, and now the young man who was like her son was threatening to never speak to her again. For the first time I began to truly feel sorry for her.

"We shouldn't sweat it too much," I said. "Once we get him to Shri for the visit, he'll come around . . . at least a little."

Molly opened her eyes and stared at me with the most hollow, sad gaze.

"Will he?"

48

NURSING HOME

We met Hanne at the coffee shop and briefed Arlo on what Hanne had learned from her phone call. For reasons of interpreting, Arlo let go of his previous refusal to touch Molly or me. We had become mere tools, conveyors of information, which, in reality, was our role. After purchasing another blank notebook and large Magic Marker for Arlo, I walked with him to the nursing home, while we told Molly and Hanne to meet us back at the car in an hour.

As we approached the front of the facility, Arlo lifted his sunglasses, his eyes straining to comprehend where we were. His body shook from excitement, and a smile appeared and disappeared on his face every other moment.

"Nursing home nice?" he asked.

"It's okay," I signed. "To be honest, it looks a little run-down, but maybe it will be nicer inside."

Ten feet from the entry, Arlo winced at the smells of the nursing care facility: disinfectants, medicines, recently cleaned-up incontinence, aging and wounded bodies. Even Snap sniffed the air and gave a small whine. I was familiar with the odor, having done jobs in such facilities many times. While it didn't appear to be the best of residential rehabs, it certainly wasn't the worst. The receptionist sitting at the front desk wore powder-blue scrubs with a teddy bear pattern. She appeared to be in the middle of a personal conversation. When we approached her, I coughed lightly so she knew we were there. While we waited for her to finish her call, I noticed a man through an open window in what appeared to be a nurse's office. He was surrounded by open medicine bottles. The man, middle-aged and bald, had dark circles under his eyes and hollowed cheeks. With his thick fingers, he doled out pills into rows of pink blister packs as he watched what looked like a Russian-language soap opera on a nearby television. When he looked up at us, I smiled at him, hoping to create a positive vibe with everyone in the home, but instead he raised his eyebrows, shrugged, and retreated farther back into the nurse's office.

I described what I saw to Arlo, which made him grow concerned. Finally, after a full three minutes of us standing there, the receptionist paused her phone conversation to look up at us.

"Can I help you?" she asked in a thick New York accent.

"Sorry to interrupt," I said, simultaneously interpreting for Arlo. "We're here to visit Shridevi Mukherjee."

She told her telephone interlocutor to hold, and looked us up and down, suspiciously.

"You wanna visit Shri?" she said, picking up a logbook in front of her. "I don't see any note. There needs to be permission from her family or the supervisor. Sorry."

The receptionist returned to her call and swung her rolling chair toward the wall.

"What do?" Arlo asked, panicking. "Must see Shri!"

"Calm down," I signed, then once again coughed to get the receptionist's attention. "Excuse me?"

The receptionist mumbled something to her caller and then slowly spun her chair around, looking even more annoyed than just a moment before.

"What?"

"I'm sorry to bother you . . . Bella?" I said, checking her name tag. "We're a little confused, because Shri's auntie was supposed to call and let you know that we were coming to visit."

The receptionist raised her eyebrows and exaggeratedly looked us both up and down before letting out a sarcastic snort.

"Relatives? What part of India are *you* from?"

"Ha ha. Funny," I said. "I know. But we are relatives. By marriage. I'm Shri's brother-in-law, Doug, and this is my little brother, a good friend of Shri's—Walter."

I regretted the lie as soon as I said it and hoped she wouldn't remember it the next time Arlo came for a visit a year hence.

"Sorry," Bella said. "I can't let you in until she calls. I'm sorry."

As I interpreted this, Arlo groaned loudly and ran his hand through his hair. Bella grimaced at the sound and went back to her call.

"Okay," I said, even louder than before, still trying to keep the situation amiable. "I'll call now and let you talk to her aunt. Hold on a minute."

I punched in ten numbers, put the phone to my ear, and complained it had gone to voice mail.

"Hey, Auntie!" I said loudly into the phone. "This is Doug. Walt and I came up to visit Shri, but you forgot to leave our names at the front desk. When you get this message, could you do that for me? Thanks."

I turned back to the receptionist with a disappointed look on my face.

"I forgot today she's volunteering at the Hindu temple all day. I have no idea when she'll call. You have to understand, we've driven a really long way. Isn't there a way to make an exception? Please. My brother and Shri have been best friends since they were kids."

The receptionist shook her head no. I signed to Arlo without voicing.

"We need to make the receptionist feel really sorry for you, okay? Pretend you're really upset."

I turned Arlo so he was directly addressing Bella. In an instant, Arlo turned hysterical, signing dramatically and using his voice. He told her how it was actually his birthday and how Shri was his best friend, and *"please, see friend, please."* He was even able to produce tears that he wiped on his sleeve. The performance was impressive. Bella, ending her personal call, appeared overwhelmed by having a weeping DeafBlind man in front of her.

"Poor kid," Bella said, her expression softening. "Tell your brother not to be so upset. Maybe the aunt will call back with permission. It's nice you know that Deaf hand stuff so you can talk to him. Sometimes I wish we had someone who could make signals to that Mukherjee kid. Most of the time they just write on a piece of paper."

As soon as I interpreted what Bella had said, Arlo's fake, weepy face was instantly replaced by one featuring incredibly real anger.

"What?" Arlo snapped. "Shri can't read English good! Shri from other country!"

"Hey. Take it easy," I begged him without voicing. "Your sad performance was starting to work. Let's just get you in to see Shri first. I'm sure they get interpreters in when they need. While you two are talking, I'll speak to whoever runs this place and explain about the language issues. Now go back to looking sad."

He did.

"Is something wrong?" Bella asked.

"He's just upset. Like he said, it's his birthday, and he's being sent to live out west so he may not be able to visit Shri again for years."

Bella shook her head sadly. "Hold on a minute."

Bella dialed the phone and let it ring for a while. She looked frustrated, but on the brink.

"The assistant supervisor isn't picking up as usual. Oh, well . . . I really shouldn't, but next time just make sure the family calls first and leaves a note. Go to room twenty-five. Down that hall on the right. But the rule is only one person in the room at a time. Otherwise the kid throws a fit. We don't need any drama this week."

Bella leaned in and whispered from her rolling throne. "Don't be fooled by that girl. You look in that room and see those big pretty Indian eyes and think she's a precious angel. And then bam, you get clocked on the head with a can of Ensure. Or worse."

Bella pulled her right eye bag down with her pointer finger to indicate she was giving me the inside scoop. I suddenly grew concerned that Larry may not have painted a complete picture of Shri's condition.

"Got it," I said. "We'll go one at a time."

"Mmm-hmm. But sign the logbook first."

As I flipped through the book, I paid special attention for the last time anyone had actually come to see Shri. There were no recorded visits until I went all the way back to December, when someone, who I assumed was her aunt, stopped by for just thirty-five minutes. *No one else for eight whole months.*

When I signed our names, I wrote *Doug and Walter Whitman.*

Snap whimpered as her calloused paws slipped and slid on the tile floor as we made our way down the grayish-pink hallway. Two older female patients with some sort of dementia wandered along the hall with vacant looks. One of the women pulled up her gown, exposing her naked lower half like a neglected toddler. Surprisingly, there were very few attendants around, especially for a place that was responsible for doing rehab as well as skilled nursing care. Other than the echo of our footsteps, the only sounds were the random groans and mutterings from behind half-open doors. Snap's ears pushed back, and her eyes echoed my own concern. At one point Snap planted her paws, stubbornly resisting going any farther. Arlo shook the harness aggressively, then reassured Snap with a pat on the head.

"Snap nervous," he signed. "I nervous too."

Me too, buddy, me too, I thought.

When we arrived at Shri's room Arlo took a deep breath. A woman pushing a cleaning caddy reminded us about the one-at-a-time rule. They were watching us.

I pushed the door open and was stunned by what I saw and smelled. A rank decaying effluvium wafted from the dimly lit room. A tray filled with what looked like breakfast and lunch dishes was stacked on a table against the wall. There were at least two empty Ensure cans on the floor. While the sheets looked clean, the room had very little character, with no photographs or posters on its walls. And the window faced another cinder-block wall, letting in very little light. But most shocking of all was the figure in the bed. Shri's body looked too thin and at the age of twenty-two looked the size of a twelve-year-old. Her legs were disproportionally small, atrophied from lack of use. Because she faced away from the doorway, all I could see of her head was a pile of thick black hair on the pillow.

"Shri seems to be sleeping," I signed, containing my reaction. "I think she might be sicker than we thought. She's very thin."

Arlo smiled. "Ha ha. High school, Shri always smaller and skinny. Wow. Still small? Okay. I go in now. See you later."

I gave him directions to the bed, and Arlo nudged Snap forward. Her nose was going crazy with the smells. I wanted desperately to follow them, but just as Arlo arrived at the edge of the bed, that cleaning woman came up behind me and pulled the door closed.

"Is best if crazy deaf-dumb kid doesn't even see two people," she said in an Eastern European accent. "She is very dangerous."

"Actually, Shri is a grown woman," I said. "And just a heads-up, you should never use the word 'dumb.' The proper word is—"

Before I could finish talking, the housekeeper shrugged her shoulders and moved on.

I stood outside Shri's room for fifteen minutes, making sure I didn't hear any screaming or glass breaking. I quickly texted Molly and Hanne.

The eagle has landed! They are in the room together. All seems cool. However, this place is not at all set up to work with the Deaf. The people I've met seem a little clueless. Cultural mediation time. Gonna go find a manager and make sure they get good interpreters and understand about Shri's language needs. Wish me luck.

49

IN YOUR EYES

Shri's room is too dark to see anything. Standing at the edge of the bed, you touch the cool sheets. A slight vibration means a living body lies there, inches from you. On Judgment Day, Jehovah God is supposed to bring the dead back to life. That's what this feels like. Only Shri is real. Shri is true.

You take a big breath and let the tips of your fingers slide across the bed until they meet the warmth of Shri's back. Gently, gently, you let your fingers touch her shoulder. Bones and skin. Much thinner than you remember. Still her warm body rises and falls with each breath. *Alive. Shri is alive.*

Wake up. Wake up, Shri! You tap her small shoulder. Nothing. You tap again, harder. Shri's body jolts awake. You are so happy that you throw your arms around her. A split second later you feel a small fist hit you in the side of your head. The blow, more shocking than painful, makes you stumble backward. Snap scratches your leg and tries to pull you to the door, but you pull her back to the bed. When you reach out for Shri you feel the slaps and punches of tiny hands like the beating wings of a furious butterfly. Shri is too weak to cause any real pain, except to your heart, which is in agony.

"Shri, please!" you sign. "Why hit? Don't you recognize? Remember? A-r-l-o. Name-sign Arlo! I understand you angry. Before I didn't know. If know . . . I run here fast. Please, punching me, stop! Talk with me!"

You press your crying face into the sheets as her blows continue on your head and back, and you raise your hands in case Shri wants to speak to you. After the longest moment, the punching stops and Shri's thin, dry fingers sign angrily into your hands.

"Where? Where?! I waiting, waiting for you. So long! Many years! You never come! All alone! I hate you! Go away!"

But you don't leave. You pull your body farther onto the bed and Shri's tiny, crying body pulls itself into your lap and you wrap your arm around her. Her bony back is like a basket of sticks. Her hair is still thick, and longer than before.

Sniff.

You breathe in. All you can smell is the hard soap used to clean Shri's hair, the strong detergent used to disinfect her sheets and pajamas, the scent of medicine on her breath. *Gone? Is Shri still gone?* No. Underneath it all, Shri is there, in the shape of her fingers, the cadence of her signs, and your own longing to protect. Ghost child is here. You are crying, Shri is crying. Snap puts her front legs on the bed and licks the tears from both your faces.

"You dream?" Shri asks. "You dream or real, which? Tell me!"

Over the next hour, you tell Shri the story of your last five and a half years. You tell her about being pulled from the Rose Garden School and sent to live with Brother Birch, about their lies, about trying to forget, about writing the essay, about getting in contact with Big Head Lawrence who is now called Larry, about Cyril and Hanne (but not everything about Hanne). The words will not stop flowing. It is just like your nighttime conversations back at the Rose Garden School.

When you finish signing, Shri's fragile hands, like wild horses freed from their pens, buck and twist beneath your fingers. What of *her* five and a half years?

"Five years and one half ago I sent hospital. Stay how long? One month, two month, three month. Almost die, but not die. C-O-M-A. When I wake up, I look around. Recognize nothing. *Where?* Rehab hospital. Can't move. Why? Whole body covered bandages, braces. Shocked. Everyone ask: Why you fall from roof? I say, I don't remember. Psychologist tell everyone I jump, try kill myself. Not true."

"Truth . . . what?"

When Shri tells you the whole true story, the one to replace all the made-up stories that have filled that spot in your brain, it doesn't start on the Day That Changed Everything. Her story starts months before. She reminds you about that day when Crazy Charles attacked you after you peed in his locker, and how Shri confessed that she let Crazy Charles kiss her behind the gym if he would agree to leave you and your friends alone.

"Yes, yes. I remember," you say.

"But before I didn't tell whole truth," Shri says, her hands shaking and growing cold. "When I kiss Crazy Charles, he want more. He says, *I love you, I love you. You my girlfriend.* I say, *No, no.* But Crazy Charles not accept so . . ."

She couldn't tell Crazy Charles about you and her being sweethearts. If she had, he and the Deaf Devils would have hurt you again. So Shri lied to Crazy Charles and said that her mama made a promise to the Blue God and the Elephant God that she would not date anyone and by even kissing Crazy Charles that one time she was doing a very bad thing.

"Crazy Charles very sad," Shri signs. "Crazy Charles said, *Okay, okay, I understand.* But he heartbroken and express himself—can't. No words. After that, I frightened to let other people see you and me together. Dating, we must secret. Then what happened? Marla, very jealous, she video you and me kissing behind cafeteria and show Crazy Charles. She tell him, *Arlo and Shri sweethearts long time. Sex together.* That night Crazy Charles and Deaf Devils want to beat you. They go looking for us in Secret Forest."

A tornado of feelings swirls inside your body as Shri continues the story: fury at what Crazy Charles might have done, fear for what Shri is about to relive, and utter humiliation that you are unable to go back in time and protect Shri. But underneath it all is unbelievable joy that the fingers telling you the horrible story, at this very moment, belong to Shri, not a ghost, not a demon, but a living breathing human. *Shridevi Mukherjee is alive.*

"When Crazy Charles and the Deaf Devils find us in Secret Forest, I run very fast and force Crazy Charles chase me all over. Then I hide on roof of Magnolia House, but he find me. Crazy Charles shows me cell phone video. He asks, *You and Arlo sweethearts?* I say, *Yes, yes, long time.* He heartbroken, starts to cry. I say, *Okay, okay. Sorry sorry.* He tell me he loves me very strong. Again I tell him: *Sorry sorry, but I love Arlo.* Crazy Charles—crying crying but also very angry. He screams at me, *You bitch! You whore!* And many other mean things about you and me. Then he says he will kill you, and I say, *No! If you hurt Arlo I will tell!*"

Shri stops signing. She is shaking. Telling the truth after holding it inside your body for so long is very, very painful. So you wait until Shri can continue, and when she does she signs much more slowly. She tells you how Crazy Charles told her he wanted to have sex with her on the roof, and unzipped her coat and pulled at her blouse, causing it to rip, which made Shri very angry because it was a shirt she liked very much.

"Then I kick him and punch him, and Crazy Charles begs me, *Please please, I love you, I love you,* again and again. What happens? He push me off the roof? No. I try run away again. Crazy Charles grabs back of my coat and swings me around in circle, like he's playing. We too close to edge of roof. But he keeps swinging very very hard like swing ride at amusement park. Crazy Charles laughing and crying. My feet lift off the ground. Finally I wiggle, trying to escape, but then my coat comes off and I can't control myself and . . ."

Shri's index finger and middle finger become the legs of her body as she stumbles over the side of the roof, falls down down down like in your nightmare, hits her back on the edge of an overhang, and then lands on the pavement. All the air is gone from her body, she signs. She shows her foggy eyes looking up at the trees but unable to move. Then she says she doesn't remember what happened after that until she woke up in the hospital, unable to move.

"Shh, shh," you blow into her hair, and rub her back, trying to quiet all the tremors of truth telling. You have to stop yourself from screaming that if Crazy Charles were in the room at this very moment you would kill him. It doesn't matter if Crazy Charles didn't push Shri. It was *his* fault. *Wasn't it? But if you had been there for Shri? If she hadn't been afraid of him knowing about you? If you were able to protect her?* Your head starts to spin. But then you have to force yourself to remember: a miracle just happened. *Shri is alive. Revenge can wait. Blame can wait.*

"When you woke up you didn't ask for me, why?"

"I try!" Shri explains.

Then she tells you how a week after she came out of her coma, a nice hearing woman came to the hospital with an interpreter and asked Shri if she had been raped. She assumed they were asking if Crazy Charles had raped her. She told the woman no, and then even denied that he had done anything wrong for fear that he or the Deaf Devils might again go after you.

"Then I ask: *Where Arlo? I want Arlo.* But you never come. Mama tell me, *Shh, shh, stop asking Arlo.* Then many days pass, weeks pass, months pass, and I think, *Maybe Crazy Charles lie to Arlo about what happen on the roof. Maybe Arlo love you never again.* So I think, *I will get better and go find Arlo.* I try to get better. Rehab nurses nice, friendly. Interpreter come. Mama visit every day, bringing delicious food, sweets. They take casts off arms and legs. Rehab counselor teaches me exercises, says I must practice every day. I do. I stronger. Can lift myself from wheelchair to bed, bed to wheelchair. My arms grow muscle. But walk . . . still can't. I think, *But if I can't walk . . . find Arlo, how?*"

Shri's signs grow slower, sadder. She tells you how she eventually gave up hoping that you would find her and forgive her. She tells you how eighteen months after the accident, Shri's mama suddenly stopped coming to the rehab hospital. Shri didn't know why for weeks, since no one would tell her. Then one day, Shri's auntie came with an interpreter and explained that Shri's mama had to move back to India and would not be coming anymore. Then, because there wasn't enough money to stay at the nice hospital, and because Shri needed more care than Auntie could provide, Shri was sent to live here, at the terrible long-term nursing home and rehab.

"Rehab?" she signs bitterly. "Ha! Here P-T almost nothing. Exercise almost nothing. Only few minutes pull rubber bands, then finish. P-T person here fake. I become weaker. Food disgusting. Staff not friendly. Many times I try run away with wheelchair. Three months ago my wheelchair break, they say will get fixed, but never fix. Wheelchair locked in closet. If I scream loud, they give medicine make me sleepy."

Shri's auntie, who is too busy with her own children, only pays short visits on some holidays, and leaves containers of food, but always looks sad and angry to Shri. It used to be that Shri would try to make contact with her auntie on the videophone, but her auntie didn't want to hear her complaints about the food, about the lack of exercise, about no one visiting her. And when the videophone broke two years ago no one would replace it. Then Shri tells you more stories—worse stories—and the rage in your stomach becomes unbearable.

"Not fair!" you yell. "Must tell boss! Must report! Next time interpreter comes demand you want wheelchair back! Demand fix videophone! Demand boss fire mean staff!"

"Can't," Shri explains. "Whole time, interpreter come . . . never. Boss's face always angry."

"Never interpreter?" you clarify. "But communicate, how?"

"Communication—none," Shri signs, using double zeros, and blows air through each one for emphasis. "Staff moves their lips or writes big words on paper. I understand, can't. Staff angry. Must get out of here! Please don't leave me alone again forever!"

Shri presses her head into your chest, and both of your bodies vibrate from two sets of tears.

"Promise," you sign, "I will never leave you alone again forever."

50

CULTURAL MEDIATION

In the best of all possible worlds I would have let the Deaf person speak for themselves. But Shri was obviously not living in the best of all possible worlds, and from what Arlo had said, without an interpreter she couldn't advocate for herself. Before finding a manager, I texted and googled, trying to compile a list of good local ASL interpreting agencies. My basic rule of thumb was, if possible, to try to make it easier for a business to hire good interpreters. Without any guidance at all, a business might drop the ball or end up hiring some shitty spoken language agency that had no clue about ASL interpreting and made things worse. I also reminded myself to approach whoever was in charge in a win-win way. Make the head honcho feel like they're the consumer's ally. Tell them everyone would be happier with regular visits from a qualified (preferably certified) interpreter. Try not to let the conversation bleed into how the nursing home was failing miserably, or the shabby, deaf-unfriendly condition of Shri's room. That wasn't your business. Most importantly, I told myself: *Do not lose your temper.*

When I arrived back at the front desk, Bella was deep into another phone conversation about someone named Radley who was stepping out on someone named Donna the Tramp.

"Can I help you?" Bella asked, acknowledging me faster than before.

"Sorry to interrupt again. Before we head out, I was wondering if I could speak to a manager?"

"You mean the assistant supervisor? I'll see if she's available."

Bella dialed into the office phone and mumbled that some family member wanted to speak to her, and no, she didn't know the reason.

"She'll be right with you," Bella said, and then returned to her conversation.

Five minutes later the assistant supervisor finally appeared. She was a thick squat woman in her thirties with bleached blond hair, a pastel pink suit, and makeup applied so generously it bordered on 1960s burlesque queen. In her hands she held a plastic Big Gulp cup. She told me her name was Durdona. I introduced myself (or, rather, my fake self) and told her that I was Shri's brother-in-law.

"Is the supervisor also in today?" I asked.

"There is no supervisor, only me, the assistant supervisor," she said, in a sarcastic singsong voice, widening her eyes to indicate her annoyance at this fact.

"How can you be an assistant supervisor if you don't have someone to assist?" I joked, trying to pour on the charm. "I guess that makes *you* the supervisor."

"No," she said humorlessly. "I am just the assistant supervisor doing the work of a supervisor at only half the pay. Come."

Durdona gestured me into her office. Once we were seated, Durdona explained in a weary voice that she had been working at the nursing home for only two months and was working overtime most nights.

"It's overwhelming," she said. "Staff turnover is ridiculous. The last assistant supervisor worked only four months before disappearing in the middle of her shift. That was it. Just gone."

"That's crazy," I said, doing my best empath face. "How is that even possible?"

So Durdona told me. She explained that the nursing home had been in the process of hiring a new supervisor for over two years, but they weren't willing to pay enough to actually get someone—despite how much the rehab facility was billing the insurance companies. She rolled her eyes and mimed locking her mouth with a key. Then she went on and on about how it was so unfair for her, who had only just graduated with her master's in social work from Queens College, to be shoved into a management role.

As she continued to complain, I mm-hmmed my head off, saying how well I understood her situation. Then I steered the conversation back to my purpose, explaining my background as an ASL interpreter, and said that I noticed there seemed to be some challenges with Shri in the nursing home, and said that I had some suggestions that could make their lives easier.

"First, I was wondering how you communicate with Shri here at the facility. Language boards? And does she have access to a videophone?"

Durdona gave a nihilistic snort and squeezed a little stuffed unicorn she kept on her desk, picking at its eyes with her French manicure.

"I'm very well acquainted with Ms. Shridevi Mukherjee. And we communicate just fine. Back when she had that videophone thing she just wasted time calling the same numbers over and over. Her mother or aunt never picked up. In fact, you're the first family member who has visited in forever. It's no surprise. No offense, but your . . . cousin?"

"In-law," I clarified, lying like a champ. "Sister-in-law."

"Right. Your sister-in-law can be a handful."

"I see," I said, trying to neither confirm nor deny her estimation. "You know, I'd bet a lot of the trouble is because of a communication breakdown."

"Oh please." Durdona snorted dismissively. "Shri knows exactly what's going on. She's not dumb, that's for sure. She reads lips very well."

"Actually, I don't believe Shri *can* read lips," I said.

"Sure she can. She reads lips fine, but she likes to pretend she doesn't so she can manipulate people or worse. That's why I'm extra careful with her. I don't want to make you worry, but last week one of the aides went into her room and Shri didn't like something, so next thing you know a dinner tray goes flying. Hits the aide and Shri laughs. So I went in and not only did I talk slow so she could read my lips but I also wrote it down on paper: 'If you do that again you're not getting any dinner.' Of course, Shri gives me that big brown-eyed, innocent weepy-baby look, and the next thing I know the little devil takes a swing at me. Oh, she knows exactly what's going on."

My insides were convulsing in anger. I had encountered stupid shit like this from hearing people my whole career. They believed their mind-reading of the Deaf was a more valuable tool than hiring a goddamned interpreter.

"Wow, that's not like Shri to hit anyone," I said, gritting my teeth, trying to stay calm. "I'm so sorry. But I should explain. Shri doesn't read English well, or much at all."

Another scoffing laugh from Durdona.

"If you ask me, the real problem with your sister-in-law is . . ." She lowered her voice. "She's spoiled and has been allowed to get away with murder because of her disability. We have to be firm with her."

My fingers grabbed the edge of my chair, the knuckles whitening.

"Um . . . wow," I said, no longer even able to fake a smile. "I think you've made a lot of unfounded assumptions about Shri. Everything would be clearer if you'd get an interpreter in here to actually *talk* with her and see what might be causing the blowups. I've written down a list of good agencies you could call—"

"That's okay," Durdona said, waving off my list. "First, as I said, we communicate just fine with Shri. Second, there's no way the company will pay for a translator. Of course, if your family actually wants to visit more and translate, go for it."

And that's what made me lose it.

"Oh, come on!" I snapped. "That's bull. Besides being unethical, you have no idea if her family even has those skills."

Durdona raised her eyebrows suspiciously.

"Aren't you her family? Don't *you* have translation skills?"

Not even catching my own gaffe, my index finger jabbed down onto the metal desktop like a tiny flesh hammer.

"It's called *interpretation*, not translation, Durdona! And it's the nursing home's responsibility to provide an *interpreter*! Do you even know what the ADA is?"

Durdona's face went blank as she stood up and opened the door to her office.

"Soon it'll be Shri's bedtime," she said with a forced smile. "Visiting hours are over."

Fuck me, I thought, *I probably just made things worse for Shri.* I was desperate to fix it.

"Sorry if I lost my cool, it's just that we both obviously want what's best for Shri. Look, I have an idea, you're right. While I'm here, let me interpret a meeting between your staff and Shri? Then maybe the blowups will stop. That would be good, right?"

Durdona shook her head. "I'm sorry, sir. My staff really doesn't have time right now. They've got meds to give out and bedtime to get started, and a mountain of other responsibilities. One of our older residents passed last night. Which means they have to disinfect the room, and I have to do even more paperwork, and I'm leaving in like forty minutes. I understand you're concerned about your sister-in-law, but we really are doing our best. If you ask me, the problems we have with Shri are more due to the fact that your family is barely in the picture. The audacity you have, showing up out of nowhere, blaming us for *her* behavior problems and then trying to accuse us of not following the ADA? I have an idea. On your way out you can use your translating-interpreting skills to tell Shri to stop being a little monster. Okay? Now, as I said, I have a pile of paperwork so . . ."

Just as Durdona was closing the door in my face, two very loud crashes came from down the hall. Durdona's eyes widened and her sculpted eyebrows contorted themselves like rageful minks as she pushed past me, running as fast as her high heels could take her. I followed. A second later came another crash, followed by the sound of Snap barking furiously, and then what I assumed was Shri's horrific guttural scream echoing through the building. Pulling the walkie-talkie from her belt, Durdona yelled for the orderlies to go to "Mukherjee's room." I imagined Arlo being physically injured. I imagined blood. I imagined an emergency room, and me having to explain it all to Brother Birch.

But as we turned the corner to where Shri's room was located, we could see it wasn't Shri who was throwing a fit. It was Arlo. There he was, standing in the middle of the hallway, his face a mask of fury, groaning loudly, throwing punches in the air. He had just turned over the housekeeper's yellow supply caddy, covering the floor with trash, dirty mop water, and cleaning supplies. Furious tears rolled down his cheeks. Snap barked and scratched at Arlo's leg, trying to calm him down.

"Not fair! Not fair!" Arlo vocalized as he signed violently to anyone who might be around. "Where boss? Tell me where boss! Nursing home terrible! Shri suffering! Where boss!"

It was the first time I had heard Arlo vocalize full sentences. It was not the voice I had imagined for him. It was a primal, barely intelligible, heartbroken voice. I ran to Arlo and pushed my name quickly into his hands.

"It's okay. Calm down, it's gonna be all right. You're frightening Snap. Tell me what's wrong."

Three other staff members ran up beside Durdona, including Bella, all staring at Arlo like he was some kind of monster.

"What is he doing?" Durdona screamed at me. "And that dog should not be in here at all! It's time for you all to leave!"

I interpreted what Durdona had said, but Arlo ignored me and continued to rage.

"They hurt Shri! Punish her how? They not give food! Only drink milk shake! All the time, Shri stuck in bed! Have sores on backside. Bleeding. Family stop visiting. No interpreter come. They not follow ADA law! Not fair!"

"Easy. Easy," I signed to him, tapping his shoulder in the Protactile gesture for *understanding*. "The boss is right here, looking at us. She's very angry. Calmly tell her what you just told me, and then we definitely need to leave."

"Can't leave! Shri needs our help!"

"We can talk later," I begged. "Right now, try not to freak out any more or they'll never let you visit again. Just say what you want to say, and we'll say goodbye to Shri. But try and stay calm."

Arlo asked me to turn his body toward Durdona and *just interpret*. He repeated what he had said to me forcefully but more calmly than probably I would have been able to if I were in his shoes. As I voiced, I tried to make sure my own anger toward the situation did not infiltrate the tone. When Arlo finished, I added, "This is me, the interpreter, talking now. Look, we're sorry for the outburst. But Arlo is right. You are in violation of the ADA all over the place here. But we're happy to help you make it better. Like I said, I can interpret a conversation with Shri right now. Trust me, it will help. We all want to be heard, right?"

Durdona raised her hand to my face, indicating she had heard enough. Suddenly her eyes turned into angry slits.

"You just called this man 'Arlo'?" Durdona said, her eyes narrow. She turned to Bella. "I didn't see that name in the log. The aunt gave these two permission to visit, right?"

Bella, looking guilty, started explaining what I had told her about it being Arlo's birthday. Durdona scolded Bella about following rules.

Snap barked and took a step toward Durdona, who jumped back with a scream.

"Snap! Down!" I commanded. "Look, sorry, I mean . . . Okay. We aren't Shri's family, but Arlo is like family to Shri."

Durdona pointed to the front of the building.

"Out. Now."

"Please, just let Arlo say goodbye to Shri," I pleaded.

Durdona told two large male staff to show us the door. When I described this to Arlo, he planted his legs, refusing to move.

"They need promise bring interpreter!" he cried. "They need promise give better food! Give wheelchair back! Must get doctor help Shri! They must respect! Tell them!"

Before I could interpret anything more, one of the bruisers grabbed Arlo's arms, causing Snap to leap toward the attendant, growling. Releasing Arlo, the attendant kicked Snap, shouting that she had bitten him. (She hadn't.) Durdona pulled out her cell phone like it was a gun.

"That does it! I'm calling the police!"

"Look, we're sorry. Can you please just take it easy? Snap wouldn't hurt a fly. Look at her. And Arlo just didn't know Shri was in this condition. He's DeafBlind, for chrissakes. Can we all just calm down!"

Durdona motioned for the two male aides to get Arlo, who was headed back into Shri's room. Snap growled angrily again. I threw my body between Arlo and the attendants. Meanwhile, I heard a scream coming from behind me in Shri's room. Shri had seen the attendants grabbing for Arlo. I quickly turned to look. It was the first time I actually saw Shri's face. While she was clearly frail-looking, with a sickly crust around her mouth from dehydration, her wild black eyes were fierce and beautiful. I quickly signed that I was Arlo's friend. Then, when one of the attendants pushed me out of the way to get to Arlo, Shri threw a plastic water bottle, hitting the attendant on the head with perfect aim.

"Stop it! Stop it!" she signed. "Don't touch!"

Durdona ran into the room.

"Calm yourself now!" she shouted, wagging her finger and overexag- gerating her mouth movements. "Or else no dinner!"

Shri's black eyes widened in a furious glare. Then, in one quick move- ment, she reached under her blanket and pulled out a semi-full, blue plas- tic bed pan and lobbed it, full force, at Durdona's chest. Shit and piss flew everywhere, but mostly onto Durdona. Everyone went silent, except for Durdona, who, looking down at the brown and yellow mess covering her pastel pink suit and white blouse, gave out one long, rageful scream. Then, coldly and calmly, she pressed the button of her walkie-talkie and ordered the nurse to bring a sedative and to call the police.

"Tell them we have intruders, and we need a car here immediately."

I told Arlo we had to leave right away, but he jerked himself away and walked right into a service aide who grabbed him around the waist. A second later I felt a different set of thick hands grab the back of my shirt and pants. Snap went wild, barking and baring her teeth. The orderlies swung both Arlo and me around, making us a barrier between them and Snap, and started pulling us down the hall. A third aide grabbed Snap's harness and quickly thrust her out a side door. Arlo, now panicking without Snap, let his body go limp, so the aide started dragging him.

"Hey, go easy!" I screamed. "You're looking at a lawsuit, buddy! That was his guide dog! Someone is going to get hurt!"

As we got to the main entrance, Arlo grabbed onto the doorframe, stop- ping himself from being pulled outside. The aide started yanking at Arlo's fingers to make him let go, but Arlo was too strong to be moved.

"If this DeafBlind motherfucker doesn't let go," the service aide snarled, "I'm gonna break his damn fingers with my foot!"

Fearing for Arlo's safety, I elbowed the aide who was dragging me, and then threw a punch at the guy who just threatened Arlo. Sadly, I only grazed his shoulder, but it was enough to set both of them against me.

Before I knew it, I was outside, and a moment after that they yanked Arlo out by his collar, swinging and screaming. When the aide released his grip, Arlo lost his balance and fell onto the pavement, ripping his shirt and khakis and opening a wound on his leg that gushed blood. I ran over to help him up, just as Snap ran around the side of the building. When I looked back at the doorway, Durdona was snapping our photo with her cell phone camera. My hands trembled into Arlo's.

"We have to get out of here, now!"

51

AFTERMATH

When we were within half a block of the car, I saw Molly leaning against it but no sign of Hanne anywhere.

"No, no, no!" Molly cried upon seeing Arlo's roughed-up appearance. "Why are his clothes ripped? And his leg is bleeding—is he in pain?"

"Where's Hanne?" I asked.

"I don't know. She said she was going for a walk."

"Great," I said, cutting Molly off angrily. "I told Hanne to wait here! This is not what I need right now. The nursing home was a disaster. We need to get out of here."

I tapped Arlo to explain what was happening, but he pushed my hands away and said he didn't want to listen. He looked a mile deep inside his head, and I assumed he was just ruminating over what had happened. I quickly texted Hanne, telling her to get back so we could leave. Then I recounted the whole mess to Molly.

"And now who knows if he'll ever be allowed to visit her again," I said.

"So what happened with Shri?" she asked, pointing at the part I had left out.

"Oh, right. Sorry. Better than I expected. At first, anyway. I mean, they talked together for a long time. But then I don't know what happened. Whatever she said made Arlo lose it."

Arlo, emerging from his thoughts, waved for me and asked to speak in private.

"Without Molly," he emphasized.

"I'm sorry," I said to her.

"It's okay," she replied, with a hurt but understanding smile. "I'll take a walk around the block."

As soon as I let Arlo know we were alone, he began screaming at me.

"You lie! You lie so much!"

"What are you talking about?" I signed, trying to remain calm though I wanted to scream back. "I just helped you visit Shri like I said I would. If anyone should be angry, I should. You messed that up big-time. You may not get another chance to visit Shri for a long time."

Arlo lowered his head, thinking. He appeared to accept what I had just said, and I figured he was going to apologize for blowing up. But then out of nowhere he declared, "We must rescue Shri!"

Sign RESCUE *(same as the sign for* SAVE *and* FREEDOM*): Two fists held together, crossed, as in shackles, then they twist outward as if the chains are broken.*

"You are not serious," I signed.

"Yes! Serious! We must go back to nursing home. Shri and I long talk. Discuss plan. Her idea. She knows best time and way escape. Shri says we run away, find apartment, and live together. Remember, you promise will help? So help!"

"No, no, no! I did not promise that. We are not helping Shri escape from the nursing home!"

"But Shri has plan!"

"Forget it. Besides, we can't get within ten feet of that place thanks to you!"

"Shri like prisoner! They abuse! Not provide interpreter! ADA law says illegal! Must tell police!"

I took a deep breath and tried to see the whole thing from Arlo's point of view. The person he loved was in danger, was hurting. She convinced him of some lame plan that would let them be together. Of course he wasn't thinking clearly.

"Yes. You're right," I signed. "But the police aren't going to help us. There are dozens of steps she has to take. First, we can report the situation to Adult Protective Services. Once they get involved it will still take some time. But it's the best we can do at the moment. And remember, we have to get you back to Poughkeepsie so Brother Birch doesn't find out. And then you'll go to Ecuador tomorrow and let the situation here cool down. I can make sure someone follows up on getting help for Shri, even if it has to be me. I promise."

All of a sudden, Arlo let out a guttural scream and swung at me, nearly hitting me.

"No!" he yelled. "I refuse wait! I refuse fly to Ecuador. Understand? Shri will kill herself if I leave her there. She fell off roof because of me. She suffers because of me!"

I grabbed his hands and tried to sign calmly.

"Just please listen for a moment. And please do not try to hit me again. You shouldn't be blaming yourself for any of this."

"You don't know!" Arlo yelled. "We must help her get out tonight! Must!"

"We can't. Don't you understand? Shri's under guardianship like you. I know this isn't fair, but the state has said that neither of you can make decisions for yourselves. If we took Shri tonight, we could be accused of kidnapping."

A look of pure hatred filled Arlo's eyes.

"Go ahead and hate me," I signed. "I'm trying to be a good friend by NOT letting you do something stupid."

At that moment I saw Hanne rushing down the block toward the car, clutching a large tote bag to her chest.

"You went shopping? Are you kidding me?" I shouted, my anger at Arlo projected onto her. "Now he wants us to help break Shri out of the nursing home like we're in a fucking prison escape movie!"

"Would it be okay if I talked to him?" Hanne asked.

"Good. Please talk some sense into him."

I felt certain Hanne would be able to reason with Arlo better than me, since their bond was different and didn't involve interpreting.

"Hanne wants to talk to you," I signed and voiced. "Remember, she's almost a nurse. She's going to explain to you how dangerous it would be to take Shri from the nursing home. We don't even know the extent of Shri's injuries. Go ahead, Hanne. Tell him."

Hanne smiled and then held out the tote bag she had been carrying, letting Arlo feel it. I could finally see that the bag contained a large plastic three-ring binder filled with hundreds of pages and colored tabs.

"This is what I need to tell him," Hanne said, her voice growing more excited. "While you and Arlo were causing such a mess, I talked to that nurse, the big burly Russian guy? You won't believe what I found out!"

I stopped interpreting and glared at Hanne, an uneasy feeling seeping into my gut.

"Hanne?" I said. "Please tell me you didn't do anything stupid."

"Tell me what Hanne say!" Arlo demanded, before angrily grabbing my dormant hands and shaking them. I proceeded to interpret.

"Morally questionable?" Hanne said, shrugging. "Perhaps. But effective. It turns out the Russian nurse is from a town I've visited on the Black Sea."

"Hanne, for chrissakes," I said, shaking my head.

"Oh, stop it," she said, rolling her eyes. "I was chatty, that's all. Maybe a little flirty. Period. We mostly just talked nursing school stuff, bedsores, and wound drainage. Also, where I can buy the best frozen pierogi in Queens.

You think I would whore myself out? Shame on you. Anyway, when he went off to give a patient some medicine, he left me alone in the medical office. And guess what? I found Shri's medical file just lying out unattended on the nursing station counter with several other files. That's a serious violation of HIPAA rules! They could definitely be sued. I was so appalled at the under-staffing and blatant disregard for medical file protocol, I walked out, and somehow Shri's unprotected file fell into my tote bag! Can you imagine?"

Arlo started rocking with excitement, then he reached out for Hanne, who embraced him. That's when I blew up.

"Hanne! What the fuck?" I shouted. "You stole medical records? That's a felony! Did he know you were with us?"

"Oh, stop making such a big deal. No, he had no idea I was with you. I said I was there researching possible jobs postgraduation. And he won't even know the file has gone missing by the look of the place, which is a disorganized mess. And to respond to Arlo about the danger in helping Shri to leave that place, in my *nearly* professional nursing opinion, I think it would be far more dangerous to let Shri stay."

At that point, I was so furious at what Hanne was saying, my hands froze, and once more I stopped interpreting.

"We have to get her out of there," Hanne said. "And that's not all. Hey, aren't you supposed to be interpreting everything I'm saying? Isn't that a rule?"

"Yes," I snapped, reanimating my hands. "I love how you're only con-scious of rules when other people break them."

I quickly caught Arlo up on anything he had missed, including Hanne's admonition when I had stopped interpreting. Arlo sneered at me when I got to that part.

"Anyway," Hanne continued. "I read through Shri's file and then I called one of my nursing school teachers who has a lot of experience work-ing with spinal injuries. Yes, Shri's paralyzed, but that's all. Her file doesn't indicate any other condition that requires her to be in a nursing home."

"Are you sure?" I asked.

"From what her file says, yes. But you want to know the worst part?"

Hanne reached into the bag that held the medical binder and pulled out a full blister pack of pills with the initial S and the last name *Mukherjee* written with marker. She shook the blister pack like a maraca.

"Besides the mild bedsores from them not getting her out of that bed enough, they've also been sedating her with antianxiety pills that aren't even prescribed by a doctor. Including enough Xanax to knock out a forty-year-old man. Talk about a felony."

Hanne then explained the dangers of giving someone Shri's size that kind of dosage. Arlo pulled his hands from mine as his face became a mask of rage.

"How is this fucking possible?" I asked.

"We have to do something, Cyrilje," she pleaded.

"I agree," I said, and I meant it. I got Arlo to put his hands back on mine.

"Calm down," I told him. "We'll take care of this. First, we need to call Adult Protective Services! And I'll do that immediately. Hopefully they can get Shri to a safe place soon."

Once again Arlo went off about Shri having a plan. Again I attempted to explain the impossibility of taking Shri from the facility, but he immediately shoved his hands into his armpits, silencing me.

I was furious.

Hanne pointed at Molly, slowly walking back toward us. Molly looked tentative, wanting to make sure Arlo and I had finished our private discussion.

"Come on! We need to talk!" I called out to her. "Hurry!"

I filled Molly in on everything Hanne had discovered. She took the news of Shri's situation even harder than I had, and nearly broke down. She agreed that we should let the proper authorities know about the nursing home ASAP.

"As mandated reporters, we must," Molly insisted.

"Yeah, I know," I said. "And I will."

"Surely they'll move her someplace safer?"

"I hope so, but first we need to convince Mr. Escape From Alcatraz here that we can't take her out ourselves. And she won't be leaving tonight."

Then I had an idea of something that might change Arlo's mind: guilt.

I tapped Arlo's arm. "Molly's back," I signed. "I need you to understand something. If we go back there tonight and take Shri out without the proper permission, it's not only you who will get in trouble. You understand me? Molly and Hanne could go to jail. Do you want that?"

Arlo's eyes narrowed; he squeezed his fists and adjusted his position as if he were ready to plead his case in front of a judge.

"Pay attention," he demanded, more sober and steady than he had been all evening. "Save Shri? Save me? No! We don't need! Shri and I save ourselves . . . will! We have plan. If Hanne wants, she can stay away. Safe. But you worry if help me will get in trouble, right? But you and Molly both interpreters . . . understand? Molly also my SSP. Means what? You told me before, remember? Interpreter and SSP must interpret whatever a Deaf person says. Boss who? Me! Me! Not you! It's not your job make decisions for Deaf person. Cyril, you think you must become hero? No! We don't need hero. Understand? We hero ourselves."

My head wanted to explode. I tried to think of something to say, but my fingers became stuck in the word *but*. Molly took Arlo's hands from mine and tried to explain, in her way, the dangers of Shri leaving with Arlo that night. She said something about God's law and the need to obey man's law. Arlo pushed her hands away and picked up Snap's harness.

"Fuck you. I go myself!"

After walking ten steps down the block with Snap, he stopped and almost howled in sad frustration. Snap joined him. It was the most pitiful lamentation I had ever heard. None of us knowing what to do, we all went to him. Molly rubbed his back; Hanne threw her arms around him and hugged him. I finally approached his shoulder and tapped in Protactile understanding. At my touch, Arlo's face turned crimson with rage, angrily freeing himself from everyone's touch.

"Know something? Cyril . . . Molly . . . you both cowards! But Cyril . . . you worst coward ever! You refuse Shri's plan? Why? Because long time ago your boyfriend die. You hurt so bad. After that you never want hurt again. Cyril so much pain . . . push it down deep inside! That's why you drink so much wine every night. I smell it. I smell it on you every day. You drunk! That's why you lonely, sad man. You same as JWs! *Careful, careful, don't have sex, don't read books, don't make friends. Happiness for future. Judgment Day!* Bullshit! Your sweetheart dying cancer . . . You visit? No! Why? Cyril scared everything! Frozen! Understand? Suppose Shri and me try escape and fail? Or suppose we not try at all? Doesn't matter. Right? Doesn't matter! Everybody still hurt! Cyril think, *Avoid, avoid everything. Stay out of it. That safe. Just wait and see. Nobody get hurt.* But you wrong! If we don't try, then everybody hurt worse! Worse! Forever!"

When Arlo had finished, I just stood there, barely able to breathe, feeling exposed like every centimeter of skin had been flayed from my body. Molly's eyes filled with pity. Despite not knowing any sign language, Hanne could see that whatever he had said, Arlo had gone deep.

"He's right," I said. "I didn't visit Bruno because I was scared. I couldn't save him. I couldn't."

I don't recall the exact details of what happened next. I gather Molly described to Arlo what was happening, because it wasn't until he came over and put his arms around me that I realized I had been crying. I wiped my face on the hem of my T-shirt and looked at Molly and Hanne, both reflecting my heartbreak back at me.

"Are you all right, Cyrilje?" Hanne asked.

"Yeah," I said, wiping my face. "I'm all right."

Arlo walked back over to Molly and asked her to interpret, which meant he was starting to trust her again.

"Arlo is right about something else too," I said. "We work for Arlo, and he says he can't leave Shri in there tonight. I'm not gonna tell a man what he can and can't do. But something has to be done."

Arlo clarified with Molly if he understood me correctly. Molly herself wasn't sure.

"You mean we're calling the authorities?" Molly asked.

"Yes, absolutely we'll call the authorities," I responded. "But we've all dealt with social services long enough to know they won't do anything tonight, and maybe not for weeks or months. So let's do what Arlo says. Let's follow Shri's plan and try to get her out of there tonight."

Arlo smiled and punched the air with his fist, speaking a "Yes!"

"We'll have to figure out a safe place to take her later," I said. "But I don't want either of you to get in trouble. My career is already down the toilet, so I'll take this on with Arlo. Hanne, you should take the train back to Poughkeepsie. Molly, you can just tell Brother Birch you followed us here to try to stop us."

Molly and Hanne looked at each other and had a very quick wordless conversation with their eyes, the gist of which was: *Is he serious?*

"*Godverdomme*, Cyrilje," Hanne said, rolling her eyes. "Suddenly it's the two men riding off to war? Fuck that. I'm helping too!"

"Me too," Molly added nervously.

Molly covered her face with her hands and both Hanne and I assumed she had devolved into tears once again, but then we could see that she was actually laughing, which made the three of us start to laugh really hard. Then, as our nervous hysteria was dying down, we heard the ting of a message coming into Molly's phone. As she read the text, all sense of joy drained from her face. She passed the phone to me to read. The long, angry message was from Birch, the gist of which was: he knew what Molly was up to, and if she didn't have Arlo back to Poughkeepsie in two hours he was calling the police. The end of his text, though calmer, was clearly meant to leave some damage.

That you would do this to punish me is clearly the bitterness of a scorned woman. Satan was truly the puppet master of our horrible mistake, and I will continue to pay for it as will you. But we can't just act like what you've done never happened. I've spoken to the other elders and we all agree that when Arlo and I return from Ecuador next year you will no longer be working with Arlo and will no longer be welcome at the Kingdom Hall in Poughkeepsie. It's for the best. Now please bring back my nephew immediately and may Jehovah God have mercy on you.

Molly hugged her thin arms around herself as if she had suddenly been surrounded by a blast of arctic air. I had no idea what to say. Luckily, after also reading the text message, Hanne went to Molly and placed her hands on the older woman's shoulders.

"Forget him," Hanne said. "He's just a selfish prick. In Belgium they'd call him a *kloothommel*, which basically means toilet drum, but it sounds worse in Flemish."

I interpreted the entirety of Birch's text message for Arlo. When I finished, he went to Molly and pulled her into his arms. Molly crumbled into a pile of sobs. After she gathered herself, Arlo asked if he could borrow Molly's phone.

"What for?" she asked.

"Send video message to Brother Birch. Cyril will voice for me so Brother Birch understand."

"To say what?" I asked. "If we're going to do this, we already have less than two hours."

"Just do it!" Arlo demanded. "I'm boss, right?"

And that was that. Arlo asked Hanne to shoot the video since *she was the artist.* Molly fixed Arlo's hair. I stood next to the camera so I could be heard. Yes, I was aware I was creating evidence of my violation of the restraining order. I didn't care. My focus was on matching Arlo's calm, direct tone with my voice.

"Hello, Uncle Jonathan. I need to tell you something. Honestly, Molly and Cyril didn't kidnap me. I made the decision to run away on my own. Cyril and Molly are just working for me as interpreters. I'm an adult now and I have a right to decide. So, what's my decision? I'm not going to Ecuador with you, and I don't want to live with you anymore. You've been a bad guardian. First, I know you thought you were doing Jehovah God's will, and that you needed to protect me from the goats, from the internet, from new technologies that would connect me to the world and my old friends. You did this to protect me from the Devil's influence, right? But that wasn't protection. Access to the world is not only when hearing-sighted people think it's okay. Access is my right! Second, you've lied to me repeatedly, not telling me my mama was sick, and why I had to leave the Rose Garden School. Third, on more than one occasion you've physically not let me leave the house, and two or three times locked me in my room, which is very hot. That's called abuse. You were also mean to my mother and to Molly. You pretend to be the nice, spiritually strong man that everyone should look up to, but you're a phony and a bully. My intention now is to go to court and seek . . ."

I clarified the word Arlo fingerspelled, and when I understood, my voice cracked with emotion.

"I intend to go to court to seek *emancipation*. It means I will be free. I will marry my sweetheart, Shri. Remember Shri? That was your worst lie. You told me she was dead, causing me to live for years with the worst broken heart. Now Shri and I will live together. We will both be independent. I know you tell everyone you love me, and did what you thought was best, but it wasn't best. It was hurtful. From now on you need to stop causing problems for us. If you leave us alone, I will not tell the elders at the Kingdom Hall or the police how you lied and abused me. You should just go to Ecuador like you planned. Go tell all the poor people about Jehovah God. He's your God now, not mine. My God is bigger and better than your God. My God believes in me and knows I can succeed. Goodbye and . . ."

Arlo held up both hands with his middle fingers extended toward the camera. Voicing wasn't necessary.

Hanne stopped filming and handed the phone back to Molly. Molly looked at me, uncertain, and then asked Arlo if he was sure he wanted to send it.

"Definitely."

Molly stared at the little blue up arrow like it could launch a nuclear weapon. Then she hit Send and, as the video began to upload, a faint smile returned to her face.

52

OUTLAWS

10 p.m.

We cannot see Manhattan from this part of Queens, but the night sky to the west has a glow that reminds us it's there. Sitting in the hot car with the doors flung open, we stare at the New Bridge Gardens Nursing Home and Rehabilitation Center across the street, the mighty fortress where Shri still doesn't know we are about to put her own escape plan into motion. Soon she will be awakened by her knight in shining armor—or, rather, a button-down shirt and torn khakis. His gallant steed: an aging guide dog, long in the teeth. His weapon: a white folding cane, a keen mind, and three hapless middle-aged vassals—a religious zealot, a Belgian madwoman, and a redheaded homo.

The plan:

1. Contact Adult Protective Services about the abuse we witnessed in the nursing home. (Done. We already left a message and sent an email.)

2. Extract Shri from the home unnoticed. This is more complicated. Shri had explained to Arlo that every night at ten forty-five, the 3 p.m. to 11 p.m. staff go to the front of the nursing facility to do "shift change," where they share information with the graveyard shift about anything of importance that happened during the day. So for just thirty minutes, between ten forty-five and eleven fifteen, the back of the nursing home is

unattended—unless, of course, one of the patients calls for help, but at that time of night, Shri assured Arlo, all the patients would be asleep. Thus, it's the perfect time for Arlo to help Shri escape via an emergency exit out the back of the facility. Shri had even drawn Arlo a map, which he shows us proudly for the third or fourth time.

"Shri very brilliant," Arlo reminds us.

The map, drawn with Arlo's Magic Marker in his notebook, shows dots from Shri's room, left down the hallway past three other rooms, and then to the emergency exit, which she's marked with a star on it. On the other side of the door she has drawn trees and sunshine to indicate the outside: aka *freedom*. Shri also told Arlo there are railings on the wall he could use to get to her room. One thing she hadn't considered was how we would get the emergency exit open from the outside.

3. This part Arlo and Hanne worked out. First, we'll leave Snap waiting in the car with the windows open. (We don't want to risk any dog drama like earlier in the evening.) Then Arlo and I will make our way across the adjoining empty lot to the back of the nursing home. When we are close to the emergency door, we'll text Hanne and Molly. Then the two women will go to the front desk on the pretext that Hanne had lost her ID at the facility when she had visited earlier. While Hanne looks for her lost ID and schmoozes with the Russian nurse again, her "friend" Molly will ask to use the bathroom, which is down the hall in the direction of the emergency exit. Molly will just need to go an extra thirty feet to open the emergency door for me and Arlo. Then Molly will return to the front and she and Hanne will meet the rest of us at the gas station a block away where we parked the car.

Comfortably, we'll have a full twenty minutes to get in, get out, and get to the car.

If everything goes perfectly.

If.

"Let's go," Arlo signs, unfolding his cane like a whip.

◇ ◇ ◇

10:35 p.m.

Arlo takes my arm and we begin to walk across the empty lot, which is littered with rocks, potholes, and debris. With Arlo's balance issues, it might as well be one of those Iron Man obstacle courses. I text Hanne and Molly and tell them it's going to need to be a little bit longer before they head inside. The two-minute walk takes us nearly seven minutes, with Arlo tripping several times, once falling and cutting the heel of his hand on a piece of glass. He's so focused he doesn't notice the pain or the bleeding. When we are close enough to see the emergency door, I text Hanne for them to go in.

◇ ◇ ◇

10:45 p.m.

We wait.

And wait.

And wait.

Something is wrong. According to the plan, Molly should have opened the door for us by now. But we are standing there outside in the darkness and I think I hear something inside the building that sounds like loud voices. I have a bad feeling and tell Arlo I think maybe we should head back to the street. He refuses.

◇ ◇ ◇

10:47 p.m.

Just when I'm about to demand that Arlo and I get out of there, I hear footsteps and see Molly running toward the emergency door. (Running was not in the plan.) She pushes the door open and looks in a major panic.

"What happened?" I whisper.

"It's a mess," she whispers back, pulling Arlo and me inside. "Just go. Hurry. Get Shri. I need to go back and help Hanne."

"What's wrong?"

She's gone. I can now clearly hear yelling at the front of the building. No time to think about whatever is happening. I take my two fingers and quickly draw our path on Arlo's back, from the emergency door, four steps, turn right, pass three doors, the fourth door is her room, and then I tell him to remember that we'll reverse the directions when we leave, and then quickly draw that map on his back: out the emergency exit door, across the lot, and back out to the street.

"Clear?"

"Clear!"

We make our way down the hallway. Unfortunately, Arlo is swinging his cane and slapping his feet loudly in that cautious way of his, testing the surface. Even though no one is supposed to be back there, I tell him to walk on his tiptoes. He does.

◊ ◊ ◊

10:50 p.m.

Finally inside Shri's room, and without turning on the light, I lead Arlo to her bed and place his hands on Shri's shoulder. He shakes her and shakes her again. Shri groggily comes to. Realizing it's Arlo, she begins to quake with excitement. As Arlo explains what's happening, I turn on my phone's flashlight and run around the room, jamming everything that looks necessary into a pillowcase, including cans of Ensure, diapers, wet wipes, a few items of clean clothing in her drawers. It all feels in slow motion because I'm freaking out and my hands are shaking. When I look to Arlo and Shri, they seem way too calm. Lucky for them, they can't hear the sound of yelling coming from somewhere in the front of the building. My heart is scraping at my chest, and I consider the possibility of how bad it would be to have a heart attack at this moment. I tell Arlo and Shri we have to get moving. But then my phone rings and it's Hanne.

"Hanne?" I whisper into the phone. "Are you okay?"

There is no response, but instead I hear her screaming in garbled tones, and then someone screaming back at her: "Stay where you are! Don't move!" I get it. Hanne's in trouble and she turned her phone on to signal she needs help. Maybe she was wrong about the Russian nurse. What happened to Molly? I text her but get no response. For a second I'm paralyzed. I don't know what to do.

◊ ◊ ◊

11:00 p.m.

Still no word from Molly or Hanne. If I leave with Arlo and Shri I may not be able to get back in the building. I think about what Arlo had been saying, about this being his and Shri's plan, about respecting their choices. I tell them that Hanne and Molly appear to be in trouble and that I need Arlo and Shri to make their way out of the facility on their own so I can help the two women. I quickly explain how Shri's going to need to look out for obstacles outside so Arlo doesn't trip. She tells me she understands and that she has lots of experience guiding Arlo. I tell them to go very slowly and meet us at the gas station a block away. Once more, I draw the escape route on Arlo's back: pass three doorways, turn left, then out the emergency door, diagonal across the empty lot to the pavement, turn right and follow the pavement until Shri tells him to stop. Before they go, I give Arlo a quick hug and wish him luck. He looks nervous but also excited and is smiling.

◊ ◊ ◊

11:03 p.m.

Arlo lifts Shri onto his back and immediately she starts using some sort of touch communication from when they were younger, tapping his shoulders like she's steering a truck. As they head out into the hallway, Shri waves the nonromantic sign for *I love you* at me.

I sign it back. Then I take a deep breath before running to the front of the building to help Hanne and Molly.

53

WHAT HAPPENED NEXT

As I neared the front of the facility, I could see and hear it was mayhem. The staff were all standing around watching Hanne, whose arm was being held by the Russian nurse, and he was demanding to know if Hanne had taken the file, where it was, and who she was. I hid myself around a corner.

"Just give it back," the nurse demanded. "I'm serious or I'm calling the police."

"Why don't you call the police then," Hanne demanded. "I don't have your stupid file. I just came back to pick up my ID."

I saw no sign of Molly. Had she bailed? Then things managed to get worse. Right outside the side window, just behind the backs of the entire staff, I could see Arlo and Shri stumbling across the open lot where a bright streetlight was illuminating them and bouncing light off Arlo's white cane. All that had to happen was one of the staff turning around and they'd be caught. I considered my options. I could rush the Russian guy, which, by the size of him, would not end well. But then maybe Hanne would have a chance to run, and that might cause enough of a distraction to give Shri and Arlo time to reach the street. And then I had a meta moment: *Am I really thinking about physically attacking a Russian nurse so I can free my friend and aid a DeafBlind man to escape with his Deaf wheelchair-using lover? Has being a sign language interpreter really come to this?*

As I prepared myself to act extremely out of character, I felt my phone vibrate. It was a text from Molly, finally: *Pull the fire alarm!*

Just as I received her text, Molly appeared at the front glass doors, banging and screaming:

"Fire! Fire! Your dumpster! It's on fire!"

And sure enough, the dumpster in front of the building had been set ablaze, smoke was billowing and orange licks of flame were crawling up the old mattresses. The perfect distraction from Shri and Arlo, who at that very moment were crossing the lot just outside the window next to where everyone was freaking out.

"Holy shit," one of the attendants screamed. "My car is right there!"

"Someone call the fire department," another shouted.

As Molly instructed, I pulled the nearest fire alarm. Immediately strobe lights and sirens went off, and the sprinklers created a massive deluge throughout the hallways. The Russian nurse released Hanne, who immediately bolted out the front door, grabbing Molly's hand and running. Not wanting any of the staff to possibly recognize me from earlier, I headed back through the waterfalls of sprinklers and out an exit on the other side of the building.

When I arrived at the street, soaking wet, I ran as fast as I could until I met up with Molly and Hanne, who were huffing and puffing and walk-running. All of us had that look of stunned joy, that we actually pulled off Shri's plan, or thought we had.

"Molly, that was brilliant," Hanne said, catching her breath.

"Good job, Molly!" I added.

"Let's not talk about it now," she said, barely able to breathe. "Where are they?"

We assumed we would pass Shri and Arlo en route, but five minutes later we arrived at the car parked at the gas station and there was no sign of them. All of us were worried and puzzled. Had they taken a wrong turn? Had Arlo fallen? Did they catch him and we just didn't notice?

Snap, looking for her human, anxiously scratched at the window.

"I'll go back," I said.

But then Snap started going crazy, and when we turned around to see what she was barking at, there was Arlo, still carrying Shri. Shri was slapping Arlo's back, creating a tactile experience of applause. Hanne started clapping. Molly held a hand over her mouth to contain her sobs of joy. Snap was wagging the lower half of her body, whimpering and joyously licking everything she could, the seats, the door, the window.

"Okay," I shouted. "Let's get them in the car and get the hell out of here!"

I got into the driver's seat while Molly and Hanne helped Arlo and Shri get settled in the back. Once they were buckled in, Hanne jumped in the passenger seat, and I signed to Arlo to move over so Molly could get next to them. He did, but then Molly closed the door instead, reached through the window, and started interpreting to Arlo as she spoke to me.

"No. It's too crowded. I'll take the train back. But you better get going."

"Are you kidding?" I said. "You need to come with us!"

"I'm going to head back to the nursing home. When they see Shri is missing, they're going to figure it out. I can be a witness when the police get there. I want to tell them about the abuse—the unprescribed medicine."

"But you just kind of committed arson?" I reminded her.

"Oh please, it was a little trash fire. They'd never be able to pin it on me, anyway. And if we all just run away then for certain it will look even fishier. No matter what, it will buy you some time and at least persuade them not to shoot you."

Arlo grew upset and begged Molly to come with us.

"We escape to Seattle," he signed. "We get house. All live together with Martin and Big Head Lawrence!"

"I'm tempted." Molly squeezed her eyes closed. "But I can't."

Then Molly kissed Arlo on the cheek and embraced him long and hard through the window. When they broke the hug, Arlo signed:

"I sorry you get into trouble. I love you."

Molly kissed his hands, then signed, "I love you too. You are a good man."

"We better hurry," I said. "Thank you, Molly. We couldn't have done this without you."

Molly stepped over to my window.

"I know you thought I was just an old, stupid JW who had no heart. But I do have a heart. I also have Jehovah God, who woke me up. Just get Arlo and Shri somewhere safe. I'll try to smooth things over. I can't promise there won't be a disaster ahead for all of us, but let's all just try our best. And please don't tell me where you're going so I don't have to lie anymore. I think I've committed enough sins today."

I reached up to give Molly a hug, but she pushed me away and waved for me to go. But then Hanne got out of the car as well, taking the tote bag filled with Shri's file, and came around to my window.

"I better stay with Molly," she said. "She'll need help explaining. I have no problem lying. Also, I have things I can say to blackmail the hell out of that place."

She lifted the tote bag. I looked at Hanne, my eyes begging her to come. Hanne kissed me on the lips, and then reached through the back window and stroked Arlo and Shri on their cheeks, her sad, shimmering eyes trying to smile.

"Come on, Hanne," I said, my voice catching in my throat. "Please."

"Cyrilje, you know I have a kid who has to graduate high school, not to mention my mess of a husband. And, of course, I still intend to be the greatest world-traveling artist-slash-nurse this country has ever seen. But not today. What an adventure this all was. I love you, my little red-haired gay Viking. Now go!"

Then I did the next right-wrong-ethical-unethical thing: I stepped on the gas and left.

EPILOGUE

STORY FINISH

CYRIL

For the first two days after we left New York I constantly looked behind us, waiting for the police to stop us any minute. But it never happened. Somehow, thanks to Hanne and Molly's intervention, plus calls to Shri's family, and the investigation by APS social workers, it looked like there would be no great chase scene, no DeafBlind Bonnie and Clyde, with Arlo shooting bullets out the window indiscriminately. At least not yet.

For much of our trip west, Snap sat in the passenger seat, her nose sticking out the window, sniffing the cattle ranches and ripe earth. Sometimes she'd look over at me with curiosity, toss her gray muzzle in acknowledgment, just one support animal to another. Then, just like me, she would periodically peer into the back seat at Arlo and Shri, who were either chatting or wrapped in each other's arms. Cleaned up and off the unprescribed meds, Shri, the stunning soul that Arlo had first been able to discern in the darkness merely through her hands, turned out to be an all-around beautiful human being, loquacious, funny, and smart. While driving through Cleveland we got her a checkup at a free clinic. Shri's bedsores were healing nicely. We were also able to score a used wheelchair at a thrift store and Shri began tooling around in it like she had owned it forever. Eventually she worked out a system where, if she got tired, Arlo could push and steer while she gave directions via tapping on his hands. Arlo explained about Protactile, but their hands rarely left each other's bodies anyway. It was and is an unending dance of communication.

At four in the morning on the day we are to arrive in Seattle, the two lovebirds are sleeping in the back, and I reach over and scratch Snap's head. The old girl looks up at me with those big brown service dog eyes as if to say, *You have no idea what you're doing with the rest of your life, do you?*

"No, Snap. In fact, I don't. Any ideas?"

She doesn't answer, thank God.

Hanne and Molly update me daily. Social workers and lawyers are involved, including a disability rights lawyer Tabitha had suggested. Weirdly, Tabitha's interpreter, Flirty Zach, also texted me, offering support, and suggested we grab a coffee when he's back in Seattle in October. I haven't responded yet.

Everything is in a holding pattern. But as long as I get Arlo to the Laura Bridgman Center by this afternoon, I will probably not face any charges, or that's what people tell me. Arlo's other school friend, Martin Van Ness, is planning to help me get Arlo and Shri connected to services in Seattle, so they can start looking for housing and get set up with the right equipment, including an iPhone with a brand-new portable refreshable braille display for Arlo. While there may be some kind of pushback from their families in the future, for the moment Arlo and Shri are okay. Birch, it turns out, left as scheduled for his mission to Ecuador. The lawyer said this "abandonment" of Arlo will work against him if he ever does try to exercise his guardianship rights. It seems Birch's concern for the next life clearly outweighs his concern for this one—or, as Molly suggested, maybe Birch really did see the light about Arlo's right to independence.

This was the good news. The bad news is all the money I have saved will be gone in a matter of weeks, and I am still set to lose my certification if Clara Shuster has anything to say about it. Molly is trying to help with that, but the outcome is definitely not certain. Now my future is one big messy question mark. What will I do if I'm not an ASL interpreter anymore? Stay in Seattle? Go back to the East Coast? To what? Hanne has sent me phone numbers for a couple of her AA friends out in Seattle, so I plan to check out some meetings. I haven't had a glass of wine in the two weeks of traveling and getting out of bed has been a lot easier. Bruno would have been proud of me.

◇ ◇ ◇

Those of us who can see look at the sun's rays reflecting off a flock of geese alighting on a field in the distance. Those of us who can hear listen to the whoosh of the air and the hum of the engine and the silence that fills the car. Arlo watches the streaks of light across the car's ceiling and feels the warmth of his love's hand on his face. Shri can feel the cool morning breeze with the warmth of the rising sun on Arlo's cheek. They probably know, just like I do, that our freedom is precarious and everything still might fall apart. It could, right? In real life, things don't end so happily, right? But, at the moment, we are just moving forward, swinging our white cane right, then left, dodging obstacles, taking one more step, finding our way.

ARLO

Shri is curled up in your arms, and every once in a while you place a kiss on that thick mane of black hair, you stick your face into the space between Shri's head and neck and breathe in the smell of her body, holding it inside your lungs, wanting it to become part of you. Jehovah's Witnesses believe Judgment Day is coming soon, that all of us who will be left behind, and all those who have died and are not the chosen 144,000, will sit before Jehovah God and Jesus and be judged. Those who refuse to come to Jehovah God, or those who have done red star sins their whole life—people like you—they will cease to exist. No more body. No more spirit. Just gone. Oblivion.

You don't believe in this anymore.

You reach up to the front seat and scratch good-dog-Snap on her head.

You sniff the air of the mountains that Cyril says are S-U-B-L-I-M-E.

There are so many ways you could sign *the sublime*. One day you will realize even the English words fail to fully contain that which truly fills your body and mind with awe. A complete understanding of the sublime will always be just beyond your grasp, but still you will reach for it.

But today, the word that fascinates you is much simpler. That word is *home*. A number of places in your life have worn that name: Mama's small apartment, your room at the Rose Garden School, Brother Birch's house, the city of Poughkeepsie. Molly once told you the sign for *home* was originally a combination of the signs for *food* (bring your hand to your mouth, fingers closed, as if you were putting food in your mouth) and *bed* (hands in prayer position lifted to the side of the head as if you were sleeping on them). *Home* was the place you ate and slept. That old sign was like your previous homes. But ASL signs evolve, often foreshortening or migrating on the body for ease of use. Frequently they will be replaced by a brand-new sign altogether. Today, the sign for *home* is done by gathering the fingertips, but instead of bringing them to the mouth as before, the signer just touches the side of the chin and then, keeping the same hand shape, touches the top of the cheekbone. The funny thing is that same hand shape (the gathered fingers touching your face or body) is almost exactly like the sign for *kiss*. So the sign for *home* is like someone kissing you twice, once near the mouth and once on your cheek just below your eye. *Home* went from being a place where you eat and sleep to the place where someone loves you. You take your fingers and make the sign for *home* on Shri's face.

Home.

STORY FINISH (END)

ACKNOWLEDGMENTS

I could not have written this book without the help of many, many people. First and foremost are the DeafBlind and Deaf, low-vision individuals who allowed me to interview them by email, in-person Tactile interviews, or both. The DeafBlind disability activist Divya Goel; Jeremy Best and his good dog, Ryley; the writer John Lee Clark (read him, you must!); Bob Morales; Koko Thomas; Julio Cornejo; Kathleen Walter; and my good friend Martin Greenberg, who guided me and introduced me to so many of these wonderful, generous people. I'd especially like to acknowledge my early readers (Deaf, DeafBlind, and hearing) who kept me honest: Angela Palmer (who read the entire manuscript in braille on her iPhone!); Angela Piteris; Gary Jones, Monique Holt; Silvia Stramenga; and my thesis advisor at CCNY, David Groff. A special thanks to Colin Lentz, who logged a ton of hours offering invaluable feedback (you're not easy, but you're worth it and I love you a LOT). I'd also like to thank the other experts in their fields who advised me: Gene Bourquin; Emmanuel "Mani-Jade" Garcia; Walei Sabry; Ann Marie (for her stories of her JW, Queer, CODA youth); Heather Archibald; my Flemish friends (Bernard, Marc, Karen, Barbara); and the helpful folks at the Helen Keller National Center and RID.

There is no way this book would be what it is without the guidance of probably the best book agent in the world, Doug Stewart at Sterling Lord Literistic Inc. (thanks for the introduction, James Hanaham!). Doug corrected my grammar and my misspellings and gave the kind of insightful feedback I didn't know agents did or could do. Also Maria Bell, Doug's assistant, who suggested one of my favorite changes and truly gave me a eureka moment.

A gigantic thanks to Emily Bestler, my publisher and editor, for taking on this project, and also to the invaluable Lara Jones for answering my countless questions. And to all the other incredible folks at Emily Bestler Books/Atria: Libby McGuire, publisher of Atria; Dana Trocker, associate publisher; Karlyn Hixson, marketing director; Falon Kirby, publicist; Maudee Genao, marketer; Paige Lytle, managing editor; Tamara Arellano, copyediting manager; Dominick Montalto, copy editor (thank you thank you thank you); and Jimmy Iacobelli, art director.

To the many other folks along the way who supported this work I send my great appreciation, including Gary Lennon, Jessica Ames, my teachers and classmates in the MFA Creative Writing Department at the City College of New York, Enrico Gomez for always being there to talk me down, and Bryan Thornton for our Joshua Tree writing retreats.

I'm especially grateful to the Lippman and Himmelfarb families for their generous support through the Doris Lippman Prize in Creative Writing, which afforded me some much-needed time (and validation) to finish the book.

And finally, I really couldn't and wouldn't have written this book if it wasn't for my Tuesday night writing group and the brilliant writers past and present: Marian Fontana, Louise Crawford (who basically wrote my query letter), Kent Shell, Jennifer Berman, Aaron Zimmerman, Don Cummings, Mila Drumke, Kim Merrill, Gabriel Amor, Rosemary Moore, and anyone else who passed through that magic room with their brilliant feedback and encouragement. I am very lucky.

the sign
for home

Blair Fell

This reading group guide for The Sign for Home *includes an introduction, discussion questions, ideas for enhancing your book club, and a Q&A with author Blair Fell. The suggested questions are intended to help your reading group find new and interesting angles and topics for your discussion. We hope that these ideas will enrich your conversation and increase your enjoyment of the book.*

INTRODUCTION

When Arlo Dilly learns the girl he thought was lost forever might still be out there, he takes it as a sign and embarks on a life-changing journey to find his great love—and his freedom.

Arlo Dilly is young, handsome, and eager to meet the right girl. He also happens to be DeafBlind, a Jehovah's Witness, and under the strict guardianship of his controlling uncle. His chances of finding someone to love seem slim to none.

And yet, it happened once before: many years ago, at a boarding school for the Deaf, Arlo met the love of his life—a mysterious girl with onyx eyes and beautifully expressive hands that told him the most amazing stories. But tragedy struck, and their love was lost forever.

Or so Arlo thought.

After years trying to heal his broken heart, Arlo is assigned a college writing assignment that unlocks buried memories of his past. Soon he wonders if the hearing people he was supposed to trust have been lying to him all along and if his lost love might be found again.

No longer willing to accept what others tell him, Arlo convinces a small band of misfit friends to set off on a journey to learn the truth. After all, who better to bring on this quest than his gay interpreter and wildly inappropriate Belgian best friend? Despite the many forces working against him, Arlo will stop at nothing to find the girl who got away and experience all of life's joyful possibilities.

TOPICS AND QUESTIONS
FOR DISCUSSION

1. When Arlo learns the concept of "the sublime," it leads him to profound personal revelations, both happy and sad. Reread Arlo's own definition of the concept in chapter 11. Have you experienced the sublime? In what ways did that experience change your life?

2. If you began reading *The Sign for Home* without much familiarity with the DeafBlind community, what did you learn about DeafBlind culture that surprised or interested you?

3. A recurring theme in *The Sign for Home* is exploring how people lead ethical lives. Brother Birch and Molly follow the tenets of their faith, Arlo is influenced by a mix of religion and his gold star/red star system, and Cyril acts according to the professional code of conduct for ASL interpreters. Toward the end of the novel, Cyril says he "did the next right-wrong-ethical-unethical thing" when he drives off with Arlo, Shri, and Snap. How and why do other characters go against their personal codes of ethics to do the "wrong" thing that is actually right?

4. Arlo narrates that the ASL sign for *home* was originally a combination of food and bed, but then it evolved to something that also resembles

the ASL sign for someone kissing your face — "home went from being a place where you eat and sleep to the place where someone loves you." If you were to make your own sign for *home*, what would it be? When you think of "home" what concepts or physical objects do you instantly envision?

5. While the novel tackles big questions and tragic moments in the characters' lives, much of it is also very funny. What lines made you laugh, and how does Blair Fell use humor to help define his characters?

6. Cyril narrates that the "quintessential" interpreter face says *we reside in a liminal world*. At this point in the novel, why is Cyril more comfortable occupying a liminal space? In what ways does he demonstrate more personal agency in his life as a result of knowing Arlo?

7. What characteristics make Arlo and Shri a good match? How do their distinct personalities complement each other?

8. When Cyril takes the interpreter job with Tabitha, she tells him, "I can be independent and still need other people." While Tabitha says this regarding the DeafBlind, it also holds true for Cyril. In what ways throughout the novel does he come to understand his own simultaneous need for independence and help from others?

9. When Molly admits to Cyril, Hanne, and Lavinia that she lied about Shri's fate to Arlo, she tells them she now wants to put things right, otherwise she will never be able to forgive herself. Many characters in *The Sign for Home* struggle to forgive others and themselves. Who do you think is able to do so by the end of the novel?

10. Blair Fell depicts the secondary characters as vibrantly as he does the main characters. Which secondary characters did you connect with most, and why?

11. Arlo bravely and wisely tells Cyril that he and Shri don't need him to be their hero: "Shri and I save ourselves. . . . We don't need hero. Understand? We hero ourselves." How is Arlo his own hero? What qualities and actions lead him to saving himself by the end of the book?

12. The novel ends with all our main characters embarking upon a new chapter in their lives. What do you imagine the future holds for them? What do you think they'll be doing in the next five years?

A CONVERSATION WITH BLAIR FELL

While you have years of experience working as an ASL interpreter for the Deaf, did you do any specific research for this novel?

I did a lot of specific research for this novel, like speaking to ophthalmologists and attending a weeklong DeafBlind interpreting workshop at the Helen Keller National Center. I spoke to orientation and mobility trainers, as well as experienced one of the O/M trainings myself. I spoke to a couple of DeafBlind tech experts as well. These folks were extremely helpful. I also read a number of nonfiction books about the DeafBlind, including books by and about Helen Keller, as well as Laura Bridgman who preceded her. I also researched a lot online, reading more contemporary personal accounts of DeafBlind folks, especially those who are working in the area of Protactile and disability rights. So many people were very helpful. But the bulk of my research was one-on-one interviews with DeafBlind individuals, either in person or via email; people like the poet and essayist John Lee Clark (a breathtakingly good writer who is DeafBlind) as well as Divya Goel, a DeafBlind activist, and many others. A good DeafBlind friend of mine, Martin Greenburg, introduced me to many of the folks I interviewed, and he also helped me to understand some of the day-to-day challenges he faces. When the manuscript was finished, I also asked both a top interpreter for the DeafBlind and a DeafBlind woman out west to do a sensitivity read for me.

Was there a character you found easy to write? Who was most challenging to write?

Arlo was more of a slow discovery for me, and thus harder. I literally wrote hundreds of pages I cut trying to get to know him, including a hundred and fifty pages before he was born learning who his parents were. I had really written enough for two books, but had to cut it down. Cyril was a bit easier since he's a middle-aged gay interpreter like me—although he has red hair and psoriasis, which I don't have. (He also has more patience than me to be honest. I would have lost it in the lunchroom way earlier.) When I write, like many writers I basically allow the characters to tell me who they are and what the story is. Molly was a challenge, as was Brother Birch—a challenge because I didn't want them to be only evil. I had to find their motivations and their heart. Molly was especially a challenge because of the evolution she goes through. Hanne, one of my favorite characters, was a total surprise. She just had coffee with Cyril one day and she saw Arlo through the window and it was like *bam!*—I need her!

What does the sublime mean to you? Do you and Arlo share the same definition?

I think what I share with Arlo on my understanding of the sublime is that I cannot fully know how to solidify it easily in my mind, and when I try to sign it, I feel like I fall short. Words and signs are vessels that strive to express everything that we experience . . . and they can't. Not fully. I like that Arlo refuses to settle on a sign or a series of signs for the sublime. Like him, I appreciate the search for that full meaning, but also respect its ineffability—its refusal to be captured.

What did you most hope to express about the DeafBlind experiences through your depiction of Arlo?

Arlo is an individual character. I don't mean him to represent all Deaf-Blind people or experiences. His being an orphaned Jehovah's Witness who is kept isolated from the world is just as much part of his identity. But I did also want to give a window into both a DeafBlind world and that of an interpreter. So I talked to a lot of my DeafBlind friends about their desires, struggles, and frustrations with the world, and what they felt were their biggest challenges. Audism is a common theme—how the hearing world looks at everything through that lens, as if being hearing is the one and only way to find happiness or have value. This is why one should never say "hearing impaired"; it implies the Deaf need to be fixed and are somehow substandard. I guess I wanted to show how Arlo wants to live his life to its fullest and how the hearing-sighted world, among other things, can get in the way or worse. But also, how he, like many DeafBlind people I know, can and do find meaning, love, sex, fun, and fulfillment—and must also fight against oppression. I wanted to show that DeafBlind folks have the right to be wrong and can be flawed as well as heroic. But this, as I said, is a story about an individual—not a political idea or a way of presenting deaf-blindness as a monolith. It's about Arlo Dilly, and his friendship with his interpreter and his best friends, and his love for Shri.

Do you have a favorite book written by a DeafBlind person? What Deaf-Blind writers do you recommend for people eager to read and learn more about this culture?

One of my favorite writers (period) is the poet and essayist John Lee Clark, who is DeafBlind and has Usher syndrome. For starters, he's brilliant. His first book of essays is called *Where I Stand: On the Signing Community and My DeafBlind Experience*. I'm afraid that title might be off-putting. It doesn't express how great these essays truly are or how broad their topics. His DeafBlind experience is only part of it. He has one chapter on how he might interpret the national anthem that is breathtaking and made me actually interested in the lyrics and backstory for the first time. He has a new book of essays coming out in spring 2023 called *Touching the Future* and another book of poems from Norton called *How to Communicate: Poems* in fall 2022. I can't wait to read both!

Why did you decide to use Walt Whitman's poem as the basis for Arlo's assignment? Were there any other poems you considered using instead?

Good question. I did consider other poems, but I really love Whitman, and interpreting him is, as Cyril learns, hard but also doable because of the raw physicality of them. The more I can physically see something in my head the better I can interpret it. Whitman shows us the grass, the battlefield, the boys swimming. I can't remember the other poems I considered. Been a long time.

Snap is such an important character, despite not being human. How did you approach writing her and her relationship with Arlo?

Snap was a little hard for me. I love dogs so much, but I've never had a service dog. To be honest, I would think of the expressions my late pit mix Sophie used to make, but more often I'd contact another DeafBlind friend named Jeremy Best about his yellow Lab Ryley. I'd periodically get stuck and send him an email asking how Ryley behaves in certain circumstances. Things like, "When you go into a bathroom how does Ryley help you?" And he'd say how she can help him get to the toilet, but she wouldn't be able to help him find the restroom. I'd also study guide dogs whenever I'd see them. Keeping my distance of course since they'd be working.

Did you ever consider having Arlo not forgive Molly? Why, ultimately, did you decide to have him do so?

That was one of the most difficult aspects of the novel. It wasn't just hard to have him forgive her, but having Molly be worthy of his forgiveness was such a tricky thing. I struggled. I work with a lot of Jehovah's Witness interpreters, and most, to be honest, are great interpreters and very kind. They also believe I'm headed for oblivion if I act out on my sexuality. (I've been told, like Arlo tells Cyril, that as long as I don't have sex with another man then I can still get into heaven even though I'm queer. No thanks.) I really wanted to make Molly a whole person and not just an evil trope of zealotry. I had to find a reason she would do such horrific things to Arlo while still loving him. I also love the topic of forgiving the unforgivable because, hell, that's our task in this world where so many seemingly unforgivable things are happening. It's hard for me to forgive, that's for sure. But Arlo is better than me, Cyril is better than me. I write for what I aspire to be. But, yes, there was an early thought to have him not forgive her—but I prefer where it ended up even though it was way harder. I keep intending to write something easy, but it never works out that way. Damn it.

Do you think Cyril will take a chance on love again with Zach?

We shall see. I think Cyril is going to try to get sober, and then who knows. He's not capable of truly loving before he goes on this journey, but if he sobers up and gets honest with himself anything is possible. I suspect he will find love.

Can you tell us what you're working on now?

I'm working on two new novels. One is a completed draft of a very different book, *Disco Witches of Fire Island* (a working title), which is about the seasonal workers on Fire Island in 1989 during the AIDS crisis and a coven of (you got it) Disco Witches. I really wanted to capture the difficulty of being a young man, like I was, trying to cope with that hopeless period of the AIDS crisis and to find love, and also create a mythology around the dance floors of the '70s, '80s and '90s. Despite the magical realism in the book, it steps into a bit of fictionalized autobiography for me. I was a bartender on Fire Island in the 1990s and share other things with the protagonist. My agent has the most recent draft, and the early readers seem to be really jazzed about it. There are also two other novels in the works, neither of which I'm ready to talk about. One also features a DeafBlind character and several interpreters. I wrote a rough draft of it in the middle of writing *The Sign for Home*. I had given up on *The Sign for Home* halfway through the first draft because it was really hard and taking forever. So I thought,

I'm going to write something faster and a little lighter. So this other novel popped out. There are murders. I'll say that much. There's also a third book I'm writing just because I really, really want to write it. I also have a memoir I've dabbled with over the years, focused on the films that inspired me as a kid, especially *The Singing Nun* and the 1937 *Lost Horizon*. And then there are dozens of other books that are swimming around on my TO BE WRITTEN list. I like to stay busy, and it's never about what I've written but what I'm currently writing. I get depressed if I'm not writing something new. To be honest, I never knew I could write a novel before, it was quite a surprise, and I loved it. So I'm not going to waste any more time.

ENHANCE YOUR BOOK CLUB

1. Research Helen Keller's books and choose one that interests you to read as a group. Discuss how Helen's descriptions of living as a Deaf-Blind person compare to Blair Fell's descriptions in *The Sign for Home*.

2. In recent years, there have been many more movies, TV shows, and documentaries exploring Deaf and DeafBlind culture, such as *Deaf U, Audible, The Sound of Metal,* and *Coda.* Pick one to watch for a book club screening.

3. Watch the documentary *Through Deaf Eyes* produced in association with Gallaudet University (which Blair Fell attended) to learn more about Deaf culture in America.

4. Visit Blair Fell's website at www.blairfell.com.